THE SILVER SHOOTER

ALSO BY ERIN LINDSEY

THE ROSE GALLAGHER SERIES

Murder on Millionaires' Row

A Golden Grave

THE BLOODBOUND TRILOGY

Bloodbound

Bloodforged

Bloodsworn

THE NICOLAS LENOIR MYSTERIES
(WRITING AS E.L. TETTENSOR)

Darkwalker

Master of Plagues

THE SILVER SHOOTER

A Rose Gallagher Mystery

ERIN LINDSEY

MINOTAUR
BOOKS
NEW YORK

First published in the United States by Minotaur Books, an imprint of St. Martin's Publishing Group

THE SILVER SHOOTER. Copyright © 2020 by Erin Lindsey. All rights reserved. Printed in the United States of America. For information, address St. Martin's Publishing Group, 120 Broadway, New York, NY 10271.

www.minotaurbooks.com

Designed by Omar Chapa

Map designed by Catarina Cunha

Library of Congress Cataloging-in-Publication Data

Names: Lindsey, Erin, author.
Title: The silver shooter / Erin Lindsey.
Description: First edition. | New York : Minotaur Books, 2020. | Series: A Rose Gallagher mystery ; [3]
Identifiers: LCCN 2020031673 | ISBN 9781250623447 (trade paperback) | ISBN 9781250623454 (ebook)
Subjects: GSAFD: Mystery fiction.
Classification: LCC PR9199.4.L564 S55 2020 | DDC 813/.6—dc23
LC record available at https://lccn.loc.gov/2020031673

Our books may be purchased in bulk for promotional, educational, or business use. Please contact your local bookseller or the Macmillan Corporate and Premium Sales Department at 1-800-221-7945, extension 5442, or by email at MacmillanSpecialMarkets@macmillan.com.

First Edition: 2020

10 9 8 7 6 5 4 3 2 1

This year has been a tough one everywhere. New York, especially, has been hit hard by COVID-19. But the city is no stranger to crisis, and once again, New Yorkers are rising to the occasion. This book is dedicated to the city of New York: to the health workers, scientists, public servants, and volunteers on the frontlines of the crisis; to the essential workers of all stripes, from teachers to bus drivers to grocery store clerks putting themselves at risk to keep the city running; to the ordinary New Yorkers going out of their way for their friends and neighbors and strangers in need. You are, as always, an inspiration.

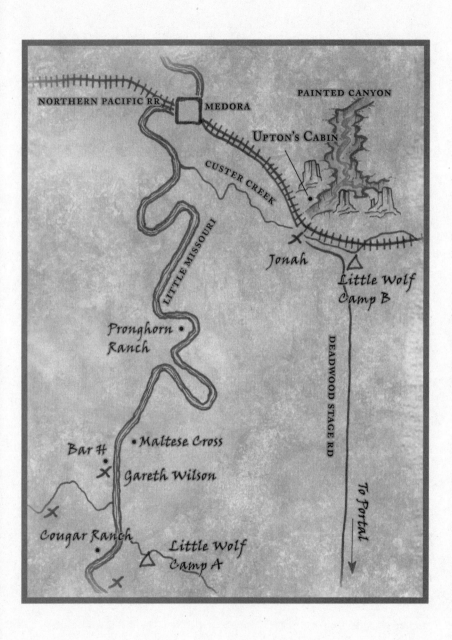

THE SILVER SHOOTER

CHAPTER 1

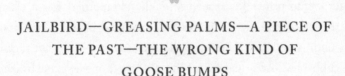

JAILBIRD—GREASING PALMS—A PIECE OF
THE PAST—THE WRONG KIND OF
GOOSE BUMPS

When you're a detective, certain things come with the job. Getting shot at, for example, or tossing a man twice your size over your shoulder. From time to time, there might be a little light burglary. If you're with the special branch of the Pinkerton National Detective Agency, you can add to the list the occasional tussle with a ghost or a shade, or a person endowed with the sorts of uncanny powers that people in my line of work refer to as *luck*. These things come with the territory. You expect them.

One thing you do *not* expect is to spend the night in jail, and I can't say that I much care for it.

I'd never set foot in the Tombs before that night, not even for work. Even though I grew up a stone's throw away, in the heart of Five Points, I harbored a slum dweller's natural suspicion of the law, and I'd always given the place a wide berth. I'm not sure what I expected it to be like, but as it turns out, the name says it all. That's not its real name, of course—officially, it's the New York City Halls of Justice—but I've never heard a soul refer to it that way. Even the coppers call it the Tombs, and a more dismal place you'd be hard-pressed to find, at least on the island of Manhattan.

As to how I ended up there, I blamed Thomas.

My partner was a brilliant investigator, but he had a peculiar affection for breaking and entering—or, more precisely, for getting *me* to sneak onto premises where my presence was not strictly legal. This time, it was the home of a certain prominent businessman whose name was often in the papers. Like many of New York's elite, this gentleman was *lucky,* though of course that particular detail never made it into print. The existence of the paranormal was a closely guarded secret, known only to a few thousand New Yorkers, most of whom were lucky themselves. That exclusive list did not include the coppers who arrested me, or the chief matron who came by every so often to shine a lantern between the bars of my cell and scowl at my degenerate ways. How could I explain to them that my theft—or rather, my attempted theft, since I'd been caught before I could fin-ish the job—was for the public good? *The thing is, ma'am, that artifact is magic. Powerful magic that shouldn't be in the hands of a ruthless shark like Edmund Drake. The Pinkertons will take good care of it and see that it can't do any harm.*

No, that sort of speech would land me straight back in the cranky-hutch, and one visit to the Lunatic Pavilion at Bellevue Hos-pital was quite enough for me. (That, dear reader, is a whole other story, one I would rather forget.)

I might have tried to plead my case by pointing out that the arti-fact in question didn't belong to Edmund Drake, either, having been stolen earlier that week from Wang's General Store. But the odds of a pair of immigrants like Mr. Wang and me being believed over a man as powerful as Edmund Drake were slim to none. So there I sat, hud-dled on the damp floor as far away from the flea-riddled mattress as

I could get, scratching myself raw and thinking very dark thoughts about my partner, Mr. Thomas Wiltshire, whose grand scheme had landed me in this horrible place.

Thankfully, I wouldn't have to endure it much longer. An echoing *boom* sounded at the far end of the corridor, followed by approaching footsteps. I sat up a little straighter, listening. No jingle of keys, which meant it wasn't the matron. I felt a flicker of hope, followed by a flood of relief as I recognized the familiar rhythm of the footfalls coming down the corridor. A moment later, Thomas appeared on the other side of the bars, looking very sheepish indeed.

"Hello, Rose."

I stayed where I was, scowling up at him and trying very hard not to show how glad I was to see him. He looked wildly out of place in that grim dungeon, trimmed in his usual elegant tailoring, silk hat on head and griffin-headed walking stick in hand, darkhaired, pale-eyed, and irritatingly handsome. I wasn't the only one who thought so, apparently: a wolf whistle sounded from one of the nearby cells, followed by peals of feminine laughter up and down the cellblock. Thomas lifted an eyebrow but didn't turn his head.

"Good morning," I said. "At least, I assume it's morning. It's hard to be sure, what with the lack of windows in this cell."

He sighed. "I can't tell you how sorry—"

"You can and you shall, but right now I'd quite like to *leave*."

"Yes, of course." He fidgeted with his jacket in his very English way, casting an awkward glance down the corridor. "The matron is coming just now."

She grunted when she arrived at my cell, shaking her head as though she considered it a terrible mistake to set me loose on the world. "Got yourself a real fancy lawyer here, Miss Gallagher," she said, indicating Thomas with a jerk of her chin. "Can't imagine why he'd have truck with the likes of you." She took her displeasure out on the door, clanging and banging her way through the business until the bolt shot aside and the squeal of rusting hinges signaled my freedom. "You should look to a more savory breed of client, sir," she opined. "Thieving Irish are surely beneath you."

"Reckon she's making it worth his while," a voice called from the cell above me, to more laughter. "Hey, mister, I'd be happy to trade too, if you get me outta here."

Thomas pretended not to hear, but I could tell he was annoyed. I wondered if he'd ever been catcalled before. I don't suppose most men have had the pleasure, especially not wealthy Fifth Avenue swells like Thomas. The laughter followed us all the way out of the women's prison and into the courtyard, only to be drowned out by the grim clatter of timber hitting the flagstones as workers took down the gallows from the morning's hanging. Thomas and I hurried past, and we didn't slow until we'd reached the entrance, where I paused in the shadow of the faux-Egyptian columns to let my eyes adjust to the sunlight. Morning was well under way, from the look of things. Centre Street was crowded with pedestrians, and the streetcar that rumbled past was full of New Yorkers on their way to work. That meant I'd spent at least ten hours in that wretched place.

"We're over here." Thomas gestured at a carriage parked across the street. Not our usual battered hack, I saw, but a shiny new brougham—an awfully fancy way of getting around in this neighborhood. He must have been feeling very guilty indeed. A clutch of ragamuffins had already gathered around the vehicle, waiting for its presumably rich owner to return; I shooed them away gently before accepting a hand up from the coachman. Thomas climbed in beside me, and we were off. "I presume you wish to head home?"

"Yes, please. Mam will be worried sick." My mother was still in the dark about my new life as a Pinkerton agent. As far as she knew, I was still Thomas Wiltshire's maid, and for now at least, I saw no good reason for that to change. My mother's health was fragile, mentally and physically, and it wouldn't do her any good to know that her only child was breaking into homes or spending nights in jail. "I have no idea how I'm going to explain not coming home last night."

"You needn't be concerned about that. As soon as I left Drake's, I sent a note to your mother explaining that I was giving a last-minute soiree and needed you to work overtime."

"Thank you. That was thoughtful of you." I glanced at him out of the corner of my eye, already feeling my anger drain away. Try as I might, I never managed to stay cross with Thomas Wiltshire for long. It's terribly hard to argue with perfection, and though no one is *actually* perfect, Thomas did a credible impression of it. He didn't just look the part—impeccable taste, meticulous grooming, fine, aristocratic features—he insisted on being so eminently *reasonable* all the time, delivering his carefully framed thoughts in the poshest English this side of Buckingham Palace. The combined effect of it all was to make you feel as if any fault you found must surely be your own.

Also, he had an annoying habit of apologizing before you could even work up a proper head of steam. "I really am frightfully sorry, Rose. I had no idea there was so much involved in getting someone released on a relatively minor charge."

"Paperwork?"

He snorted softly. "I believe the vernacular term is *greasing palms*. A great many palms, as it turns out."

"Maybe if you'd showed up looking a little less"—I gestured at his obviously expensive attire—"a little less like *you*, there wouldn't have been so many palms to grease. You might as well wear a sign around your neck that says *free money*."

"You're right, of course. An amateur mistake. I was in a hurry, believe it or not."

"I take it you couldn't reach Sergeant Chapman?" My favorite copper would have come for me straightaway, I had no doubt. And instead of greasing palms, he'd have banged some heads.

"I telephoned him at the station, but he'd most likely gone home for the night."

"Well, it's over now, anyway." Weary to the bone, I slumped against the carriage window, watching idly as we turned up Broadway—and promptly became bogged down in traffic. At this time of day, New York's busiest street was a jostling river of hacks and horsecars, with the occasional brave pedestrian darting through the gaps between them. I'd have to wait a little longer for the hot bath I was craving.

I could feel Thomas's eyes on me. "Rose . . ."

"It's all right. I'm a grown woman. I could have said no if I'd wanted to. I just wish it hadn't all been for nothing."

"Nothing? Why, on the contrary, it was a cracking success."

I turned to find him wearing a sly smile. Reaching into his jacket pocket, he produced an unassuming chunk of rock.

"*You got it?*" I jerked upright, snatching the rock from his hands and turning it over in amazement. "How?"

"You did such a masterful job of creating a diversion that I was able to slip inside during the confusion. I daresay they still haven't noticed anything amiss. Of course, it would have been a different matter had Drake not been out of town. He'd have known who you were and what you'd come for, and he'd have secured the stone straightaway. Happily, his servants were none the wiser, and it didn't occur to anyone that you might have an accomplice."

I examined the object in my hands. To all appearances, it was an ordinary stone, smooth on one side and jagged everywhere else, as though it had recently been broken. Which it had. This was a fragment of Flood Rock, a tiny island in the East River that had been blown to bits by the Army Corps of Engineers a year and a half ago, in the fall of 1885. What the army hadn't known—what no one, not even in the paranormal community, had realized—was that Flood Rock was also a seal guarding a portal to the otherworld, the place where ghosts and shades and fae roam free. Blowing it open might have cleared the way for ships, but it also set loose a tide of spirits to wreak havoc on the city. Happily, the Pinkertons had managed to restore the seal before things got too out of hand, with most of New York none the wiser. We'd thought the matter settled until a piece of Flood Rock turned up on the black market a few weeks ago.

It was about the size of a fist and smelled a little like the sea, but if it had any power, I couldn't sense it. "Do you suppose it's even true, what they say about it?"

"We'll have to conduct the proper tests, but I expect so. It's well known that proximity to a portal greatly enhances supernatural attributes. It stands to reason that a piece of the seal would act as a sort of amplifier, magnifying the luck and magic around it. Imagine what a man like Edmund Drake could do with something like that in his pocket."

I shivered at the thought. Thomas and I had seen firsthand what Drake was capable of last year, when he'd used his luck to hypnotize us into revealing the details of our investigation. If those powers were even stronger . . . "He'd be President of the United States by this time next year."

Thomas wrapped the stone in a handkerchief and stowed it away. "I'll take this to the Astor Library as soon as I drop you off. They'll keep it safe in the special vaults until someone from the Agency arrives to secure it more permanently."

"What about Mr. Wang? Won't he be upset after all the work he put into tracking it down?"

Thomas arched a dark eyebrow. "And what about all the work *we* put into tracking down the thief, not to mention recovering the artifact? Besides, Wang must have known the Agency wouldn't allow the stone to be sold to the highest bidder. It's far too dangerous for that. I'm sure he'll be content with a finder's fee."

"Let's hope you're right. I'd hate for him to be angry with us."

"As would I. We cannot afford to alienate him. He's the best there is."

Aside from being a gifted apothecary, Mr. Wang presided over the most comprehensive stock of rare magical items in America. That, and his unrivaled network in the paranormal community, made him an invaluable ally.

But there was more to it than that. "He also happens to be our friend," I said pointedly. "One who's saved both our lives."

"Of course. I didn't mean to sound transactional. Perhaps it will soften the blow if we speak with him together. We can pay him a visit once you've had a chance to rest. You must be exhausted."

"I am," I admitted, fading back against the window. "But at least we got the stone. The only thing worse than spending the night in that place was thinking that it was all for nothing."

Thomas reached over and took my hand, giving it a gentle tug until I slid a little closer. There wasn't a lot of seat to slide along, and the move left us tucked snugly into one corner of the brougham. "I really am so sorry, Rose," he murmured.

His eyes searched mine, and I felt the familiar flutter in my belly. He rarely took such liberties, especially *after*. By which I mean *after* that night in the parlor six months ago, when we'd shared our first and only kiss. Ever since, I'd thought of our relationship in terms of *before* and *after*. I suspected Thomas did too, but I couldn't be sure, because of course we never, ever talked about it. What would be the point? We both knew there was no future for us, romantically speaking. Consorting with the likes of me would ruin Thomas socially, and get him fired in the bargain. As for me, I'd forever be known as the girl who got her job because she was involved with the boss. We weren't prepared to ask that of ourselves or each other, at least not for now. And so we pretended the kiss never happened.

Mostly.

Every now and then, though, I'd find myself staring into those pale eyes, heat washing over me as I remembered the feel of his mouth on mine. In those moments—moments like this—we were in danger of letting ourselves be swept away. Thomas's color was up, and his gaze had taken on that glassy quality that made my heart beat faster. His fingertips drifted along the soft skin between my knuckles, gliding up the back of my hand in a slow caress. My breath grew shallow, and my bottom lip slid between my teeth.

A tiny crease appeared between Thomas's dark eyebrows. He looked down. "What's this?" His touch grew firmer, more clinical.

I followed his gaze to the tiny bumps dotting my arm. "Oh, that." I sighed. "That would be fleas."

CHAPTER 2

HOME SWEET HOME—PUTTING DOWN
ROOTS—HARD LUCK

Exhausted as I was, I couldn't help smiling as I stepped out of the brougham in front of 123 Washington Place. I don't know if every new homeowner feels such pride, but for me, the sight of my tidy little redbrick house never failed to make my soul feel lighter. Number 123 was a handsome example of the Federal style, a narrow two and a half stories with arched windows, crisp white dormers jutting out from a sloping roof, and fluted Roman detail around the entrance. Built in the 1830s, it was designed for a middle-class family, which meant that for my household of three, it was positively a mansion, especially compared to the tiny flat I grew up in.

Something was different today, I noticed. It took me a moment to place it—and then I realized that Mam had hung window boxes on the second floor, full of delicate blue pansies that stood out cheerfully against the white trim. My smile grew even wider, and not just because I loved flowers. After nearly two months, Mam was finally settling into her new home.

"Good morning," I called as I walked through the door.

"Fiora!" Pietro came rushing out of the kitchen, looking equal parts relieved and annoyed. Unlike Mam, he knew the truth about what I did for a living—well, some of it, anyway—and he would have known Thomas's message about a party had been pure flimflam. "Where have you—"

"Rose, dear, is that you?"

Pietro fell silent, and we shared a meaningful look. His questions would have to wait.

"Yes, Mam, it's me. I'm coming just now." Hanging my overcoat on the rack, I followed Pietro into the kitchen, where I was met by a heady smell of garlic. Something bubbled on the stove, and little piles of chopped herbs and vegetables covered one side of the table. On the other side stood my mother, chicken in one hand and cleaver in the other, a soiled apron tied around her tiny waist.

For a second I just stood there, too thunderstruck to speak.

"Mam, are you . . . *cooking*?"

Pietro arranged himself at the other end of the table and resumed chopping, casual as you please, as though the sight of my mother preparing a meal were nothing special.

"Well, what does it look like, you silly thing?" Mam waved her cleaver in an offhanded way.

It looked like my often-confused mother had a very large knife in her hand, but it wouldn't do to say so. "I'm just . . . a bit surprised, is all."

"You act as if you've never seen me cook before."

I glanced at Pietro, but he was no help; he just winked at me and kept chopping. "Well, it has been a while, Mam." By *a while*, I meant *years*, ever since her dementia had made the task too dangerous to contemplate. The main reason I'd found her a boarder three years ago was to take care of the cooking while I was away at work. Fortunately for Mam, Pietro had proved to be more than competent in the kitchen, and had even managed to coax her into trying something other than the bland cabbage-and-potatoes fare she'd grown up with. These days, Mam enjoyed garlic and tomatoes nearly as much as our boarder. "What are you making?"

"*Pollo alla cacciatora*," Pietro replied. "I like to make this sauce with rabbit, but I couldn't find it nowhere."

"Couldn't find it *anywhere*, Peter." As a former schoolteacher, Mam never tired of correcting his grammar. It had been the same with me when I was a child, except Pietro handled it with a lot more grace than I ever had.

"Sorry, Mama," he said affably. "One day I will learn."

"Are these fresh tomatoes?" I picked up a juicy-looking specimen. "Where did you find hothouse tomatoes around here?" Plenty of posh grocers uptown carried them, but I couldn't think of any place between Washington Square and . . . "Ah," I said, spying a link of salami hanging from the ceiling. "I see you made a trip to Augusto's."

There must have been something in my tone, because Pietro looked up. "*Sì*, I wanted to buy some seeds for the garden. Actually . . ." Setting his knife down, he gestured at the door leading out to the courtyard. "Come, Fiora, I show you."

He led me out into the small yard behind the house, where he'd already started removing some of the paving stones to plant a garden. The shade-loving plants would go here, he'd informed me, while he planned to try growing tomatoes and such on the roof. "I bought a few different kinds to try, and they also had these." He pointed to some baby plants wrapped in burlap. "I will put them in a bucket for now."

"What are they?"

"*Melanzana*. I'm not sure how you call them in English." He made a shape with his hands. "Like a squash, but purple?"

"Aubergines. At least, that's what we call them. Americans call them *eggplant*." Folding my arms, I added, "And you can find them a lot closer than Augusto's."

He folded his arms right back at me. "*Va bene.* You tell me where you were last night, and I tell you why I went to Augusto's."

"I was . . ." Peering around his lanky frame, I checked that the door to the kitchen was firmly shut. "I had a spot of trouble, and . . ." *Oh, just spit it out.* "I spent the night in the Tombs."

Pietro's eyebrows flew up, and for a moment I thought he was going to scold me. Instead, he burst out laughing. "The Tombs! *Non ci posso credere.* Beautiful!" Leaning forward, he sniffed at me. "You don't smell too bad for all that."

"I'm glad you find it so amusing."

"Sorry." He didn't look sorry. His dark eyes danced, and he didn't even try to hide his smile. "But it is a little ironic, no? A detective spending the night in jail? I don't remember things like this happening when you were a maid."

"I don't remember a lot of things happening when I was a maid. Being able to afford my own home, for example."

"Careful. You don't want Mama to hear."

There was a hint of disapproval in his voice, and I knew why. Pietro didn't like keeping secrets from my mother. I wasn't very happy about it either, but I didn't see much choice. Mam's health was improving, but she certainly wasn't back to her old self, and I doubted she ever would be. Part of her condition was down to the amount of time she'd spent communing with the ghost of her dead mother—a practice Thomas had thankfully convinced her to curb—but another part was what the doctors referred to as *dementia,* and it left her confused and forgetful. As it was, Pietro and I had to remind her regularly that she lived here now, instead of in the tiny flat on Mott Street where I'd grown up. Just last week, I'd come home to find her sobbing in Pietro's arms. She'd woken up from her nap with no idea where she was or how she got there. What Mam needed right now was familiarity and routine, and that did *not* include find-ing out her daughter was a Pinkerton.

"Are you going to tell me why you were in jail?" Pietro asked.

"It's a long story, and you probably don't want the details."

"You always say that."

"I do, and we agreed it was for the best." As far as I knew, Pi-etro wasn't the superstitious sort. Though he humored Mam about her ghost, he didn't really believe her, and I saw no need to burden him with the truth about the supernatural world. "Anyway, it's your turn. What were you doing down in Five Points?"

"Just saying hello to some friends at the grocery."

"Anyone I know?"

Pietro's mouth took a wry turn. "Subtle. No, I didn't speak to Augusto."

"I don't know what you mean. I was just curious, that's all."

"I'm not stupid, Fiora. I know that part of the reason you brought me here was to keep me away from Augusto and the Mul-berry Street Gang."

"I brought you here so Mam wouldn't start asking questions about how I could afford a house on a servant's salary." We'd told her the place was rented, and that Pietro was contributing as a boarder, just as he'd done in Five Points.

"*Sì*, and as a nice coincidence, that means there is someone around to help her while you're out. And, oh, by the way, another nice coincidence: it means your friend Pietro won't have time to be hanging around that shady Italian grocery. It's all very tidy, no?"

I couldn't help laughing, even as I blushed. "Was it that obvious?"

He shrugged. "I know how you love your clever little schemes."

Not as clever as all that, apparently. Sheepishly, I said, "I hope you don't feel too manipulated."

"I used to work for Augusto. Believe me, compared to that, you don't even know what manipulating means."

"Then why go back there?"

He sighed. "Please, Rose, you're not my mama. If I want to see my friends, I will see my friends."

"Since when is Augusto a friend?"

"He's not. He's one of the most important businessmen in Five Points—"

"Who also happens to be a ruthless criminal."

"—who also happens to have a lot of influence in my community, even with respectable people. I'm Italian, Fiora. Family is important to us, and loyalty. I cannot just go away and expect them to welcome me back when I decide it's time to make a life for myself. If I want a business of my own one day, and a family, I cannot afford to make an enemy of Augusto."

I sighed. I might not like it, but I knew he was right. It was true of most immigrant communities to one degree or another. Italians shopped at Italian businesses and married Italian spouses and had Italian children. To them, it even mattered what region you came from, and which village. The fact that a Bolognese like Augusto wielded such influence even over southerners like Pietro was proof of the man's reach. If Pietro wanted a life among his people, he'd have to stay in Augusto's good graces. "Just promise me you won't get mixed up with his business."

"I'm not the one who spent the night in jail."

"Maybe not this time, but I'll bet you have."

"*Certo*. And since I have some experience, you should take my advice and have a bath."

I smiled wearily. "I thought you said I don't smell too bad."

"No," he said, "but you probably have fleas."

I took the longest bath of my life, after which I sat down to a nice meal, so I was feeling more or less right with the world by the time I struck out for the el. It wasn't a long journey. My new house was just half a block from the Sixth Avenue line, which ran the length of the island from the Battery to Central Park. That nearness had its downsides: the only thing noisier than a steam train is an elevated steam train, and Pietro's rooftop tomatoes would probably end up sporting a healthy dusting of ash. That didn't bother me. I had thick windows, and besides, those little faults were part of the reason I could afford a house in such a nice neighborhood. You certainly couldn't beat it for convenience: in no time at all, I was descending from the platform at 58th Street, from which it was a short walk to Thomas's house.

I took my time, strolling along the edge of Central Park and enjoying the warm sun on my face. Last night's events already seemed a distant memory, and I marveled at how easy it was to recover from life's little hiccups when everything else was going smoothly. The worries that had plagued me for so long—about my mother's health, our finances, my lack of real prospects—were gradually fading into memory. Mam was doing so much better, and now she had a proper place to live. I had money in my pockets and good friends to spend it with. I had a job with real purpose. I was, in other words, happy.

So naturally, when I spied an unfamiliar brougham parked outside 726 Fifth Avenue, I viewed it as nothing less than a harbinger of doom.

I hurried up the steps and let myself in after a cursory knock. Until recently, I'd lived here myself, first as a housemaid and then as a guest, so I didn't feel the need to stand on ceremony. "Hello?" I called. "Thomas?"

"They're up in the study."

Clara appeared in the hallway, a ledger tucked under her arm. That, and the fact that she wasn't wearing her usual cook's apron, told me that she was on housekeeper duty at the moment. How she managed to juggle cooking with running a household, I never understood, but manage it she did, and without a lick of nonsense. "Who's they?" I asked, giving her a quick hug.

"Mr. Burrows is with 'em, but I didn't catch the other fella's name. It was Louise answered the door, since I was busy doing the inventory. Did you know there's four hundred bottles down in that cellar? What's a bachelor need with that much booze, anyway? Ain't like he's throwing any parties." Pausing, she looked me up and down. "Rose, honey, you feeling all right? You look like a fresh-scrubbed beet."

I glanced down at my arms, which were indeed rather pink. "You're not far off. I may have gotten a little carried away in the bath this morning."

"I bet you did. Mr. Wiltshire told me all about your little adventure at the jail."

"How thoughtful of him."

She laughed. "Nobody ever said this Pinkerton business was gonna be ribbons and puppies." Clara was my best friend, and one of only a handful of people who knew the truth about what I did for a living—ghosts and shades and all. She didn't much like it, but she'd made her peace with it, and even lent a hand now and then. Especially when I needed stitches, which was more often than I would have liked.

"It was awful," I said.

"And I wanna hear all about it, but you best get on up there with the others. Looked like business to me."

I headed upstairs, pausing on the landing to check my reflection in the mirror. Rosy complexion aside, I looked fresh and presentable, my clothing crisp and my strawberry blond hair pinned neatly in place. Thus reassured, I made my way to the study. The door stood ajar, and just as I was about to knock, a high, hoarse laugh sounded from within.

"Good heavens, Burrows, what a rascal you are! Mr. Wiltshire and I are shocked, are we not, sir?"

I knew that voice. It was one of the most recognized in the city, and it belonged to Theodore Roosevelt.

"Miss Gallagher!" He propelled himself out of his chair with his usual vigor. "Good to see you again!" Seizing my hand in both of his, he gave it a hearty shake, sending a familiar buzz of energy up my arm. Most people who met Mr. Roosevelt put that strange tingle down to charisma, but I knew better. Theodore Roosevelt was lucky, and his powers were perfectly suited to a politician. Brilliant though he might be, it was the uncanny magnetism of his luck that drew people to him like moths to a flame. Though he'd lost the mayoral election a few months ago, there was little doubt he had a bright future in politics, and I was very proud to have saved his life. (Twice, not that I was counting.)

"You're looking well, sir."

"I suppose you mean well-stuffed," he said amiably, patting his belly. "I blame the exquisite restaurants of Europe."

If he'd put on weight, I didn't see it; his stocky frame looked as powerful as ever. A lingering suntan and hints of red in his hair and mustache only added to the impression of vitality. "And what brings you to us this afternoon?" I asked, though I had a sinking feeling I knew the answer.

He flashed a toothy grin. "Why, have you forgotten? I did warn you back in October that I'd have some business for the two of you come spring."

"In Dakota. I remember." Forgetting something and putting it out of one's mind are not *quite* the same. Taking a seat next to our other guest, I added, "I didn't realize that business involved Mr. Burrows."

"Does my presence offend you, Miss Gallagher?" The gentleman in question gave me a lazy smile, as though he didn't much mind about my answer. Which he probably didn't. Jonathan Burrows had the sort of good looks and careless charm that routinely sent Fifth Avenue princesses to the fainting couch, and he knew it. Add to that a fortune to rival the Rockefellers, and you had a man too pleased with himself by half. He was also brave and loyal and generous, but he could be thoroughly exasperating, and hardly a week went by that I didn't want to break something over his pretty golden head.

I made sure my gaze said as much. "Don't be silly, Mr. Burrows. I'm only thinking of our client."

"We did discuss the need for discretion when we spoke last fall," Thomas put in, shooting a warning glance of his own at his mischievous best friend.

"Much appreciated, both of you," Mr. Roosevelt said. "But few gentlemen of my acquaintance are safer with a secret than my old college chum here."

"There we cannot argue," Thomas said. "Moreover, I gather from what you said before Miss Gallagher came in that the two of you have discussed the matter already."

"A little, yes. It came up in a roundabout sort of way. Burrows and I were having luncheon earlier, and I mentioned that I'm completely ruined." Mr. Roosevelt's laugh was even higher-pitched than usual. "Then I recalled that the three of you were close confederates, so I felt free to unburden myself."

"Ruined?" I exchanged a look with Thomas. "Do you mean financially?"

"That was my principal meaning, but at the risk of sounding sentimental, I will confess that I am also utterly heartbroken. We've had a terrible winter at the ranch, you see. I lost a great many of my backwoods babies. Cattle, that is."

"I'm sorry to hear that," I said. "Was it a very large herd?"

"Thirty-two thousand head," he replied wistfully. "Plus more than a thousand calves. That was last fall, mind you. As of now, I couldn't give you a number. We're still rounding up the stragglers, but we estimate the losses at about sixty-five percent."

Thomas jerked forward in his chair. "*Sixty-five percent?* Good heavens! I'd read in the papers that the industry had taken a blow, but this . . . why, it's staggering!"

"I fared better than most, if you can believe it. And though perhaps *ruined* is a touch overstating the case, I am exceedingly strained, and I don't know that I can sustain the investment."

"It's hard luck, Roosevelt," Mr. Burrows said.

Our guest grunted. "What an interesting choice of words, old fellow. It's *some* kind of luck, if I have any nose for it."

Thomas narrowed his eyes. "Are we to understand that something more than nature was at work here?"

"I will not claim to master all the secrets of Mother Nature, Mr. Wiltshire, but one thing I know for certain: Something strange is going on in the Badlands. Something evil. And the way things are going, by this time next year, there will be no one left to stop it."

CHAPTER 3

CAMPFIRE TALES—POWDER KEG—A
MURDER, A MONSTER, AND MAGIC

Evil?" Thomas arched a dark eyebrow.

"It sounds dramatic, I know," Mr. Roosevelt said. "Please believe I use the word quite deliberately. There has simply been too much death and mishap to put it down to chance. This horrid winter is just the latest episode. When I came to you last fall, I would have sworn things couldn't get much worse, and now here we are."

"Perhaps you'd better start at the beginning," Thomas suggested.

"Indeed." Mr. Roosevelt sank deeper into his chair, as if settling in for a long tale. "Misfortune comes in threes, isn't that the saying? It certainly has in this case. It all began last spring, or thereabouts."

"Thereabouts?" I echoed. "You can't be more precise?"

He shook his head. "What you must understand, Miss Gallagher, is that the Badlands is a rough bit of country in every sense of the word. Calamities big and small blow through town like so many tumbleweeds. That being the case, it's hard to say for certain when it all started, but it seems to me that it was around this time last year when things began to feel . . . off."

"How do you mean?"

"I don't know quite how to describe it. A turn in the air. A sense of foreboding. I put it down to restlessness and melancholy, to which I confess myself occasionally prone. It's only with hindsight that I realized this period coincided with two very unhappy events. The first was a murder. At least, that's the theory; they never did find a body."

"Who was the presumed victim?" Thomas asked.

"A prospector by the name of Benjamin Upton. He'd only been in town for a few weeks, but he was already quite the local celebrity. He'd made a great success of it in the Black Hills. One of the last lone wolves operating down there, as I understand it. Didn't need a geologist to tell him where to look for gold. Cut from the same cloth as your forefathers, Burrows."

"My foremothers, actually," Mr. Burrows said. "It was my great-grandmother who had the nose for gold. I'm told it smelled like sugar, but perhaps that was a metaphor."

"What does it smell like to you?" I asked, my curiosity momentarily getting the better of me. Mr. Burrows had earth luck, of a sort that allowed him to sense the elemental composition of anything he touched. I'd often tried to imagine what that would be like. He usually referred to it as tasting or smelling, but I suspect it was neither, or maybe something in between.

In answer to my question, he said, "Why, it smells like money, of course."

Thomas cleared his throat impatiently. "Back to Mr. Upton. Do I take it he was lucky?"

Mr. Roosevelt shrugged. "I couldn't tell you. Lucky or not, he was rumored to have a hundred thousand in gold squirreled away somewhere nearby, and I'd call that plenty of motive for murder."

"I'll say." I couldn't help picturing the cartoon image of a robber baron frolicking in a mound of coins. "But if you never found a body, how do you know he's dead?"

"I don't, for a certainty. But given how many people have seen his ghost, I feel fairly confident in the diagnosis."

"*Hmm*." Thomas cut me a look. "Forgive me, Mr. Roosevelt, but are you sure that isn't merely—"

"Campfire tales? I thought so too at first. Cowboys are a superstitious breed, and given to spinning yarns. But some of the witnesses had never met the man, yet they described him to a T. Tall, rugged, outlandishly bushy mustache. And the circumstances of the sightings were all the same. Always in the mirror of the hotel room where he'd been staying."

That certainly sounded like a ghost. Unlike shades, they couldn't manifest physically, so they tended to rely on images and sounds. Mirrors were a favorite medium for haunting, along with photographs, paintings, and of course, dreams.

"Even then," Mr. Roosevelt went on, "I might not have taken much notice of the affair. Murder is hardly unusual out west, and with murder comes restless spirits. Except that our Mr. Upton was only the first to go missing. After he disappeared, Medora caught gold fever. Everyone and his pony wanted a piece of that hundred thousand he'd supposedly stashed somewhere nearby. Treasure hunters swooped in from every corner of the territory—and now half a dozen of them have vanished too. Anyone who gets close to his trail just"—he snapped his fingers—"gone."

"Good heavens, what a tale!" Mr. Burrows laughed. "Murder. Ghosts. Treasure hunters disappearing on the trail, never to be heard from again. Why, it's the stuff of yellowback novels!"

"Just wait. I haven't even got to the part about the monster."

"I'm sorry." Thomas leaned forward again. "Did you say *monster*?"

"I did, and only half in jest. That's the second of our trio of mysteries." Mr. Roosevelt removed his pince-nez and began cleaning them with a handkerchief. "Another frequent occurrence in the Badlands is cattle rustling, so here again, it's hard to be sure exactly when it all started. I became aware of it when about a dozen of my own went missing. I mentioned it to the Marquis de Morès, and he reported having suffered a similar loss some weeks before. This was back in, oh"—he squinted at the ceiling—"call it the second week of July last year. I convened a meeting of my stockman's association, and lo and behold, virtually every man there was missing at least a few beeves.

"Well, naturally, we assumed it was the Indians. They'd been making mischief in the area for a while, setting fires, that sort of thing. There was a . . . *discussion* . . . on the prairie. A few of us, a few of them, more than a few Winchesters. They denied it all fiercely, and since we had no proof . . ." Shrugging, he replaced his pince-nez. "Then, not a week later, that same band comes thundering into Medora, furious, claiming half a dozen horses have been stolen from their camp. Well, the ranchers didn't take to being called thieves any better than the Sioux had. It looked set to be a terrible show-down. I don't like to think about what might have happened had they not come across that clearing." He fell silent for a moment, gaze abstracted with memory.

"Clearing, sir?"

"I beg your pardon, Miss Gallagher. Yes, the clearing. Just when things were looking rather dire between the ranchers and the Sioux, a group of their hunters came across a clearing littered with carcasses. Their horses, our beeves, not to mention elk, deer, virtually every hoofed creature you can name—all of them ripped apart by something monstrously powerful. I saw them myself. Rib cages cracked open, skulls and femurs shattered . . . Genuinely horrific to look upon."

"Could a mountain lion be responsible?" Thomas asked. "Or perhaps a bear?"

Mr. Roosevelt smiled. "You're not a woodsman, are you, Wiltshire?"

"Very far from it, alas. I take it my question is naive?"

"In the general order of things, perhaps, but even seasoned hunters have mooted unlikelier theories, for lack of anything better. The reality is that none of us, Sioux or white, has ever heard of such a thing. I mounted a hunting party myself, but we found no trace of an animal capable of that sort of violence. To say nothing of its appetite. The sheer scale of the slaughter beggars belief. Hundreds of animals over the course of a single summer. That's why I came to you last October. By that point, I was convinced this was no ordinary wild animal. Even so, I didn't feel a great deal of urgency, since I presumed the killings would slow over the winter, if not stop altogether. And so they did, only now that the snows have melted, the beast is back—and this time, it's killing men, too. I received word just this morning that one of the boys from Pronghorn Ranch was jumped on the trail a few days ago. Dragged right off his pony, and the both of them mauled to bits."

"How awful!"

"It is indeed, Miss Gallagher. As bad as things were last summer, it's immeasurably worse now. Whatever this thing is, it's covering more ground than ever before, killing everything in its path. It's got the whole Badlands in an uproar. Some of the most hard-bitten, God-fearing fellows I know are convinced it's a demon."

Mr. Burrows scoffed. "Surely you don't believe such nonsense?"

"What I believe, Burrows, is that something in those woods can crack open the rib cage of a thousand-pound moose like a squirrel splits a sunflower seed."

"*Christ.*" Mr. Burrows made a face. "What an image."

"I'd hoped that if there was one silver lining to this awful winter we've just had, it would be that this beast, whatever it is, perished along with everything else. Instead, it's just having more trouble finding prey."

"So now it's preying on people," I said, shuddering.

"Precisely."

A bleak silence drifted over the study.

Thomas cleared his throat again. "About this winter, then. I presume that is the third of the misfortunes you referred to?"

Mr. Roosevelt nodded. "The Winter of the Blue Snow, they're calling it. The worst anyone can remember. Tens of thousands of animals perished, to say nothing of the human casualties. They say when the river finally started moving again, it unleashed a black tide of animal carcasses that flowed for days."

Thomas shook his head in grim awe. "It will ruin a great many ranches, I suppose."

"It already has, not to mention the businesses that depend on them. Medora is in danger of becoming a ghost town, Mr. Wiltshire. Which is why I need your help, both of you. People are saying the place is cursed—unless they dismiss that as superstition, in which case they blame the Indians, and vice versa. It's already a powder keg out there. I fear this could be the match. Something must be done."

"What of the local law enforcement?" Thomas asked.

"The sheriff is a fellow by the name of Hell Roaring Bill Jones. A thoroughly competent frontiersman, at least when he's sober. But he's quite out of his element here."

"*Hell Roaring Bill.*" Mr. Burrows laughed, delighted.

"I serve as his deputy now and then, and I can promise you the moniker is well earned. But as I said, this matter is beyond his expertise. He's not one of *us,* you know." Mr. Roosevelt raised an eyebrow, making his meaning plain. Sheriff Jones, however hell-roaring, wasn't a member of the paranormal community. "I don't care to have him directly involved."

"We understand, sir," Thomas said. "We'll certainly do our best to get to the bottom of the matter."

"Good, good." And just like that, Mr. Roosevelt was on his feet, watch in hand. "You'll leave tomorrow?"

"*What?*" I jerked upright. "So soon?"

"We may require a *little* more time to get our affairs in order," Thomas said diplomatically.

"Very well. I'll make the necessary arrangements. And here." Mr. Roosevelt drew a stack of letters from a leather case at his feet and deposited them on the desk. "From my men at Elkhorn and Maltese Cross. A little light reading for the train." Looking Thomas up and down, he added, "You ought to pay a visit to your tailor before you go. You'll want something a good deal sturdier than what you're wearing. You can ride, I trust?"

"Passing well."

Mr. Burrows snorted. "Don't believe a word of it, Roosevelt. He joined us for polo once, and he rode circles around the lot of us."

"I daresay you'll find this a bit different," Mr. Roosevelt said. "They'll call you a dude, Wiltshire, but don't you bother about it. Show them what you're made of, and they'll shut up soon enough, trust me. And what about you, Miss Gallagher? Can you sit a horse?"

"Passing well, and I'm not being modest." I'd learned only recently, as part of my training with the Pinkerton Agency. I could lope around a ring and jump a low fence or two, but that was about the extent of it.

"Well, then, this will be quite the adventure for both of you. I'm only sorry I can't join you. I've a manuscript to deliver to my publisher, and given the state of my finances, I don't dare disappoint them. But my men will take good care of you, and I'll expect regular updates on the wire."

"You'll have them, sir," Thomas said, shaking hands.

"Excellent. In that case, I wish you good hunting, and . . ." His smile faded, and his blue eyes grew solemn. "Be careful," he said. "Both of you."

"So," Mr. Burrows said, "what's your theory?"

He sat across from Thomas and me in the landau, which he'd summoned to the house as soon as Mr. Roosevelt left. He claimed to be interested in the case, but I didn't believe that for a second. I'd seen the glint in his eye when Mr. Roosevelt suggested new clothes; he wanted to be there when Thomas visited his tailor. Not that I blamed him. I'd met Mr. Jennings, and he was nearly as posh as his best client. Watching those two painfully English gentlemen try to work out how to outfit Thomas for the Badlands would be worth the price of admission. Alas, a gentleman's tailor was no place for a woman, but I had no doubt Mr. Burrows would merrily relate the details afterward. For now, we were headed down to Wang's General Store—to procure supplies and, hopefully, smooth things over with the proprietor.

"My theory?" Thomas arched an eyebrow. "It's far too early for that."

"Come now, we both know you have one. You're just reluctant to show your cards in case you're proven wrong later."

Thomas *tsk*ed. "Do you think my pride so fragile? There's a difference between theories and rampant speculation, and I see no benefit in indulging in the latter."

"Oh, let's do indulge." Mr. Burrows thumped his cane playfully on the floor of the carriage. "Tell him, Rose."

"Much as I don't like to encourage him, Thomas, I am curious what you think. The murder seems straightforward enough, but a monster? And what do either of them have to do with a harsh winter?"

Thomas started to answer before checking himself. "Let's wait until we reach Wang's. I do have a thought—"

"I knew it!" Mr. Burrows thumped his cane again.

"—but I'd like to hear Wang's reaction first. If he has a similar notion, then I'll know there's merit in it."

Traffic was light this time of day, and it didn't take us long to reach Five Points. It felt strange visiting the old neighborhood these days—especially arriving in a landau, of all things. If a tidy little brougham was conspicuous, Mr. Burrows's six-seater vis-à-vis was positively outrageous. People stopped to stare as the three of us descended from our grand vehicle, as though maybe they expected to see the mayor. That was silly, of course. The mayor wasn't half as rich as Jonathan Burrows. I fought the absurd impulse to wave, as though I were the Queen of England. Instead, I hurried awkwardly into Wang's General Store.

As always, the scent of the place hit me as soon as opened the door, a unique cocktail of incense and dried mushrooms and heaven knew what else. The shelves were so crowded that it was impossible to keep track of all the exotic items lending their perfume to the place. The grocery section was interesting enough, but it was the dry goods—the silks and the porcelain, the lacquer boxes and jade talismans—that drew me most. I'd spent hours browsing these shelves with wandering eyes and fingers. It reminded me of a museum—or, more accurately, the basement of a museum, where they keep all the curiosities crammed haphazardly in high, overstuffed shelves. How Mei kept track of it all, I couldn't imagine.

Just now, she was sweeping up some broken bits of pottery near the counter. "Oh dear," I said. "I hope they paid for it, whoever they were."

Mei smiled, showing her dimples. "He left with a full ear and an empty purse."

"That's my girl," I said, laughing. Mei Wang was a gentle soul, but those who mistook her soft-spoken ways for weakness learned their lesson very quickly.

The bell on the door tinkled again, and her glance went over my shoulder. "Hello, Mr. Wiltshire, Mr. Burrows. Shall I fetch my father?"

"Miss Wang." Thomas doffed his hat. "If you wouldn't mind."

She ducked through the silk curtain separating the front of the store from the back, reappearing a moment later with her father in tow. I could tell straightaway that Mr. Wang had heard what happened to the stone we'd recovered, because the look he gave Thomas and me was slightly south of frosty. His mouth was a thin line under his drooping mustache, and he folded his arms over his frog buttons as if to say, *Explain yourselves.*

"Good afternoon," Thomas said breezily, as though he didn't notice. Drawing a money purse from his jacket, he deposited it on the counter. "For your troubles, Wang. Thank you again."

Mr. Wang didn't even glance down. He just stood there like a statue, arms folded.

Thomas sighed. "Look, Wang, it's not as though we had a choice. The Agency has spent thousands of dollars dredging that site to recover every last fragment of Flood Rock. There was no chance they were going to let it go."

Mr. Wang said something bone-dry in Chinese.

Thomas blinked. "Well, I hardly think *that's* called for."

Mei cleared her throat awkwardly. "Would anyone like tea?"

"That would be lovely, thank you," Mr. Burrows said, making no attempt to hide his amusement.

"We really are very sorry, Mr. Wang," I said. "Of course Mr. Wiltshire and I know you wouldn't have sold it to just anyone, but we couldn't convince Chicago. They don't know you like we do. It's terribly unfair, but we were under direct orders." More or less.

That seemed to appease him a little. He picked up the purse, hefting it experimentally. Then he grunted and tossed it back down.

With another sigh, Thomas reached into his jacket once more. "You drive a hard bargain, Wang. There now, can we consider the matter settled?"

Mr. Wang glanced down at the stack of bills on the counter. "Settled," he said grudgingly. "But not happy."

"That will have to do, I'm afraid. Miss Gallagher and I are on a very tight schedule. We're headed out west, and we've a list of supplies we need to procure. In addition to which, I'd be grateful for your thoughts on a rather fascinating tale we've just heard."

That piqued Mr. Wang's interest. He cocked his head.

"What kind of tale?" Mei asked, reappearing with the tea.

"Three sorts, actually," Thomas said, with the bright-eyed look of an intrigued detective. "A murder, a monster, and magic."

CHAPTER 4

AN ELEMENTARY THEORY—THE LUCKIEST
MAN ALIVE—A NEW HABIT

Mr. Wang took a long, meditative sip of tea. Then he asked a question in Chinese.

Thomas shook his head. "I'm afraid not. From what our client told us, it doesn't sound as though anyone has actually seen the beast."

Mr. Wang hummed a skeptical-sounding note and said something else.

"A fair question," Thomas said. "Mr. Roosevelt did mention that frontiersmen are a superstitious lot, and given to tall tales. It's possible, even likely, that some of the details have been exaggerated. On the other hand, Roosevelt saw some of the carcasses himself, and he was quite insistent that the predator responsible had to be as strong as a grizzly, if not stronger."

Mei Wang shuddered as she poured her father another cup.

"This is very hard to imagine. I saw a stuffed grizzly bear at the museum once. It was the size of an ox."

"An ox with four-inch claws, and it's preying on humans," Mr. Burrows said, eying his own tea as though he wished it were something stronger.

We'd decamped to one of the dozens of rooms behind the store, the better to keep our discussion private. Mei had left a boy in charge of the counter so she could join us, and I was happy to have her there. Aside from acting as a translator for her father, she had a way of asking the right questions, and today was no exception. "Do you believe these things are related? The ghost, the creature, and the winter?"

"Mr. Roosevelt seemed to think so," I said. "But if there's a connection, I'm not seeing it. Could any of it be explained by magic?"

Mei considered that. In practice, she was only an amateur witch, but her knowledge of lore ran deep. "I have heard of magical experiments on animals from ancient times. They say Empress Wu Zetian kept a tiger with fangs as long as swords, but this is probably legend."

"What about the winter?" I asked.

She shook her head. "No magic is that powerful. Not mortal magic, anyway."

Mr. Wang narrowed his eyes. He said something to Mei, and she fetched a map from the back of the room and spread it out before us. Crudely drawn and smudged in places, it depicted the North American continent as it might have looked before the arrival of Europeans. There were mountains and rivers and lakes, but not much else. No state lines or borders or even cities. Instead, a single Chinese character appeared at a handful of sites across the continent, and they didn't match any place I could name. None, that is, except one: Mr. Wang took a pencil and drew the same character over the familiar shape of New York, in the place where Long Island meets the rest of the state.

That's when I understood. "These are portals, aren't they?" The one he'd just drawn was Hell Gate, the portal in the East River we'd discovered last year.

"Those we know of, at least," Thomas said. "As Hell Gate proved, there are almost certainly others that have disappeared from modern memory. But this will be the lion's share, and as you can see, they are thankfully few and far between."

I counted seven, three of which looked to be in Canada, and another that might have been in Mexico, or maybe Texas. "This one," I said, dropping my finger near the middle of the map. "Where exactly—?"

"Dakota," said Mr. Wang. "Bad lands."

I groaned. "That can't be a coincidence."

"It *could* be," Thomas said, but his tone was more than a little skeptical.

"I don't understand," Mr. Burrows said. "Portals lead to the realm of the dead. It would explain the ghost, but what does it have to do with monstrous predators or a freakishly harsh winter?"

Thomas and Mr. Wang exchanged a look. The latter said something in Chinese, and his daughter gasped.

Dread prickled along my skin. Mei Wang was not easily alarmed. "What is it?"

"I . . . I don't know the word in English."

Thomas sighed. "The word is *elemental,* and I had very much hoped I was being fanciful in considering it. But if you're having the same thought, Wang . . ."

I wracked my brain for any mention of elementals in *Pullman's Guide to the Paranormal,* but came up empty. "Is that some kind of fae?"

"Not exactly," Thomas said, "but neither is it a mortal being.

They dwell in the otherworld, past the realms of the dead but before the realms of the fae."

"But what are they?" Mr. Burrows asked. "I've never heard of such a thing, and I thought myself relatively conversant in the paranormal."

"Their exact nature is a source of much debate. The ancient Greeks thought of them as embodying the four classical elements of earth, air, fire, and water."

"But they forgot wood," Mei put in, "and metal, which are also part of the *wu xing*."

Thomas nodded. "Perhaps. The Hindus and the Japanese add æther. Where all the major traditions agree is that elementals command tremendous power over the earth's great forces. You can be forgiven for not having heard of them, Burrows. They haven't been encountered since the Great Hurricane of 1780. Conventional wisdom has it that elementals disappeared from the earth along with the fae when the portals were sealed centuries ago. The incident in 1780 was the result of a breach in the Matawi portal in Venezuela."

"Does that mean we have another leaking portal on our hands?" The thought made me ill.

Thomas raised a cautioning hand. "Let's not get ahead of ourselves. It's one possible explanation, but by no means the most probable. It's far more likely that we're dealing with more mundane forces. An unusually harsh winter may simply be that. This so-called monster, if it exists at all, might be nothing more than a relic of a species thought extinct. A saber-toothed cat, perhaps, or a giant bear."

I felt some of the tension go out of my shoulders. "The missing prospector might be an ordinary murder case."

"Precisely. The only way to find out is to begin our investigation, and on that note . . ." He drew out his Patek Philippe. "Good heavens, it's already half two. We'd best be getting on. May I leave you with this list, Wang? Miss Gallagher and I have another stop in the neighborhood."

"Another stop?" I couldn't think of any other business we had in Five Points, unless it was in . . .

"Chatham Square," Thomas said. "We are in need of our wizard."

Nikola Tesla was not technically a wizard. He was, however, an inventor of astonishing genius, who also happened to be the luckiest man alive, having inherited two separate strains of luck. One of these allowed him to manipulate electricity at will, shaping it as easily as Clara kneaded dough for her famous biscuits.

All of which I tried very hard to remember whenever it seemed as if we were about to explode.

"I say, Tesla, is that entirely safe?" Thomas took a step backward, his gaze fixed warily on the shimmering web of electricity that was presently weaving itself across the center of the lab. He'd have to take a few more steps to join me, since I was already pressed up against the back wall having a few discreet words with Our Lord and Savior.

"Please excuse me, Mr. Wiltshire," the inventor replied, "I am concentrating."

"Yes. Quite." Thomas took another step back.

Mr. Tesla closed his eyes, his sharp features bathed in the eerie glow of his electric web. Before him, a hulking copper mushroom—the device he referred to as his "coil"—crackled with power. Tongues of lightning lashed out in all directions, some as thick as an arm, others as delicate as gossamer. Wild and terrifying, they were gradually being tamed, woven together into a sort of rope at a wave of the inventor's hand. A gesture to his right plucked a strand from the nest; a sweep to his left guided it into place. He swayed a little with each movement, looking for all the world as though he were conducting a symphony orchestra. The more threads of electricity were joined together, the thicker the rope became and the brighter it grew, until I was forced to shut my eyes against the glare. Even then I could *feel* it—whispering along my skin, standing the hairs of my arms on end.

And then, without warning, it was over. The light faded, and I opened my eyes. The inventor stood in front of his coil looking annoyed—and decidedly luminescent.

"Tesla," Thomas said. "You're glowing."

The inventor made a dismissive gesture, his long fingers tracing moonbeams through the shadows. "It will pass." He threw a series of switches, silencing the machine and setting the room aglow with electric lighting. Then he heaved a frustrated sigh.

"What were you doing?" I asked, peeling myself away from the wall.

"I am attempting to develop electric forces on the order of those found in nature."

"You mean like lightning?"

"Precisely." His blue-gray eyes sparked like one of his oscillators, bright with enthusiasm. "If I can re-create lightning, the possibilities are almost limitless. We could power such machines as the mind can scarcely conceive. Even the very rains in the sky would be ours to command. But I fear I am a long way off. I cannot seem to keep the current stable. I thought perhaps if I . . ." The gleam in his eyes faded, and he sighed again. "Another time, perhaps. I'm sure you are in a terrible hurry, yes?"

Thomas smiled. "You know us too well."

Waving us toward his little office in the corner, he said, "Tell me."

"What do you know of portals?" Thomas asked.

"To the otherworld? A little. As you may recall, I once attempted to create one. That is how Scarlett came to me." As soon as he spoke the name, a burst of red flame went up from his desk, and Mr. Tesla's pet fireball sprang into the air. Scarlett hung there a moment, as if deciding whether Thomas and I were safe. Then she floated over to the inventor and settled on his shoulder. As always, I half expected to see his clothing catch fire, but of course it didn't. The otherworldly flame ball wasn't actually hot. For that matter, she wasn't even really a flame. Nobody knew what she was or where she came from, and Mr. Tesla had given up trying to find out.

"Of course," Thomas said, "how silly of me. In that case, you must have conducted all manner of experiments. Would any of that work be useful in trying to determine whether a portal is leaking?"

"Leaking?" Mr. Tesla considered that. "Yes, I have a device that would serve. You have used it yourself, in fact." He gestured toward a humble-looking bit of machinery on his desk. About the size of a loaf of bread, it resembled a metal box with a cord attached to it, at the end of which was a probe that looked a little like the earpiece of a telephone.

I recognized it straightaway. "The luck detector?"

"Indeed. The miniature version I gave you last fall was not very powerful, but this larger apparatus is much more sensitive and has a greater range. You are welcome to take it. I have reverted to the theoretical phase of investigation on that particular project." He tapped his head, which was where most of his *investigating* took place.

"That's very kind of you," I said. "But how does a luck detector help us with a portal?"

Mr. Tesla smiled patiently. "The intended purpose of a device does not represent the limit of its potential applications. The machine works by detecting the electromagnetic waves emitted when a person uses his luck. These waves can be distinguished from other forms of radiation by the specific frequencies at which they oscillate."

"I remember. You explained that to us last time." I hadn't really understood the explanation, but that was another matter.

He gave a professorial nod. "Yes, good. Now, to understand

how that relates to portals, we have only to recall that luck comes to us from the fae, traced back to ancient times when fae and mortals occasionally coupled."

I remembered that too, and in its own way, it was even harder to grasp. What would it be like to know that one of your ancestors had a fling with a fairy? Or, in Mr. Tesla's case, more than one of your ancestors?

"Therefore," he went on, "if certain electromagnetic waves indicate the presence of luck, and luck is of the fae . . ."

"Then the fae would presumably give off the same type of radiation." Thomas nodded. "I see. Meaning that if a portal to the realms of the fae were leaking, that radiation would be spilling out into our world."

"Precisely. So . . ." The inventor indicated the tin box once more. "A luck detector, yes. But also a fae detector, and therefore a leaky portal detector."

"Brilliant," Thomas said. "It's exactly what we need. But how shall we power it? Electricity will be in very short supply where we're going."

Mr. Tesla shrugged. "Batteries."

"I beg your pardon?"

"Batteries. I have recently perfected a dry-cell variant of the Leclanché cell, which is quite convenient for portable use."

My mouth fell open. "Why, but only six months ago, we had to go to all sorts of trouble to transmit power wirelessly!" By *all sorts of trouble*, I meant risking our very lives to attach an antenna atop the Statue of Liberty. To this day, I can't even look at Lady Liberty without feeling a little weak in the knees.

"Such is the relentless march of progress, Miss Gallagher. It is what makes science so very exciting. Now, is there anything else you require?"

"That should do nicely, thank you." Smiling, Thomas added,

"Unless you happen to have a device that might prove useful against an alpha predator of mythic proportions."

He'd been making light, but Mr. Tesla took him quite seriously, tilting his head with interest. "Are you referring to werewolves?"

"Wait." I felt the blood drain from my face. "Werewolves aren't real, are they?"

"Of course not," said Thomas.

"*Hmm*," said Mr. Tesla.

Thomas laughed, but it sounded a little nervous. "Come now, Tesla, the matter has been thoroughly investigated by science."

"My dear Mr. Wiltshire, nothing in this world has been *thoroughly* investigated by science."

Which remark has haunted my nightmares ever since.

We parted ways after that, Mr. Tesla returning to his experiments while Thomas and I saw to our outfitting needs. Thomas would visit his tailor while I headed back uptown in hopes of borrowing a riding habit from my friend Edith. I might look a little strange prancing about the Badlands in a frock designed for a stately ride through Central Park, but I was pretty sure none of the stores on Ladies' Mile had a cattlewomen's department. And whereas Thomas's tailor could just adapt his existing designs to a more rugged fabric, I'd need more time than I had to find a pattern and a team of seamstresses ready to stitch it together in a day.

Boots, I thought as I made my way to the el. *I'll need sturdier boots, and a riding coat.* And there was one more thing, I realized, recalling the yellowback novels I'd read about the Wild West.

I was going to need a bigger gun.

CHAPTER 5

LITTLE MISERY—STONE AND SAGEBRUSH—A FANCY FELLER

The train pulled into Medora at two o'clock in the morning, a full four days after we'd departed New York. I was sleepy and stiff from the journey, so it took me a moment to absorb my surroundings, and when I did, my first thought was that we must have missed the station.

The window beside me framed a dark canvas of wilderness. Not a single building obstructed the view, which stretched unbroken to a distant horizon sketched in starlight. Thomas was obliged to open the door of our sleeping car himself, and I had to pick my way carefully down the steps in the dark. It wasn't as though I'd expected white-gloved ushers to help me from the train, but a platform would have been nice. Instead, I hitched up my skirt and jumped down onto dry grass, sending a puff of dust into the night air. The station, such as it was, revealed itself to my left, in the form of a log cabin about the size of Augusto's Grocery. It stood dark and shuttered, and I realized that Thomas and I were the only passengers getting off the train.

This really is the middle of nowhere, I thought. Then I glanced up, and what I saw took my breath away. "Thomas," I whispered, instinctively reaching for him.

The night was ablaze with stars, tiny pinpricks of cold white light scattered across an impossible canopy of sky. The moon had sunk below the horizon; in its place, a glittering band of light traced a clear path through the heavens. At its center, a black void yawned, as though the sky itself were torn. I knew this for the Milky Way, but I'd never seen it. In New York, you could barely make out the stars at all, what with the smoke and ash of steam trains and factories, not to mention hundreds of thousands of homes heated with coal and wood. They were clearer in Newport, but *this* . . . The sky wasn't just above us, it was *all around us,* as if poised to swallow us whole. The thought made me a little dizzy, but Thomas was there to steady me.

"Magnificent," he murmured as I leaned against him.

We stood there a moment in perfect silence, contemplating the vastness of the universe. Then the train blasted its whistle and I nearly leapt out of my skin.

With a clang of bells and a puff of smoke, the train chugged away, leaving Thomas and me alone in the grass. On the far side of the depot, the blocky outline of a town carved itself out of the gloom.

"Thomas Wiltshire?" A figure stepped out of the shadows. "Charlie Morrison. I'm the foreman down at Maltese Cross. Mr. Roosevelt asked me to see to you. These yours?" He nodded at a jumble of trunks in the dirt. Some thoughtful soul must have dumped them from the train while Thomas and I were admiring the sky.

"A pleasure to meet you, Mr. Morrison," Thomas said. "Thank you for making the journey, especially at such an uncivilized hour."

"No trouble. Wagon's over here." Grabbing a trunk at one end, Morrison started dragging it through the dust.

Thomas hastily picked up the other end. "Apologies, but there is some rather delicate equipment in here."

The foreman grunted. "Boss says you're a photographer?"

That was the cover story we'd agreed on with Mr. Roosevelt. Pinkertons being about as popular as plague in these parts, we figured it would be best for all concerned if we kept our true business here under wraps. Usually, Thomas posed as an attorney when he was on a case, but this time, we'd decided on a wildlife photographer and his assistant. Rumors of the mysterious beast prowling the Badlands had reached New York—so our story went—and Thomas and I were there to capture it on film. "I can't tell you how exciting it is to be here," Thomas said brightly. "I've long wanted to document the great American frontier."

"Well, you're welcome to it," the foreman said, sliding the trunk into the back of the wagon. "What's left of it, anyways."

We finished loading up and climbed onto the buckboard. "So," Thomas said as the wagon rattled into motion. "This is Medora."

"What's left of it," Charlie Morrison said again, with a sour twist of his mouth.

"We've heard about the difficulties out here," Thomas said. "Hard times."

"You could say that. Half the town's upped stakes. Newspaper's gone, and the hardware store. Not to mention the billiard bar, the oyster grotto . . . These days, about the only concern going is Granger's Saloon. That and the hotel. Speaking of which . . ." He hauled on the reins, bringing us to a halt outside a white clapboard building.

"We're here already?" I glanced over what would be our home for the next few weeks, a bland structure of two floors with small, grimy-looking windows.

"Ain't a big place, ma'am." Mr. Morrison jumped down and offered me a hand. "I'll be here midmorning to take you down to

Cougar Ranch. If you're looking to get a photo of whatever's been taking them animals, that's the best place to start."

"Tell me, Mr. Morrison, what do you make of all this business?" Thomas asked. "What are we likely to find out there?"

The foreman was silent a moment, his features inscrutable in the dark. "Whatever it is, I'd stay out of its way if I was you. I seen my share of blood and guts—begging your pardon, ma'am—but what that thing done to young Gareth Wilson . . ." He shook his head. "Best keep a shotgun on you, is all I can say."

"Sound advice. We'll procure one first thing in the morning."

"Sleep well." The foreman touched his hat and was on his way.

The mention of *sleep* hit me like a spell. Suddenly, it was all I could do to keep my eyes open. Thomas and I headed into the hotel, and about half an hour later, I was curled up on a sagging bed, dozing off.

I dreamed of monsters.

"A lion," I told Thomas over breakfast the next morning. We sat in the small dining room on the ground floor of the hotel, pushing vaguely oatmeal-shaped sludge around in our bowls. "A lion the size of a mountain."

"Indeed? I didn't realize *mountain lion* was quite so literal."

"Easy to make fun when you're well rested." I reached for the sugar, but decided against it when I saw the line of ants marching up and down the side of the bowl. I followed the procession with my gaze, tracing it across the ill-fitted floorboards all the way to a crack in the wall. From the look of it, ants weren't the only thing coming and going through that crack, and I resolved to make sure my trunk stayed tightly sealed.

"Actually," Thomas said, "I couldn't sleep either. I spent much of the night on the balcony, taking in the night air."

"Balcony?" I frowned. "My room barely has a window."

"Yes, it would appear that aside from being haunted, my room has the additional distinction of being the Presidential Suite." Thomas's eyes twinkled with amusement. "Apparently, there was some hope of President Cleveland stopping here at one point, so they erected a balcony for him to oversee the parade they were planning. Alas, the townspeople were disappointed. He never came. A great shame for Cleveland, too, I should think. That parade would have been something to witness."

I glanced around the dining room, packed with whiskered ruffians who hadn't seen a bath this side of Easter. "I think you're right about that."

"Ah, here's Roosevelt's man." Thomas waved at a figure in the doorway.

We abandoned our breakfast without regret and headed outside, where Charlie Morrison waited with the buckboard and an extra horse. By the light of day, our guide revealed himself to be just the sort of hard-bitten fellow you'd expect of a cowboy, with craggy features and a bushy mustache that hid a great deal from the world.

"Nice-looking bit of iron you got there," he said, inclining his head at Thomas's shiny new 12-gauge shotgun. "That the new repeater folks is all lathered up about?"

"Indeed." Thomas hefted the weapon, looking pleased. "It seems the gunsmith is moving on as well, so he was keen to unload his inventory. I made a number of splendid purchases."

"Lucky you. Anyways, we oughta hit the trail. You two take the wagon. I got Fletch here." Morrison patted his horse and mounted up. Thomas took the reins of the buckboard, and we were off.

We'd arrived in the dark, so I had yet to form much of an impression of the town, but the morning light revealed a glum scene. Medora lay scattered across a flat expanse of dust and sagebrush, hemmed in on either side by looming walls of rock. The main street was a muddy track flanked by false-front buildings, many of them boarded up. Behind them, chickens and the occasional stray hog picked their way between scruffy shacks of graying wood. Some of those looked abandoned too. *Medora is in danger of becoming a ghost town,* Mr. Roosevelt had said, and he hadn't been exaggerating.

The picture improved as we passed the outskirts of town, following the gentle arch of the Little Missouri River. Tufts of green started to appear in the parched earth, and the muck of the main road gave way to a hard-packed wagon trail. The cliffs blocked much of our view, but as we passed beyond their embrace, the landscape erupted into violent relief. Towering bluffs of rock and clay studded the horizon, forming a chaotic tableau of gold and green and rust. Rugged peaks glowed white under the sun, while shadows carved deep troughs in the clay. Coulees lined with cottonwood and willow cut between the buttes, carving a million branching pathways through a maze of stone and sagebrush. I'd grown up in a different kind of maze, one of brick and peeling paint stuffed with so many people that it could be hard to breathe. This vast, empty country was vaguely terrifying—and exhilarating in a way I can hardly describe. I'd never seen such a wild place. It made me want to unhitch the horse from the wagon and ride, just *ride,* until both of us were exhausted.

"It's quite remarkable," Thomas said, his lean frame swaying along with the wagon. "If there's any trace of civilization out there, I can't see it."

"There's a few ranches nearby," Morrison said. "Normally, we'd be coming across some cattle by and by, but things is pretty quiet nowadays, what with the Great Die-Up."

The Great Die-Up. Like roundup, only deader. I recognized only too well the bleak humor of the destitute. We Irish practically invented it. "Were you here during the winter?" I asked.

He nodded. "Worst I ever saw. Lost a lotta good folks."

Thomas and I exchanged a look. How could we ask more

pointed questions about the winter without sounding strange? *By the way, did it seem supernatural at all?*

"Was there a particular storm?" Thomas asked. "Or was it just generally very cold?"

"Both. Mercury fell below fifty more 'n once. And there was this blizzard in January . . ." He shook his head. "Three full days, wind screaming like demons unleashed."

Demons. As analogies went, it seemed eerily on the nose.

"Wind wasn't the only thing screaming, neither." Morrison's gaze had taken on a faraway look. "Every night, you could hear the cows bellowing. Like they was begging for help. Until they wasn't. After that it was so quiet. Quiet enough to drive you mad. Some folks decided they preferred the business end of a rifle rather than go on with it."

I shuddered. Suddenly, the rugged landscape didn't seem quite so inviting.

We continued on in silence, hugging the riverbank for several miles until eventually we came to a shallows. "Cougar Ranch is just over yonder," Morrison said, indicating the far side of the river with a nod of his head. "We can cross here. Normally, I'd've done it a ways back, but the Little Misery is high this time of year."

Little Misery. More bleak humor, or was that just the local pronunciation of Missouri? I figured it would be rude to ask.

We splashed across into a lush meadow. Squinting, I could just make out the bulky outlines of cattle scattered across the green. Even from a distance, they looked thin and listless. "These are the strong ones," Morrison said. "Those as could hold up through the weather. Or at least, they was."

A few minutes later, the ranch house came into view, a long bungalow sheltered in a stand of cottonwood trees. Behind it, the working part of the ranch was a hive of activity. Men crisscrossed the yard like ants, ferrying wheelbarrows and pails and bushels of feed. Someone was shoeing a horse in front of the barn, while another man loaded his pony with rope and branding irons. Meanwhile, on the far side of the yard, a young stallion pranced nervously in a riding arena, while a colored fellow in worn leather chaps approached the animal slowly, murmuring something consoling. A pair of ranch hands leaned against the fence, watching; Morrison rode over, and they chatted for a spell, their laughter carrying on the wind. Money was exchanged, and then Morrison headed back to us, calling, "Good luck to you, John," over his shoulder. The cowboy in the arena nodded, but his eyes never left the stallion. The animal was watching him too, hooves stuttering against the hard earth.

"Is he trying to break that horse?" Thomas asked. "It looks awfully agitated."

Morrison swung down from his saddle. "He's full of piss and vinegar all right, but my money's on John all the same." He paused, looking embarrassed. "Beg your pardon, ma'am. Ain't used to having ladies about."

I'd barely noticed, too busy watching the fellow in the arena. "Is it dangerous? Breaking a horse?"

"Can be, but John's been doing it since he was in short britches, so I reckon he'll be just fine. This way."

We found the ranch owner, one Mr. Fergus Reid, reclining on a wide verandah overlooking the river. I could smell bread baking inside, but if there was a Mrs. Reid, she didn't come out to greet us.

"Mornin', Gus," said Charlie Morrison. "This here's the photographer I was telling you about, Thomas Wiltshire. And his assistant, Miss Gallagher."

The rancher looked us over, but he didn't get up from his chair. "Roosevelt's friend."

"That's right," Thomas said. "Thank you for taking the time to see us."

"Englishman." Reid grunted. "Figures."

"Does it?" Thomas smiled blandly. "Do you mind if we sit?"

"Suit yourselves." Our host continued to eye Thomas, taking in his silk ascot tie and engraved silver belt buckle, his perfectly tailored trousers and still-shiny boots. Even in the reinforced cotton known as denim, my partner somehow managed to look stylish, which probably wasn't a point in his favor in these parts. I'm sure he knew that, but Thomas simply wasn't capable of anything less than impeccable grooming, even if it marked him out as a *dude*.

"As Mr. Morrison has no doubt explained, we're here to photograph the mysterious creature everyone is talking about. I gather your stock has fallen prey more than once. If you have any information—"

Reid cut him off with an impatient gesture. "Like I told Charlie, and Roosevelt before him, there ain't no *creature*. Nothing in these woods is near strong enough to do what's been done to them animals. This is the red man's work, but if they think they can scare me off with all that hocus-pocus hoodoo of theirs, they are very much mistaken. All that jawin' about a serpent-demon?" He leaned over and expelled a squirt of tobacco juice, in case we'd missed the contempt.

"Serpent demon?" Thomas tilted his head.

"Something to do with the Sioux," Charlie Morrison explained. "A couple of their elders is saying it's down to this demon from their folk tales. That's the word, anyways, but nobody knows if they really believe that or if it's just smoke."

"Meanwhile, preacher in town's going on about the *end times*." Reid waved his hands elaborately before treating us to another volley of spittle. Apparently, he didn't discriminate when it came to religion; they were all equally worthy of the spittoon. "Ripe bunch of hogwash, all of it. This here's a straightforward affair. The Indians got it in for us, plain and simple."

Why, Mr. Reid, I can hardly imagine why anyone would have it in for you. Aloud, I said, "Weren't some of their horses taken too? The Sioux, I mean."

"So *they* say."

"Mr. Roosevelt saw the carcasses himself."

"How's he gonna tell one set of horse bones from another? And even if it was their horses, what's that prove? I can get Charlie here to sock me in the eye and say I was jumped by bandits, but that don't make it so."

I didn't know much about life out here, but it was plain to see that horses were important. The idea that the Sioux would slaughter their own animals just to throw some white ranchers off the scent seemed pretty far-fetched to me.

Thomas thought so too, judging from the starch in his posture. "Mr. Morrison mentioned some tracks," he said coolly. "Perhaps you might tell us about those?"

"I weren't the one saw 'em. That'd be John." Reid hooked his thumb in the direction of the riding arena.

"Want me to get him?" Morrison offered.

"No need," said a new voice, and I turned to find the man in question coming toward us. He looked a little wary at hearing his name mentioned, but when his gaze settled on Reid, he grinned. "Got him, boss."

The rancher whooped and slapped the arm of his chair. "Hot damn!"

Morrison was grinning too. "Them boys owe me some money," he said, inclining his head at the pair of ranch hands he'd been chatting with earlier.

"I warned 'em," John said. "Today's the day, I said. He won't take nobody but me just yet, but it won't be long now."

"Well goddamn, John Ward, if you ain't the finest bronco buster in the territory." Reid slapped his chair again. "That pony's gonna fetch me a pretty penny. You see 'im, Wiltshire? That there's a prime Missouri Fox Trotter."

Thomas smiled politely. "I'm not familiar with the breed."

"Strong as a standardbred, pretty as an Arabian." He paused, eyes narrowing shrewdly. "Horse like that'd be perfect for a fancy feller like yourself. Interested?"

Thomas laughed. "I enjoy a challenge, but a freshly broken horse doesn't seem like a very practical choice."

"Not him. Got another one, same sire. Three-year-old."

I could tell Thomas was tempted. On the whole, he lived modestly for a man of his means, but he did have a weakness for certain indulgences. Elegant tailoring. Fine wines. Swiss timepieces. And, apparently, horses. "As it happens, we are in the market—"

The rancher didn't even let him finish. "John, why don't you show these nice people what we got in the stables?" Smirking, he added, "You can tell 'em all about your monster."

CHAPTER 6

JOHN WARD, COWBOY—A NEW ROMANCE—
ANNIE OAKLEY—AN UNEXPECTED VISITOR

He really is magnificent," Thomas said, displaying all the bargaining skills of a rich man. He patted the stallion's neck, and it gave him a friendly snuffle. "I've never seen coloring like this."

Neither had I, and I couldn't deny it was striking. The coat was a sooty brown, almost black, but the mane and tail were silver.

"It's different, all right." John Ward had a deep, rasping voice that hinted at Southern roots and a fondness for tobacco. Late twenties, I guessed, though it was hard to be sure, lean and sinewy as he was. "Mr. Reid bred him special. Had a buyer lined up, but he went back east. Guess you could say Gideon here got stood up at the altar."

"Gideon." I could tell by the wistful look in Thomas's eye that he was going to buy that horse, whatever the price.

"Chose the name myself. It was me trained him to saddle, too.

He's young yet, but if you know what you're about, he's as smooth a ride as they come."

Thomas smiled. "You're a skilled salesman as well as a skilled horseman, I see."

"Don't know about that, but I sure would like to see him well situated. He'd be wasted around here. Horse like this is meant for running." Patting the animal's neck, he added, "And for lookin' fine."

As diverting as it was to watch two grown men fussing over a pretty pony, we had business to attend to. "Mr. Reid says you're the one who found the animal tracks," I said. "The ones left by the mysterious animal, I mean. Mr. Wiltshire and I are hoping to photograph it."

"Photograph it?" The ranch hand looked at me as if I were a few straws shy of a bushel. "Ma'am, anybody finds that thing, they need to put it in the ground."

"So you do believe the beast exists?" Thomas said. "Your employer seemed doubtful."

"All due respect, he ain't seen what I seen. There's *something* out there. I been hunting it for weeks, ever since the snows melted."

"Have you found anything?" I asked.

"Not much, but I only make it a few miles at a time before I gotta turn back. Boss don't consider it ranch work, and I ain't got too much free time on my hands, 'specially since I'm doing the foreman's job half the time."

I took out a notebook and a pencil. "What did the tracks look like?"

"Strange. Sorta like cat tracks, but huge." He made a shape with his hands, as big around as a supper plate.

I swallowed. Thomas's fancy shotgun seemed a whole lot less comforting than it had a minute ago. "Could it be a freakishly large mountain lion?"

Mr. Roosevelt had laughed at that question, but the look Mr. Ward gave me was deadly serious. "All I know is, I never saw nothing like it before. On top of which, I'm a decent hunter, but I can't seem to track this thing for more than a couple hundred yards before I lose the trail."

"*Hmm.*" Thomas stroked Gideon's neck thoughtfully. "Could the tracks be faked? Perhaps your employer isn't completely off the mark after all."

"You mean about the Sioux?"

"Or at least about cattle rustlers."

The ranch hand hesitated. "I don't like to contradict, but if you're asking my opinion . . ."

"Indeed, we defer entirely to your expertise."

"Well, in that case . . . I been running cattle all my life, and I seen my share of rustling. It don't usually involve killing. Slaughtering is a whole lotta work. Transport too. It just ain't practical. Better to move 'em on the hoof."

"Unless they wanted the meat for themselves," I pointed out. "Maybe they were just hungry."

"Plenty of hungry mouths around here, no doubt. But *that* much meat? And what about them horses the Sioux lost? You'd have to be pretty desperate to eat that."

"Your boss figured the dead horses were just for show," I said. "To throw the ranchers off the scent."

Mr. Ward shook his head but otherwise held his peace.

"Does he have any evidence to support that claim?" Thomas asked.

Another pause. I was getting the idea that John Ward was a cautious sort, at least around strangers. "Gets to a point where a man just needs someone to blame," he said finally.

"And he's decided to blame the Sioux," I said.

"No more 'n they've decided to blame him."

My eyebrows went up. "You've spoken to them?"

"Couple of 'em, anyhow. There's this group I keep running into out on the trail. Hunting party, led by a young fella called Little Wolf. They're real insistent that it's ranchers stealing their horses, and the rest is nothing but tricks."

Well, that made about as much sense as the reverse. Which was to say, none at all.

"By all accounts, cattle are being butchered by the hundreds," Thomas said. "The ranchers would hardly jeopardize their own livelihoods for some elaborate ruse. Especially now, after the winter has left them so vulnerable. Surely the Sioux can see that?"

"My thinking is, there's a whole lotta things the white man does that don't make sense to them, and they don't put nothing past him no more. Begging your pardon."

Thomas sighed. "Understandable, perhaps, but it does make things difficult. It's hard to find common ground where there is no trust."

"No trust around here, that's for sure. Just a whole lotta bad blood."

"So it would seem. Though it sounds as though you and this Little Wolf, at least, have managed to maintain a dialogue. Do you think he would be willing to speak with us?"

Mr. Ward's gaze shifted between Thomas and me, and I could see the wheels turning in his head. What did a photographer and his assistant want with a Sioux hunting party?

"I suppose you're hoping to take their photographs, Mr. Wiltshire?" I prompted.

"Indeed. A photograph of Sioux hunters ought to be of interest to any number of magazines and newspapers."

It would probably be a whole lot less interesting to the Sioux.

How would they react to a pair of white strangers asking questions? The idea made me more than a little nervous, and Mr. Ward's reply did nothing to ease my mind.

"Not sure this is the best time to be asking them for favors."

"Perhaps not," Thomas said, "but we have little choice. We're under a great deal of pressure, you see."

The ranch hand didn't look convinced, but he was too polite to argue. "Well, if you're set on it. Little Wolf speaks good English, and his sister too. Can't promise they'll talk to you, but I expect you'll be all right so long as you mind your p's and q's. I can show you on a map."

"Excellent. Thank you, Mr. Ward, you've been tremendously helpful." Thomas extended a hand, and they shook. "And now, back to transport. Miss Gallagher is also in need of a horse."

John Ward cocked his head. "Follow me. I got just the pony for you, ma'am."

Her name was Luna, and I was in love.

I hardly noticed the countryside on the way back to Medora. Barely listened to Thomas chatting with Mr. Morrison. I was too busy murmuring sweet nothings to *my very own horse*, a statuesque saddlebred that had briefly belonged to Mr. Reid's daughter. She was a palomino, Mr. Ward had explained, which meant she had a gold coat and a flaxen mane and tail. Tall and graceful, she was every inch as lovely as Thomas's stallion, but it was her manner that had stolen my heart: mild and curious, with attentive ears and soulful eyes that seemed to understand everything around her.

"You seem quite taken with her," Thomas observed as we reined in outside the hotel. Mr. Morrison had gone his own way at a crossroads a few miles outside of town, heading back to Maltese Cross.

"She's perfect. I could stay in this saddle all day." But of course that wasn't *quite* true, as I learned a moment later when I hopped down and a jolt of pain ran up my side.

"Stiff?"

"Sidesaddle is murder on the back." Not to mention the knees, the neck, and just about everything else. Yet another way in which women were forced to endure discomfort in order to protect their modesty. I hadn't noticed it much during my Newport training, but I'd only been in the saddle for an hour or so at a stretch. "I'm going to be a human pretzel by the time we're done here."

"Have you considered trousers?"

I blinked in astonishment. Not at the idea of wearing trousers—I'd thought about it plenty of times—but that it would be Thomas Wiltshire, the very model of starchy English propriety, who suggested it. "You wouldn't be embarrassed to be seen with a woman in trousers?"

He laughed. "Why should I be? Look around, Rose." He gestured at the street in all its makeshift, manure-lined glory. "I daresay you won't offend anyone's delicate sensibilities. Besides, we have a job to do, and it makes little sense for you to be inhibited out of deference to some arbitrary social convention."

Well, when he put it *that* way. "Where would I get them?"

"Trousers?" He looked me up and down. "You might manage with a pair of mine, actually."

That brought a furious blush to my cheeks. I could only imagine what Mr. Burrows would say. A dozen jokes about getting into my partner's trousers flitted through my mind—which of course just made me blush harder.

Thomas pretended not to notice, loosening the cinch around his horse's middle. "I'm ravenous. Shall we find ourselves some supper?"

I wrinkled my nose, recalling our so-called breakfast that morning. "Please tell me the hotel isn't our only option."

"I believe cold oatmeal represents the limit of the hotel's culinary ambitions. According to Mr. Morrison, the only real restaurant left in town is Granger's Saloon." Thomas gestured down the street. "Let's see what's on offer, shall we? We'll get the horses settled afterward."

I'd never set foot in a real Wild West saloon, and I expected to find a raucous barroom full of gamblers and gunslingers. As it turned out, though, Granger's was pretty tame, even by New York standards. The joints I was used to had names like One-Eyed Johnny's and Tub of Blood. They were unruly affairs, thrumming with noise and the threat of violence. The only thing thrumming in this place was the flies. Fewer than half the tables were occupied. An elk head hung crookedly on the wall, as if nobody could be bothered to straighten it, and the piano in the corner sported a generous layer of dust. The patrons looked dusty too, beaten down and exhausted, hunched over their drinks as if their sorrows didn't even have the decency to be properly drowned.

One group, at least, seemed to be enjoying themselves. A rabble of about half a dozen rough-looking men clustered around the bar, drinking and swapping tales at a volume that suggested they'd been at it for a while.

"Treasure hunters, I'd wager," Thomas said in an undertone. "Roosevelt mentioned that a number of them were still in town. I wonder if any more of their colleagues have gone missing."

If so, they didn't seem too worried about it, judging from the collection of empty whiskey bottles on the bar. "Should we try talking to them?"

"Once they've sobered up, perhaps. For now, I'd like to go over what we heard at the ranch while it's still fresh in our minds."

We chose a quiet table in the corner and ordered supper, a greasy stew with potatoes and root vegetables that looked like the sort of thing Mam used to make when we had no money. Still, at least it was hot and filling.

"So," I said. "What do we think about the creature? Real or not?"

"Too soon to say. Mr. Ward certainly seemed convinced, but it does strike me as odd that he would have such difficulty following its trail. He claims to be a proficient tracker, after all."

"Maybe he's not as skilled as he thinks."

"In which case, can we rely upon his judgment either way?"

A good point. Something didn't add up there. "What if you and Mr. Wang were right about it being an elemental? Could that explain it?"

Thomas made a skeptical sound. "We know so little of them, it's hard to be sure, but I'd be surprised if their tracks resembled those of a cougar or any other known animal. If the creature does exist, I'd be more inclined to favor the idea we discussed before, of a predator thought to be extinct."

"Like a saber-toothed tiger?"

"For example. We saw for ourselves how much wild country is still out there. It's not so outlandish to imagine that a handful of zoological relics could have survived beyond the gaze of science. It might even explain some of the creatures that appear in the local folklore."

"A serpent demon?" I arched an eyebrow.

"Very well, perhaps not *that* one. But I've seen too much in my career to dismiss anything out of hand. Hopefully, we'll learn more from this hunting party."

The reminder of our plan for tomorrow brought a flutter of nervousness to my belly. "Thomas, are you sure it's a good idea to drop in on a Sioux hunting party unannounced?"

"If they have evidence that can assist our investigation, I don't see that we have much choice. We'll just have to be on our guard, and make sure we don't give them any cause for alarm."

"But won't we be armed?"

"Most assuredly. It would be the height of imprudence to strike out in these parts without taking proper precautions, especially if there's a man-eating predator on the loose. But we'll keep our weapons holstered and our hands in plain sight. Which reminds me . . ." Reaching into his satchel, he produced a revolver and set it on the table. "I bought this earlier today, when I picked up the shotgun."

"A Colt?"

"Forty-one caliber. They call it the Lightning. More powerful than my old Webley, and it weighs substantially less than the Peacemaker, which I thought would suit you."

That was a polite way of saying I was rubbish with the .45. I'd nearly killed a man with a Peacemaker once, and not on purpose. Though in my defense, that was before I'd been trained in the proper use of a firearm.

I hefted the Lightning experimentally. It was well balanced, and handsome in the bargain, with engraved blued steel and a pearl handle. Even so . . . "I don't suppose this is going to be much help against a saber-toothed tiger."

He smiled. "Probably not. I intended it primarily as a deterrent for the local ruffians." Thomas's gaze shifted meaningfully to the nearest occupied table, where a greasy fellow sat with his back to the wall, watching us.

It wasn't a casual gaze. Whoever he was, he wanted us to know he was looking. And he also wanted us to know he was armed, having placed a big bowie knife on the table, where we'd be sure to see it. He had a pair of six-shooters strapped to his waist too, grips facing out for a cross-draw. Only a certain kind of man carried his guns like that. The message was clear: *I've got my eye on you, and you don't want to cross me.*

Maybe Granger's Saloon was a little more Wild West than I'd thought.

If Thomas was worried, he didn't let on. "For the wildlife, prehistoric or otherwise, we have the shotgun, and I also picked up the latest Winchester repeating rifle, which you're welcome to."

I couldn't help laughing. "Trousers and Colts and Winchester rifles. At this rate, I'm going to look more like Annie Oakley than a photographer's assistant."

"I very much look forward to seeing that," Thomas said, and the glint in his eye was better than a shot of whiskey.

It was around then I decided I liked Medora.

We got back to the hotel just after nightfall. The corridor was dimly lit, and I stumbled a little on the crooked steps. Thomas put a hand on the small of my back to steady me, and he didn't take it away until we'd reached the top of the stairs. It was more than a little familiar, and I expected the usual polite apology, at least, but he didn't even seem to realize he'd done it. He looked perfectly relaxed—more so than I could ever recall seeing him. "This place seems to agree with you," I said, a little bemusedly.

"It does, rather."

"I'd have thought it a little rough around the edges for someone like you."

"Someone like me?" He arched a playful eyebrow. "Dare I ask?"

I felt myself blushing. "I just mean . . . It's very different from Fifth Avenue, that's all."

"That's what I like about it." His glance drifted over the rustic hallway, with its peeling wallpaper and poorly fitted doors. "The constraints of formal society feel very far away indeed. It's refreshing. Liberating, even. Out here . . ." His pale gaze fell to mine. "Out here, one is whoever he wishes to be, isn't he?"

And who is that, Thomas?

I knew better than to ask. Glimpses into the inner sanctum of

Thomas Wiltshire were few and fleeting, and offered only when you weren't looking for them. Try to barge your way through, and he would shut you out faster than you could blink.

Instead, I just smiled and said, "I like it here too."

We bade each other good night and retired to our respective rooms. I say *respective*, but we might as well have shared one for all the privacy they afforded. The wall between us was so thin and shabbily built that the lamplight from Thomas's room leaked into mine; I could see his shadow moving across it, feel the floorboards creaking under his weight.

I slipped into my nightgown and put out the lamp. Then I turned—and yelped as a figure moved in the shadows.

"Who's there?" I demanded, backing toward the nightstand where I'd left the Colt. "How did you get in here?"

He stepped out of the shadows, revealing a middle-aged man with a mustache. He was well over six feet, with the rugged physique of an outdoorsman. For a moment I took him for one of the roughs from the saloon. Then I looked into his eyes, and a searing chill knifed through my ribs.

I knew that sensation, though it had been a long time. You never forget how it feels when you're about to die.

I didn't bother with the gun. It wouldn't do me any good. "*Thomas!*" I pounded the wall between us, fighting down a sickening wave of fear. "*Ghost!*"

CHAPTER 7

A GHOULISH GIFT—PERSONAE NON GRATAE—BEWARE OF SHALLOW WATERS

'd never seen a ghost before, and I was completely unprepared for how terrifying it would be. You'd think one spirit of the dead was the same as another, but you'd be wrong. Shades—the sort of dead people I was used to—were incredibly dangerous, capable of killing at a touch. But at least that was a threat I understood, one I'd faced before and knew how to fight. Ghosts, on the other hand, used madness and suggestion to overcome their victims. Theirs were weapons of the mind. How did you fight that? Already, I could feel it: a skittering along the surface of my brain, as if a hundred spiders made of frost had been set loose inside my skull. My hands flew to my scalp, scratching furiously, but of course it made no difference. The spiders were inside, crawling, crawling . . .

Do something.

But what? My mind was a terrible blank. The prickling turned to probing, icy fingers prodding and grasping as if testing my brain for ripeness. I whimpered, clutching at my head. *Get out get out get out* . . .

"Rose." Thomas's voice sounded from the other side of my door, tense but calm. "Don't panic. You've trained for this."

Training. Remember your training. I drew a breath, forcing myself to think rationally. *Avoid looking at the ghost. If it tries to speak to you, hum or talk to yourself.*

Squeezing my eyes shut, I backed into the nightstand and fumbled about for my hairpin, the one with the jade rose. It was enchanted and made of ash wood; if necessary, I could use it to banish the ghost back to the otherworld, though that would only buy me a few moments. Ghosts were just projections, so banishing them did about as much good as dropping a pebble through a reflection in the water. The image would disperse, but it would only take a few seconds to resolve itself. Even so, I felt a little steadier with the hairpin in my hand.

"Your door is locked." Thomas again. "Can you find the key? I'd rather not have to kick it in."

"Just a minute." My voice sounded thin and warbling, a humiliating contrast to the cool, measured tones coming from the far side of the door. *Calm down,* I scolded myself. *Just keep your wits about you and you'll be fine.* The tendrils of frost still brushed against my brain, but there'd been no whispering so far, no visions of any kind. I was in command of my faculties. Mostly.

I found my key and backed toward the door, keeping my hairpin pointed in the vague direction of the ghost. My fingers groped about for the lock, and a moment later Thomas rushed in. "Where is it?"

I opened my eyes. Thomas stood like a shield before me, ash walking stick at the ready. But there was nothing to protect me from. The corner where the ghost had been was only shadow.

"Gone." I sagged back into the wall in relief. "You must've scared him off."

"Are you all right?"

"I think so." My knees felt a little wobbly, so I sank down onto the bed. "Did I wake the entire hotel?"

Thomas peeked out into the hallway. "All clear," he said, closing the door. "Are you sure you're well? You're . . ." He glanced at me before looking away hurriedly. "You're terribly pale."

"Just unnerved." Literally. Parts of my brain still felt numb.

Thomas went to the window and looked out, as though he might spot the ghost fleeing into the night. "I assume it was our missing prospector, Mr. Upton?"

"He didn't introduce himself, but that would be my guess. He matched the description in Mr. Roosevelt's letters." I shuddered. "I *sensed* him, Thomas. Just the same as if he were a shade." I'd been able to do it ever since the Hell Gate incident, when the shade of Matilda Meyer had accosted me in my bedroom. A fragment of her spirit had become lodged in my breast, and it had nearly killed me; ever since, a pang of cold warned me when shades were near. "I didn't realize it would be the same for ghosts."

"Neither did I."

"I could see him, too, and not just in the mirror. He was right over there." Thomas didn't turn around, so I added, "In the corner. And even from over there, I could feel his touch. Like icy fingers in my head. Is that normal?"

"No. Or rather . . . Not exactly." He didn't elaborate, and that worried me.

"What was he doing here, anyway? It was supposed to be your room that was haunted." We'd paid extra for the privilege, since apparently Benjamin Upton's old room was a hot commodity among treasure hunters looking for clues as to the whereabouts of his missing gold. We'd expected the ghost to show up sooner or later, but Thomas had been confident he could handle it when the time came.

"Maybe the fellow at the front desk got it wrong. Maybe this was the haunted room all along."

"It's possible, though I rather suspect . . ." Thomas started to turn around before checking himself abruptly.

Why does he keep doing that? "What's the matter?" I asked, exasperated.

He cleared his throat. "Perhaps you ought to put on something a bit warmer. You don't want to catch a chill."

I looked down.

Sweet Mary and Joseph. In all the excitement, I'd forgotten what I was wearing: a thin cotton nightgown that was practically see-through in the moonlight. I snatched up the blanket at the foot of my bed and wrapped it around my bare shoulders. "Sorry," I muttered, my face burning. "You were saying?"

He turned around at last. "I've been wondering about something ever since I met your mother for the first time. Do you recall that night? She mentioned something that has stayed with me ever since. About smelling the dead."

"I remember. She told me I smelled like them. Which I suppose I must have, with Matilda Meyer's shade attached to me."

"Exactly. Mrs. Meyer left a sort of imprint on you, and somehow your mother sensed it. That's highly unusual, and it makes me wonder if perhaps she has the gift."

"What do you . . . *Oh.*"

That gift. The one that let you hear the dead, and talk to them, and apparently smell them, too. Though if that's a gift, I couldn't tell you what a curse looks like.

"Wouldn't she know it?"

"Not necessarily. The signs are not always apparent to those who don't know what to look for. And if she passed something of that gift on to you, it would explain a great deal. Why Mrs. Meyer chose you, for example, and perhaps even how you survived your encounter, when so many others would not have."

I digested that. Unsettling as the idea was, I couldn't deny it might come in handy. "If you're right, maybe I should try to talk to the ghost of Mr. Upton. Find out if—"

"Absolutely not." Thomas stared at me as if I'd lost my mind. "Rose, consider what communing with ghosts has done to your mother. Her health is irretrievably shattered. It takes years of practice, not to mention a strict regimen of precautionary measures, to interact safely with ghosts."

"But how else are we going to find out what happened to him? It's been almost a year since he went missing."

"We'll work it out somehow. Or if we can't, we'll send for a professional medium. We're in no hurry, after all. Poor Mr. Upton isn't getting any deader. Right now, our priority ought to be locating the creature."

I supposed that made sense. Of the three mysteries we'd been sent here to solve, only one was actively killing people. "What about in the meantime? He's bound to come back sooner or later."

"And when he does, we'll be ready. We know how to defend ourselves."

One of us does, anyway.

He saw it in my expression. "The first encounter is always difficult, but you'll know what to expect next time. Still, I'm happy to switch rooms, if you'd prefer."

"If your theory is right, that's not going to help. He'll latch onto me wherever I am."

"True enough. Well, I suppose we could . . . Ah, that is . . ." Thomas's glance strayed about the room before falling, inevitably, on the single bed. He swallowed.

Dear Lord, that's all we need. "Er, no thank you, I'll manage."

The relief on his face was almost comical. "You're quite sure?"

"It just caught me off guard, that's all. You're right. I know how to defend myself."

"Still, given your sensitivity, I think it would be a good idea to drink a glass of saltwater each night before going to bed. It fortifies you."

"That's easy enough." Every agent in the special branch kept a pouch of salt on hand at all times. Like ash wood, it had protective qualities that made it an essential part of the arsenal against ghosts and shades. "I'll make some now."

Thomas nodded and reached for the door. "Get some sleep. We've an early start tomorrow. And remember, I'm just on the other side of that wall."

As though I could forget.

Early morning found me standing in front of the mirror, giving the waistband of my borrowed blue jean trousers an experimental tug. They'd stay up, thanks to the suspenders Thomas had given me, but just barely. I'd already had to punch an extra hole in my new gun belt, and I'd need to sew some darts into Thomas's shirt when I had a moment. About the only thing that actually fit was my boots, and they were all but invisible under the too-long hem of my blue jeans. I grabbed my hat and rifle, posing in the mirror as though for a photograph. I looked like one of those lady outlaws you sometimes saw in *Harper's* or *Frank Leslie's*.

Oh, Mam, if you could see me now. Shaking my head, I headed off to find my partner.

Dawn was just breaking as we hit the trail. The place John Ward had marked on the map was many miles south of Medora—and yet still a very long way from the Great Sioux Reservation. That worried me. "Do you suppose Little Wolf and his hunters have permission to be out here? Away from the reservation, I mean?"

"I don't know." Thomas gazed idly over the landscape, taking in the wildflowers and sagebrush as though we were out for a leisurely morning ride. "Is that any of our affair?"

"It might be, if they're expecting trouble. Things are already tense with the ranchers. If they're worried about the authorities descending on them at any moment . . ."

"We don't look like soldiers."

"No, but we probably look like Pinkertons, and around here, that's practically the same thing." The Agency had made quite a name for itself chasing outlaws and protecting the railroads from bandits. That made us personae non gratae in these parts.

"It's unlikely anyone would identify us as agents. Besides, as I said before, I don't see that we have any choice. We'll simply have to proceed with caution. That's assuming we find them at all. This terrain isn't exactly to our advantage."

That was putting it mildly. The surrounding hills looked like the perfect place to hide, for people and for predators. In truth, Little Wolf and his hunters were probably the least of our worries. I'd bet my new britches there were more than a few banditos around here—and, oh yes, a *monster*. Something allegedly strong enough to tear a horse in half.

I gave Luna's neck a nervous pat. Then I loosened the holster at my hip, making sure the Colt was ready to hand. The Winchester, meanwhile, was slung in a scabbard along the side of my saddle; Thomas had done the same with his shotgun. Armed to the teeth, both of us wearing Thomas's finely tailored denim, we most definitely looked like Pinkertons—or very fancy outlaws. But there was nothing to be done about it now.

Sometime after eleven o'clock, Thomas drew up. "We ought to let the horses rest for a spell, and I'd like to check the map again. This shady spot by the river should do nicely."

We tied the horses off under a tree, loosening their cinches and letting them crop at the lush grass sloping down to the riverbank. The water looked cool and inviting, so I headed down.

Grasshoppers whirred in the long grass. I crouched at the riverbank and splashed some water on my face. Somewhere in the trees, a squirrel chattered.

Behind me, I could hear Thomas muttering over his map. "As I thought. We've been in the area Mr. Ward indicated for at least an hour. Perhaps we ought to veer east . . ."

The insects fell suddenly silent. My head snapped up. A figure stood on the opposite bank, his features shadowed under the brim of his hat. Long, dark hair spilled down his back, some of it tied off in braids. He wore a button-down shirt and buckskin leggings, and he held a rifle in one hand, its stock resting in the grass.

Swallowing past a dry throat, I raised a hand in greeting. "Hau."

"Good morning."

A brief silence, filled with the burble of water and the buzzing of grasshoppers.

"You should not drink in this place," the man said.

"I'm sorry." I kept very still, acutely aware of the rifle in his hand. "Is it yours?"

He laughed. "How can a river be mine?"

"I, er . . ."

"There's a beaver dam just south of here." He gestured upstream. "The water is not good."

"Oh," I said, feeling ridiculous.

He stepped closer to the bank, bringing his features into view. His bronze skin was smooth, his hair a youthful, glossy black. About my age, I judged, maybe a little older. The dark eyes that met mine sparkled with amusement. He'd chosen the perfect moment to show himself, catching Thomas and me off guard. That wasn't a coincidence, I felt sure.

Thomas cleared his throat behind me. "Good morning. I hope we aren't intruding."

The young man's mouth twitched, as if he were holding back a wry response.

"I wonder if you might be the fellow we're looking for. Little Wolf?"

Dark eyes narrowed. "What do you want with Little Wolf?"

"We were hoping to consult him about an animal we're tracking. A man-eating predator. We were speaking with a Mr. John Ward yesterday—perhaps you know him? He mentioned that Little Wolf and his hunters might have some information about this creature." Thomas took a careful step forward. "May I?"

The young man nodded. Slowly, I straightened from my crouch, keeping my hands in plain sight as Thomas made his way down to the riverbank. The young man, meanwhile, said something over his shoulder, and two more hunters appeared out of the brush. They were armed too, one with a bow and the other with a rifle, but neither weapon was raised.

"This is Red Calf." The young man gestured at one of his companions. "And this is Two Horses. I'm Little Wolf."

Thomas inclined his head formally. "Pleased to make your acquaintance. My name is Thomas Wiltshire, and this is Miss Gallagher. We're photographers."

"Photographers." Little Wolf's gaze fell to the gun at my hip. "My mistake. I thought you were Pinkertons."

I gave Thomas a flat look.

Little Wolf laughed. "I hope that was not rude."

"No." Thomas sighed. "I'm the one who's been rude. Miss Gallagher and I are in the habit of concealing the true nature of our work. Pinkertons are not always warmly received, especially in this part of the world. Still, that's no excuse. Lies are a dreadful way to begin a relationship. You have my heartfelt apologies." He gave a very English little bow.

Little Wolf looked like he didn't quite know what to make of us, and I couldn't really blame him. "You are friends of John Ward?"

"We met him yesterday," I said. "He told us about the tracks he found. The rest of what Mr. Wiltshire said is true. About the animal, I mean. We are trying to find it—just not for a photograph."

Two Horses said something in their language, and Red Calf laughed. Little Wolf translated. "He says the animal you seek walks on two legs and has white skin."

Thomas nodded. "Mr. Ward thought you might say that. He disagrees, as I'm sure you know. Either way, something strange is going on, and we hope to find out what it is."

"I will take you to one who knows more."

"We should be very obliged," Thomas said.

"Do you need to rest more before we go? Or drink, maybe? I have good water." Little Wolf glanced at me, his eyes dancing again.

I felt myself blushing. "Thank you for telling me about the dam."

"There is an old saying among my people. *Beware of shallow waters*."

I had a feeling he was teasing me, but I couldn't be sure, so I just smiled and said, "That sounds like good advice."

Little Wolf tilted his head. "This way," he said. "Your horses can cross over here."

CHAPTER 8

DAKOTA DOUGHNUT—A COUNTERFEIT
CURSE—HORSESHOES

My father had a horse like that once." Little Wolf glanced over my shoulder at Luna as we walked. "Gold, with a white mane and tail. I was very young, but I remember her well. She was taken in a raid. I cried for days."

"How awful."

He laughed. "I should not admit that, but as I said, I was young. Five, or maybe six. Old enough that I already had my first bow. I remember that, because I wanted revenge. I thought that if I had skill enough to shoot an arrow through a rolling hoop, I was ready to be a warrior." He shook his head, smiling.

"Did such things happen often?" Thomas leaned past me to address Little Wolf. The three of us walked abreast, leading the horses, while Red Calf and Two Horses trailed behind, keeping a close eye on Thomas and me.

"Capturing horses was the way of things in those days," Little Wolf said. "Before the Lakota were herded off to the agencies."

"Lakota?" I echoed, confused. "Are you not Sioux?"

"That's what your people call us, but it is not our word. The people you know as *Sioux* are actually many different tribes. Even within the Lakota, we have Seven Council Fires. We are the Hunk-papa, *those who camp at the end.*"

"And this area was your homeland?" I asked. "Before the reservation, I mean?"

"This was not the place where we camped, but we have hunted here for a long time. These lands were set aside for us by treaty. *Unceded Indian Territory*, they called it. Then they found gold in the Black Hills."

Even I knew what came after that. The Great Sioux War, and especially the Battle of the Little Bighorn, had riveted the nation. To this day, I can hear my da's voice reading aloud from the papers, Mam scolding him for filling my eleven-year-old ears with such violence.

I didn't know what to say. *I'm sorry* was so inadequate that it almost felt insulting. I said it anyway. "I've read a little about what happened out here. How you were forced from your lands. I can't imagine what that must have been like."

"You speak as if it was the past." Turning, I found Red Calf looking at me with hard eyes. "For us, it is not the past."

There was an uncomfortable stretch of silence. Then Little Wolf continued. "With the buffalo gone, we have had to range farther each year to hunt. These lands have been good for the past few years. Plenty of deer and elk. The annuity food is never enough, so when the time comes to make meat for the winter, we send hunters out from the agency. Small groups, so there is no trouble with the government men." He didn't mention whether they had permission or not, and I didn't ask. As Thomas said, it was none of our affair.

"And the ranchers?" I asked.

"We have learned to avoid each other. We were not friendly, but there was peace, of a kind. Until last year. That's when the animals in this area started disappearing, and it made things very bad between us."

"We'd like to hear more about that," Thomas said. "When did you first notice something was wrong?"

"Right away. We came here to hunt, as we have for many summers. But for the first time, it was not easy finding game. A few deer here and there, but nothing bigger. Instead, we found only bones. At first we thought white hunters were to blame, but then we started to find fresh kills. Animal kills. Only these were not made by a cougar or a pack of wolves."

"How could you tell?" I asked.

"The signs were wrong. Especially the tracks. We had never seen anything like them before."

"Because they were false," Red Calf put in from behind us.

Little Wolf nodded slowly. "Some said so. Others did not agree. There were arguments in the camp. It was not long after that our horses were stolen."

"Stolen?" Thomas echoed. "Not killed?"

"Both, eventually. But first they were stolen."

"How can you be sure?"

"We would have heard an animal attack. When a horse is afraid, it will not stay silent. It will scream and kick. And there would have been signs. Blood. Hair. Marks in the earth. We found none of these things."

"Interesting. Where exactly was this?"

"I will show you on your map when we reach the camp. It's not far now."

A few minutes later, the smell of woodsmoke pricked my nose, and we came to a clearing dotted with tents. At its center, a campfire burned low, surrounded by blankets and furs for seating. Strips of pounded meat hung on a rack under the sun, and a pair of hides had been stretched over hoops to dry. From the look of things, Little Wolf and his hunters hadn't been here long: The grass was still green, the meat rack little more than a few logs propped together. The horses grazing at the edge of the camp were saddled and ready, their beaded bridles throwing flashes of color between the blades of grass. It looked as though the hunters could pack up and leave at a moment's notice.

Little Wolf called out a greeting, and a woman's head poked out of one of the tents. She froze when she saw us. Surprise quickly gave way to anger, and she said something sharp in their language, but Little Wolf just laughed. "Always fierce. Just like our mother. This is my sister, White Robes. She is the one who can tell you more about the horse thieves. Sister, this is . . . uh . . ." He looked at me apologetically.

"Rose. And this is my partner, Thomas. We're detectives, and we're trying to find out what's happening to the livestock in this area. Your brother thought you might be able to help."

White Robes emerged from the tent, but her expression didn't soften. "My brother speaks for himself. He does not speak for me."

"No one speaks for you, Sister. Not even your husband."

"Especially not me," said Red Calf, and the hunters all laughed.

White Robes pretended to glare at them, but I could see she was wrestling with a smile. Little Wolf's easy humor seemed to have a disarming effect on everyone around him, for which I was grateful.

"Are you from the government?" White Robes took in my un-conventional attire with a bemused expression. She herself wore a calico dress, moccasins, and a no-nonsense look that reminded me a little of Clara.

"Not from the government, no. We've been hired by a local rancher, a Mr. Theodore Roosevelt."

"A rancher." Her tone frosted over again.

"I know that name," Little Wolf said. "He was one of the hunters we took to the clearing, to show them the carcasses. High Back Bear said he was an important man among the whites at Medora."

"That's him. He believes there's some sort of monstrous predator lurking in these hills."

"Does he truly?" White Robes narrowed her eyes. "Or is that just a story he wanted you to tell us?"

"He believes it," I said firmly. "And I believe him."

"Then you believe in monsters also?"

I hesitated. We'd only just met these people, and I knew nothing of their ways. How would they react to talk of elementals and fae? "I don't know about monsters," I said carefully, "but I do think there are things out there beyond our understanding."

"Like God?"

Little Wolf gave an incredulous laugh. "They have not even hitched their horses and already you are talking about God." He took my reins and gave them to Red Calf. "Please, sit. We will eat something. After, we can smoke a little and talk about God."

"That's very kind of you," Thomas said, handing over Gideon's reins. "Though we'd rather discuss what happened to your horses, if you don't mind."

"*Sit*." Little Wolf herded us to the fire. "Eat. Then we will talk." We arranged ourselves on the blankets, and he gave us each a chunk of fried bread, along with a small crock of what looked like berry preserves. "*Wajapi*," he said in answer to my curious glance. "Chokecherries. Like the bread and jam they gave us at school, only better."

It *was* better, sweet and wonderfully tart; paired with the fried bread, it was like eating a jelly-filled doughnut. "I wish we could get this at the hotel," I said. "It's the best thing I've eaten since we got here."

"White Robes is a good cook," Little Wolf said. "It's the only reason we let her come along." He ducked expertly as a slug of *wajapi* sailed over his head, flung from the tip of White Robes's knife.

"They *bring* me along because I know where the game will be, and because I am a better tracker than any of them."

"That's only because you spent all your time alone in the woods when we were children."

"How else would I have any peace? I had a noisy baby brother."

"He is still noisy," Red Calf said, and they all laughed.

"And I still seek peace in the woods. It gives me a good eye for the land." Her smile faded. "Which is how I know our horses were taken by men and not monsters."

"Perhaps we might start at the beginning," Thomas said. "Little Wolf mentioned that the first disappearance was last year. Do you recall when, exactly?"

"In the Moon of Ripening Berries." She glanced at her brother. "July?"

"June," he corrected.

"We had been here only a short time before the thieves found us. It was our own fault. We were careless. The horses were allowed to graze too far from camp, with only a boy to watch them. He fell asleep, and . . ." She made a frustrated gesture.

"Where were you exactly? Can you show me?" Thomas spread his map out on the blanket.

"Here." Little Wolf tapped a finger on the map. "By this creek, where the hills meet the prairie."

"There is a wagon trail there," White Robes said, warming to her tale. "It runs all the way to Deadwood, so it is well traveled. We should have known better than to camp so close to it. And we were too many. Fourteen of us, and more than twenty horses. We brought too much attention to ourselves."

Glancing around the camp, I saw only three tents.

White Robes followed my gaze. "There were more of us last week. The rest decided to leave."

"Why?" I asked, though I had a feeling I knew the answer.

"They think this land is cursed," Little Wolf said.

White Robes snorted softly. "If it is cursed, it is the same curse as everywhere."

I had a feeling I knew what she meant by that, too.

"This has become a place of death," Little Wolf said. "There is no meat, only bones. What we have managed to gather"—he gestured at the drying rack—"is barely enough to feed us, let alone our families. And now we hear rumors that men are being killed as well. Some of us believe this talk of curses and demons. Others think white men are to blame. Either way, there is nothing for us here, so our hunters went south. The four of us stayed behind to learn the truth."

"I know the truth," White Robes said. "Someone is trying to frighten us away from this place. We will find out who, and we will have justice."

"You believe the tracks are meant for you?" Thomas asked. "To persuade you to leave?"

Little Wolf looked uncertain, but White Robes was firm. "Not only the tracks. Someone is slaughtering the game so that we cannot hunt. And they are stealing our horses."

"They *are* stealing. Not they *were*." Thomas took in the grim expressions around the fire. "I take it there's been another incident?"

White Robes nodded. "A few days ago. They came in the night, as before. Near the Deadwood trail, as before."

"And you're certain it was thieves and not—"

"I'm certain. Last year, we found many signs that white men were to blame. The ends of their cigarettes. The tracks from their horseshoes. But this time I did not need to look for signs in the dirt. This time, I saw them with my own eyes."

I sat up a little straighter. At last, we had an actual witness. "What exactly did you see? Any detail you remember could be helpful."

"I was asleep, but they woke me with their coughing. I went outside and saw three men on horseback. They were leading two of our packhorses away."

"Did you get a look at their faces?" I asked.

She shook her head. "But one of them had a beard, so I knew they were whites. And they were cowards. When I shouted for them to stop, they ran like deer. I grabbed the nearest horse and chased them through the trees, but it was dark, and my horse tripped and fell. By the time our hunters caught up, it was too late. The thieves were gone, and it was too dark to follow."

"We had to shoot that horse," Little Wolf said.

"I'm so sorry." I couldn't help glancing at Luna, feeling a pang. "I know what horses mean to your people."

"No," Little Wolf said, "you don't."

Another uncomfortable silence. "We will have justice," White Robes said again. "The ranchers will pay for what they have done."

"You're convinced it was the ranchers, then?" Thomas asked.

"Who else?" Red Calf put in. "They blame us for the loss of their cows. They blame us for setting fires. Some of them even blame us for the winter, as if we could call magic down upon them."

"I care nothing for their reasons," White Robes said. "I know it was ranchers because I saw the marks."

Thomas leaned forward eagerly. "What marks are those?"

"The kind they burn into their animals." She patted her haunch. "It was dark, but the moon was good. I could still see the white scars on their horses."

"What did they look like?" Thomas asked.

White Robes picked up a stick and rubbed it in ash from the fire. "One horse had a mark like this." She drew a horseshoe, curled up a little at the edges. "And the other two were like this." Using the tip of her stick, she drew a bullet-shaped cluster of dots, a little like a drawing of a raspberry.

Thomas took out his notebook and copied them down. "The idea of a tit-for-tat theft is plausible, I grant you. But what do you make of the other evidence you've found? The animal carcasses and the tracks?"

"We told you," Red Calf said. "The tracks are false. There is no such animal."

White Robes took up her stick again. "Here, it is a cougar." She traced the outline of a paw. "But here, it is a bear." She added a toe, and extended the claw marks out several inches. "That is the front foot. The back is even more foolish." Another paw print, this one with faint lines between the toes. "This is . . . what? A giant beaver?"

Red Calf and Two Horses laughed. Little Wolf, though, looked thoughtful. "Tracks can be faked, it's true. But we have also seen droppings, and scratching on trees. The carcasses we found had no meat left on them. Even the bones had been cracked open for the marrow. Why would the ranchers do this? Not only to horses, but to all sorts of creatures? This is what I can't understand."

White Robes sighed impatiently, as if they'd had this conversation many times before. "Why do they do anything? They kill everything they see. They can't help themselves."

"Their own cows?" He made a skeptical face.

"Tell me," Thomas said, "are there stories associated with this area that feature unusual creatures? Myths, folklore, that sort of thing? You mentioned demons, and one of the ranchers we spoke to said something about a serpent."

"*Unk Cekula?*" White Robes shrugged. "A myth, as you have said. One of many tales the old ones tell to children."

"Is it possible it's more than that?" Thomas's gaze took in the others. "Do any of you believe there might be some truth to these tales?"

Little Wolf's expression grew thoughtful again. "There are many different ways to believe. Many kinds of truth. Some say we make our bows from the ash tree because it protects us from evil. Others say it is just good, strong wood."

My hand drifted reflexively to the hairpin at the nape of my neck. Ash wood. Could it be a coincidence?

"Either way," Little Wolf went on, "I will make my bow from ash, because that is the way it is done. The way it has always been done. We have always told stories of *Unk Cekula,* of *Iktomi* and *Wakinyan.* They are a part of who I am. I believe them, in my way."

"And the ranchers want to use that against you," White Robes said. "They want us away from this place forever, and they will use whatever tricks they can to frighten you. It is a lie, Brother. But soon everyone will know the truth."

"It sounds like you have a plan," I said.

"We do." She didn't elaborate, and I didn't ask her to. White Robes didn't completely trust us, and why should she? We were strangers, and we'd been hired by a rancher. Even leaving aside all the history between our peoples, she had reason enough to be cautious.

"We will catch these horse thieves," Little Wolf said. "But there are questions that still need answering. *Something* tore our horses apart and ate their meat. I would like to know what."

"We'll certainly do our best to find out," Thomas said.

"As will we. If you need to find us, we will be near the Deadwood trail."

Thomas nodded. "In the meantime, do take care. The rumors you've heard are true. Whatever is killing these animals is also killing men. This area may not be safe."

"Thank you for the warning," White Robes said. "But whatever comes, we are ready."

CHAPTER 9

SCAVENGERS—OF PINSTRIPES AND
PIG-STICKERS—THE FIVE POINTS VARIATION

t was past dark by the time we reined in outside Granger's Saloon, and I crawled off Luna's back with the supple grace of a ninety-year-old. Ten hours in the saddle was not a thing to be undertaken lightly. "I don't think I've ever been so stiff in my life."

"It is rather humbling, isn't it?" Thomas rolled out his shoulders. "Even these enormous Western saddles can only do so much. One gets used to it, presumably, but for now . . ."

For now it felt as if my backside had been paddled by an over-zealous schoolmarm. "Do you suppose we could stand at the bar to eat?"

"Capital idea."

It was a Friday night, so I expected things to be a little more lively, but I was completely unprepared for the wall of noise and cigar smoke that greeted us inside. I hardly recognized the place, and not just because my eyes were watering. Nearly every seat in the joint was taken, and much of the standing room too. A card game was going on in one corner, dice in another. Stargazers in heavy rouge and faded frocks plied their trade at the bar, while just a few feet away, a pasty fellow in a pinstriped suit conducted another kind of business, handing a pen and paper to a resigned-looking cowboy sitting across from him.

"It's as busy as the Bowery in here," I said incredulously. "Something must have happened."

"Perhaps the barkeep can enlighten us."

We haggled our way between the tables, trying our best to ignore the eyes following us. Even in this crowd, Thomas and I stood out. "Get a look at this dude," someone slurred, waving a half-empty bottle in Thomas's direction.

"Never mind the dude. Get a look at the filly! Why the trousers, darlin'?"

"Careful. She's liable to stick a gun in your face."

"I know where I'd like to stick my gun."

Thomas's stride faltered, but I touched his arm. "Leave it," I murmured.

The drunks continued their heckling, but it was drowned out soon enough by the rowdy laughter coming from the bar. The mob of treasure hunters had only grown since last night, leaving little room for anyone else. Thomas and I wedged ourselves in as best we could. The stench in those close quarters was almost overwhelming, a miasma of unwashed bodies and sour whiskey breath. All that hard riding to be back in time for supper, and I'd about lost my appetite.

We ordered anyway, and Thomas slid a few extra bills across the bar. "Much obliged," the saloonkeeper said, managing to sound both grateful and wary. "To what do I owe the generosity?"

Thomas blinked, the very picture of New York naïveté. "Are gratuities not customary in these parts? Forgive me, sir. I'm afraid I'm quite out of my element."

I had to hand it to Thomas: he slipped into character flawlessly. The saloonkeeper relaxed. "You're that photographer, ain't you?"

"Thomas Wiltshire." He extended a hand. "And this is my colleague, Miss Gallagher."

"Lee Granger." They shook. "Don't get many gratuities in here, that's for sure. Especially with so many folks fallen on hard times."

"You have a full house tonight, at least," I said.

"True enough. Guess I oughta be thankful." He didn't look thankful, eying his patrons without much enthusiasm.

"Not locals, I take it?" Thomas asked.

"Some of 'em. It's payday for most of the cowboys around here, so that always means a busy night. The rest is newcomers. Stage come up from Deadwood this afternoon, so we got us a fresh crop of vultures."

Thomas tilted his head with interest. "Vultures?"

Granger lowered his voice, leaning against the bar conspiratorially. "Seems like all we get around here these days is scavengers. First it was the bone pickers, gathering up the skeletons of all them cows and selling 'em to the fertilizer companies. After that came the treasure hunters. Now we got this pinstriped pecker from Bismarck"—he nodded toward the pasty fellow I'd noticed earlier—"buying our land on the cheap. Vultures."

Our host was chatty. Good. Chatty barkeeps were always useful.

Wide-eyed easterner seemed like the right approach here, so I affected a nervous glance at the treasure hunters down the bar. "They seem like a rough lot," I said in a worried undertone. "Though I suppose you'd have to be in their line of work. It must be awfully dangerous, mustn't it, if they keep disappearing like that?"

"Disappearing, or cutting each other's throats?" The saloonkeeper lifted an eyebrow meaningfully.

"Is that what's going on?"

He shrugged. "Can't say for sure, but a hundred thousand is an awful sight of money, and most of these rambling types would sell their own mother for a nickel. I reckon each and every one of 'em sleeps with one eye open and a gun under his pillow. 'Specially now, with everybody so worked up over this cabin."

"Cabin?" Thomas and I exchanged a look.

"You ain't heard? That's what brought most of this rabble to town. Local trapper come across it the other day, just south of Painted Canyon. Some shack they're saying Ben Upton used while he was out on the trail." He started to say more, but someone caught his attention down the bar. "Keep your shirt on, Willy. I see you. 'Scuse me, folks."

I waited until Granger was out of earshot before turning back to Thomas. "Sounds like we'd better get a look at that cabin, ideally before this lot descends on it and ruins any evidence."

"Agreed, though if these fellows are as cutthroat as our host makes them out to be, we'd do well to be careful."

It was starting to feel as if we had to be careful everywhere we went around here. *Rough country,* Mr. Roosevelt had called it, and he wasn't wrong.

As we stood waiting for our supper, a familiar figure walked through the door, and I touched Thomas's arm discreetly. John Ward stood on the threshold, eying the crowded barroom with a bemused expression.

"Shall we ask him to join us? A table just opened up in the corner there." Thomas started toward the door, but I put my hand on his arm again, and he gave me a quizzical look. "Is there a problem?"

"Do you suppose we were a little too quick to trust him yesterday?"

"Why, because he works on a ranch? The same could be said of half the men in this bar."

"Maybe, but what about the animal tracks? Mr. Ward insisted they were real, but after what we saw today, I'm not so sure."

"Little Wolf also believes them to be genuine," Thomas pointed out. "It's difficult to reconcile their views, I grant you, but isn't that all the more reason to dig deeper?"

True enough, I supposed. And besides, I'd come to rely on my instincts when it came to reading people, and nothing about John Ward had given me pause. If anything, he came across as the sort of quietly righteous hero you found in the yellowback novels. "All right, let's talk to him. Why don't you catch him before he sits, and I'll wait for the stew?"

I kept an eye on my partner as he made his way through the tables, in case the drunks gave him any more grief. Instead, it was one of the stargazers who accosted him, seizing him by the lapels and looking him up and down with a sultry little smile. "Oh my," she purred, fingering the fine fabric of his suit. "*Oh my*." I didn't hear Thomas's reply, but she sighed theatrically and sauntered away, to much laughter from the surrounding patrons.

One of the onlookers wasn't laughing, though, and I stiffened as I recognized the greasy gunslinger who'd been staring at us the night before. His eyes tracked Thomas all the way across the room.

"Stew's up." Crockery landed heavily on the bar behind me.

"Pardon me, Mr. Granger. That fellow near the window over there. Black hair, oiled mustache. Who is he?"

The saloonkeeper flicked him a glance. "Been calling himself William Ford, but he ain't fooling nobody. That there's Bowie Bill Wallace. So-called on account of that pig-sticker he's always waving around. 'Scuse me, that's a—"

"I know what a pig-sticker is," I said grimly. I'd seen a man stabbed once, in an alley off Mulberry Bend. That sort of thing leaves an impression on a nine-year-old. "Let me guess: he's a wanted man."

"In three territories, so they say. Rumor has it he's the one robbed that stage coming outta Deadwood last month."

I cursed under my breath. "Why hasn't the sheriff taken him in?"

"Asked Bill Jones that very question, not two days gone. He tells me he ain't got no quarrel with the man, on account of that stage was robbed in Montana. I guess he wired Sheriff Bullock down in Deadwood and reckons that's his duty done." Granger glanced at the outlaw again. "I'd stay well clear if I was you, ma'am. He'd gut you like a fish soon as look at you, him and his boys."

"I'll be very happy to stay clear of him, thank you." Whether he'd stay clear of us was another matter. I couldn't think of any reason he'd be staring at Thomas that didn't spell trouble. Resolving to keep an eye on him, I picked up the stew and headed for the table in the corner, where Thomas had settled in with John Ward.

Mr. Ward didn't recognize me straightaway, not that I blamed him. I'd left town looking disrespectable enough, and only acquired a patina of dust and horse grime since then. When he realized who I was, he leapt up and snatched off his hat. "Pardon me, ma'am. Let me get that for you."

"Thank you." I smiled awkwardly and handed him the stew. "It's so nice to run into you like this."

"Can't help but run into folks in this town," he said as we took our seats. "'Specially now all the other restaurants is closed."

"I suppose that's true. In which case you must be acquainted with many of these fine gentlemen." My arm did a sweep of the room.

He smiled. "Some. And there ain't a gentleman among 'em."

"Hey." One of the other patrons had overheard, and he glared at us from a neighboring table. "Show some respect, boy."

John Ward met his gaze coolly. "Mind your business. And don't be calling me *boy*."

The stranger scowled, and for a moment I thought there'd be trouble. But I guess he figured he'd bitten off more than he could chew, because he looked away, muttering into his beer.

"You must encounter that sort of thing often out here," Thomas said.

Mr. Ward shrugged. "Not as much as you might think. Out on the range, things is different. Colored or Indian or Mexican, it don't matter, long as you can ride 'n' rope. In town, though . . ." He shook his head. "Just one more reason to avoid it where I can. Only reason I'm here now is to pick up some supplies."

"Are you going somewhere?" I asked.

"Hunting." The grim look in his eye left little doubt what he'd be hunting for. "Managed to convince Mr. Reid to give me the day off tomorrow. After that it's Sunday, so I oughta be able to cover some decent ground. Which reminds me—how'd you all get on today? Did you find the Sioux?"

"Lakota," I corrected automatically. "And yes, we did."

"You were right," Thomas said. "They're quite convinced their horses were stolen by ranchers. And I must say, in view of the evidence they presented, we're inclined to agree." He watched our companion carefully, absorbing his reaction.

Mr. Ward's mouth tightened, and he glanced away. "All right, then."

"Though that doesn't necessarily preclude the possibility that the creature is real."

John Ward frowned. "Beg pardon?"

"Little Wolf thinks both things are true," I said. "That the horses were stolen by ranchers, *and* that they were eaten by some sort of wild animal."

"'Spose that could be. All I know is, them tracks was left by *something*."

"White Robes believes the tracks to be forged," Thomas said. "The product of human trickery, designed to frighten them."

Mr. Ward sighed. "So I hear. Is that what you think, then?"

"The paw prints she drew for us were certainly implausible. Little more than a pastiche of unrelated traits. Though to be fair, I imagine any creature outside the ordinary would appear that way when glimpsed for the first time. I've no idea what the spoor of a prehistoric bear-dog or giant mustelid would look like, for example. Not having seen the tracks for ourselves, it's difficult to judge. Wouldn't you agree, Miss Gallagher?"

I might have done, if I had any idea what a mustelid was. As for whether the prints were authentic or not, I still wasn't sure what I thought. It was hard to reconcile White Robes's certainty with Mr. Ward's—or for that matter, with her own brother's. Little Wolf was convinced something was out there too, but people had a way of seeing what they wanted to. Until Thomas and I got a look for ourselves . . . "I'm trying to keep an open mind."

"Those tracks don't make no kinda sense," the ranch hand said. "I ain't saying otherwise. But I learned a long time ago that just 'cause a thing don't make sense don't mean it ain't so."

Thomas smiled. "On that we agree, Mr. Ward."

"You can go ahead and call me John."

"In that case, Thomas will do just fine."

"And Rose," I said. "And now that's settled, may I ask an indelicate question, John? If all this *were* some sort of elaborate ruse, can you think of who might be behind it? Theoretically speaking."

"Theoretically speaking?" He raised his eyebrows and blew out a breath. "S'pose it could be anybody. No love lost between ranchers and Indians."

"What about between the ranchers themselves? Are there rivalries?"

"Squabbles, sure. Nothing like the range wars down south,

mind." John frowned. "You asking me if one of 'em might be doing all this to poke the others in the eye?"

"I suppose that is what I'm asking, yes."

"Like I said, anything is possible. But unless one of 'em's got a lion locked up in his barn, I still don't see how it explains them bones."

"No." I sighed. "Neither do I."

Then there's Ben Upton and his ghost, and the disappearing treasure hunters, not to mention this mysterious winter. I couldn't figure any of them, let alone how or even if they were connected. The whole thing gave me a headache.

John excused himself to get supper, and as soon as he was out of earshot, Thomas said, "Well? Are you convinced?"

"That he's telling the truth? Yes, but you've just given me an idea. I'll be right back." I headed outside to check the horses hitched up in front of the saloon. None of them bore the brands White Robes had drawn, but virtually all of them had some sort of identifying mark. I'd bet my britches John Ward could identify most of them, at least if they were from around here. Might he recognize the horseshoe and the cluster of dots as well? Probably, I decided, though we'd have to be discreet in our questioning. It was too early to start throwing accusations around.

I headed back inside, but I hadn't got far before a hand shot out from one of the tables, seizing me by the wrist. "Well, hello there." The man looked up, and I recognized one of the drunks who'd cat-called me earlier. "Where're you off to in such a rush?"

"Excuse me," I said coldly, twisting out of his grasp. "I'll thank you to keep your hands off me."

"Don't be like that, darlin'." He grabbed me two-handed, pulling me down into his lap. "Let me get a look atcha."

I sprang to my feet like a scalded cat, but he was right behind me, arm snaking around my waist. Sour breath warmed my neck, and his hand crept up under my breast.

Looking back on it, I may have overreacted.

I'd only ever been manhandled like that in jujitsu training, and I responded accordingly, grabbing his arm and driving my hip into his middle. He went over my shoulder cleaner than my sparring partners ever had, hitting the floorboards with a *whump*.

For a moment he just lay there, blinking at the ceiling. Then a roar of laughter went up from the surrounding tables. That's when I knew I'd made a mistake.

He lurched to his feet, scarlet with humiliation. "You think that's funny, bitch?"

I might have pointed out that I wasn't the one laughing, but he didn't seem like the negotiating type. Instead I backed away, bracing myself for whatever came next. He made a clumsy grab, but I batted him away easily. I had the sense he wanted to throw a punch but couldn't quite bring himself to hit a woman. Instead he charged at me again, arms spread like he was trying to corral a stray hog. He made it only a few steps before something jerked him back.

"That will do, I think," Thomas said, hauling the man by the collar and throwing him into a chair.

The drunk shot right back up again. Now he had a suitable target for his rage, and he took a swing at Thomas that would have done real damage had it landed. Thomas sidestepped—and couldn't resist sticking his foot out while he was at it, sending the drunk face-first into the table.

Well, things turned into a real mess after that.

The drunk's friends leapt into the fray, surging at Thomas like a pack of hounds. He ducked under one before spinning to face another, catching the fist aimed at his head and using it like a lever to send the man cartwheeling over his shoulder. A third man came at him swinging a bottle; Thomas grabbed his arm and tumbled backward, planting a foot in his attacker's middle and launching him through the air before rolling smoothly to his feet. Again they came at him and again they met the same fate, careening off him in all directions as he redirected their momentum with clinical efficiency.

The rest of the patrons whooped and jeered at the spectacle, but nobody stepped in. As for me, I had problems of my own. The first drunk, the one who'd started this whole bag of nails, was back on his feet and looking for blood. He reached into his boot and pulled out a knife, which I guess was his way of saying he was done being a gentleman. He held that blade like he knew how to use it, and my pulse skipped a beat. But when he came at me I was ready, batting his arm aside and grabbing his wrist. That was the easy part, but when I tried to wrench the knife free, he was having none of it, grappling and swearing, one hand clamped around my wrist like a vise. He was stronger than me, and heavier; the blade started to pivot toward my middle. I did the only thing I could think of, driving my knee into his groin and dropping him like a sack of potatoes.

He curled over himself on the floor, whimpering in a register mainly discernible by dogs, and I can't pretend I didn't find it just a little gratifying.

"Are you all right?" Thomas appeared in front of me, out of breath but otherwise unruffled. Behind him, those of our attackers who could still walk were limping away with their tails between their legs, shepherded off by a stern John Ward. "You know damn well he had that coming, Earl," I heard him say. "Now go on and get yourself dried out."

I gave myself a quick once-over, but aside from a sore wrist, everything seemed fine. "I think I'm finally getting the hang of this jujitsu thing. I must have had a good teacher."

"*Hmm.*" Thomas hoisted an eyebrow at the poor sod crumpled at my feet. "I don't recall covering that particular technique in class. A Five Points variation, no doubt."

I smiled, a little embarrassed. "You might have to go over disarming for me again. I never can get it right." Picking up a broken chair, I added, "Thank you for stepping in. But I could have handled it, you know."

"I have no doubt. Believe it or not, my initial intention was to de-escalate the situation. I'm afraid my temper rather got away from me." He sighed, glancing around. Every pair of eyes in the saloon was riveted on us. "And now it seems we have some explaining to do."

CHAPTER 10

THE TRUTH HURTS—A LITTLE MORE
EXCITEMENT—NO STONE UNTURNED

You don't say. The Far East?" Lee Granger leaned on the bar, looking pretty unperturbed considering the mess we'd just made of his joint. It helped that his pockets were lined with more than enough cash to pay for the damage, courtesy of Thomas.

"The adventure of a lifetime," Thomas said. "I only wish I could show you the photographs. Miss Gallagher and I soaked up everything we could, including jujitsu. Though I must say, I hadn't thought to put it into practice outside the sparring ring." Leaning in conspiratorially, he added, "It was rather invigorating!"

Granger laughed. "You're an odd duck, Wiltshire, but I like you." He poured us both a whiskey and walked away, still chuckling.

"He seems satisfied enough," I said. Hopefully, he would spread that story around, and anyone with a mind to ask how a photographer and his assistant made short work of four hard-bitten cowboys would have his answer.

"Not everyone will be quite so credulous, I fear." Thomas inclined his head at John Ward, who was still trying to smooth feathers with some of the locals.

"I'm more worried about the rest of these roughs." Bowie Bill hadn't moved a muscle during the commotion, but he wasn't the only shady character in here. "What happens if they don't buy it?"

"Let us hope we don't have to find out. In the meantime, I think perhaps it's time to bring Mr. Ward into our confidence. Are you comfortable with that?"

I sighed. "I wouldn't call it *comfortable,* but I don't think we have much choice." Neither of us were trackers, and that meant John Ward was our best chance of finding the creature. We needed him to trust us, and I doubted he'd fall for any flimflam about photographs in Japan. Not after we've spent the past two days peppering him with questions. Of course, the truth might not suit him any better. Would he want anything to do with a pair of Pinkertons?

Here's hoping. I picked up my whiskey and tossed it back—and promptly succumbed to a fit of coughing.

"Good heavens, that was brave of you." Thomas patted my back. "Are you all right? I shouldn't wonder if that was half kerosene."

In a fit of Irish cussedness, I drank his too.

We took John Ward aside to deliver the news, stepping out into the street to avoid prying ears. Thomas kept the details to a minimum, just as he'd done with the Lakota. No point in overwhelming the poor fellow with ghosts and strange winters all in one go. Livestock rustling and a possible man-eating monster were enough to be getting on with for now.

"Pinkertons, huh?" John's expression was unreadable in the shadows. "Guess I figured it had to be something like that."

"I hope you can forgive us for not being more forthcoming," Thomas said. "We thought it likely the locals in this area would be less than cooperative if they knew."

"No doubt."

I still couldn't get a bead on him, whether he was angry or disappointed or something else. I had the impression John Ward kept his cards pretty close, even by cowboy standards. "We're here to help," I said, hating how trite it sounded. "We're chasing a lead on a separate matter in the morning, but we'd be happy to join you on the hunt afterward, if you're willing. We're not trackers, but we can shoot, and from the sounds of things, having a few extra guns might not be a bad idea." *Also, I have a few more questions to ask about your fellow ranchers.* I knew better than to push our luck any further tonight. Hard to read he might be, but John was clearly a cautious sort. Better to give him a chance to digest things first.

"Lemme think on it a spell," he said.

Thomas nodded. "That's more than fair. You can leave word for us at the hotel if and when you're ready. In the meantime, we should be very grateful if you kept this information to yourself."

"I surely will. I don't need no blood on my hands."

With that comforting remark, he headed back inside. I watched him mount the steps, and that's when I noticed something that made my stomach drop.

"Thomas." I inclined my head at the saloon. One of the windows stood open, releasing a wisp of cigar smoke into the night.

He sighed. "This just isn't our day. I don't suppose you recall whether anyone was sitting near that window?"

I did recall, only too well. "Bowie Bill Wallace. Wanted in three territories, I'm told."

"Of course."

"I guess there's no way of knowing whether he heard."

"Nor anything to be done if he has. Let's just get the horses settled and head back to the hotel, shall we?"

It was busy there too, a few of the treasure hunters having splurged on rooms instead of bunking in at one of the boardinghouses in town. "We should try to get ahead of this crowd tomorrow," I said as we stopped outside my door. "Before there's nothing left in that cabin to find."

"Agreed. We'll leave before dawn. Just remember to drink some saltwater before you go to bed, in case Mr. Upton should decide to pay another visit."

"Thanks for the reminder. I don't think I can handle any more excitement tonight."

"It has been an exhausting couple of days, hasn't it?"

"Still enjoying it?" I asked wryly.

"Immensely." He took my hand, turning it over under the light. "Though I do wish our evening had been less eventful. That's going to be a nasty bruise, I fear."

Already, dark smudges were forming on my wrist, and I couldn't help shivering, recalling how close my attacker had come to wrenching the knife free. "I had my revenge, anyway."

"You certainly did."

Something in his voice made me look up. He stood perilously close, head bent toward mine, his pale gaze drifting idly over the contours of my mouth. Warmth crept into my cheeks. I had only to lift my chin, and—

"*Ahem.*"

We both started. A middle-aged woman in a traveling cloak stood at the top of the stairs, a dramatic arch of her eyebrow conveying her disapproval at this shocking behavior. Thomas dipped into a formal bow as she passed, and I bit my lip to keep from smiling.

"Good night, Miss Gallagher." My hand was still in his, and he raised it to his lips, eyes shining with laughter.

"Good night, Mr. Wiltshire."

A door opened and closed; the woman disappeared into her room, leaving the hallway deserted. Thomas hesitated a moment.

Then he lifted my hand again, this time pressing a kiss to the inside of my wrist. He lingered there, his breath thrilling along the delicate skin. "Good night," he said again, this time in a whisper.

By the time I'd closed the door behind me, my knees were weak, and my pulse frolicked like a day-old colt. There'd been something dangerous in Thomas's eyes a moment ago. Something I'd never seen before. It was terrifying in the best possible way.

My thoughts churned deliciously. I daydreamed my way through disrobing, through unpinning and brushing my hair. I turned down the lamp and pulled the curtains, and then I climbed into bed, still picturing that forbidden look in Thomas's pale eyes.

I forgot all about the saltwater.

The sweat on my lips tasted of blood. Or maybe the blood tasted of sweat; there was plenty of both streaming from my brow. I was sticky with it, drawing flies from every corner of the room. The drone of their wings blended with the ringing in my ears, a steady buzz that would've put me to sleep if I hadn't already been asleep.

I'm asleep.

A fly landed on the tip of my nose. I tried to swat it away, but my arm wouldn't move. Hadn't moved in hours. My hands were past numb, and my legs too. *Ropes are too tight,* I thought. I couldn't remember why there were ropes, but I could see them, banded about my chest and ankles, binding me to a chair.

"Just tell me." The voice came from behind me. Boots tolled against the floorboards as he circled around. "Just tell me and it'll all be over."

I tried to speak, but it turned into a cough—a wet, bloody cough that left foam on my lips. Every breath scorched with pain. Vaguely, I recalled something to do with a shotgun, the butt end of it meeting my ribs. It seemed like the sort of thing I ought to remember clearly.

"I'm going to find it one way or another," he said.

"You're dreaming," I rasped.

I'm dreaming.

"Am I? I might not have your touch, but I have ways of my own. I read, Ben. I *learn*. I have resources you'll never understand, do you hear me? *Look at me, goddamn it.*"

I tried to lift my head, but it was so heavy. The room spun on a sickening axis. *Who is he?* I felt as if I should remember. His face swam before me, unfocused, unrecognizable.

"I'm through waiting on you to do the right thing. You're going to die here, and for what? You don't even need the money. You have more than you could ever spend. Just show me on the map, and you can be on your way. You can go off and buy a mansion and a yacht and whatever else your greedy little heart desires. You can live your life, and we never have to see each other again, do you hear me? *Do you?*" He was practically screaming now. His face was inches from mine, and the manic gleam in his eye struck terror into my heart.

I tried to reason with him. "It don't have to be like this. We can talk about it. If you let me go, I'll—"

"*LIAR!*" The gun he pointed at my face was my own, the silver-plated one with the pearl handle. His hand trembled so badly that the cylinder rattled in its frame. "*YOU'RE A BASTARD LIAR!*"

Panic flooded my breast. I wriggled against my bonds—a useless, instinctive gesture. As if I hadn't tried it a hundred times. As if now, weak and exhausted, with a six-shooter pointed at my head, I was going to miraculously break free and overpower my kidnapper.

He leaned over me, and when he spoke again, the hysterical note was gone, replaced by an icy calm that was more terrifying still. "You're the most selfish sonofabitch I ever met."

I tried to think of something to say. Anything.

"Past time you got what's coming to you." He put the gun to my head and clicked the hammer back.

I screamed.

Bang.

I waited for the pain, but it didn't come. There was only blackness—and then light, a searing glow as a lamp was lit, sending me scurrying against the headboard in terror. For a horrible moment I didn't know where I was. Then Thomas dropped onto the bed beside me and I threw myself into his arms, drawing deep, shuddering breaths that were just short of sobs. "He shot me. He killed me."

"It's all right. You're safe. You're safe, Rose." He repeated it over and over, rubbing my back as if I were a small child.

An unfamiliar voice sounded from the doorway, startling me all over again. "What in blazes?"

Thomas's arms tightened around me. "She had a nightmare, but she'll be all right. Terribly sorry for the fuss."

"What happened to the door?"

"I'll see that it's repaired first thing in the morning. Now, please, if you wouldn't mind . . ." Thomas's voice smoothed out into a meaningless drone. I could feel myself being dragged back into sleep; it closed around me like quicksand, toxic and heavy.

"Not yet, Rose. Drink this first."

A cup was pressed into my hand. I tasted salt.

"That's it. A little more."

I was falling backward, but slowly this time, gently. Darkness wrapped around me, warm and soothing, enfolding me like a lover. I felt safe, protected.

I fell asleep, and did not dream again.

I woke to an empty room and a pounding headache. Sitting up, I found a cup of tea at my bedside, still warm, and a glass of water that smelled faintly of rotten eggs. Sunlight filtered between the curtains, and I could hear the murmur of breakfast going on downstairs.

Damn. So much for getting ahead of the crowd. Ben Upton's cabin would be swarming with treasure hunters by the time we got there, and it was my fault. I'd been careless, too wrapped up in silly romantic fantasies to take proper precautions against the ghost. Upton had taken full advantage, showing me the moment of his murder in horrific detail. I'd tasted the blood and sweat, felt the terror thrumming in my veins. I'd even heard the gunshot . . . Or had I? Twisting in bed, I found the door to my room propped against its frame, hinges askew. *There's your bang.* After taking such care to spare my door the night before, Thomas had been obliged to kick it in anyway.

"Another top-notch performance, Gallagher," I muttered, swinging my legs over the side of the bed.

I washed up and got dressed, huddling into a corner to avoid being seen through the gaps in my doorframe. Then I headed downstairs, where I found my partner loading up the horses. A wooden crate full of dry goods sat beside Luna, and a thick canvas roll had been strapped behind my saddle.

"How are you feeling?" Thomas paused in his preparations to look me over. "Did you find the mineral water I left at your bedside?"

I nodded sheepishly.

"I'm sorry about the sulfur. Wang was out of the brand I usually prefer, but it's better than nothing. I only wish I'd brought more. We'll have to ration it carefully."

"Thomas . . ."

He raised a hand. "No need. What matters is that you're all right." He resumed his task, stuffing a can of beans into his saddlebag.

"That's not all that matters. You should be able to count on your partner. Instead you're having to rescue me all the time."

"Don't be ridiculous. By even the most charitable accounting, I'm decidedly in the red in the rescuing department."

"How about the careless mistakes department?"

He sighed. "Try not to be so hard on yourself. One can't expect to develop a whole new set of reflexes overnight. Centuries ago, dealing with ghosts and shades was a matter of routine, but we're brought up differently these days. Eventually, these things will become second nature to you, but in the meantime, you've been paired with a more experienced agent precisely in order to cushion the impact of such inevitable lapses."

Did he really believe that, or was he just making excuses for me? I wasn't sure I wanted to know.

"In any event," he went on, "I think perhaps solving Mr. Upton's murder is a little more urgent than we thought. I'm assuming what you saw last night was the moment of his death?"

I shuddered, which I figured was answer enough.

"That suggests the ghost is impatient to see his killer brought to justice. Which makes him dangerous. He'll keep trying to intrude into our minds, and if he becomes sufficiently aggressive, he may succeed in breaking through no matter what precautions we take. I've already wired for a medium, but I expect it will take several days, depending on who's available and how far they have to travel. In the meantime, we now have two pots on the boil, which means we may be in for some very long days."

"Hence the canvas bedrolls?"

"Tents, actually. Upton's cabin is only a few miles away, but who knows where the day will take us? I've packed everything we can carry, just in case." He patted one of his saddlebags, where a bulky rectangular object testified to the presence of Mr. Tesla's luck detector. The pocket camera, meanwhile, had been strapped awkwardly behind his saddle. "I'd like to take some books along as well, but I fear that would be too much to ask of my faithful steed, and I don't fancy navigating some of those canyon trails with a wagon."

We finished loading up and rode out. Already, the trail bore signs of heavy traffic; what was hard dirt yesterday had been beaten to mud, and a few new trails branched off the main route, left by riders keen to avoid the muck. I swore under my breath. "It's going to be Grand Central Depot out there, isn't it?"

As it happened, I was only half right. It wasn't just Grand Central Depot, but the whole of Fifth Avenue at rush hour, with a steady stream of riders clogging the trail in both directions. What could Thomas and I possibly hope to turn up this many hours later, with so many bodies polluting the scene?

Finding the place wasn't hard, but only because there were voices to guide us, and the smell of woodsmoke and bacon. Otherwise, the dense brush would have kept the trail well hidden, and the cabin was set far enough back that a casual passerby would never notice it. No doubt that explained why it had taken the better part of a year for someone to discover it.

But discover it they had, eventually, and in the two days since, a bustling camp had sprung up around the place. Tents and bedrolls dotted the clearing like so many mushrooms. A few trees had been felled, and some enterprising soul had even erected a makeshift privy. A pair of treasure hunters cooked breakfast over a fire, while another poured a canteen of water over his head, sweating in spite of the cool morning air. The surrounding brush was alive with the sounds of digging, branches crackling and spades singing as they met the hard earth.

"Good lord," I murmured in dismay. "They're tearing the place apart."

If there was any rhyme or reason to their searching, I couldn't see it. Holes pitted the ground in seemingly random locations. Rotting logs had been pried up from the earth, and rocks too. They had literally left no stone unturned.

We hitched up well away from the others, and Thomas made a great show of unloading his pocket camera. There was plenty of glaring and grumbling, but nobody seemed inclined to interfere with us, so we started toward the cabin.

I'd taken only a single step before I sucked in a breath, my hand flying to my chest as a blade of cold knifed through me.

"He's here," I whispered. "The ghost. And there's something he wants me to find."

CHAPTER 11

CABIN IN THE WOODS—THE BALLAD OF
POOR JONAH—HELL WITH THE FIRES OUT

can't see him," I said, doing my best to keep calm. "But I can feel him."

Thomas put a reassuring hand on my arm. "Don't worry. Even if he tried to show himself, neither of us would be capable of perceiving him, not in our current state. Between the saltwater and the mineral water, we're quite protected for now. Even so, we shouldn't linger. Let's see what the scavengers have left behind, shall we?"

What they'd left behind was a right royal mess—not that the place had been a palace to begin with. Dry leaves and mouse turds littered the floor. The rafters were festooned with cobwebs, the walls spackled with bird leavings. A dingy bedsheet served as a curtain, and the furniture, such as it was, consisted of a crooked table and a pair of mismatched chairs, one of which was actually a stepping stool. For a moment I wondered if there'd been some mistake. What would a rich man want with a place like this? But no, this had to be

Upton's cabin. Certainly the treasure hunters thought so, because they'd torn through it like a tornado. Every cupboard hung open, and every drawer. The floorboards had been pried up, the mattress slashed. Even the stovepipe had a gaping hole in it.

"One has to admire their thoroughness," Thomas said dryly. "Do you recognize anything through the clutter?"

I didn't, and it wasn't just the clutter. Everything about the place was wrong. The door was to my left instead of my right. The rafters were too low, the walls too narrow. "I don't think this is it."

"I don't understand. I thought you sensed him?"

"I do. It's definitely Upton's cabin, but . . ." I trailed off as a man stuck his head through the doorframe. He took one look at the mess, cursed, and withdrew, apparently deciding he'd missed his chance. I knew how he felt. "This isn't the cabin from my dream. At least, I don't think so. It was hard to see properly. Everything was muzzy. I think Upton might have been hit on the head before he . . ." I swallowed. *Before we were shot.*

"It's possible, though it might simply have been a feature of the dream. From what you described on the way here, it sounds as though you were deeply immersed, but not so deeply that you experienced the event exactly as he did. The detachment you mentioned, the confusion, suggests that you retained a part of yourself throughout." He glanced over. "Which is terribly fortunate. If he'd dragged you down any further, you might never have awoken."

I shivered, resolving then and there to drink a glass of saltwater every night before bed for the rest of my life.

Thomas did a slow tour of the room, taking in the details with a detective's eye. "You're right, the murder most likely didn't take place here. No trace of blood anywhere."

"But if this isn't the scene of the murder, what does the ghost want me to find?"

"The gold, perhaps?"

"Why would Ben Upton want a complete stranger to have his gold? Besides, if there was gold anywhere in this cabin, the scavengers would have found it by now."

"Perhaps it isn't gold as such, but rather the means of finding it."

"You mean like a map?"

"You tell me. Can you feel anything?"

Mostly, what I felt was hungry—at least until my eye fell on the jars lining Bill Upton's shelves, at which point I promptly lost my appetite. They were so black with rot that even the treasure hunters had left them alone. So I thought, at any rate, but when morbid curiosity got the better of me and I picked one up, what I found surprised me. "What on earth?"

Thomas came over for a closer look. "I took these for preserves."

"So did I, but . . ." I showed him what the jar contained, which was . . . well, *earth*. "What kind of grown man keeps jars of dirt on his shelves?" I turned one of them on its side, but if there was anything buried in there, I couldn't see it. "Do you suppose he stored earthworms in here, for fishing?"

"Look here. They're labeled, one through three. Soil samples, perhaps?" Thomas dropped his satchel on the table and started loading the jars inside.

As I watched him, my eyes narrowed.

Seeing my expression, he said, "One never knows when the most humble piece of evidence might come in handy."

"It's not that." I pointed at the stool tucked under the table where he worked. It was serving as one of two mismatched chairs, or so I'd assumed by its placement, but now I wondered. "I can't imagine Upton had many guests out here. What did he need with two chairs?"

"Perhaps he didn't. This one is actually a stool."

"Exactly. Do you remember the description of Upton in Mr. Roosevelt's letters?"

Thomas paused. "Middle-aged, rather rough-and-tumble looking, and . . ." His brow cleared. "Extremely tall."

"The ghost I saw was well over six feet, but look." I rested my hand on the top shelf. "I don't even need to stand on my tiptoes to reach. There's nothing hanging on the walls. So what did he need a stool for?"

We both looked up. Above the rafters, the peaked roof stretched into shadow. There was no ceiling, and no place to conceal anything, except . . .

"Stand guard, would you?" I grabbed a broom from beside the door and started prodding along the tops of the rafters. Dust and mouse filth and heaven knows what else rained down on me, but eventually something more substantial slipped free, tumbling to the floor in a whirr of pages. I scrambled to collect it, and not a moment too soon: Thomas coughed just as another stranger barged through the door. He eyed us suspiciously, but all he saw was a photographer framing the scene with his hands while his assistant scribbled away in a notebook.

"Yes, I believe this angle will do nicely. Although . . . Really, Miss Gallagher, could you kindly step aside? It's frightfully difficult to imagine the oeuvre with you standing in the middle of the frame."

"Yes, Mr. Wiltshire. Sorry, Mr. Wiltshire."

The treasure hunter skulked around for less than a minute before stomping out, muttering in disappointment.

The moment he'd gone, Thomas whirled on me, eyes shining. "Is that what I think it is?"

"A journal, from the look of things." I flipped through the pages. "There are drawings in here and everything."

"Rose Gallagher, I could kiss you." And then he did just that, pressing his lips triumphantly to my forehead.

As many times as he'd said that, he'd never actually done it, and it sent champagne bubbles through my blood. *It doesn't mean anything, you goose. He's just excited.* Well, that made two of us now, and I turned for the door, hoping he wouldn't notice my blush. "Let's get out of here before somebody gives us trouble."

Alas, it was not to be. No sooner had we stepped outside than we were accosted by a trio of treasure hunters. "Gonna have to search you," one of them said.

Thomas's reply was mild enough, but I felt him coil beside me. "I'm afraid that won't be possible."

"It weren't a request." The ringleader took a threatening step forward.

"Careful, Silus," another man called from the campfire. "That's the pair tore up Granger's last night."

The man called Silus scowled. "That s'posed to scare me?" He did, in fact, look a little nervous, but that was hardly a comfort. Nervous men were dangerous men, especially when they had guns in their belts and liquor on their breath.

"You don't look like a man who scares easily," Thomas said. "Which is why you're absolutely perfect. Don't you agree, Miss Gallagher?"

"Perfect," I echoed dutifully, having no earthly idea what he was talking about.

"I'm afraid I can't allow anyone to handle this most delicate machine." Thomas gave his camera a reverential little pat. "But I would be so very obliged if you would allow me to take your photograph, all three of you. The interior of the cabin is rather a fright. No newspaper is going to print that. But a photo of three intrepid adventurers? That would look very well in *Harper's*, don't you agree?"

Silus grunted. "*Harper's?*"

"Or perhaps *The Atlantic*. They're simply mad about such images back east. You'd be seen by thousands. Hundreds of thousands, even." The trio exchanged glances, and the next thing I knew I was helping Thomas set up his telescoping tripod.

Half an hour and half a dozen poses later, Thomas and I were ready to make our getaway when a new rider came up the path, grim-faced and spattered with blood.

"Shit, Eli," said our new friend Silus. "What in hell happened to you?"

"Found Jonah out on the trail. What was left of him, anyway."

Thomas and I exchanged a blank look. One of the treasure hunters, presumably.

"Torn up from root to stem," the rider went on. "Wouldn't even have recognized him except for that fancy six-shooter of his. It was still in the holster. That *thing* must be awful fast."

The others had started to gather round now; Thomas and I drew closer to listen. "You sure it was the monster?" one of them asked.

"What else would it've been?" said another.

Eli seemed to be enjoying his audience a little more than was seemly. "It dragged Jonah's pony off into the bush," he said, raising his voice for all to hear. "I tried to get what was left of him up on my horse, so he could be buried and whatnot, but it was too much of a mess." He shook his head. "I sure wasn't gonna hang around waiting for that thing to come back for the rest. I'm telling you, boys, it's time to get out of this place."

"Excuse me," Thomas said. "Where was this, exactly?"

"Not two miles south, where the crick meets the Deadwood trail. I'd stay well clear if I were you, mister."

"Oh yes, we certainly shall." Thomas turned back toward the horses.

"Straight there, then?" I murmured.

"Of course."

We lit out at a lope and didn't slow until we saw the ravens. They circled lazily overhead, rustled and cawed in the trees. We reined in, and Thomas slid his 12-gauge out of its scabbard. I did the same with my rifle, letting Luna's reins go slack as we scanned the surrounding undergrowth.

I'd had my doubts about the creature, wondering whether it could possibly be real, but let me tell you: it's one thing to be skeptical when you're sitting in the snug confines of a saloon, and quite another when you're out on the trail, exposed, surrounded on all sides by dense brush. I thought I'd encountered every shade of dread by then, but I'd never felt anything quite like this. As if death could literally pounce on me at any moment, from any direction. Every creak of a branch, every shiver of a leaf, sent a spike of fear through my veins.

There was no body. Instead, a swath of broken branches marked the place where the carcasses had been dragged off. Blood soaked the muddy earth, pooling in the half-moons gouged out by horse hooves. This, it seemed, was all that was left of poor Jonah, whoever he was, and I crossed myself, whispering a prayer for the dead.

Thomas swore under his breath and lowered his shotgun. "Whatever did this certainly wasted no time coming back for the rest."

Which was why I was keeping my rifle right where it was. "If this is a forgery, it's a very good one."

"Too good. No, I think we can officially discard that theory. This was certainly an animal attack of some kind. These furrows in the mud . . . Claw marks, I presume."

"Should we try to track it?"

"If we had the appropriate skills, perhaps. As it stands, we'd simply be offering ourselves as *digestifs*." He walked his horse in a tight circle, scanning the ground. "Hopefully, we can return with Mr. Ward, but in the meantime let us focus our efforts where they may do some good. I want a look at that portal. We've all but ruled out our earlier theories, but I'd like to be sure." Glancing at me apologetically, he added, "It will be a long ride."

"Good thing we have those tents," I said, and put my heels to my horse.

We continued south, cutting a twisting path through the Badlands. Castles of rock towered over us on all sides, ramparts and turrets and rugged keeps baked under a punishing sun. The heat, combined with the long afternoon shadows, conspired to give the landscape a vaguely sinister air. The earth looked flayed, bone-white and bloodred, shot through with layers as black as ash. I could almost imagine the faint smell of sulfur. It was like riding through—

"Hell," Thomas murmured. "With the fires out."

"Pardon?" I glanced at him, a little unnerved at how in tune our thoughts were.

"That's how General Sully described this area when he first rode through in the sixties. A fitting description, don't you think?"

"I'll say. I can practically smell the sulfur."

"That's not your imagination." He pointed at a hill just ahead.

At first glance, it was no different from the others: a layered mound of gold and rust separated by veins of black. This one, however, was *on fire*. Smoke billowed out from one of the dark seams, curling lazily into the afternoon sky. If I squinted, I could almost imagine a craggy old cowpoke with a sunburn enjoying a cigar, letting the smoke leak out of his toothless mouth.

"Is it a volcano?"

Thomas shook his head. "Burning coal, apparently. That's the geological explanation, at any rate, but it certainly can't be a coincidence that it's in the immediate vicinity of . . ." He reined in abruptly, and this time I didn't need him to point.

Before us loomed the most striking butte I'd seen yet. A soaring column of sandy white, it reminded me of a cathedral spire—except it was the size of the Statue of Liberty. A memory came over me, of sitting in a back room of Wang's General Store, having portals explained to me for the first time.

"Aren't they sealed with magic?"

"Nothing quite so impressive, I'm afraid."

Holding his hands a couple of feet apart, Mr. Wang said, "Big rocks."

"Just a minute. You're telling me that the gates separating the dead from the living are sealed with—"

"A monolith," I murmured.

"And a rather obvious one at that." Thomas jumped down from his horse. "Any member of the paranormal community would know it for a portal straightaway."

"If it were leaking, wouldn't there be shades and heaven knows what else all around here?" I couldn't help looking over my shoulder as I said it, even though I hadn't sensed anything. In my experience, the dead can be awfully sneaky.

"Not necessarily," Thomas said, already rummaging in his saddlebag. "Still, we'd do well to be on our guard. You have your hairpin, I presume?"

"Always."

"Good, because I'm quite unarmed, spiritually speaking. Bringing my cane along wasn't practical. If we're in the territory for any length of time, I'll see if I can have a gun stock made out of ash, but in the meantime . . ." He hauled out Mr. Tesla's luck detector. "I'll operate the device while you keep an eye out for trouble."

As science experiments went, it wasn't very exciting. Thomas spent the better part of two hours wandering around the base of the butte, waving the probe hither and thither. He climbed as high as he dared, leaning out so far that my stomach did backflips. He shuffled about on his haunches, in case the leak was below ground. He scanned every crag and crevice. All the while, the dial stayed stubbornly at zero, and the box failed to emit so much as a single *click*.

Finally, Thomas was forced to admit defeat, jamming the luck detector back in his saddlebag with enough force to set Gideon dancing. "No radiation," he growled. "The seal is quite intact, apparently. Whatever we're dealing with, it doesn't appear to involve the portal."

"Isn't that good news? You said you wanted to rule it out, after all."

He sighed. "You're right, of course. I'd just hoped for . . . *something*. If not an answer, at least a clue about the creature, the winter . . . anything at all. If the portal isn't involved, then I struggle to see what connection there could possibly be between the Winter of the Blue Snow and the animal attacks, or indeed between any of our three mysteries. Two days' worth of investigating, and what do we have to show for it?"

"We have the journal," I reminded him. *And three jars of dirt.* I figured that last bit wouldn't help my case.

Thomas passed a weary hand over his eyes. "Apologies, Rose. I'm being needlessly pessimistic. It's only that after this morning . . . That poor fellow on the trail . . ."

"I know. I feel it too. Like we're running in place, and people are dying because of it. But we'll figure it out." I tried for a comforting smile. "Let's head home and get some rest. Then we can look at this journal with fresh eyes."

Thomas nodded, and some of the tension went out of his shoulders.

As for me, I couldn't help looking out over the horizon. Thunderheads gathered in the distance, roiling slowly westward against an otherwise pristine sky. To another pair of eyes, they might have looked like buttes, or a herd of buffalo.

All I saw was monsters.

CHAPTER 12

X MARKS THE SPOT—ELECTRICITY—AN
ARRESTING DEVELOPMENT

t's more of a sketchbook than a journal," I said, scanning yet another drawing that meant nothing to me. "If I didn't know who
this belonged to, I'd guess he was an inventor." I turned the book
around to show Thomas.

The two of us sat in the shade, resting our horses—and our
rumps—for a spell. We were still well south of Medora, and with
afternoon fading into evening, I had a feeling we were going to be
putting our new tents to good use.

Thomas glanced up from the map he'd been poring over. "What
am I looking at?"

"No idea. It looks like a design for some kind of pulley mecha-
nism. Maybe for a new mining technique?"

"That would make sense. Roosevelt did say that Upton was one
of the last lone wolves operating in Deadwood. Most of his ilk were
pushed out by corporations long ago, not least because the gold is

becoming increasingly difficult to extract. It's not a business of pick-axes and shovels anymore. There's machinery involved."

"So maybe Upton was trying to figure out a way to stay in the game." I flipped to another sketch, a tool of some kind that vaguely resembled a war club. "But then why come to Medora? There isn't a gold mine within a hundred miles of here."

"Perhaps those soil samples tell a story after all." Reaching into his satchel, Thomas pulled out one of the jars and gave it a contemplative shake. "I'm half inclined to send for Burrows. His luck would tell us everything we need to know about these jars."

"Where would that get us?"

"It would help us trace Upton's movements, which is always useful in a murder case. A bit of a long shot perhaps, but we're stretched thin at the moment. The creature is still our most urgent priority, and we've scarcely touched on the Winter of the Blue Snow. We need all the help we can get."

"Would Mr. Burrows really spend four days on a train just to help us with a couple of jars of dirt?"

"In a twinkling," Thomas said with a wry smile. "He has altogether too much time on his hands. The slightest whiff of adventure will have him packing his trunk. Or at least, have someone packing it for him."

"Worth trying, I guess. In the meantime, I'll have to go through this book more carefully. *After* I get something in my stomach." I set the sketchbook aside in favor of a can of peaches, which was the first thing I'd eaten all day. "How about you? What exactly are you doing with that map, anyway?"

"Now that we're convinced our predator is real, I've been jotting down the locations of the attacks. It's not good news, I'm afraid."

"Oh?" I shuffled closer to look.

"We have Cougar Ranch, here." He showed me a wide circle drawn in ink. "Their stock ranges far and wide, which makes it difficult to be precise about where the attacks took place, but I've assumed a radius of a few miles in each direction. I've done the same for Pronghorn Ranch, as well as Roosevelt's Maltese Cross. That leaves us with a radius of about fifty square miles. Now, within that . . ." He pointed at an *X*. "These denote predator attacks on humans. The ones mentioned in Mr. Roosevelt's letters are here and here. Then there's young Gareth Wilson, who died two days before we arrived. According to Mr. Morrison, he was killed approximately here, in the vicinity of the Bar H. And finally, we have the site of poor Jonah's demise this morning. The attacks occurred in that order, which means . . ."

The peaches turned over in my stomach. "It's getting closer."

"I fear so. Jonah's death is the only one that doesn't fit the pattern. The rest have been concentrated south of town. Assuming the animal remains in the area, it's probably hunting somewhere among this dense cluster of ranches, including Roosevelt's Maltese Cross. In other words, just outside of Medora itself."

"You don't think it would venture into town, do you?"

"If it were any other wild animal, I would say no. But we still don't know what we're dealing with here. It's terribly difficult to predict next moves when one doesn't even know the rules of the game."

Speaking of rules . . . I frowned, looking closer. "There's another pattern here. Do you see?" I traced my finger along the map, drawing a line between the *X*s. Each and every one sat directly beside some kind of waterway—the Little Missouri, or one of its offshoots. The rivers and creeks ran like roads between destinations, almost as if . . .

Thomas closed his eyes briefly. "Of course. Is it any wonder John Ward keeps losing the trail?"

In my mind's eye, I saw again the tracks White Robes had drawn. The front foot like a cougar, with claws as long as a grizzly's. The back foot clawed as well . . . with lines between the toes.

"Webbed feet. It's *swimming*." Our eyes met. In his, I found the fascinated gleam of the scientist. In mine, he found abject horror. "Thomas, what in the name of God is this thing?"

"Perhaps a giant beaver wasn't far from the mark after all."

"I can't believe you're joking about this."

"I'm not. At least, not entirely. An otter-like creature existed in the Miocene that weighed more than four hundred pounds. *Enhydriodon sivalensis*. Native to East Africa, mind you, and one doubts it had claws like this creature."

I stared at him. "You just knew that off the top of your head?"

He laughed. "Hardly. Did you not notice my reading materials on the train?"

"Which ones? You were practically swimming in books the whole time."

"Fair enough. In any case, I waded through two full volumes on prehistoric creatures. There were a number of interesting specimens, though nothing quite *this* intriguing."

Intriguing wasn't the word I'd use. "We need to take this information to John Ward. And the Lakota too."

"Agreed. Let's see how far we can get before nightfall."

He'd just started to fold the map away when a sudden gust of wind tore through the ravine, startling the horses and whisking the hat clean off my head. Shielding my face with my arm, I looked up. "Er, Thomas? I don't think we need to worry about nightfall."

The wind had changed direction sometime in the last hour or so, and the storm I'd seen in the distance was nearly on top of us. It looked even more menacing now, iron-gray and billowing, its underbelly flashing with lightning.

"That's going to be on us in a trice." Thomas sprang to his feet. "We need to get those tents up as fast as we can."

I hurried to untie my canvas roll, but I'd never assembled a tent in my life. "Please tell me you know what you're doing."

"Not a clue."

"You didn't ask?"

He shot an annoyed look across his saddle. "I didn't imagine we'd be in *quite* such a hurry."

The wind picked up. Fat drops of rain started to hit the dust. I glanced despairingly at Ben Upton's sketchbook. It would be ruined in a downpour. Then there was Thomas's map, and Mr. Tesla's luck detector . . . "There's no time," I said, dragging the saddlebags off Luna's rump. "We've got to get these things under cover. I'll use my tent like a blanket. You do what you can with yours." Unrolling the canvas, I stuffed everything I could underneath and tucked the corners under our saddles. Then I tried to help Thomas.

The special branch of the Pinkerton Detective Agency has a rigorous training program. It includes riding, shooting, fighting, poisons, disguises, and even ballroom dancing. It does not, however, include basic outdoor skills, a fact that was grimly in evidence that day in the Dakota Badlands. Thomas and I fumbled and floundered our way through the business, so that by the time we'd finally hammered the last peg in place, we were so thoroughly soaked that our teeth were chattering. We had a single dry blanket and not a stick of firewood. The two of us barely even fit inside the tent; we had to curl into little balls with our arms over our knees, and even then, our heads brushed the canvas.

We huddled there a moment, shivering. Thomas and I looked at each other—and burst out laughing.

"What a sorry pair we are." He dropped his head between his knees, raking his fingers through his dark hair. It was extra wavy in the damp, which I thought looked very well on him. For that matter, the shirt plastered to his body looked very well on him too.

He caught me staring, so I said, "Your lips are blue."

"So are yours. And you're shaking like a leaf. I think we'd better get under this blanket before we make ourselves ill."

We shifted around awkwardly. Draping the blanket over our shoulders didn't offer much warmth, so we lay down on our sides. Thomas wrapped his arm around my waist and gathered me close, and we tucked ourselves in like a pair of spoons in a silver cloth. He was shaking just as badly as I, but after a moment or two we both settled, and I could feel my fingertips again. Sadly, there was nothing to be done about Gideon and Luna; the poor animals just bowed their heads, turned their rumps to the wind, and resigned themselves to being soaked.

Meanwhile, a magnificent drama unfolded all around us. Lightning forked between the hills, searing white against the black belly of sky. Thunder shook the valley. The rain was coming down so hard that it made a thunder of its own, drumming against the canvas above our heads. Even the nervous stirring of the horses was eerily beautiful, their forms blurred and wraith-like in the downpour. "It's incredible," I said, my voice all but lost in the din.

"Yet another way in which this place is wild." Thomas's smooth tenor was honey in my ear; his breath lifted the hairs at the nape of my neck. "The weather shifted so suddenly."

"I noticed the clouds earlier, but they seemed to be moving away from us. I should have said something."

"And I should have included rain slickers among our supplies." I felt him shrug. "We're here now. And . . . it's not so unpleasant, is it?"

"No." I burrowed in a little deeper. We were pressed so close now that I could feel the watch in his breast pocket; I fancied I could even feel it ticking, like a soft heartbeat against my back.

The storm continued to rage, all violence and raw power. It was exhilarating, even a little frightening. Lying here like this, curled up together, felt deliciously forbidden. Yet there was something familiar about it too, and the longer we lay there, the more a sense of déjà vu came over me.

"Thomas?"

"*Mmm?*"

"Last night, after you gave me the saltwater. Did you stay with me?"

"For a little while."

I almost left it at that. Did I really need to know the rest? What if I ruined this perfect moment? Already, the storm was waning, retreating as quickly as it had come upon us. The lightning had withdrawn into the clouds, and the rain slackened. All too soon, it would be over.

But I had to ask. "Did you stay with me . . . like this?"

A long pause. Thunder rumbled in the distance. More than once, I felt him start to answer, only to falter. Finally, he said, "Not exactly like this. But yes, I held you. I wanted you to feel safe." Another pause. "Was it wrong of me?"

I rolled over. Pale eyes searched mine, as if trying to read my thoughts. I'd never seen him so unsure of himself, and it was strangely thrilling.

He reached for me, his fingertips brushing my hairline. "Was it wrong of me, Rose?"

"Does it feel wrong?"

And then he was cradling my head, his mouth seeking mine, and I sighed into him, surrendering to the longing that had tugged at me for so long. His kiss was gentle at first, soft and searching, but it grew deeper as our limbs twined around one another, and when I threaded my fingers through that thick, damp hair, it brought him rolling onto me in a rush.

Reader, I almost came undone.

My hand found its way under his shirt. I'm not sure which of us was more surprised. The muscles of his back knotted, and I half expected him to pull away; instead I felt gooseflesh break out along his skin, and his kiss grew harder. Suddenly I had a fistful of buttons, and I blush to think what I might have done next if he hadn't broken off suddenly. He hovered there a moment, breathing hard, and then he rolled as far away as he could without knocking the tent down.

"I think," he said breathlessly, "I had better get that other tent up, don't you?"

To this day, I wonder what he would have done if I'd said no. If I'd tested the limits of his restraint, and my own. But even then, in the heat of the moment, I knew it would be a mistake. So I just watched as he clambered out of the tent, missing his warmth already and wondering how on earth we were going to pretend *this* never happened.

At least it had stopped raining.

We made an early start of it, riding into Medora at a little after ten o'clock on Sunday morning. We hadn't discussed last night's . . . *incident*. Already, it felt strangely distant, like a dream, or something I'd read in a scandalous novel. That was probably for the best. We needed to stay focused on the task at hand. The creature was less than five miles from Medora, stalking the banks of rivers and streams. People's homes lined those same waterways. Men fished in them. Women drew water for laundry and livestock. Children played in them, swimming and catching frogs. We had to find that thing before it killed again. Ben Upton and the Winter of the Blue Snow would just have to wait. As for Thomas and Rose . . . that was probably best left alone entirely.

"I hope there's a message from John Ward waiting for us," I said as we hitched up outside the hotel. Otherwise, we'd have to hire a tracker, and who knew how long that would take—assuming we could even find anyone willing to take on the task.

Thomas didn't answer, too busy squinting at something over my shoulder. Turning, I found a trio of riders heading toward us at a jog. They rode three abreast, and the man in the middle didn't seem to be holding on to his reins. It took me a moment to process what I was looking at, and even longer to accept it. The man in the middle was a prisoner, and though we'd only just met, I considered him a friend, or at least an ally.

Two Horses sat rigid in the saddle, arms bound in front of him. If he recognized Thomas and me, he gave no sign, staring straight ahead as the three of them trotted past.

Exchanging a grim look, Thomas and I followed.

The riders hitched up outside the jailhouse. Already, they were drawing a crowd; townsfolk clustered on the boardwalk, looking on with approving nods and even a few jeers.

"Softly, now," Thomas warned in an undertone. "These people are desperate for someone to blame for their troubles. Things could unravel quickly."

I did my best to heed that advice, but the smug look on the faces of Two Horses's captors made my blood boil. As if they expected the town to throw them a hero's parade. "Stand back, ma'am," one of them said self-importantly as we approached. "Indian's dangerous."

"He most certainly is not. His name is Two Horses, and he's a friend of ours."

The rider gave Thomas a wry look, as if to say, *Get your woman in line*. Two Horses, meanwhile, didn't acknowledge my presence, or anybody else's; he sat perfectly still, his expression blank. "Don't seem like he knows you," the other man said.

"He doesn't speak English." He seemed to understand it well enough, from what I'd seen, but these men didn't need to know that. "What have you done with the others?"

"You mean the rest of his band? We ain't found 'em yet."

I breathed a little easier. The other three were safe, at least.

"On what grounds are you holding him?" Thomas asked in his poshest lawyer voice.

"He's wanted for cattle rustling," the first man said.

"Wanted by whom?"

"Gus Reid."

"I'm acquainted with Mr. Reid," Thomas said, "and to the best of my knowledge, he doesn't wield any judicial authority."

"This here's a citizen's arrest."

"Based on what evidence?"

"What in hell is going on out here?" A heavy tread sounded on the boardwalk, and a man stepped out of the jailhouse, donning his hat as he squinted in the morning light. He wore a badge, though he didn't really need it; it was obvious from the way he carried himself— lazily domineering, with just a hint of latent menace—that this was Hell Roaring Bill Jones, sheriff of Billings County.

"Morning, Bill," said the first man.

"Jed." The sheriff took in the scene with a sour expression. He was a striking fellow, with arresting blue eyes, heavy brows, and a drooping mustache. He might even have been handsome were he not in dire need of a wash; as it was, he looked like the sort of rough who'd start a saloon brawl purely for the fun of it. "You wanna tell me why I got an Indian on my porch?" The accent was Irish, the tone tinder-dry.

"This here's one of the Sioux been rustling Mr. Reid's stock."

"I was just inquiring how the gentleman supports this contention," Thomas said.

The sheriff gave him a cold look. "Do I know you?"

"I beg your pardon. Thomas Wiltshire, and this is my assistant, Miss Gallagher. We're acquainted with this fellow. His name is Two Horses, and I can assure you—"

"I can assure *you* I ain't interested in the say-so of some dude been in town all of twelve seconds." Then, to Reid's men: "I'll take your Indian, for now. But the tenderfoot ain't wrong. You need some kind of evidence if you want me to keep him."

"Keep him?" Jed snorted. "Cattle rustling's a hanging offense, Bill."

I felt sick to my stomach. What kind of barbarians would hang a man over some cows?

"It's a hanging offense if and when a judge says it is," the sheriff replied. "I don't wanna see you or any of the rest of you Cougar Ranch boys outside my office with torches, you hear?"

Jed scowled. "Fine, then. We'll get a judge to sign off on it."

"You do that. Meantime . . ." Jones jerked his head, and Two Horses was pulled down from his horse and bundled off to the jailhouse.

Thomas started to say something, but the sheriff stayed him with a gesture. "Unless you got evidence of your own, I don't wanna hear it."

"And if we obtain such evidence?"

"Do as you like. But if you mean to set this boy free, you'd best hurry. Might be they decide to let him go, but I wouldn't count on it. Judges round here don't take a whole lotta convincing when it comes to Indians." Glancing back at the jailhouse, he said, "I'd give it . . . oh, three days. A week at the outside."

"And then?" My voice trembled with anger.

"And then it's over," said Sheriff Jones. "One way or the other."

CHAPTER 13

NATURAL LAW—THE BUCKSHOT OUTFIT—
HIDE AND HAIR

We have to do something," I said as we walked away.

"And so we shall." Thomas's features were grave but composed. "We're going to find that animal and put a bullet in it, and if we have to have it stuffed and presented to the good sheriff with a bow around its neck, then that's what we'll do. This doesn't change our plans, Rose. It merely adds urgency."

He's right, I thought. Righteous outrage wasn't going to do Two Horses any good. We needed to think rationally about this. "Should we try to find Little Wolf and White Robes? Tell them what's happened?"

"My guess is they already know. Either way, if we ride out now, we risk leading Reid's men straight to them."

"What about Mr. Roosevelt? Maybe he can use his influence to help Two Horses."

"Good idea. He'll want an update in any case. We can wire him now, along with Burrows."

We split up, Thomas heading to the Western Union office while I got the horses fed and watered. After that, I made my way to the hotel, tension gnawing at me with every step. It didn't help that the whole town was on edge after yesterday's attack. Locals gathered on the boardwalk, talking in hushed tones; more than a few carried rifles or shotguns. Tempers were sour, too. The pair of cowboys loitering outside the hotel eyed me suspiciously as I passed, not even bothering to excuse themselves when one of them coughed all over me. Inside, meanwhile, I found the hotel owner arguing with the pasty pinstriped fellow from Bismarck.

"Mister, I don't wanna have to tell you again. It ain't for sale."

"I think you'll find my offer more than generous."

"I think you'll find my boot in your ass if you don't *git*." The owner gestured at the door, and the pasty fellow retreated, stalking past me in chilly silence.

I cleared my throat awkwardly. "Good morning. Have any messages arrived for us?"

"Matter of fact."

The owner pushed a folded piece of paper across the desk. There was an envelope too, and I was delighted to recognize Clara's handwriting. But her letter would have to wait.

"That there's from John Ward," the hotel owner said as I unfolded the note. "But it's me wrote it down for him, being he ain't lettered."

My gaze ran over the messy script. The scribe was barely lettered himself, but the meaning came through clearly enough, and it was exactly what we'd been hoping for: an invitation to join Mr. Ward on the hunt, with a rough description of his expected location. "When did he leave this?"

"Yesterday, just after dawn."

I looked up in dismay. "Why didn't you give it to us yesterday morning?"

"Tried to, but you all rushed out while I was dealing with breakfast."

Damn. I hurried out into the street, making for the livery at a jog. *He's got a full day's head start, and our horses are exhausted . . .* I suppose I made something of a sight—a woman in men's clothing jogging down main street, dodging horse manure as she went—and some of the locals heckled me from the boardwalk. I barely noticed, too preoccupied to pay them any attention.

Which was unfortunate, because one of them was paying very close attention to me.

We found John Ward resting in the shade near the river, not far from where we'd met Little Wolf two days before. He sprang to his feet the moment he spotted us, flicking the remains of a cigarette into his campfire and scraping dirt over the embers with his boot. "Thought to be seeing you folks yesterday. Figured you might need the smoke to find me."

"Apologies for the delay," Thomas said. "I'm afraid we ran into some difficulty. You've not been back to town since yesterday, I presume?"

"Been working my way down the river from where the Wilson boy got took. Why, something up?"

We told him about Two Horses, but he didn't seem all that surprised.

"I was afraid something like that might happen. When Mr. Reid starts gnawing on a bone, he ain't one to let it go." He sighed and shook his head. "Man's stubborn as a mule."

And about as bright. Aloud, I said, "That's not all. A man was killed at Custer Creek yesterday, near where it meets the road to Deadwood."

John cursed quietly. "Anybody see it?"

"Not that we know of." I explained what we'd found, how the creature had dragged horse and rider off into the bushes.

He nodded. "That's how it does. Likes to go off and find itself someplace quiet to eat. It's got its favorite spots, too. Usually, when I come across a kill, there's two or three kinds of bones in it."

"Like a leopard," Thomas mused.

"Can't say I know too much about leopards." John slung a pump-action rifle into a scabbard and mounted up, his saddle creaking beneath him.

"Nor do I, but . . ." Thomas looked thoughtful. "I do know the behavior stems from competition. Leopards share their territories with more powerful predators that might drive them off their kill, so they drag it to a safe location before eating."

John listened with polite interest. "Only other big predators around here is wolves and mountain lions. Bears, if you catch 'em on a bad day. Nothing big enough to give this thing any trouble."

"That's just it. The behavior makes no sense for an alpha predator."

John rumpled his brow. "You wanna kill this thing or study it?"

"Both, I should think."

"Mostly kill it," I said, shooting my partner a *look*. "But I think I see what Thomas is getting at. Even if this creature is some kind of animal we haven't discovered yet, or we thought was already extinct, it should still behave like an animal."

"Precisely. If it is a product of nature, then it ought to follow the rules of nature."

"What do you mean, *if* it's a product of nature?" John glanced between us. "What else would it be?"

That, Mr. Ward, is an excellent question.

"What seems clear, at any rate, is that it prefers to hunt near water." Thomas produced his map and handed it to John. "The *X*s indicate predator attacks."

The ranch hand stared at it for a long time. Then he said, "I'm a damn fool."

"You didn't have the full picture," I said.

He shook his head, as if he hadn't really heard me. "I figured we only found signs near the river 'cause that's where the prey was at. But I shoulda known it was more than that. The tracks . . . Some of 'em had these marks between the toes . . ."

"Webbed feet." I sighed. "White Robes showed us, but we didn't realize what we were looking at until yesterday."

"Yeah, well, I should have." John refolded the map in stiff, angry movements.

"I felt the same," Thomas said. "But we mustn't be too hard on ourselves. It's terribly difficult to see that which doesn't make sense."

"And it don't. Not one lick. This river"—John gestured at the Little Missouri—"ain't exactly the Mississippi. It's running high this time of year, on account of the snowmelt, but most of the time it ain't more than a trickle. How's an animal that big gonna live in it? You wanna talk about the laws of nature . . ." He shook his head again. "No use crying about it now, anyways. Let's get on up to Custer Crick and see what's what."

We headed back the way we'd come, riding single file along the narrow strip between the river and the bluffs. John took point, scanning the ground as we rode, though how he saw much of anything from the back of the massive bay he was riding was beyond me.

"That's a big horse," I called up.

"Catfish?" John patted the animal's meaty neck. "Yeah, he's a bull, all right. Got more than a little draft horse in him. Though how he come by them long whiskers, I couldn't say."

"That's why he's called Catfish, I suppose?"

"It was that or Otter. Which, speaking of . . ." John veered closer to the water, eying it critically. "If that thing's a swimmer, it's probably gonna feel safest where the water's deepest. Reckon that's where we oughta be looking."

I smiled. "You're thinking like a detective."

"Am I? Guess I'll take your word for it." There was a pause. Then, over his shoulder: "What's it like, anyhow? Being a detective?"

"Why, Mr. Ward, are you thinking of joining the Agency?"

I was only teasing, but his answer surprised me. "Thinking of finding a new line, anyways. Don't know there's much future in ranching out here, and I sure don't plan on going back to Texas."

"That's not a Texas accent I'm hearing."

Nosy, I know, but can you blame me? We had a long ride ahead of us.

He laughed. "No, ma'am. This drawl of mine's a mongrel, and no mistake. My people was from Tennessee, but my daddy moved west soon as the war was over. Heard there was work out there, and land too, but he never did settle. Guess you could say we was tumbleweeds." His hand brushed his saddle as he spoke, as if in memory. It looked comfortable and well-worn, with a set of initials stitched on the cantle.

"LJW. Was that your father?"

"Leonard John Ward. Now there was a horseman. He worked with Thoroughbreds in his plantation days, so tending livestock came natural. But he didn't have no judgment. Fell in with the Buckshot Outfit over in Kansas. I told him they'd be the death of him, and so they was. That's how I come by this." He patted the saddle again.

I winced inwardly, sorry I'd brought it up. "My condolences. Were they a gang?"

"Buckshot Outfit? In a way. They call themselves a cattle company, but they're just a bunch of hired guns. Half of 'em is wanted someplace or other. They been mixed up in just about every range war from here to New Mexico." He shook his head. "Can't understand why folks still hire 'em. Nothing but trouble. I told Mr. Reid he oughta leave them fellas alone, but he just told me to mind my own."

I sat up a little straighter. Gus Reid being involved with a bunch of notorious mercenaries sounded like the sort of thing I wanted to hear more about. "What does your boss have to do with the Buckshot Outfit?"

"Couple of the newer hands used to run with them. Boss says he don't care, long as they do the job. Bosses always say that. Then they act all surprised when their Buckshot boys start shooting up a saloon. Least the foreman keeps 'em out on the range most of the time, where they can't do much harm."

I glanced over my shoulder at Thomas. I could tell by the sharpness of his gaze that he was listening to every word. "Isn't it odd for a legitimate rancher to hire wanted men?" he called.

John laughed. "Welcome to the frontier."

Hard country attracted hard men, I supposed. The sort who might name themselves after . . .

I paused, picturing the tiny beads of lead known as buckshot. When you poured them out of a shotgun shell, they looked like . . . "Does the Buckshot Outfit have a brand?"

"Yes, ma'am."

"Is it a cluster of dots, by any chance?"

He glanced behind him. "You seen it?"

"I might have. Does one of your co-workers have a horse with a Buckshot brand?"

"Not that I seen. Most of the boys don't own their own horses, so they ride Cougar Ranch stock. But as for them Buckshot fellas, I couldn't say for sure. Like I said before, most of 'em is way out on the range, so I don't cross paths with 'em all that much."

"Does anybody else have former Buckshot boys working on his ranch?"

"Couldn't rightly say."

It fits, I thought. *Reid made it clear how he felt about the Lakota, and he sent his men to arrest Two Horses.* But why steal their horses? And how did those horses end up in the belly of some mysterious wild animal?

Those questions would have to wait. John slowed his mount and pulled his rifle from its scabbard, signaling an end to our chat. From there on, we were on the lookout, Thomas and I scanning the brush while our guide kept his eyes on the ground. He stopped for every bit of spoor he found: badger and wolf, rabbit and coyote, weasel and deer and bighorn sheep. When he wasn't watching the ground, he scanned the sky, looking for carrion birds. But after more than an hour of riding, we still hadn't found hide nor hair of our quarry.

"Thought for sure we'd've come across something by now," John said. The three of us stood ankle-deep in the water, longarms slung over our shoulders as we examined a rack of antlers tangled up in driftwood. "Deadwood trail's just over yonder. Which means we're almost at the spot where you say this Jonah fella was kilt."

"Perhaps the creature rests for a few days between meals," Thomas suggested.

John grunted skeptically. "Or maybe we're just having a bad day."

"It's about to get worse," said a voice.

We spun, all three of us leveling our weapons at the newcomer. He stood between us and the trail, a revolver in each hand and a smirk hitching one side of his oiled mustache. I recognized him straightaway. "Bowie Bill," I said, mainly for Thomas's benefit.

"So I surmised." Thomas eyed the outlaw down the barrel of his 12-gauge. "Either you're exceptionally foolish, Mr. Wallace, or you've an affection for drama. I'm going to assume it's the latter and your friends are lurking somewhere in the shrubbery."

The outlaw's smirk faded, and a moment later half a dozen armed men filtered out of the trees. "Ain't you just a smug sumbitch," Wallace said sourly.

They surrounded us in a semicircle, some upstream and some down, cutting off any escape. I kept my sights on the outlaw nearest to me, a ginger-haired kid with a .44 Starr pointed right between my eyes. He couldn't have been more than sixteen—not that it mattered. Sixteen was plenty old enough to kill, especially out west.

"Well," said John Ward. "Here we are." He wore the same expression he'd had in the saloon two nights ago, cool and grim, as if this wasn't the first time he'd found himself staring down the barrel of a gun. Which it probably wasn't.

"Apologies, Mr. Ward," Thomas said. "It appears we've entangled you in some unpleasantness. I suggest you get on your horse and head back to Medora. This needn't involve you."

In reply, the ranch hand racked his rifle. "Thought I told you to call me John."

"Ain't that sweet." Wallace waggled his six-shooter between them. "I'll tell the undertaker you all wanna be buried together."

"What exactly is your quarrel with us?" Thomas asked.

"Like you don't know."

"Actually," I said, "we don't. Just because we're Pinkertons doesn't mean we're interested in you."

"You expect me to believe that? I'm *Bowie Bill Wallace*." He let that hang in the air, eyebrows raised significantly.

Thomas sighed. "My dear fellow, I hate to disappoint you, but until two days ago we'd never actually heard of you."

"Thomas," I said between clenched teeth. "You're not helping."

The outlaw scowled. "I got a price on my head would keep a man in good liquor for the rest of his days. Bounty hunters chasing me all over creation. We hit the stage in Montana, and less 'n a week later a pair of Peckertons show up, and I'm s'posed to think that's a *coincidence*?"

"Lord spare me," said John Ward. "If I had a nickel for every peacock with a price on his head out here . . . You think you got a play, mister, go on 'n' make it. But the way I see it, once the shooting starts, ain't nobody walking away."

"That's a good point." Thomas narrowed his eyes. "What was your plan, Mr. Wallace? Not this little parley, surely."

"I expect he wanted to do it someplace quiet," John said. "To keep the law off. Most likely he was laying for you on one of them bluffs outside of town."

"Ah, I see. But then we changed course and headed east instead. How inconvenient for you. And now here we are, in an unwinnable stalemate. What is it they call that in the dime novels?"

"A Mexican standoff," I supplied.

"Is that what you see?" Wallace's smirk returned. "I see a couple of Peckertons and a cowpuncher outnumbered two to one. Hell, I bet I could put all three of you down before you got a shot off that fancy scattergun."

"An expensive wager," Thomas said, his finger tightening around the trigger.

Wallace gave a low, gritty laugh. "You got sand in your craw, Englishman, I'll give you that. But it ain't gonna save you."

To this day, I wonder how that standoff would have ended. But we never got the chance to find out.

The undergrowth rustled, and a split second later a hulking form erupted from the brush and tackled the ginger-haired kid. He barely had time to scream before a pair of jaws clamped around his throat and gave a sharp twist, and then he went limp.

He wasn't the only one. For a moment we all just stood there, gaping at the animal crouched over the kid. *A cougar*, my numb brain supplied. *Or is it a bear?* It was neither. It was both. Slim and sleek, it had the thick tail of an otter. But it was powerfully muscled too, with a long muzzle and claws like the blades of a harrow.

The horses screamed, breaking the spell.

We all started shooting at once.

The creature flinched back from the hail of bullets, but the only blood I could see was the kid's. Then it reared up on hind legs, towering over us all and roaring its rage. The outlaws on either side of it scattered, but not fast enough; a massive paw lashed out, and I flinched away from the spray of blood even as I pulled the trigger. A man went down screaming, clutching at what was left of his midsection. As for my bullet, it did no more harm than the one before it, or the one after, or any of the others we unloaded in a steady stream of fire. I pumped the lever of my rifle again and again. Thomas emptied his shotgun and grabbed his sidearm, fanning the hammer until that was spent too. We could hardly see for the smoke, and yet all we succeeded in doing was making the thing angrier. It crouched defensively on its forepaws, snarling and snapping like a rabid wolf and looking for a place to pounce.

"The water!" John grabbed my arm. "Get out of its way!"

Thomas dove one way, John and I another. The moment its path was clear, the creature sprang into the creek, slicing through the water like an arrow and darting away, leaving a plume of blood in its wake.

The three of us sat sprawled on our behinds, breathing hard as the cold water seeped into our britches. The horses were still screaming and straining against their tethers, but all else was quiet. Wallace and his boys had lit out, leaving their two dead comrades bleeding in the dust.

"Jesus," John whispered. "Jesus."

I levered myself up onto wobbly legs and waded back to dry land. I kept my gaze on the ground, unwilling to look at what the creature had done to the ginger-haired kid. He never even knew what got him.

John leveled a finger at the creek. "What in the hell *was* that?"

Thomas squinted into the distance where the creature had disappeared. "You know," he said, "I thought it would be bigger."

CHAPTER 14

A TRICKY TELEGRAM—BAITING THE
TRAP—A LETTER FROM HOME

John Ward knelt over the scattering of spent bullets, staring at them with a numb expression.

"We're fortunate no one was injured," Thomas said, running a hand down Gideon's forearm. "I thought the horses, at least, would have taken a stray." Rising from his crouch, he patted the stallion's neck and murmured consolingly in his ear. Gideon's eyes were still white-rimmed, his ears swiveled back, but he'd stopped bucking, at least. Luna had taken it a little better, and Catfish was already cropping at the weeds, his nerve apparently as sturdy as the rest of him.

"I suppose we missed our chance to follow it." I was surprised how steady my voice sounded, considering that my heart was still hammering in my chest.

"I'm not sure we ever had one. Did you see the way it moved in the water?" Thomas shook his head in awe. "Remarkable."

"So what now?"

"We found it once. We'll find it again."

"And then what? We unload more of those?" I gestured at the fresh shells he was snapping into his 12-gauge. "There were seven of us shooting at that thing and we didn't even make a dent."

"True. Could we catch it, perhaps?" He looked to John, but the other man was in a world of his own, turning a shattered bullet over in his hand.

He's shaken. Which made two of us. Thomas, meanwhile, was his usual businesslike self, flipping out his notebook and scribbling down a few lines, cool as you please, as if we hadn't nearly been gutted by a man-eating monster. If this was what a few years in the special branch did to a person, maybe I was in the wrong line of work.

"We'll need to wire the Agency straightaway. And start looking through those books of the arcane. There, you see? You mocked me for a bringing a trunkful of books, but we'll be very glad of them now."

I struggled to imagine how he'd explain all this in a telegram. *Have located creature, stop. Appears to be bulletproof cougar-bear, stop. Please advise.*

"A telegram isn't exactly private. Hadn't you better send it in a letter?"

"I think we can manage, provided we choose our words judiciously. But Jackson will probably have to respond by post, which means we'll be waiting a couple of days for an answer."

Jackson? If Thomas was planning to consult the Agency's senior necromancer, that could only mean . . . "You think we're dealing with magic."

That got John's attention. His head snapped up. "Beg pardon?"

Thomas demurred, but I didn't see much point in sugarcoating it now, not after everything John had just witnessed. "Magic," I repeated firmly. "Witchcraft. Sorcery." When my partner still hesitated, I added, "You're the one who suggested we bring John into our confidence, remember? I think we're past half measures."

Thomas sighed. "Very well, then. Yes, I think it's possible. Chiefly because I can't think of any other explanation. That thing isn't just unfamiliar, it's unnatural. Any member of the animal kingdom, prehistoric or otherwise, would be vulnerable to bullets. Yet as you pointed out, we didn't even graze its hide. What else but magic could account for that?"

John's gaze cut between us, as if trying to decide whether we were joking. "What kind of Pinkertons believe in magic?"

"The kind who work for the special branch." I handed him a silver business card embossed with the single staring eye of the Pinkerton Agency.

He flipped it over, frowning. "There's no writing on this."

"In case it should fall into the wrong hands. The special branch is . . . well, it's a secret. Most of our fellow Pinkertons don't even know we exist. We handle cases of a supernatural nature."

"Supernatural. As in hoodoo and haints and such." His tone was inscrutable as usual. John Ward, I decided, ought to take up poker.

"We didn't mention it before, because . . ."

"Because it would sound crazy." He was quiet for a spell, digesting this. "So you knew all along this thing wasn't . . . What did you call it? A product of nature?"

"Not exactly," Thomas said. "We toyed with a number of theories, including an outright hoax, or perhaps some sort of prehistoric animal. But it would be fair to say that our minds remained open to the possibility that we were dealing with the paranormal."

"What about you, John?" Maybe it was rude, but I had to ask. If you're going to be working with a person, it's helpful to know whether they think you belong in the cranky-hutch. "Is your mind open to the possibility?"

He sighed and shook his head. "Guess it don't much matter what my mind is open to. My *eyes* is open to this." He showed me the collection of shattered bullets in his hand.

It was just the sort of thing Sergeant Chapman might say, and it occurred to me that the two men had more than a little in common. My favorite copper was a man of few words and cast a wary eye on the supernatural. Half the time, I wasn't sure he even believed what Thomas and I were telling him. But when you got right down to it, he was ready to get on with the business, and I figured that went for John Ward, too.

"A pragmatist, then," Thomas said approvingly. "Does that mean we can continue to count on your assistance?"

"Far as it goes. But you was right in what you said before. We ain't putting that thing down without a Gatling gun, and maybe not even then."

He started to say more, but a thudding of hooves sounded from up the path. At first I thought it was Bowie Bill and his gang come to finish what they'd started, but then I recognized Little Wolf, followed closely by White Robes. They looked ready for a fight, hunting rifles tucked under their arms, but we all relaxed when we recognized each other.

"We heard shooting," Little Wolf said. "It sounded like a battle."

"So it was," Thomas said. "Of a sort."

"In that case, I'm glad you're safe."

"What about you?" I glanced up the path, but there was no sign of a third rider. "Where's Red Calf?"

"Back at camp. When we heard the guns, we thought maybe Two Horses had escaped. We came to help, but Red Calf stayed behind to guard the horses in case it was a trick." Little Wolf's glance passed over the grim scene on the ground. He looked drawn, as if he'd aged a year since we saw him two days ago. Worried sick, no doubt, about the fate of his friend.

I did what I could to put his mind at ease. "We saw him. Two Horses. He's safe, at least for now. They took him to the jailhouse in town."

Relief passed over Little Wolf's face—followed by bitter anger. "He was only trying to buy a horse. They had no right to take him."

"They've accused him of cattle rustling," Thomas said.

"Lies. We have not even seen a cow in days." He didn't ask what the sheriff would do next, which was a relief. I didn't want to be the one to tell him they were talking about hanging his friend—though he probably assumed as much anyway. His people had learned long ago to expect the worst from the law.

White Robes climbed down from her horse to take a closer look at the bodies in the dirt. "Who are they?"

"Outlaws," I said. "They ambushed us on the trail."

"And then? These men were not shot."

"*It* got 'em," John said. "That *thing*. It jumped out of the bushes there, went straight for the kid."

Little Wolf's eyes widened. "You saw it? What was it?"

The three of us looked at one another. Where to even start?

"It weren't no product of nature," John said, succinctly.

We took turns describing what we'd seen. We must have sounded completely barmy, but the siblings listened without comment, only exchanging glances every now and then.

"You say it *swims*?" Little Wolf muttered something in his own language. "The peoples to the east speak of an underwater panther that lives in opposition to the Thunderbirds. Its body is that of many creatures blended together. A cougar, but with horns, and the tail of a serpent."

"Indeed?" Thomas arched an eyebrow. "That certainly sounds similar to what we saw. Fascinating."

White Robes, meanwhile, looked decidedly unconvinced, observing this exchange with a frown.

John smiled ruefully at her. "I know what you're thinking, and I don't blame you. But I saw what I saw. I about emptied my rifle into that thing. We all did, and this is what we got to show for it." He held out a hand as if to give her something, and when she opened hers, he let the shattered bullets fall into her palm. "Now you tell me what coulda done that besides a brick wall."

She shook her head. She had no answer for him.

"My people have hunted here for a hundred years and more," Little Wolf said. "If there was such an animal, why have we not seen it before?"

"That," said Thomas, "is a very good question. Why here, and why now? Until we find answers, it may not be possible to destroy it."

Little Wolf didn't even hesitate. "Then we must catch it. We must catch it and show it to everyone in town, so they will see Two Horses is not to blame." He turned to his sister, and they conversed for a moment in Lakota. "We have a plan. We meant it for the men who stole our horses, but it should work for this creature as well."

"A trap," White Robes said, "using horses as bait. We can let them graze in places we know the creature hunts."

John nodded slowly. "That oughta get its attention, but then what? I'm good with a rope, but I don't like my chances of lassoing that thing."

"We will find a way," White Robes said. "We must, for Two Horses. But first we need bait. That's what Two Horses was trying to do when he was taken. We were foolish to send him. We should have known the ranchers would not sell to Lakota. But they will sell to you, John Ward."

"We are poor," Little Wolf added, "but we have things to trade."

"That needn't be a concern," Thomas put in. "The Agency will cover our expenses. Will this do for now?" Reaching into his jacket, he produced a few crisp bills and handed them to John. I didn't see the denominations, but the arch of John's eyebrow suggested they were generous. "For our part, Rose and I will consult our resources in Chicago and New York to see if we can find any record of such a creature."

John glanced at the Lakota. "They reckon it's magic," he explained, hooking a thumb at us.

That was a whole lot more blunt than I'd have suggested, but they took it pretty well, considering. Little Wolf looked thoughtful, and White Robes just sighed. I suppose they'd heard it all before, and besides, there wasn't much point in arguing about it now. What mattered was catching the thing, and then we'd see what we could see.

"Well, then," said John. "If I'm going on a buying spree, I best get started. Might be we'll find a place that's got more than one or two ponies to sell, but most likely I'll be all over creation. What with the distances and all, that's gonna take time."

"What about the livery?" Thomas asked.

"They'll have a few, at twice the price, but not enough. I reckon it makes most sense to start around here, see how we do."

"What about your boss?" I asked. "I don't suppose he'll much like you taking time off."

"Don't suppose he will. He can send me packing if he likes. This here's more important than any job."

"You will need help to herd them, once you have enough," Little Wolf said. "When you are ready, you know where to find us."

John nodded. "Will do."

I didn't like abandoning our friends out here in the wilderness, but we didn't have much choice. Thomas and I had our part to play, and we'd only slow them down anyway. "Just promise us you'll take care of yourselves, all of you."

"And you must do the same," Little Wolf said. "The creature may not be the only thing stalking you." He inclined his head meaningfully at the dead outlaws.

He's right, I realized with a sinking feeling. Men like Bowie Bill Wallace wouldn't let something like this go.

"This will be answered," Little Wolf said. "Answered in blood."

It was late afternoon by the time we got back to Medora. I was filthy and exhausted, so when Thomas told me I wasn't needed at the Western Union office, I was happy to let him go, already dreaming of the hot bath I would take. *Lavender water,* I promised myself. *Candles.*

Imagine my disappointment when I arrived back at the hotel to find blood everywhere.

It took me a moment to notice it. The lobby was deserted, so I went to ring the service bell; that's when a flash of crimson caught my eye. The hotel registry lay open, its cream-colored pages marred with a single, perfect drop of blood. There was more of it on the desk, I realized, a wide smear that wasn't quite dry.

My hand strayed to my gun. "Hello?"

Silence.

I walked around to the other side of the desk. The drawers hung open, and the cupboards too. The safe was dappled with bloody fingerprints, though it didn't look to have been opened. A door marked PRIVATE stood ajar. Warily, I stepped through, and that's where I found the body. It sat slumped against the wall, almost as if it had been propped there. *The owner,* I realized, recognizing his straw-colored hair. Stabbed, from the look of things, and not long ago. I swallowed down a surge of nausea. No matter how many times you see it, murder is always horrific.

I'd just knelt for a closer look when the door swung open.

Quicker than you could say *tough day,* I had my gun pointed at the man's face. He yelped and threw his hands up; we recognized each other in the same instant.

"Damnation!" The night clerk clutched at his chest. "You about scared the life outta me!"

I lowered my gun, but only because I didn't want him to see my hands shaking. "What happened here?"

"Mr. Oliver got kilt."

"I can see that. Do you know who killed him?"

"No, ma'am. Looks like he was robbed, though. His pockets was turned out, and they took his belt buckle. Probably they was laying for him just outside the back door, and jumped him on his way home." Seeing my puzzled expression, he added, "It was me brung him in here while I went to fetch the law. Didn't want him just lying there for any old Peeping Tom to see."

"Is the sheriff on his way, then?"

"Not yet. He were . . . *indisposed,* I guess you'd call it. Best to catch Hell Roaring Bill early in the day, if you take my meaning."

Drunk. Doesn't that just figure. "What about his deputy?"

"We'll track him down. Don't you fret."

I clucked my tongue in disgust. *No wonder Wallace and his boys chose this place to lie low.* I wondered if Bowie Bill might even be to blame. He was famous for using a *pig-sticker,* after all. "Does this sort of thing happen a lot around here?"

"Now 'n' then. Gets to where you can smell it coming on. Folk is all nervy and ill-tempered. They get to drinking and gambling, and then . . ." He gestured vaguely at the body. "Anyhow, you don't need to worry about it none. Like I said, the law'll be here by and by, and they'll sort it all out. Now, I'm gonna have to take care of this, but is there anything you need? Cup of tea? Hot bath? Splash of laudanum? I know you got the delicate nerves and all."

"I . . . pardon?"

"That nightmare you had the other night musta really been something. I've heard plenty of hollering up there on account of this place being haunted, but that scream you did . . ." He shook his head. "No offense, ma'am, but I don't need to be replacing that door again. So why don't you let me have Lucy fix you some chamomile and draw you up a nice, relaxing bath?"

I hesitated, but there wasn't much point pretending I could be of service here. Even if I wanted to get involved in a stray murder case, Thomas and I were in over our heads already. And besides, from the sounds of things, this would be nothing new to Hell Roaring Bill Jones. *Just another day in the Wild West,* I thought, holstering my gun. "When you do speak to the sheriff, tell him he ought to question Bowie Bill Wallace. And that fellow from Bismarck, too. I saw him arguing with Mr. Oliver earlier today. I think he was trying to buy the hotel."

After which I accepted the tea and the bath, though I drew the line at laudanum.

It's a strange sensation, soaking in lavender water when you know there's a corpse one floor below. I couldn't stop thinking about it. The detective in me went over the crime scene, while the former housemaid couldn't help wondering how they'd get the bloodstains out of the floorboards. Neither train of thought was especially relaxing, so I decided to read Clara's letter, which I'd kept tucked in the pocket of my trousers. It did my heart good to see her familiar neat hand. She must have had a meticulous schoolmarm, someone just like Mam who clucked and tutted over every loop and line. But there was nothing fussy about the prose. That was pure Clara, and it brought a smile to my face.

Dear Rose,

I hope it didn't worry you to find a letter from me so soon. Everything is all right here, but I figured you ought to know what happened the other day so you got your story straight by the time you come home.

I was down at the Eighteenth Street station, and who do I bump into coming off the el but your friend Pietro, and right behind him your mama. How strange is that? I finally meet them after all this time and not a month later I run into them on the street. Anyhow, your mama gets to asking if I've heard from you all, and I forget what the story is supposed to be, so I go and say something addlebrained about the weather in Newport. Well, she gives me this funny look because of course you all are not supposed to be in Newport. So now she's worried, and Pietro is practically dancing a jig because I'm messing it up so bad, and all I can think to do is skedaddle before I make things worse.

But don't worry, your friend Edith fixed it. I got to admit, Rose, I wasn't sure about her at first, but she's all right. She came around yesterday, asking if you'd written yet. I told her how I messed things up with your mama, and she said not to worry, she'd take care of it. And that's just what she did. She went straight down to your place with some flimflam about needing to pick up a few things for you, and oh by the way, Mr. Wiltshire started his holiday in Newport but you all was in Long Island now, and that's where she was headed because he was throwing some big fancy party. So it's all fixed up, and all you need to remember is that bit about Newport and your mama will never know the difference.

I hope you're enjoying Medora. I started to read about it and then decided it would be best for my nerves if I didn't. All I can say is it don't sound like a place any good Christian soul would want to live. You all be careful, now.

Love,
Clara

CHAPTER 15

EXODUS—*CUI BONO*—A DILEMMA DEFERRED

f I'd had time to answer Clara's letter, I'd have told her I didn't think there was a soul, Christian or otherwise, enjoying Medora just now.

Word of the monster sighting at Custer Creek tore through the town like wildfire. Bowie Bill, or one of his boys, must have ridden through the streets like Paul Revere, because by the time I'd finished my bath and put on a fresh shirt, the commotion outside was audible. The stage to Deadwood wasn't due to leave until tomorrow morning, but there it was, parked on the street below my window as it loaded up with passengers. There was a queue outside the Northern Pacific ticket office, and when I headed downstairs, I found the clerk struggling to handle a crowd of guests waiting to check out. Medora was clearing out faster than a typhoid town.

Thomas had left word to meet him at the saloon. For supper, I presumed, but it would be a working supper, judging from the mountain of books I found him poring over. Granger's was busy, but that hadn't stopped my partner from claiming two tables for himself, over which he'd spread half the Astor Library.

"No wonder it took two men to lift your trunk," I said, sinking into a chair across from him.

He paused in his note taking, his hand sliding across the table to take mine. "How are you feeling? It must have been a terrible shock to find a body waiting for you at the hotel."

"Not my first murder scene."

I'd been trying for professional indifference, but I guess I didn't quite manage it, because Thomas arched an eyebrow. "Perhaps not, but the first you weren't prepared for, surely? It's perfectly natural to be shaken, Rose."

"Has it ever happened to you? Stumbling across a murder scene, I mean."

I'm not sure why I asked, and I sensed immediately that it was a mistake. Something dark passed through Thomas's eyes. "I have," he said, returning to his notes.

"Have you seen what's going on outside? Safe to say everybody knows what happened at Custer Creek."

"Indeed. They're calling it the Medora Monster. Frightfully unimaginative, if you ask me. Judging from the snippets of conversation I've overheard, half of these fine fellows"—he gestured at the crowded barroom—"are planning to drink their way through to the 8:35 Atlantic Express tomorrow morning."

"So much for keeping things quiet. I don't suppose our client will be pleased." To say nothing of the United States government. The special branch was under strict orders to keep paranormal matters out of the public eye. We called it the Containment Protocol, and it was one of our most important directives. "What if the story hits the papers in Bismarck, or even Chicago?"

"It's not our tidiest operation, to be sure, but you needn't worry.

Breaches like these aren't as uncommon as one might think, and we always manage to control them. The Agency will take care of the newspapers and any stray officials who need to be brought back into the fold."

"And what about everybody else? The treasure hunters and the cattlemen and the rest?"

"The dust will settle eventually. It always does. Once the shock wears off, people drift back to their natural corners. They sort the facts according to their worldview, and anything that doesn't fit within that framework is simply cast aside. Most will dismiss the paranormal aspects in favor of some more prosaic explanation."

That, at least, I knew to be true. I'd done it myself, when my mother told me she talked to my dead granny. Ghosts didn't fit within my *worldview,* so I blamed it all on her dementia—and almost had her committed to the insane asylum on Blackwell's Island.

Not a helpful turn of thought, Rose. I tried to focus on more immediate matters. "Did we hear back from Mr. Burrows?"

Thomas nodded. "He says he'll try for the six o'clock train, though I'd be surprised if he manages it. Either way, he'll wire us from Chicago to let us know of his progress."

Assuming he did catch the overnight Western Express, that would put him in Medora on Thursday, four days from now. Four days of waiting for an extra pair of hands to help us solve Ben Upton's murder—and four nights of fending off his pushy ghost.

Just then, a commotion broke out on the far side of the room, a man erupting from his chair with enough force to send it skittering back. At first I took it for a saloon brawl, but then I recognized the scowling face of Gus Reid. "*I told you, I don't give a damn what Roosevelt says!* He ain't here! He went back east, remember?"

"I got his proxy," said one of his companions, and I recognized the back of Charlie Morrison's head. "And seeing how he's the chair of this here association . . ." He gestured at the others sharing their table.

Reid sneered. "I don't take orders from no four-eyed dude runs off with his tail between his legs at the first sign of trouble."

Morrison's chair creaked as he rose up out of it. "If he was here, he'd knock the tar outta you for disrespecting him like that. But since he ain't, I reckon I got his proxy for that too."

"You don't wanna do that, Charlie," said another man, pushing his own chair back in warning.

Subtly, Thomas and I did the same, ready to spring into action if the situation called for it. Morrison was Roosevelt's man, which made him our man, too.

Reid pounded the table, sending beer glasses jumping. "I'm done sitting on my ass while my stock gets butchered. Look at you all, gossiping like a bunch of old women, half of you ready to sell and run home to mama. And why? 'Cause some outlaw too drunk to tell a bobcat from a barn cat tells you he saw a *monster*? Can't you see them Indians is laughing at us? It's time to do something, god-damn it!"

"Ain't you done enough?" one of the men said. "You got that Sioux sitting in jail. What happens when the rest of his tribe comes looking, huh?"

"We'll be ready for 'em. I say we wire Fort Buford."

Morrison sighed. "Cavalry ain't coming out here on account of a few dead beeves. Chrissake, Gus, be reasonable."

"*We'll put together a posse, then!*" Reid pounded the table again. "I aim to do what needs doing. Any of the rest of you decides to grow a backbone, you know where to find me." So saying, he stormed out of the saloon.

"Meeting adjourned, I guess," Morrison said dryly.

The group of cowboys dispersed. Charlie Morrison headed for

the bar, looking very much like he needed a drink, but then he spied Thomas and me and came over.

"Please," Thomas said, gesturing for him to sit. "That looked like a lively affair. What was Reid so exercised about?"

Morrison sighed and rubbed tired-looking eyes. "His foreman come across another half a dozen dead beeves this morning. Not too far from the house, so they say."

Strange. The spot where we'd been attacked this morning was several miles northeast of Cougar Ranch. If the creature had a reliable source of food in Gus Reid's herd, what was it doing all the way over at Custer Creek?

"And of course, Gus being Gus, he's convinced the Sioux are behind it. Says he wants the cavalry out here, but I guess you heard all that."

"You told him they wouldn't come," I said. "Are you sure about that?"

"Not halfway, ma'am. Truth is, I reckon it depends who's asking. Gus, he don't have the pull. But there's others who might, and he ain't the only one losing patience."

"What of his threat to form a posse?" Thomas asked. "Would the sheriff tolerate that?"

"Can't say for sure. If he does, or if the army decides to show up . . . Well, I don't need to tell you that don't turn out well. Things like that got a way of getting outta hand mighty fast."

My skin grew hot with anger. The idea that someone like Gus Reid could call the United States Army down on the Lakota without a lick of evidence made my blood boil. "Reid is a fool."

"There's plenty agree with him."

"Then they're fools too," I snapped, ignoring the warning look Thomas was giving me. "Anyone with an ounce of sense can see what's happening to those animals isn't the work of the Lakota.

Mr. Wiltshire and I have seen the creature responsible with our own eyes."

"Sorry to say, but unless you got proof—"

"We're working on it," Thomas said curtly. "In the meantime, one thing we know for certain is that the creature hunts on the banks of rivers and streams. It would be wise to warn everyone you can, especially at Maltese Cross."

"I'll do that." Morrison pushed his chair back. "I'd best get on the wire. Hopefully the boss can have a word with the sheriff." He hesitated, his glance shifting between Thomas and me. "Listen. There's another rumor going around too, 'bout the two of you. Far as I'm concerned, that's between you and the boss. But whatever it is you're planning to do, best do it quick, 'cause things is fixing to get ugly."

Thomas sighed as we watched him go. "He's right, of course. Situations like these have a way of escalating very quickly. If conflict breaks out between the ranchers and the Lakota, we'll have failed Roosevelt completely."

"We'll have failed this whole town," I said, "and Two Horses most of all. Three days, the sheriff said, and the first one's nearly gone."

"The clock is certainly ticking. And since it would appear that our secret is out in any case, I think it's time we were more . . . *direct* . . . with the locals."

"Meaning?"

"If we can no longer conceal our association with the Agency, let us use it to our advantage. Pinkertons are disliked because they serve as the long arm of the law, and are reputed to be bullies besides. So." Reaching into his satchel, he produced a shiny piece of metal and tossed it onto the table. "If we are to suffer the consequences of such a reputation, we ought to reap the benefits as well."

"Is that what I think it is?" I picked up the metal shield, turning it over in disbelief. Made of brass, with the Agency logo stamped at

the top, it boldly proclaimed the wearer a PINKERTON NATIONAL DE-
TECTIVE AGENT, NEW YORK. It was a simple badge, but impressive—
and I'd never seen one in my life. "Why don't I have one of these?"

Thomas tilted his head. "Do you not?"

"No, Thomas, I do not." I scowled, feeling cheated.

"I'm sorry, I didn't realize. It so rarely comes up in the special
branch. In any case, it's easily remedied. In the meantime, you can
wear that one if you like."

"No, thank you," I said coolly, pushing it across the table at him.

He eyed me with a puzzled sort of amusement, but he let it go.
"At any rate, I think we ought to pay another visit to Cougar Ranch,
this time as Pinkerton agents. Gus Reid is altogether too mixed up
in this for it to be a coincidence. *His* cattle being preyed on. *His*
ranch hands arresting Two Horses. And now we find out that some
of those same ranch hands are former mercenaries."

"Not just any mercenaries, either. Buckshot Outfit. It has to be
their brand White Robes saw that night." Which meant there was a
good chance the horse thieves worked at Cougar Ranch. But were
they acting on their boss's orders, or just looking for a little something
on the side? "Reid made it clear how he feels about the Lakota, so I
have no trouble believing he'd steal from them. But then why not keep
the horses, or sell them? How do they end up in the belly of a creature
Reid doesn't even believe exists? A creature that's busy devouring his
cattle every chance it gets?"

"*Cui bono.*"

"Pardon?"

"Whom does it benefit? The questions you're asking are the
right ones. It's difficult to see how Reid benefits from anything that's
going on here."

"Unless it's all a bunch of lies, and his herd is doing just fine."
I'd blurted it out without really thinking, but Thomas pounced on it
straightaway.

"Interesting," he said, leaning back in his chair with a thoughtful expression. "Suppose you're right, and all his bluster about the Lakota is just that. A bit of smoke to throw everyone off the scent. Reid's stock hasn't really fallen prey to the creature, at least not recently. His operations are largely unaffected, but the same cannot be said for his competitors in the beef industry. Maltese Cross, the Bar H, all the others—they've been hit multiple times, and some are closing shop as a result. Reid's share of the market increases. A clear benefit."

"But would that mean he's somehow responsible for the creature?" I had a hard time imagining it. "He made his views on the supernatural pretty clear the other day. *Hocus-pocus hoodoo*, I think he called it. Unless you think that's part of the act too?"

"Not necessarily. A shrewd businessman might simply take advantage of the situation. And whipping up hysteria around the Lakota would certainly have a chilling effect on investment. Many of these ranches are financed by wealthy easterners. They're already reeling from the effects of the winter. Rumors of a looming war with the Lakota might inspire them to cut bait before they lose everything."

"Leaving Cougar Ranch in an even stronger position." I was beginning to like this theory, and not just because I *dis*liked Gus Reid. It didn't explain everything, but if it could help us clear Two Horses's name, it was a good start.

Returning to the hotel after supper, we found the place quiet as a grave. Maybe it was the unfamiliar shadows, or the creepy specter of the moose head on the landing, but I felt a skittering of ice down my spine the moment we started up the stairs, and I paused at the top, shivering.

Thomas put a hand on my waist, as casual as if I were his wife. "Are you all right?"

Why, do I seem a bit distracted? Nothing to do with the hand on my waist, I'm sure. Did he even realize he was doing it? Now I was doubly flustered, and I stammered out a thoroughly unconvincing reply. "I . . . think so, thank you. It's . . . just a chill, that's all."

Thomas narrowed one eye. He didn't believe me, oddly enough.

"It can't be the ghost, can it? I drank some saltwater just after my bath."

He hesitated. "Do you have any of that mineral water left? Perhaps you ought to take that too, just in case."

"Why?"

"This is our first night back since your dream. I think it likely the ghost will try again. The saltwater is probably enough, but one can't be too careful."

I shivered again, this time with dread. "What aren't you telling me?"

"Nothing." He put his hands on my shoulders and gave them a reassuring squeeze. "I don't mean to worry you. I would simply prefer to err on the side of caution. Events have forced us to focus on the creature once more, at the expense of investigating Upton's murder. The ghost will be impatient, possibly even angry. I don't want to leave even the slightest crack in your defenses." His gaze fell from my eyes, drifting over my features in a way that brought warmth to my cheeks. "I am rather fond of you, you know."

"Oh, really?" I managed an arch look, even through my blush. "You've never said so."

"*Hmm.* That's not *quite* true." And with no more warning than that, he leaned in and kissed me.

If yesterday's was a Saturday sort of kiss, full of passion and urgency, this was a Sunday kiss: soft, lingering, deep in every sense of the word. Within seconds of our lips meeting, I was trembling, overcome with the instinctive realization that this kiss meant more than the ones before it. The storm, that night in the parlor six months ago . . . Those had been like the bursting of a dam. A momentary loss of control. This was different. This was premeditated. And it made my heart race like nothing before.

He drew back after a moment, but his hand still rested against the nape of my neck, toying with a lock of hair that had come loose from my chignon. "I'm sorry," he said. "That was . . ."

"Perfect." I looked him right in the eye to show him I meant it. "This moment is perfect. Please don't ruin it with an apology."

"Very well then, I'm not sorry. It's the expected thing to say, though, isn't it?"

"I think we're past what's expected."

"Quite." His gaze dropped to the floor, and when he raised it again, his eyes were full of that same uncertainty I'd seen yesterday. "I'm afraid I don't know what the right thing is here. I don't want to . . . That is, I shouldn't wish you to think . . ."

That sentence wasn't leading anyplace I wanted to go, so I stopped it with a kiss.

He didn't take much encouragement, gathering me close and picking up where he left off, as though all he'd needed was my permission. Which was odd, considering that our first kiss was my doing, and I'd been the one with a fistful of buttons yesterday. My mother had firm views on the sort of woman who initiated romantic encounters, and they were not flattering. Hopefully, Thomas didn't share those views. He certainly didn't seem to just now.

I'm not sure how long we carried on, but it was only the sound of footsteps on the stairs that drew us apart. I half hoped it would be the lady in the traveling cloak again, but it was only one of the treasure hunters, and by the time he noticed us, we'd separated to a respectable distance.

Thomas gave a courtly nod, the sort I'd seen him give dozens of times at formal functions, only this one came with a wry twist of the mouth. "Good night, Miss Gallagher."

"Good night, Mr. Wiltshire."

I don't suppose I have to tell you that I didn't get much sleep that night, and not because of any ghost. Neither did Thomas, judging from the lamplight leaking between the slats in my wall. I'm quite sure none of our fellow agents would have approved of such distractions in the middle of a case. They wouldn't have approved of anything about it. Back in New York, that would have troubled me greatly, but out here . . .

Out here, one is whoever he wishes to be, isn't he?

In the three years I'd known him, Thomas had rarely let his guard down, and then only for moments at a time. All that seemed to have changed the moment the train pulled into Medora. Since then, he'd been more relaxed, more open, than I'd ever seen him. This version of Thomas Wiltshire had room for me in his life, maybe even his heart. But would he survive the train ride home? For that matter, would this version of me?

I was getting ahead of myself, of course. The real question, as I was about to be reminded, was whether either of us would make it onto that train at all.

CHAPTER 16

THE LONG ARM OF THE LAW—A LOAD OF
BULL—GIDEON PROVES HIS WORTH

We struck out just before dawn, with another long ride ahead of us. After last night, I half expected Thomas to have some sort of speech prepared, of the *It's been lovely but for both our sakes we ought to leave it here* variety. But he didn't bring it up, and that was fine by me. I understood perfectly well that what was happening between us was an indulgence, almost certainly a temporary one. Dragging it out in the open would only make it bittersweet, like anticipating the end of a holiday before it's even really begun. And what would that accomplish except to rain on our brief moment of sunshine?

I suppose that sounds like denial, and maybe it was. But if Thomas was willing to live in denial with me, even for just a little longer, it was worth it.

Gather ye rosebuds, et cetera.

It was a little after ten when we rode up to Cougar Ranch. The first to spot us was a young man rubbing a horse down near the barn. He looked friendly enough until he saw the badge pinned to Thomas's chest, at which point he nearly dropped his brush. "Can I help you?"

"Let us hope so." Thomas swung down from his saddle. "Agent Wiltshire, Pinkerton Detective Agency, and this is my partner, Agent Gallagher."

No one had ever called me Agent Gallagher before, and I quite liked the sound of it.

The young man didn't. He swallowed audibly.

"What is your name, please?" Thomas took out his notebook.

"C-Clive Weatherspoon. Sir."

Thomas wrote that down with a severe expression. "Is your employer at home?"

Clive shook his head. "Ain't back from town yet."

Probably had some whiskey to sleep off. Just as well, really. Reid's men would be on the back foot without the boss around.

"Very well, then," Thomas said. "You'll have to do. Agent Gallagher and I are here to interview the employees of Cougar Ranch."

"What, all of them?"

"Yes, Mr. Weatherspoon, all of them, beginning with the foreman. We'll require space to work. The verandah ought to suffice. Kindly ensure there are sufficient chairs. And a pitcher of water and two glasses, if you would be so good."

The young man stood there for a moment, gaping like a fish. I felt a little sorry for him, to tell the truth. But I couldn't break character, so instead I folded my arms and said, "Well? We're losing daylight."

"Y-yes, ma'am. Er . . . this way, I guess?"

He led us to the verandah overlooking the river, where we took the liberty of rearranging Reid's furniture. I couldn't help casting a nervous glance or two over my shoulder as we worked, even though we were a good thirty feet from the riverbank. If it had been up to me, I'd have suggested we conduct our interviews in the barn. With the door barred. And a shotgun.

"It'll take a while to round up the foreman," Clive said.

"Send us whoever you find, then," I said. "Just make it quick."

Our first interview was with a kid even younger than Clive. He was terrified of Thomas, his gaze riveted to that brass badge as if it might leap off Thomas's chest at any moment and stab him with the pointy bit. Thomas took full advantage, asking his questions in crisp, icy tones that sounded even more severe in his posh English accent. Not that it made any difference; the kid didn't know much. Neither did our second interviewee, or our third. They were cooperative enough, at least, plainly accustomed to following orders.

Our next interview was neither.

A cluster of curious ranch hands had collected at the far end of the verandah, and they parted like the Red Sea as a burly man with a sunburn mounted the steps, spurs ringing, a mean-looking dog trailing behind him. The foreman, obviously. He carried himself with the same swagger as Hell Roaring Bill Jones—and the same latent menace. "Who gave you permission to sit on this porch?"

Thomas didn't even look up from his notebook. "The government of the United States. Please take a seat, Mr. . . . ." He flipped a page. "Howard."

The man's expression didn't change, but his skin turned a little redder under the beard. "I don't think you understood me, mister. This here's private property. You ain't—"

"Sit down, Mr. Howard, unless you would like this conversation to take an unpleasant turn."

Figuring that was my cue, I leaned back in my chair, letting my jacket hang open in a way that just happened to show the Colt Lightning at my hip.

Howard snorted softly. "You let a woman do your heavy work?"

"Quite happily." Thomas crossed one perfectly tailored trouser leg over the other. "I'm not going to ask a third time, Mr. Howard."

The foreman hesitated a moment longer. Then he squirted tobacco juice between his teeth and took a seat, glaring at Thomas all the while. There was something familiar about that cold gaze, I decided. I'd seen this man somewhere before, but I couldn't place it. Here on the ranch, maybe? Or in the saloon?

"The carcasses you found yesterday," Thomas began. "You disposed of them, we're told."

"Sure. We don't need wolves and whatever else coming around this close to the house."

"How did you dispose of them?"

"Threw 'em in the river."

A look of aristocratic disgust crossed Thomas's features. "And did you inspect them first?"

"Come again?"

"Did you verify the cause of death?"

The foreman looked at me. "He joking?"

"I'll take that as a no," Thomas said. "Moving on. Has Cougar Ranch acquired any new horses recently?"

"Now I know you're joking. Have you seen what's going on around here? We ain't exactly in a position to buy. 'Specially not the kind of ponies Mr. Reid's got an eye for. He ain't in the business of breeding any old nag."

That, at least, we knew to be true. Luna was an exceptional horse, and Gideon would turn heads even in New York City. *Which means Reid wouldn't be interested in a couple of Lakota packhorses.* At least not for breeding.

"Still," Thomas said, "business is sure to pick up now that so many of your competitors are divesting."

"If we have a good summer, maybe. But we lost more 'n half our stock last winter. Don't much matter what the competition is doing if you can't even fill the orders you already got."

The man had a point. I'd seen for myself what the winter had done to Gus Reid's cattle. Even the survivors were thin and weak. Depending on how deep his pockets were, competition might very well be the least of Reid's worries. "What about your neighbors?" I asked. "Was everyone's stock equally affected, or did some pull through the winter better than others?" It was a long shot, but if we were entertaining the idea that someone was trying to put ranchers out of business, the winter had played an even bigger role than the creature.

"From what I heard, every rancher in the territory lost his shirt."

So much for that line of inquiry. As far as I could tell, precisely nobody had benefited from the Winter of the Blue Snow—except, perhaps, for the bone pickers.

"Very well. We're almost through here." Thomas tore a page from his notebook and handed it over, along with his pencil. "Please write down the names of every ranch hand hired within the past two years." He didn't mention the Buckshot Outfit, not wanting to tip our hand just yet.

The foreman took his time about it, scratching his beard and squinting at the sky. I had the impression he was stalling, but eventually we had our list. As he was leaving, he crossed paths with our next interview, a skinny cowboy who couldn't even be bothered to wear a proper shirt over his sweat-stained underwear. They exchanged a *look*—and suddenly I remembered where I'd seen Howard before. The two of them had been loitering outside the hotel yesterday. What business did they have in town? Hopefully, the skinny one would be more forthcoming than his boss. He dropped into the chair Howard had vacated and patted the dog, who dozed contentedly at his feet.

"Name?" Thomas asked.

"Zeke Porter. But everybody calls me Skinny."

I cleared my throat into my hand, but I managed not to laugh.

Thomas glanced at the list the foreman had made. "I see you've only worked here for a year, Mr. Porter. How did you come to be hired at Cougar Ranch?"

"George . . . That is, Mr. Howard, he hired me. We used to work together back when."

"And what are your duties here at the ranch?"

"This 'n' that. Mending fences. Mucking stables." He paused, coughing. "Whatever the foreman says needs doing, I guess."

"Didn't I see you outside the hotel yesterday?" I cut in. "You and Mr. Howard?"

Thomas glanced at me. This was new information to him.

Skinny, meanwhile, avoided my eye, giving the disinterested dog another pat. "Could be, I guess."

"What business did the two of you have in town?"

"We was with the boss."

That made sense, I supposed. Reid had gone into town for the stockman's meeting. But why did he need an escort? And then there was the timing. "It was morning when I saw you, but Mr. Reid's meeting wasn't until evening. That's a long time to be hanging around."

"We had things to do."

"Such as?"

Skinny coughed again, clearly stalling. "Picking up supplies 'n' such, you know."

"What sort of supplies?"

He could tell I was suspicious, and that made him nervous. He started coughing in earnest, a dry, wheezing hack that didn't sound feigned. The dog pricked up his ears and whined, and I didn't blame him. Skinny was making enough noise to wake the . . .

I paused, sitting up straighter.

White Robes's words came back to me in perfect clarity. *They woke me with their coughing.*

"Do you own a horse, Skinny?"

He shook his head. "I ride one of Mr. Reid's."

"And is this horse branded?"

"Yes, ma'am. Ranch horses is all branded."

"What does it look like? The brand, I mean."

"Well, there goes one now." He pointed to a horse being led out of the barn. Sure enough, it had a brand on its left haunch, and I recognized it straightaway. Not a Buckshot brand, but something just as damning: The horseshoe White Robes had drawn. Except it wasn't a horseshoe at all, but a *C*. For *Cougar Ranch*.

I took a deep breath, composing myself. "Tell me, Skinny, have you ever heard of a company called the—"

"Skinny!" One of the kids we'd interviewed pounded up the steps, red-faced and out of breath. "Come quick! That bull is out again!"

The ranch hand cursed and stood.

"Wait a minute. We're not done—" Before I could finish, two thousand pounds of angry beef went crashing through the brush near the river. The dog barked and bounded off the verandah, Skinny and the kid in hot pursuit.

"Damn it!" I stomped the floorboards in frustration. "I almost had him."

"So it would seem. Your interview technique has come a long way, Agent Gallagher."

That wasn't saying much. Not so long ago, my idea of interrogating a suspect was sticking a gun in his face and repeating the same question over and over. "I just hope this doesn't give him too much time to think."

"You believe he's our man, I take it?"

"One of them. Remember what White Robes said about being woken up by coughing?"

"Chronic coughs are common enough. And she also said something about a beard. Skinny is clean-shaven."

"Yeah, but Howard has a . . ."

Thomas and I exchanged a horrified look.

We shot out of our chairs, but it was too late. A pair of horses burst out of the barn, their riders flogging them for all they were worth. Thomas and I could only watch as Skinny and Howard thundered across our paths, heading for the meadow and the trees beyond.

Our own horses were on the far side of the yard; by the time we'd unhitched and mounted up, Howard and Skinny were halfway across the field. I drove my heels into Luna's flanks and she answered, surging beneath me with a power that scared me a little. I'd never ridden flat-out before, and I did my best to mimic Thomas's form, the way he came up slightly out of the saddle, leaning low over Gideon's neck.

Until that moment, I'd figured Thomas overpaid for that horse. I was wrong.

Within seconds, the stallion had left Luna behind, chewing up the distance between Thomas and his quarry with every stride. Skinny lagged a fair distance behind Howard, and I guess he could hear the hoofbeats coming up on him, because he threw a terrified look over his shoulder. He tried to spur his mount faster, but his shoulders started shuddering with coughs, and he slumped back in his saddle. Faced with such mixed signals, his horse started to flag.

Thomas was almost on him now. I wasn't sure what he meant to do when he caught up, but I never had the chance to find out. Howard twisted, rifle in hand, and fired off a clumsy one-handed shot. Skinny pitched backward off his saddle, forcing Thomas to swerve wildly to avoid a collision. He tried to return fire, but Howard was still more than fifty yards off. A six-shooter wasn't going to get the job done, and his shotgun would be even less use. I started to reach for my Winchester, but thought better of it; even if my aim was up to the task, my horsemanship wasn't. If I dropped my reins at this speed, I'd be more likely to break my neck than hit my target.

Howard twisted around again. Thomas broke left as the rifle cracked. The bullet sizzled past me, close enough to spook Luna; she nearly threw me as she lurched off course.

This is madness. One-handed or no, it was only a matter of time before one of Howard's shots landed. He was still well out of range of Thomas's revolver and about to hit the tree line, where his advantage would only increase. Thomas must have thought the same, because he pulled up, watching helplessly as Howard plunged into the woods and made his escape. As for me, I circled back to Skinny, hoping he might have survived.

No such luck.

I knew before I reined in that the ranch hand was dead. The shot had taken him through the neck. He probably hadn't even survived the fall.

Thomas loped up to the body, took a cursory glance, and spurred Gideon onward. "We mustn't linger! We're too exposed out here."

We didn't stop again until we were well out of range of Howard's rifle, sheltering in the trees in case anybody else at Cougar Ranch decided to try their luck. Only then did Thomas permit himself an uncharacteristically florid curse. Then he sighed and patted his horse's neck. "Just a few more seconds and you'd have had him, old boy. Bloody good show, anyway."

I looked across the meadow at the place where Howard had disappeared. "I suppose it would be foolish to try following him."

"Beyond foolish. He'll know this area like the back of his hand, and he's got a scope on that rifle. He's probably dug in for an ambush already." Irritably, Thomas started ejecting spent casings from his

Peacemaker. "Nor would it be wise to head back to the ranch. We don't know how many others might be involved, and even those who aren't won't look fondly on our killing one of their own."

Howard was the one who'd done the killing, but somehow I doubted they'd fuss about the particulars.

"A great deal of exertion for very little result," Thomas went on. He seemed to be taking Howard's escape awfully personally. "It does little good to put names to the horse thieves if we don't know why they did it or how they're connected with the creature. Nor are we any closer to ascertaining Reid's role in any of this."

All true, and yet I wasn't so sure we'd wasted our time. "I still want to know what Howard and Skinny were doing loitering outside the hotel."

"Perhaps it was their day off. It was Sunday, after all."

"Exactly. So why come into town for a meeting with the boss?"

"*Hmm.*" Thomas paused in the act of reloading. "Especially since, as you pointed out, the meeting was hours away."

"And the two of them weren't even there when it did happen. They'd probably left town already. Otherwise, they'd have had to stay overnight, like Reid did." I shook my head. "They weren't there for the meeting, and they weren't doing any shopping, either."

A ghost of a smile started to tug at Thomas's mouth. "So, what mischief could they have been about that they didn't wish us to discover?"

I had a pretty good idea.

There's only so much excitement you can take in one day before you start to feel overwhelmed. Yesterday had included a Mexican standoff, a near mauling, and an extremely distracting interlude outside my hotel room. My poor exhausted brain just hadn't had the energy to dwell on the death of the hotel owner, but it was all coming back to me now.

"What about what happened to Mr. Oliver? He was robbed and murdered not fifty feet from where I saw Howard and Skinny."

"Good heavens, I'd completely forgotten! I could certainly believe Howard capable, at least."

"Especially if he used to be with the Buckshot Outfit. Skinny fits the profile, and he did say he and Howard used to work together before they joined Cougar Ranch. I'll bet my eyeteeth it was with the Buckshot Outfit. Howard's probably the one who convinced Reid to hire his old buddies in the first place. Men like Skinny who would do whatever he asked."

Thomas grunted. "But why kill Oliver? A grudge, perhaps?"

"They tried to make it look like a robbery, but maybe that was staged. I saw Oliver arguing with that businessman from Bismarck. He was trying to buy the hotel, but Oliver wasn't interested in selling. Howard and Skinny were right outside the door when it happened."

Not loitering, I realized. *Lurking*.

"Hired muscle?"

"Why not? Like you said, Howard looks the part. He's thick as a tree trunk, and a bully besides. Handy if you're a bookish investor looking to intimidate a bunch of hard-bitten ranchers into . . ." I trailed off, my pulse breaking into a jog. "Thomas, I think I've just figured it out."

"What?"

"*Cui bono*."

CHAPTER 17

THE BONE PICKER FROM BISMARCK—FOOL'S GOLD—A SAFE CONCLUSION

Who benefits from what, specifically?" Thomas asked. "Oliver's murder?"

"Not only that. The creature, too."

Before I could continue, Thomas put a hand on my arm, inclining his head toward Cougar Ranch. A trio of riders had just struck out across the meadow, heading for the spot where Skinny's body lay in the grass. "We should move on," he said. "Hold that thought."

We rode deeper into the trees, staying well east of the house and avoiding the road. *I guess we can add George Howard to the list of people gunning for us.* Not to mention any of his friends, or Skinny's, who might be out for revenge. Between Howard's boys and Bowie Bill's, we were looking at quite the posse. And those were just the human threats. There was still a man-eating predator on the loose, and an extremely presumptuous ghost just waiting for us to let our guards down. All in all, our dance cards were a little too full for my liking.

When he judged we were far enough out of range, Thomas slowed his horse to a walk. "All right, let's have it."

I started to get excited all over again. "Do you remember what White Robes said about someone trying to frighten them away from this place? I think she was partly right. Only it isn't the Lakota they're trying to frighten."

Thomas made a thoughtful sound. "You believe someone is deliberately clearing out the town?"

"Wait, there's more. Lee Granger said something interesting too, that night in the saloon. About scavengers. He said when all those cows died over the winter, the only ones who profited were the bone pickers. After Upton died, it was the treasure hunters. And then—"

"The pasty fellow from Bismarck, buying their land on the cheap." He nodded slowly. "It's an interesting theory."

Honestly, I was disappointed. I'd expected a *Rose Gallagher, I could kiss you*, or at least a *bloody good show*. *An interesting theory* was a lukewarm reception at best. "It seems to me that scooping up thousands of acres of land at a heavy discount is a pretty big benefit," I said, a little sullenly.

"Potentially, but the benefit only accrues if the investment proves to be a good one. The local economy depends almost entirely on the beef industry. That industry is in dire straits, thanks to the Winter of the Blue Snow, and it may never recover. Our friend from Bismarck may simply be accumulating worthless land."

"Maybe he knows something we don't."

"Such as? The railroad has been here for years, so there's no chance of a transport-related spike. There's no mining in the area, nor timber to speak of. It's difficult to imagine the land increasing markedly in value even if the creature were to cease its marauding tomorrow. Still . . ." He looked contemplative as he steered Gideon around some dead brush. "It's worth pursuing. The investor obviously *believes* there's value to his purchases, and perhaps that's all that matters."

"If I'm right, does that mean he's the one responsible for the creature?"

"Let's ask him," Thomas said, and he spurred his horse.

We headed straight to the saloon, but the place was emptier than ever, with only a scattering of regulars playing poker or leaning against the bar. The man from Bismarck wasn't among them, so we waved Lee Granger over and asked after him.

"Who, Parnell? Oh, he'll be along by and by. He's about my steadiest customer these days. Usually gets here about four."

"So he just waits around for a likely prospect to show up?" I asked.

"More or less. He started out making the rounds himself, riding out to the ranches to let everybody know he was looking to buy. But it's been weeks now since he don't need to lift one pasty finger. Everybody knows where to come when they're ready to sell."

"He was making some of his own rounds yesterday. I heard him offer to buy the hotel from Mr. Oliver."

"Oh yeah?" Granger looked a little put out. "And here he told me he wasn't interested in businesses in town."

"You offered to sell?

He hitched a shoulder self-consciously. "Might've mentioned I wouldn't object to hearing an offer. Things is getting pretty tough around here, in case you ain't noticed." He gestured at his near-empty saloon.

"But Parnell wasn't interested."

"Just ranches, he said. Those, he's been picking up like grass seed. Owns tens of thousands of acres by now, scattered all over creation."

"Scattered, you say?" Thomas creased his brow. "Odd. If he means to amass land, it would make more sense for the plots to be contiguous. And if he's speculating, the safer investment is property here in town. Especially businesses like this. One imagines your saloon will be among the first enterprises to rebound once the town recovers from its current difficulties."

"*If* it recovers, you mean."

"Have faith, Mr. Granger. This too shall pass."

The saloonkeeper's glance fell to the badge on Thomas's chest. I'd forgotten about it, and I think Thomas had too, but Granger didn't seem too put out. "Guess I don't need to ask if it's true, what folks is saying." His gaze shifted to me. "You too?"

I gave him an apologetic smile. "Sorry for all the secrecy. It's part of the job, I'm afraid."

"Who hired you, then? Roosevelt?"

"I'm afraid we're not at liberty to discuss it," Thomas said. "But we can tell you that we're doing everything in our power to get to the bottom of whatever is afflicting this town."

"Well, that's something, at least." Granger turned a pair of glasses over and poured out two drams of forty-rod.

Not wanting to be rude, I took a sip. Tears sprang to my eyes, but I managed not to cough. As for Thomas, he kept his coughing under control until Granger wandered off, and even then, he managed to do it quietly. "Not exactly Madeira, is it?" he rasped, fishing out his Patek Philippe. "Half two. Let us hope Mr. Parnell keeps to form. In the meantime, what do you make of what our host just told us? If Parnell isn't interested in local businesses, why set his sights on the hotel?"

"Maybe it makes more money than the rest."

Thomas hummed a skeptical note. "Did it seem like a booming enterprise to you? Aside from the occasional treasure hunter, you and I have been virtually the only guests."

"Pretty close," I admitted, smiling inwardly at the memory of the woman who'd interrupted our moment the other night. *If she thought that was scandalous, what would she have made of last night?* I cleared my throat, blushing a little. "What exactly are you getting at?"

He ran the backs of his knuckles along the neatly trimmed line of his beard, eyes narrowed in thought. "Are you quite certain it was the hotel Parnell was looking to buy? Can you recall the details of their exchange?"

"Come to think of it, I don't know that they mentioned the hotel specifically. I guess I just assumed." But if it wasn't the hotel Parnell was looking to buy . . . "What about the safe? There were fingerprints all over it." I'd figured that was Howard trying to make it look like a robbery, but maybe I'd been overthinking it.

Thomas threw back the rest of his whiskey. "Let's see if we can get a look inside, shall we?"

We hurried across to the hotel, where we found the night clerk slumped in a chair with his hat tipped over his face. Thomas cleared his throat politely and was met with a raggedy snore, so I struck the service bell—with a little more enthusiasm than was strictly required.

The clerk started up with a snort. "*Whassat?* Oh, it's you. Sorry, folks. 'Fraid I ain't getting much shuteye just now, what with being the only feller on the desk night and day." He stretched, yawning wide enough to show the gaps in his back teeth. "What can I do for you, Mr. Wiltshire?"

"It's Agent Wiltshire, actually, and this is Agent Gallagher, Pinkerton Detective Agency. I'm afraid we're here in an official capacity just now."

"Oh." The clerk scrambled up out of his chair and smoothed his clothing, as if he were about to undergo military inspection.

"We have some questions about what happened to Mr. Oliver," I said.

"Right. I s'pose the sheriff asked you all to step in on the case, then?"

Thomas just smiled blandly. "Have you ascertained whether anything was stolen? Besides Mr. Oliver's belt buckle, that is. Any property of the hotel's?"

"No, sir. That is, I ascertained nothing was took."

"What about the contents of the safe?" I asked.

"The safe?" The clerk crumpled his brow, as if the very idea were bizarre. "Nothing in there worth stealing. Just a bunch of junk we cleared out of the Presidential Suite when the feller what was staying there went missing."

My breath caught. "Are you referring to Benjamin Upton?"

"Yes, ma'am, that's him."

Roosevelt was right. Upton is connected to all this. But how?

"When we saw he weren't coming back, Mr. Oliver had me put his personals in the safe. There weren't much, but he figured if Upton ever turned up, maybe he'd offer a reward for it. 'Course, he never did turn up. And then all these treasure hunters started coming around, saying how there was a hundred thousand in gold stashed out there somewheres. So Mr. Oliver, he reckons maybe something in that pile of junk will help him find it. 'Course, that didn't happen, neither."

I flattened my hands on top of the desk, barely able to contain my excitement. "Please tell me you have the combination to that safe."

"Yes, ma'am, but . . ." The clerk flicked an uncertain glance between Thomas and me. "Mr. Oliver's brother is coming up from Cheyenne tomorrow, and I ain't sure he'd want me to—"

"Pinkerton business," I said, barging my way behind the desk. "Open it, please."

Thomas didn't even try to hide his amusement as he watched me hover over the clerk like a bank robber, waiting anxiously for him to compose the right numbers. It seemed to take forever, but eventually the hinges creaked, and I dropped into a crouch, practically shoving the clerk aside in my haste.

Thomas must have heard my groan of dismay, because he leaned over the desk. "Problem?"

"*This again.*" I thrust a leather-bound book at him. "More sketches. Same designs, from the looks of it."

"Upton must have kept one for the trail and one for his room here at the hotel." Thomas started flipping through the pages. "Anything else?"

"Some tools. A hand drill, and a mortar and pestle, of all things. Oh, and instead of dirt, we have rocks." I picked them up, three jagged pieces of nondescript stone that were very definitely *not* gold. "This can't possibly be what Parnell was looking for."

"Unless he was in the treasure-hunting game as well," Thomas mused, "and hoped this book would lead him to the gold."

"In that case, he woulda been disappointed," the clerk said. "Ain't no clues in that book, leastways not that I found. It's like I says to Skinny the other day. If that gold is really out there, ain't nobody gonna find it."

I guess we don't need to ask how Howard and Skinny found out about the book. Did the clerk even realize the role he'd played in his boss's murder? Probably not, I decided. He didn't seem like the sharpest of pickaxes. "Why would someone like Parnell be interested in chasing after a pot of gold that might not even exist? He must be rich already, if he's buying thousands of acres of land."

"Human greed knows no bounds," Thomas said. "Some of the most avaricious men of my acquaintance are staggeringly wealthy."

"But still. Imagine what he's spent out here already. Tens of thousands at least, and for what? If you ask me, it sounds like he already has more than he could ever . . ." I paused, a memory washing over me.

You don't even need the money. You have more than you could ever spend.

For a moment, I was back in that cabin, tied to a chair while a madman shrieked over me. *You can go off and buy a mansion and a yacht and anything else your greedy little heart desires. You can live your life . . .*

"It was never the money," I murmured.

"Sorry?"

I grabbed Thomas's elbow and steered him to a discreet remove. "Upton's killer. Something he said in the dream. I'd forgotten it until now. He said Upton already had more money than he could ever spend. That if he gave the killer what he wanted, he could be on his way and buy himself a mansion and all these fancy things. But how could he have done that if the killer had just robbed him blind?"

"Strange." Thomas frowned.

"All along, we've been assuming Upton was murdered for that hundred thousand he had stashed away, but what if the killer had his sights on something even more valuable? Those sketches in Upton's journal . . . What if he was onto something new?"

Thomas's pale eyes lit up. "An unknown deposit. Roosevelt did say the man was lucky, or at least had an uncanny nose for gold. And we are downstream of the Black Hills."

Just show me on the map, the killer had said. He must have known about the new strike, but he'd shot Upton before he could find out where it was. Now, a year later, here was this real estate investor arranging a murder so he could get his hands on some of Upton's belongings . . .

And that's when it clicked, like a cylinder snapping snugly into the frame of a revolver. "That's why he's gobbling up all that land. Thomas, he *does* know something we don't. *He knows there's gold out there somewhere.*"

Thomas closed his eyes and let out a sigh. "Rose. You are perfectly brilliant."

Well, *that* was more like it.

"That must be why his plots are scattered all over the place, too. He doesn't know where the gold is, so he's hedging his bets." I grinned at Thomas, feeling extremely pleased with myself. He was pretty pleased with me too, judging from the gleam in his eyes.

"Our interview with Mr. Parnell promises to be very interesting indeed. What do you say, Agent Gallagher?" He offered me his arm. "May I buy you a drink?"

CHAPTER 18

A FAMILIAR PROBLEM—INITIAL SUSPECT—
DUCK AND COVER

Parnell wasn't due at the saloon until four. That gave Thomas and me some time to do a little research on our suspect, which is how we happened to be at the Western Union office when a telegram came in from Mr. Jackson.

"The Agency telegrapher is having a very busy afternoon," Thomas remarked wryly. We'd sent and received a flurry already, taking full advantage of the wonders of modern technology to acquaint ourselves with Mr. Parnell.

"And what does our favorite warlock have to say?"

"Very little, actually." Thomas frowned, his pale gaze scanning the page. "He refers us to a book on Germanic witchcraft. Specifically, the chapter on familiars."

He said that I like I ought to know what it meant, but I just shook my head blankly.

"Spirits summoned or conjured to do the bidding of the

spellcaster." He looked up, gaze abstracted. "I thought myself reasonably familiar with that brand of magic, if you'll pardon the pun. What can he be referring to?"

"Do you have the book he mentions?"

"Regrettably not, but Burrows is due in Chicago tonight. We can ask Jackson to bring him a copy at the station." Thomas dictated yet another telegram, after which we hurried back to the saloon.

Our quarry arrived right on time, wearing his customary pinstriped suit. As he came through the front, I slipped out the back, circling around the building with one hand resting on my Colt. I didn't see anyone *lurking*, at least. Satisfied that our suspect was alone, I hurried back inside.

Parnell didn't even look up as Thomas and I approached, too busy scratching out notes in his ledger. "How many acres?"

"That depends. Are you referring to the totality of my holdings, or merely the American ones?"

Now he did look up, and a flicker of worry crossed his features. "It's you."

"I don't believe we're acquainted, but perhaps our reputation precedes us. Yours certainly does."

"It . . . does?"

I pulled out one of the telegrams we'd just received from the Agency. "Mr. Wendell F. Parnell, esquire, of Bismarck, Dakota Territory. Married October 4, 1872, to Mary Wilkinson. Two children, Lily and Gregory." I folded the paper away. "It must be some time since you last saw them, Wendell."

His pasty skin flooded with color. "What is the meaning of this?"

"Impressive, isn't it?" Thomas flashed a wooden smile. "It took our colleagues at the Pinkerton Detective Agency less than an hour to find out the pertinent information. It would take even less time to arrange for your home and offices to be searched and your associates questioned. I imagine such an outcome would prove inconvenient for you, personally and professionally. Most people hesitate to engage an attorney under suspicion of murder."

Parnell's eyes widened. "What are you talking about? What murder?"

"A few of them, actually," I said. "Most recently, Mr. Oliver from the hotel."

"Why, but that's preposterous! What possible—"

"Perhaps we could adjourn to a more discreet location," Thomas said. "Mr. Granger has kindly made arrangements for us."

Parnell looked truly alarmed now. "I'm not going anywhere with you."

"You would prefer us to air your business here?" Thomas gestured at the crowded room. Already, several of the treasure hunters at the bar were staring at us; even the poker game had paused, half the players twisted around in their seats to observe the drama.

The lawyer's mouth pressed into a thin line. Gathering his belongings and what remained of his dignity, he stood.

The "arrangements" our host had made consisted of a small storage room full of whiskey barrels, beer bottles, a single chair, and an oil lamp. The cramped quarters suited Thomas and me just fine. Our suspect would feel a lot more vulnerable shut up in this tiny room without any witnesses.

Thomas gestured for him to sit. "Now, then, you were about to tell us why you murdered Francis Oliver."

"I certainly was not! It's an outrageous accu—"

"I saw the two of you arguing," I interrupted. "You wanted to get your hands on Benjamin Upton's belongings, but Oliver wasn't interested in selling. He had it in his head that something in that sketchbook would lead him to a hundred thousand in gold. And you thought so too."

The lawyer licked his lips. "I wanted to buy the book, it's true. But I didn't . . . I would never . . ." Tiny beads of sweat broke out along his receding hairline. "Do I look like a murderer to you?"

"No. Which is why you had George Howard and his friends from the Buckshot Outfit do it for you."

Parnell dabbed at his forehead with a handkerchief. "George works with me, yes. And I admit that he contributes a certain . . . gravitas . . . when negotiations become bogged down. But I never asked him to *kill* anyone."

"And yet he did," I said. "Does that surprise you?"

The lawyer squirmed in his chair. "If the allegation is true, it wasn't done on my say-so."

"A fellow of initiative, is he?" Thomas said dryly. "A desirable trait in a foreman, perhaps, but considerably less convenient in a hired thug. You must be a very tolerant employer, Mr. Parnell."

"You're mistaken. Mr. Howard works *with* me, not *for* me. We are employed by the same . . . client."

"And who is that?" I asked.

"I'm afraid that information is privileged. It would be unlawful for me to divulge it."

"I wonder, Mr. Parnell, if you've taken adequate stock of your surroundings." Thomas's tone was conversational, his posture relaxed as he leaned against a whiskey barrel. "Do you see the sheriff in this room?"

"The laws of the territory still apply, sir," Parnell said primly.

"Perhaps, but as an attorney, you'll no doubt appreciate the distinction between *de jure* and *de facto*. At the moment, the only law you need to be concerned with is ours."

Parnell drew himself up a little straighter, trying righteous indignation on for size. "So you mean to bully me into complying, is that it?"

That got my back up. "You have the nerve to accuse *us* of bullying? After you've terrorized everyone within fifty miles just so you could get your sticky little fingers on their land?"

"Terrorized? Madam—"

"What would you call it? Hundreds of cattle and horses dead. Ranchers forced into bankruptcy. People being mauled on the trail, and Two Horses sitting in jail waiting to hang. How much blood is on your hands, Mr. Parnell? How much bloodshed yet to come if the ranchers and the Lakota start shooting at each other because of what you've done?"

"I don't know what—"

"How did you do it? Is the magic yours, or someone else's?"

My anger was genuine, but it served a purpose, too. Parnell was truly distressed now, which gave Thomas an opening.

"Agent Gallagher," he said in his most eminently reasonable tones. "Let us not be premature. We don't know for certain that Mr. Parnell was directly involved in these matters. If he was merely acting on behalf of his client, there may be scope for cooperation."

"Cooperation? He should hang for what he's done!" Lord help me, I actually meant it.

Parnell swayed a little in his seat, as though he were in danger of swooning.

"Someone will certainly hang," Thomas said mildly, "but we must be sure it is the party or parties responsible, and not merely their agents."

"Th-that's right!" Parnell leaned past me, appealing to the more rational of his tormentors. "I'm just an agent! All I do is acquire the land! I don't know anything about the rest. Magic?" He gave a hysterical little titter, as if to say, *Is she mad?*

Much as I hated to admit it, he was awfully convincing. "How long has this been going on?" I growled.

The lawyer hesitated, but when he saw the unforgiving look in Thomas's eye, he answered. "Since last summer."

"You've been here a year, then?" Thomas asked.

"Not continuously. I only stayed for about a week, to inform prospective sellers that my client was in the market. It wasn't until this spring that I was obliged to return. That's when the floodgates truly opened."

"And what do you suppose opened those floodgates?" I asked coldly. "Are you going to sit there and tell us you didn't know what was going on?"

He gave a helpless little shrug. "What's going on is that a terrible winter has decimated the beef industry, and all but the stubborn and the well financed are getting out. It's a pity for those concerned, but it's the way of the world."

"And the animal attacks? I suppose you didn't know anything about those?"

"Of course I heard the same rumors as anyone. I admit the attacks were convenient, but I don't see how we can be blamed for that. It's a wild animal, for heaven's sake!" That nervous titter again, as if this whole conversation were ridiculous. I wanted to throttle him, and I made sure my expression said as much.

"Who's *we*? Who's the client?"

"That information is—"

"As God is my witness," Thomas murmured, "if you say the word *privileged*, you will regret it."

Parnell dropped his face in his hands. "Please, sir. You will ruin me."

"You are already ruined," Thomas said. "The only question now is whether you will live. You weren't merely preying on the desperate like any red-blooded capitalist. You knew perfectly well that your client was employing immoral tactics in pursuit of his greed. You admitted as much when you acknowledged working with Howard.

Whether his coercion involved a marauding predator or the barrel of a gun is quite immaterial. You are accountable, sir, and you will face justice. Your only hope for leniency is cooperation."

The lawyer was weeping now, still shielding his face with his hands. "God," he said. "Oh, God."

The Bible tells us the Lord forgives all sins, but I found myself hoping He might make an exception in this case.

Thomas leaned over our sniveling suspect. "For the last time, *who is your client*?"

"I don't know," he wailed. "I've never even met him! Everything was done through Howard. The payments, the transfer of deeds—all of it!"

"What name did he give you? You would have needed one for the property deeds."

"He only gave me initials. *CA*. I was to leave the rest blank, so he could fill it in himself. He was adamant that he remain anonymous."

Thomas glanced at me, and I answered his unspoken question with a reluctant nod. I didn't want to believe the lawyer, but I did. Which made two of us, apparently. I could sense Thomas's frustration behind the icy mask he wore.

"This ledger." He snatched the leather-bound book from the lawyer's lap. "It contains the details of each transaction?"

Parnell nodded miserably.

I was feeling pretty miserable myself by that point. We'd finally managed to put the pieces together, to connect Ben Upton's murder with the mysterious marauding predator, and what did it get us? A set of initials and yet another book. At least we'd have the satisfaction of throwing this bloodsucker in jail.

We tied the lawyer's hands and walked him out the back, the better to avoid any trouble in the saloon. Rumor spread faster than smallpox in this town, and I had no doubt there would be plenty of cowpokes itching to use Parnell for target practice when they found out what he'd done. The sheriff would have his hands full protecting the lawyer from a lynch mob, assuming he had any mind to do so.

The jailhouse was a little down the way, on the other side of the main street. "Let's hope the good sheriff isn't *indisposed*," I said sourly as we started across. "It is nearly five o'clock, after—"

A gunshot rang out, punching a hole in the clapboard behind us and sending passersby scrambling. Parnell shrieked and tried to hightail it; Thomas could barely keep hold of the man, grabbing him by the scruff and fairly throwing him at the nearest cover, a wagon loaded with goods from the general store. We'd just hunkered down when the second shot came, striking a sack of flour and sending a fine white cloud into the air. The draft horse hitched to the wagon grunted and stamped, but he stayed put—for now.

There are some things you never get used to. Whatever they say in the dime novels, I can tell you that getting shot at is one of them. Every nerve in my body buzzed, as if Mr. Tesla had attached some of his wires to my bones and thrown the switch. Even so, my voice was surprisingly steady as I said, "We can't stay here."

As if to prove the point, a bullet tore through the side of the wagon, showering us with splinters.

"A rifle," Thomas said. "That gives us a moment to break between shots."

"Assuming there's only one."

"If there were a second shooter, one of us would be dead already."

Parnell whimpered.

"When he fires again, we break for that alley." Thomas pointed at a gap between the buildings. It was only about twenty feet away, but it might as well have been a mile. "Are you ready, Parnell?"

The lawyer nodded feebly.

The next shot was aimed at the feet of the draft horse, and it did the trick: The animal spooked and lunged against his harness, dragging our cover with him. By that time, Thomas and I were legging it to the alley, shoving Parnell as we ran; we made it just as another shot whizzed past, ricocheting noisily.

I dared a peek around the corner, but I couldn't see anyone. The shooter, whoever he was, had found cover of his own. "Howard?"

"Most likely. He has reason to want all three of us dead."

"What?" Parnell glanced between us, wide-eyed. "Why me?"

"To keep you from talking." As I spoke the words, it dawned on me that the bullet that took Skinny might not have been a stray. Which would make Howard a pretty crack shot, considering he'd been firing a rifle one-handed. Behind his back. At a full gallop.

I swallowed.

Thomas started to lean out from cover, only to jerk back when a bullet bit a chunk off the wall. "Damn! He's somewhere across the street, but where?"

If only we had something we could use as a . . .

My gaze fell on just the thing. Holstering my weapon, I reached for Thomas and started unbuckling his belt.

"Good heavens," said Parnell.

"Er," said Thomas.

Yanking his belt free, I removed the buckle, a silver disc about the size of a dinner roll, and flipped it over, revealing a smooth, polished surface. I couldn't help grinning when I saw my own reflection staring back at me, a little warped from the curve of the buckle but otherwise clear as a bell.

"Rose Gallagher, you crafty little . . ." Thomas snatched the buckle, turned his back to the street, and gingerly eased the makeshift mirror around the corner.

The rifle cracked again. Thomas flinched back, but he'd seen what he needed to. "The roof above the hardware store. Cover me."

I fired off a couple of blind shots, and quicker than you could say *Jack be nimble,* Thomas was across the street and scrambling hand-over-hand up a drainpipe. I thought I'd seen every trick up those impeccably tailored sleeves, but apparently I was wrong. He reached the parapet in moments, racing across the roof of the gun shop and leaping over the gap between buildings like he did this sort of thing every day. I dared a look around the corner when I heard his Peacemaker fire, and I saw the sniper break cover and start running.

Not Howard, my brain registered. I was about to take a shot of my own when a *bang-bang-bang* from the street sent the sniper tumbling behind the false front of the hardware store. A burly man stepped into view, his revolver trained at the rooftops. He took aim at my partner next, and my heart froze.

"*Stop!*" I cried. "*Pinkerton Detective Agency!*"

How I wished for that badge then—but as it turned out, I didn't need it. "I know what you are," said Hell Roaring Bill Jones, holstering his weapon. He kept his gaze on the rooftops, watching as Thomas advanced warily toward the place where the sniper had fallen. "Hoy up there! He dead or what?"

Thomas disappeared from view as he crouched over the body. "Quite dead, I'm afraid." Straightening, he added, "Which means we shan't be able to question him."

The sheriff snorted. "Next time I'll let 'em have you, ungrateful bastard. Now get your arse down here." Turning to me, he added, "I guess it's time we had a talk."

CHAPTER 19

A THOROUGHLY COMPETENT
FRONTIERSMAN—SMELLS LIKE MONEY—THE
HAND THAT FEEDS

Sheriff Jones locked our prisoner up in the same cell as Two Horses. Parnell looked terrified at the prospect of bunking in with a Lakota. Two Horses, meanwhile, didn't so much as glance up, not even when I said his name. As before, he just stared straight ahead, determined not to acknowledge any of us. "Ain't spoken a word in twenty-four hours," the sheriff said. "Suits me just fine."

Thomas could tell my temper was coming to a boil again, and he headed me off before I landed us both in hot water. "I imagine you have questions, Sheriff."

"Oh, I got questions, all right. Starting with how come me own deputy don't see fit to tell me he's gone and hired Pinkertons to see after this business with his missing beeves."

"I can neither confirm nor deny—"

"Spare me." Jones made a curt gesture for us to follow, leading us into an adjoining room separated by a heavy door. A rumpled cot and the reek of stale whiskey suggested he'd taken this side of the jailhouse for his private quarters. "Sit," he instructed, rapping his knuckles on a table. He himself perched on the edge of the bed. "So, you wanna tell me who that fella is I got Snyder scraping off the roof of the hardware store?"

Thomas sighed. "I wish we could."

Hell Roaring Bill Jones considered us with an irritable expression. He was a big man, with a cold gleam to his eye; I had no doubt he could intimidate most of the roughs in this town just by looking at them. But we'd faced down the toughest coppers in the New York City Police Department. We weren't about to be cowed by a small-town sheriff, and I made sure my gaze said as much.

"What does your outfit want with the lawyer?" The question was put to Thomas, as the man of the operation.

"Mr. Parnell is a key player in a conspiracy to intimidate local ranchers into selling their land."

"*Conspiracy*, is it?" The sheriff raised his eyebrows wryly.

"Indeed, one that includes the foreman at Cougar Ranch. Mr. Howard has been acting as hired muscle."

Jones grunted. That part, at least, didn't seem to surprise him. "George is a mean enough cuss for the job, sure enough. But what's this about forcing ranchers off their land?"

Thomas and I glanced at one another. Mr. Roosevelt had explicitly asked us not to involve his friend the sheriff. On the other hand, Bill Jones wouldn't take kindly to being given the stone wall.

Thomas tried to finesse the matter. "We would require express permission from our client to discuss the details. What we can tell you is that Mr. Howard and some of his associates, formerly of the Buckshot Outfit, have been employing various unlawful and immoral techniques in order to persuade local ranchers to sell their land to Mr. Parnell on behalf of parties unknown."

The sheriff made a sour face. "I don't speak tenderfoot. You wanna try that again?"

"Howard and Skinny murdered Francis Oliver," I said, since that seemed simpler.

He glanced at me. "Frank Oliver wasn't a rancher."

"No, but he had something Parnell wanted. A book with some valuable information in it. Parnell offered to buy it first, and when Oliver refused, Howard and Skinny murdered him and tried to break into the safe. My guess is they were interrupted before they could finish the job."

"Your guess."

"There's still a lot we don't know." It sounded thin even to me, and it certainly didn't impress the good sheriff. His gaze shifted between Thomas and me, as if he couldn't decide whether we were a burr under his saddle or something much worse.

"I could believe Howard and Skinny robbed Frank Oliver. But the rest of it? I've not had a single complaint about being tricked or bullied into selling, by the Buckshot Outfit or anyone else. Meantime, I don't see what none of this has to do with cattle rustling, which is why Roosevelt hired *your* outfit. My point being, you're herding somebody else's beef, friends."

"I can certainly understand how it would appear that way," Thomas said. "But these matters are closely related. You see—"

"Let me tell you what I see. I see a pair of *New Yorkers*"—he pronounced the words with roughly the same inflection as *sewer rats*— "who been nothing but trouble since they turned up. You're in town all of a day before you start busting up Lee Granger's place. Three days later you're having a hoedown in the middle of main street. In between, you go and kick the hornet's nest with a rambler I been keeping warm for Seth Bullock—who ain't the most understanding fella, by the way, so the two of you can be the ones to explain to him why Bowie Bill Wallace is in the wind again."

I sputtered in protest. "Why, but you can hardly blame us for that! Couldn't you just have arrested him?"

"This ain't New York City, girl. Did you see how many boys he's got riding with him? Roosevelt ain't here, so that leaves me 'n' Snyder, unless I'm gonna deputize a bunch of cowpunchers and watch 'em get gunned down like prairie chickens."

Well, there wasn't much I could say to that. I'd all but dismissed Hell Roaring Bill Jones as a drunk and a buffoon. He might be the former, but he certainly wasn't the latter. *A thoroughly competent frontiersman*, Mr. Roosevelt had called him, and it seemed to me a careful choice of words. Not a good man, necessarily, or even a competent sheriff. A *frontiersman*—with all the rugged, cold-eyed pragmatism that implied. He'd rather let a notorious outlaw slip through his fingers than risk the lives of ordinary townsfolk by picking a fight he didn't think he could win. I suppose I even understood it, up to a point. But that didn't mean I had to like it.

"We regret the inconvenience," Thomas said. "And we shall certainly endeavor to maintain a lower profile from now on."

"You do that. I'll keep your lawyer in the cage for now, but like I told Gus's boys, you best come up with some real evidence."

Except as far as I could tell, Gus Reid wasn't bothering with evidence. Instead, he was planning to round up the rest of the Lakota, too. "Did you know Reid is threatening to bring in the cavalry? Or even hired guns?"

I felt sure Jones would object to his town being overrun by armed men who didn't answer to him, but apparently I was mistaken. "I already had Charlie Morrison in my ear about it, and I'm gonna tell you what I told him. Round these parts, it's understood that a man's got a right to defend what's his. Reid wants to hire some stranglers to keep his stock safe, I got no reason to stop him. 'Specially not if he means to drive off the rest of them young bucks prowling around where they got no business being. I know you eastern types got a soft spot for Indians, but I got a town to protect, and Indians spell trouble."

"Those *young bucks* are hunting the animal responsible for all those deaths," I said coldly.

"Yeah, well, we got hunters enough round here as it is, and we're about to get more. Couple of these rich eastern landlords figured it'd be a good idea to offer a five-hundred-dollar reward for whoever bags the Medora Monster."

My mouth fell open. *Five hundred dollars?* Not so long ago, that would have been six months' wages for me. I could only imagine how rich it would seem to a bunch of Dakota cowpunchers. A reward that size would have every fool with a rifle and a bellyful of liquid courage out in the bush looking for something, anything, to shoot. Which meant things had just gotten a whole lot more dangerous for John Ward and the Lakota.

Jones knew it, too. "If your Indian friends got a lick of sense, they'll hit the road before they end up full of lead, accidental or otherwise."

"You're just going to allow that? A free-for-all shootout in your own backyard?"

Bill Jones fixed me with an icy look. "The last thing you want to be doing is telling me how to do my job."

I started to protest, but a discreet touch on my arm held me back. I could read the meaning of that gesture as clearly as if Thomas had spoken. *There's no point in antagonizing him further. He's not going to change his mind.*

Aloud, Thomas said, "We'll get you your evidence, Sheriff. And then I trust you'll set the young man free, with the profound apologies of the Billings County Sheriff's Department."

"You do what you gotta do, Pinkerton. Just remember what I said: if I catch the two of you making trouble again, I'll have you on the next train out. *In irons.*"

With that cordial farewell, he sent us on our way.

Outside, we found the sheriff's deputy, Snyder, loading the dead man into a wheelbarrow. I hadn't got a good look at him until now, and I halfway hoped I'd recognize him, but I didn't. If he worked at Cougar Ranch, we hadn't seen him, and he wasn't one of the outlaws Bowie Bill had brought to the river. Neither of which told us very much. By all accounts, both men had foot soldiers to spare. He could be working for either of them—or neither.

"Could be one of them treasure hunters," Snyder suggested. "There's still a few of 'em about. They don't take kindly to rivals, and word is you all just picked up some of Ben Upton's things."

Thomas sighed. "Ideally, one would have a shorter list of potential assassins."

"Anyways, we'll put him in a pine box and set it up outside the jail here. Maybe somebody'll recognize him."

"How festive," Thomas said dryly.

It would be even more festive after a couple of days out in the sun. The thought made me shudder.

Thomas hefted his satchel, where he'd stashed Parnell's ledger and the strange collection of Upton's belongings. "Where shall we regroup? The hotel or the saloon?"

"Definitely the saloon," I growled. "I need a drink."

"Arrived in Medora 3 o'clock yesterday. Spent today reconnoitering the area. Ain't much to look at, but they say it's good country for running beeves, and Lord knows I had my fill of the Black Hills. Reckon I'll give it a go, at least for a season. If it don't earn like they say, maybe I'll keep on up to Canada. Hell, I'll ride all the way to the North Pole if that's what it takes to shake Kit loose." I lowered the journal. "That's it. For this entry, anyway."

"Interesting." Thomas reclined in his chair—or at least, as far as he could with his back to the wall. We'd chosen a table in the deepest corner of the saloon, away from the doors and windows, and I'd taken the added precaution of sitting next to my partner instead of across from him. We'd made too many enemies to be taking any chances. "From the sounds of it, Upton's original plan was to take up ranching. I can think of better ways to invest one's profits, but perhaps he was in a hurry. He did sound awfully eager to be away from Deadwood."

"Not to mention Kit, whoever that is. But he must have changed his mind pretty quickly, because he started sketching these within days." I gestured at the pages. Some of the drawings were hastily done, others incredibly detailed, and I still couldn't make heads or tails of any of them. They certainly didn't look like any mining equipment I'd ever seen. *Once a prospector, always a prospector? Or had you already found the gold?* I supposed it didn't matter. Whether he went looking for a new strike or just stumbled across it, Upton obviously found *something*, and spent the next few weeks obsessing over how to get it out of the ground. "It must have been some deposit, if he didn't just go at it with a pickax straightaway."

"Large enough, apparently, to make a hundred thousand dollars seem like chicken feed in comparison. Which suggests Roosevelt was right about Upton being lucky."

I tried to imagine what that would be like. "So he's out riding his horse one day and just . . ." I mimed sniffing at the air. "Gold?"

"Why not? It's how Burrows's great-grandmother struck gold in Carolina, and look where that family ended up."

Where they'd ended up was sitting atop a pile of gold, which they'd parleyed into more gold, and more after that. That's how it went with the lucky, each generation building on the success of the one before it, until they no longer even needed to be lucky at all. Mr. Burrows had inherited the family gift, but he was already so rich that it didn't matter.

"But wait . . . If Upton and Mr. Burrows have the same form of luck in their bloodlines, does that mean they're . . . ?"

"Related? Not necessarily. There are cases of similar forms of luck being found in persons who are not obviously connected. It's a bit like crossing paths with a doppelganger."

"A what?"

"Someone who bears an uncanny resemblance to someone else. Is that evidence of shared ancestry, however distant? Or is it merely that the universe has a finite number of features, and certain combinations are bound to repeat now and then? Science will provide an answer eventually, but for the moment we can only speculate."

I smiled at him. "You could have just said *no*."

"Because you generally prefer the uncomplicated answer."

"Touché." Returning to Upton's journal, I flipped forward through the pages. I'd only skimmed it so far, but if there was anything useful in there, I hadn't found it yet. "Pretty sure he doesn't mention the word *gold* in here at all."

"Perhaps that wasn't the sort of thing he wished to set down on paper."

"Yes, why would you want to write about a silly old gold strike when you could have page after page recounting your fortunes in poker?" Which fortunes had been more foul than fair, from the looks of it. That Upton would choose this, of all things, to record for posterity suggested he had more than a passing affection for gambling. "I can tell you what cards he had nearly every night, but I don't see anything that'll help us find our killer."

"It's almost as if he didn't know he was going to be murdered."

I glanced up. A more relaxed Thomas, apparently, came with a side of sauce. I'd always figured there was a dry wit lurking beneath that gentlemanly veneer, but until recently I'd only seen glimpses of it. *What else is hiding under there?* Little by little, I was finding out. It was like peeling an onion. Or removing layers of clothing. Stripping them off one piece after another, letting them fall to the floor at his feet, button after button slipping through my fingers, exposing the bare . . .

Focus, Rose.

I cleared my throat. "What about the lawyer? Anything useful in the ledger?"

"As advertised, it's a complete list of his transactions going all the way back to last year." Thomas pushed it over so I could take a closer look. "It appears Parnell initially concentrated his purchases along the Little Missouri, which would be logical if one were looking for gold. Then, after Upton's cabin was discovered, he shifted his attention to that area."

"So it all adds up."

"Not quite. It doesn't explain why so many attacks have occurred at Cougar Ranch. We thought perhaps those might have been exaggerated, but nothing we saw today supports that theory."

"No," I agreed reluctantly. Much as I would have liked to find a reason to throw Gus Reid in jail, we hadn't turned up any evidence of his involvement. On the contrary, everything we'd heard pointed to the attacks on his stock being real. "Which means he probably isn't working with the killer."

"Nor are most of his ranch hands, or they wouldn't have bothered with any subterfuge about escaped bulls. If they'd had us outnumbered, they would simply have attacked us outright."

"So it's probably just Howard and a handful of his Buckshot buddies." That explained why John Ward had been none the wiser. According to him, the former Buckshot boys spent all their time out on the range, rarely crossing paths with the rest of the ranch hands. He would have had no idea what they were up to.

Which was what, exactly?

"Seems a bit excessive, if you ask me," I mused. "Hiring a whole pack of mercenaries when all you really need is a bully or two."

"I think we can assume our Buckshot friends had a hand in the disappearance of at least some of those treasure hunters. Anyone who got too close to the truth about Upton was quietly taken care of."

I supposed that made sense. On top of which, the killer might have figured he needed professionals on the job. Howard and Skinny might be capable of murder, but they'd made a complete hash of the affair at the hotel, leaving a great big mess and coming away empty-handed in the bargain. Cowboys, apparently, did not make master criminals.

The thought gave me pause.

"Howard and Skinny seem like an odd choice of henchmen, don't they? There's no shortage of gunslingers around here, plenty of them a lot tougher than those two, and probably smarter, too. Why not hire Bowie Bill, or one of those treasure hunters? What does he want with a couple of local cowpunchers?"

"You have a theory, I take it?"

The beginnings of one, anyhow. "A cowboy's job is to look after animals. Mean ones, too, like that old bull we saw tearing through the bushes this morning. Men like that would come in handy if you needed help wrangling a dangerous beast."

"Like our unusual predator." Thomas nodded slowly. "It makes sense. I wonder, does that mean the creature lives on Cougar Ranch?"

I'd toyed with that idea too, but only for a moment. "Too close to home. It would eat every animal on the property, and probably help itself to a few ranch hands in the bargain. Even Gus Reid wouldn't be able to deny what was going on then. But I do think Howard and his buddies help themselves to the boss's cows from time to time, when the thing can't find prey of its own."

"It would be the simplest solution." A wry smile touched Thomas's lips. "It almost makes one feel sorry for Reid, doesn't it?"

It really didn't.

"I wish we knew how many of these Buckshot boys there are," I said. "It'd be nice to know what we're up against."

"That I can tell you." Thomas flipped to another page in the ledger. "Parnell also recorded his payroll in here. No names, but there are seven weekly payments. Seven hired guns, all of them working for our mysterious CA." He sighed. "What a pity C is such a common initial. Charles. Clive. Clancy . . ."

"Assuming it's a real name at all. There's a hundred nicknames starting with C." Our killer was careful; I'd give him that much. Using go-betweens at every step, keeping his true identity a secret even from them. Even so . . . "*Someone* has to know him. Maybe we could ask Lee Granger to help us put together a list, starting with Upton's friends."

"His friends?" Thomas tilted his head. "You think he knew his killer?"

I'd spoken without really thinking, and now I felt self-conscious, squirming a little under my partner's sharp gaze. "It makes sense, doesn't it? Upton was so careful. He kept two journals, one of which he went to the trouble of hiding, but he never once mentioned his secret project in either of them. And yet somehow his killer knew about it."

Something sparked in Thomas's eyes, and he sat forward abruptly, pushing the journal toward me. "Would you kindly go back to that passage you read aloud before? The one about the North Pole?"

Frowning, I flipped back to the appropriate page. "*I'll ride all the way to the North Pole if that's what it takes to shake Kit loose.*"

"Rose. You are brilliant."

So brilliant, in fact, that I had no earthly idea what he was talking about.

Was this about the initials? "Kit is spelled with a K," I pointed out, tentatively.

"Of course, and I wouldn't have paid it any mind were it not for what you said a moment ago about nicknames. Kit is short for Christopher."

Could it be? We stared at each other for a moment, neither of us daring to hope.

"Please tell me there's another reference to him in the journal."

"There is, actually." It took me a moment to find the page, and when I did, we huddled over it together, Thomas's hand resting casually over mine as we read.

Texas Sam took it all again tonight, with a pair of goddamn twos. I told him he was the worst cheat I ever seen, except maybe Kit. He said if I ever cussed him like that again he'd knock my teeth out. Ha! Guess I been bellyaching plenty about ol' Kit. Not that he ain't deserve it.

"Well, well." Thomas gave my hand a squeeze, and he lifted his gaze to the ever-present card game going on across the room. "Do you suppose one of those fine fellows is Texas Sam?"

There was only one way to find out.

CHAPTER 20

FRESH BLOOD—FAMILY FEUD—AN
IMPROBABLE OUTCOME

The gamblers didn't exactly receive us warmly.

"Pinkertons ain't welcome at this table," said a weathered fellow with shaggy muttonchops, to grunts of agreement from the other players.

"Oh, we're not here to play." I put just a touch of honey in my voice, in case it helped. "We were hoping for a few moments of your time. We're looking into the disappearance of Benjamin Upton, and we heard he was a regular at this table."

"We can make it worth your while," Thomas added.

One of the gamblers eyed him from under the brim of his black felt hat. "How much?"

In truth, Thomas had given almost everything he had to John Ward, for the horses. "I have five dollars on me, but I can obtain more when the banks open tomorrow."

The black hat tipped back down. "Come back tomorrow, then."

"Never mind him," said a third man impatiently. "You in or out?"

"I'm thinking, goddamn it." Black Hat looked over the pot, as if trying to decide whether it was worth it. I didn't blame him. It was even sadder than the one I'd noticed the other day, consisting of a small mound of chips and a battered-looking set of spurs. Not exactly a high-stakes table—which gave me an idea.

"Mr. Wiltshire, do you have the time?"

Thomas gave me a blank look. Then understanding dawned, and with the perfect amount of flourish, he produced his extravagantly expensive Patek Philippe. "*Hmm,*" he said. "Later than I thought." He angled the watch as if to show me, which just happened to offer the gamblers a bountiful view of its face, including the perpetual calendar and phases of the moon.

The Swiss really do make miraculous watches.

Four pairs of eyes locked on the timepiece, pupils dilating. One of the players shifted in his chair. Another actually licked his lips. The man with the muttonchops stared so hard that he didn't even blink.

"You're right," I said. "It is getting late. Enjoy your game of euchre, gentlemen."

Thomas didn't miss his cue. "Oh dear." He laughed. "I think you mean *poker,* Miss Gallagher. Do forgive my partner, gentlemen. I'm afraid she's not familiar with card games."

I folded my arms and pouted a little. "And I suppose you're an authority? Play much poker at the Madison Club, do they?"

"In fact, a number of us in the Fifth Avenue set have taken an interest in poker. Not for gambling purposes, of course, but as a scientific diversion."

"Ha! Where's the science in a game of chance?"

"But you are quite mistaken! Chance is not twenty-five per cent of the question. It is probability that rules in poker, Miss Gallagher.

It is a game of skill and character, as these gentlemen will no doubt attest." Thomas raised his eyebrows at the players, inviting them to agree with this manly assessment.

"Mister," said one of them, "we're trying to play this here game of skill and character, so if you don't mind . . ."

His companions, though, looked to be reassessing their positions on the matter, now that they'd had an eyeful of Thomas's gold watch. A pompous New Yorker with a fat pocketbook was simply too juicy a mark to pass up.

"Might be we could use some fresh blood," said Muttonchops reflectively. "Whaddya say, mister? You play a few hands, and we'll answer your questions."

"That there's a sensible compromise, Sam," said Black Hat.

My glance flicked over the fellow with the muttonchops. *Well, hello, Texas Sam.* At last, we'd found someone with more than a passing connection to our missing prospector.

"Got something to play with?" he asked Thomas. "Five dollars ain't gonna last the round."

As far as I could tell, five dollars would have bought everything on that table and then some, but I held my tongue.

"Will this do?" Thomas flashed the silver buckle we'd used as a makeshift mirror earlier. I figured it was worth about as much as a decent horse, but Sam was visibly disappointed, leaning back in his chair and scratching his muttonchops. I could tell he was trying to figure out how to goad Thomas into putting up the Patek Philippe.

"It's a start, anyways," he said grudgingly. "What about you, little lady?"

Black Hat looked positively aghast. "Pinkertons is one thing," he said in a stage whisper, as if I wasn't standing right there. "But a woman?"

Well, I was hardly going to refuse after that. "Certainly, I'll play."

"With what?"

Good question. I had two dollars in cash and nothing of value on my person, except my gun and . . .

"What about that?" Sam leaned back in his chair to get a better look at the hairpin holding my chignon in place. "That's jade, ain't it?"

My hand strayed to the jade rose at the nape of my neck. It was my most treasured possession, and not just because it helped me fend off the dead. That hairpin was a gift from Thomas, and Mei Wang had seen to its crafting, imbuing the ash wood with magic for added strength. I didn't care how important a witness Texas Sam might be, there was no way in creation I was going to—

"Perfect," Thomas said. "That's settled, then."

I gave him a horrified look, but the eyes that met mine said, *Trust me.* So with nervous fingers, I pulled out my precious hairpin, letting my hair fall loose. I could count on one hand the number of times Thomas had seen me with my hair down, and he watched me with something like the look the gamblers had given his Patek Philippe. I couldn't help blushing as he pulled out a chair for me, but happily, the other men were too absorbed in their hands to notice.

It probably goes without saying that I'd never played poker in my life.

Mam had a strict Catholic aversion to cards of any sort, which she'd done her best to enforce. I knew twenty-one—show me a servant who doesn't—and the special branch taught us whist and euchre, the better to blend in among high-society households. But that was the extent of my education, and something told me none of it was going to be all that helpful just now.

"All right," Sam said, dealing the cards. "Ask your questions. But first, you're the big blind, Englishman. That's a dollar."

That sounded awfully steep to me, but Thomas didn't bat an eye, dropping his chips cheerfully onto the table. That made it my turn, but when I started to reach for my chips, Thomas lifted his fingertips ever so slightly off the table.

Don't.

That puzzled me. Hadn't he wanted me to play? But I trusted my partner, so I pushed my cards away. "Fold."

"What, already?" Thomas laughed. "Dear me. Watch and learn, Miss Gallagher, watch and learn." It was completely unlike him to be so condescending, which meant he was sending me a message. His gaze skipped over the other players one by one. *Watch them. Learn them.*

Now *that* was a game I knew how to play. And in the meantime . . . "I suppose I'll handle the questions, then. Were all of you acquainted with Mr. Upton?"

"Abner and me knew him pretty good," Sam said, gesturing at Black Hat. "Enoch . . . you'd have played with him now and then, I guess. Jake here was still living in Denver, so he's no good to you." He raked out three cards and turned them faceup.

"Does the name Kit mean anything to you?"

He snorted. "Cousin Kit? Sure."

That set me back a step. "He and Upton were relatives?"

"Guess so. He never got into the details. Just kept going on about how Cousin Kit was a pain in his nethers."

"Which made him a pain in everybody's nethers," Abner put in. "Had to listen to Ben's bellyaching damn near every night."

I watched the players carefully as the betting went around, and they watched each other, looking for clues about their opponents' hands. They were detectives too, of a sort. *I could get to like this game,* I thought. Mam would be horrified.

"Did he ever describe Kit?" I asked. "What he looked like, for example? Or maybe his last name? Anything specific?"

"Naw, nothing like that." Sam flipped another card faceup. "Something you gotta understand about Ben Upton. Most of the time, he didn't have two words to rub together, least when he was sober. Then, every night about six, he'd amble in here, get a few drops of rye in his gullet, and it'd be like somebody uncorked a bad bottle and let it all come fizzing out. We just let him yammer, long as he kept the pot nice 'n' shiny."

I'll bet you did. Rich, drunk, compulsive . . . Upton would have been ideal prey for Sam and his friends.

And speaking of ideal prey . . . "I believe I shall go *all in*," Thomas said brightly, adding his silver belt buckle to the pile.

Sam's mouth quirked. "Feeling lucky?"

"Chance has very little to do with it. It's a question of probability, as I said."

I wasn't sure if Thomas was in earnest, but if so, he'd miscalculated. I'd seen the way Texas Sam eyed the cards in front of him, and though his expression hadn't changed, I could tell he liked what he saw. He'd looked at those cards just the same way he looked at the Patek Philippe: fixed and focused, without a single blink.

Even if I'd worked out a way to signal Thomas, it was too late. He'd already made his bet, and a moment later, my intuition proved out. "Three queens," Sam declared, and Thomas's silver buckle disappeared into his pocket.

Thomas sighed. "It would appear that my calculations were flawed. I shall have to be more conservative in future."

"That mean you got something else to play with?" Texas Sam was feeling mighty pleased with himself. He had a wolfish gleam in his eye now.

"Let's start with these, shall we?" Thomas removed one of his emerald cufflinks and added it to the pot. "This gets me through to the river. Agreed?"

The cards were dealt again. This time, I was the big blind, which meant I had no choice but to play. I put down my dollar and tried not to look worried.

"Now, then," said Thomas, "where were we? You say you don't recall anything specific, but if Upton was as loquacious as you suggest, he must have had his favored themes."

Sam shrugged. "Just the sorta thing any man might say about a cousin he didn't get on with. How Kit was jealous of him. How he didn't have no talent of his own. Weren't nothing but a bummer. So forth and suchlike."

"Sounded to me like they was close once upon a time," Abner put in. "And Ben had some ghosts about it."

"How do you mean?" I asked.

"Some of the things he said . . . It reminded me of a feller drowning his sorrows after he just buried his mean cuss of a daddy or something. You know, like he's got his regrets, but he don't wanna face 'em, so he just sits there rambling to anybody who'll listen how that sumbitch got what was coming to him."

Like he felt guilty about something. It would explain the drinking, and the obsessive grumbling too. "Does that mean you think Kit's dead?"

"Naw. He's down in Deadwood. Least he was back then."

"Yeah, but . . ." Sam leaned back in his chair and scratched his muttonchops, eying the newly revealed cards. "I think he mighta moved up here at one point. I've a notion that's what set ol' Ben off that night. You boys remember—when he knocked the table over?"

"Tell us more about that," I said.

"Sure thing. Just as soon as you bet."

I glanced down at my cards. As far as I could tell, all I had was a pair of tens. I knew that was *something*, but I doubted it would be enough.

I must have hesitated for too long, because Sam said, "You wanna keep asking questions, you're gonna have to play."

I matched Abner's bet. "There. I'm playing. Now, you said you thought Kit might have come to Medora. What gave you that impression?"

"Don't recall the particulars, but he said something about how the good Lord couldn't even give him one whole month without seeing Kit's ugly mug. How Kit was following him around like a dog, eating scraps from his table."

"Scraps from his table? What does that mean? Was Kit a prospector too?"

"Couldn't tell you what line he was in. Far as table scraps go, Ben was talking about some old ranch house his cousin moved into. I guess Ben, he had his eye on it first, but he passed it over. Now here was his cousin moving in there, like he was trying to buy it out from under him. You ask me, that's what drove him off."

"Sam here don't think Ben's dead," Abner explained with a toothless grin. "He keeps hoping Ben'll come back one day and sweeten the pot like he used to."

He's dead, all right. I saw him myself. As for who killed him, Cousin Kit was sounding more and more like our man. *Following Upton around like a dog . . .* He must have known his cousin was lucky, and from the sounds of things, it was an issue between them.

By this point, most of the players had folded, but not Texas Sam. He raised yet again. "Whaddya say to that, Englishman?"

"Regrettably, I must withdraw." Thomas pushed his cards away. "The odds simply aren't in my favor."

Sam looked down at the pot, fixing that unblinking stare of his on Thomas's emerald cuff link. He could practically taste the gold between his teeth, I knew. "Guess that leaves me 'n' you, little lady."

I had two pairs now, which still didn't seem like much. I'd have folded, emerald cuff link or no, but I was afraid that would bring the interview to an abrupt end, and I wasn't quite through. "Where was this place?" I asked, throwing in the rest of my chips. "The ranch house Kit moved into?"

Sam frowned. "Ain't I answered enough questions? I'm trying to play here."

"A deal's a deal. I play, you talk."

He sighed impatiently. "Alls I know is, Ben thought it was real funny. Ironic, like. Said Kit was only squatting there 'cause he thought Ben had his eye on it, but the joke was on Kit, 'cause Ben had given it the once-over and it weren't worth a nickel. Called it a fitting place for a feller who turned out to be nothing but a disappointment. I guess he told Kit he could go ahead and rot there, and they was through."

A final falling-out. That's probably what pushed Kit over the edge. He was our killer. I was sure of it. And I was equally sure that we'd got about all we could out of Texas Sam and his friends. "Speaking of through . . . Shall we show our cards?"

"We ain't done here. I raise you ten dollars."

Thomas *tsk*ed. "For shame, sir. The lady is a novice. There's no need to bully her into submission."

"That's the game, mister."

Two pairs is something, isn't it? Better than one pair, surely? Biting my lip and praying my instincts were right, I slid my precious hairpin across the table.

Sam flashed a tight smile. "You just don't know when to quit, do you?"

They'd put that on my tombstone, and no mistake.

"All right, then, I'll raise you this bit of silver." He took out Thomas's belt buckle and dropped it loudly on the table. "Too bad you can't match it."

"In fact, she can." Thomas produced the Patek Philippe. "This will more than cover it."

Oh, Thomas, what are you doing? I knew how much he loved that watch. And I also knew Sam had been trying to get it into the pot since the first card was dealt. What if he'd been playing me this whole time?

Sam sat very still for a moment. Then he said, "No staking."

That's when I knew I had him. And so did everybody else.

Abner burst out laughing. "Since when? You let Ben stake you when that fancy Chicago gambler came through."

"Sauce for the goose is sauce for the gander," Enoch agreed with a yellow-toothed grin. They'd been humbled by Texas Sam one too many times, it seemed, and were eager to see the tables turned. "Go on, then. Lay 'em out."

With trembling hands, I turned over my cards. And Texas Sam? He swore a streak that would have made any Five Pointer blush. Because he *was* a bully, and he figured he could bluff some greenhorn little girl with a pair of fours. But I'd seen the way he looked at that river of cards. His eyes, his posture, even his ridiculous facial hair had told me everything I needed to know.

The other players whooped with laughter—all except Thomas, who sat perfectly solemn. As for me, I gathered my winnings as quickly as I could, figuring we'd better skedaddle before we found ourselves in our third shootout of the day.

As soon as we were outside, Thomas let out a long, satisfied sigh. "Will you think less of me if I confess how thoroughly I enjoyed that?"

"I'd be a hypocrite if I did."

"That was profitable in every way. We have a name for our killer at last, to go along with our motive. All we need now is a location."

"Agreed," I said. "And I have an idea about how we can get that, too."

CHAPTER 21

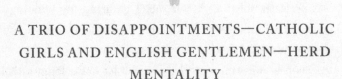

A TRIO OF DISAPPOINTMENTS—CATHOLIC GIRLS AND ENGLISH GENTLEMEN—HERD MENTALITY

Simply brilliant," Thomas said as we climbed the stairs at the hotel. "You handled him perfectly. Have you truly never played poker before, or was that just part of the act?"

"Never. But that look you gave me said to trust you, so . . ." I shrugged, still unable to wipe the grin off my face.

"Not at all. It said to trust yourself. You are singularly gifted at reading people, Rose. I had every confidence that if I played the decoy, you would handle the rest."

"Which you did masterfully. Say . . ." I spun to face him at the top of the stairs. "Maybe we're on the wrong side of all this. I'll bet we could have a brilliant career as confidence artists."

What can I say? Our success had quite gone to my head.

Nor was I the only one, judging from the glassy look in Thomas's eye. "There's a thought," he murmured, mounting the last stair abruptly and bringing his face within inches of mine. "Shall we use my room?"

"P-pardon?"

"We ought to confer, don't you think?"

"Yes." I cleared my throat. "By all means, let us . . . confer."

Thomas showed me in and set about preparing the stove and kettle. "At last, some real progress, largely thanks to you. You really have come such a long way, Rose."

"I learned from the best."

He smiled, slipping his fingers casually through mine. "I don't know about that, but you've certainly been an excellent student. Soon, there won't be anything left for me to teach you."

"I can think of a few things." The words were out of my mouth before I could stop them, and a fierce blush scalded my cheeks. Thomas's color came up too, a flash of pink beneath his dark beard. His fingers tightened around mine, and the look that came into his eyes sent a delicious shiver down my spine.

The kettle whistled. Thomas made tea. We tried to act like professionals.

"All right," he said, settling into a chair across from me. "Let's hear your idea."

I blew on my tea, stalling. He wasn't going to like it, but I didn't see any alternative. "Now that we know the killer is Upton's cousin, it seems to me that the quickest way to find him is—"

"No." Thomas set his teacup down, instantly grave. "We discussed this. Consulting the ghost is far too dangerous."

"But it would tell us everything we need to know."

"Far from certain. And even if it did, the risks are unacceptable. Need I remind you what happened the other night? You very nearly slipped under forever."

"But I didn't, because you were there to wake me."

"Rose." He closed his eyes and made a steeple of his hands. "I don't think you quite understand. The effects of these interactions are cumulative. Each one drags your mind a little further down the path to madness. That's assuming the ghost's intentions are benevolent. If they are not, and he chooses to try to bind you inside the dream, there will be virtually nothing I can do to stop it. You could be lost forever."

I took a swallow of tea, but it did nothing to banish the sudden chill. He was right: I hadn't really understood. "But we're so close."

"All the more reason not to stumble now. We've already wired for a medium. I expect we'll hear back from the Agency tomorrow, and then—"

"And then it will take days for someone to make the journey. How many people will die in the meantime? Mauled by the creature, or shot, or at the end of a rope? How much time does Two Horses have left? He's been in that jail for more than a day already, and the longer he sits there, the more likely it is—"

"I share your frustration, but that's no excuse for being reckless with your life."

"What about the Agency? Maybe they could dig up something on Kit."

"Doubtful. Tracking down a small-town attorney is one thing, but a drifter lately of Deadwood?" Thomas shook his head. "We'll ask, but I wouldn't expect much."

I growled, grinding the heels of my hands into my eyes. "That ranch house Kit moved into . . . I'd bet my eyeteeth that's the cabin I saw in my dream." Which probably meant he'd been living somewhere nearby this whole time, probably under an assumed name. "If only we had a likeness of him, we could show it around town."

"Are you sure you can't recall his face from your dream?"

"I've tried and tried. It's almost as if Upton didn't want to remember him."

Thomas sighed. "It certainly sounds as if they had a complicated relationship. Upton reads like a man carrying a considerable amount of guilt."

"And anger. That business with the cabin is downright spiteful." What was it he'd said? A fitting place for someone who was nothing but a . . .

Wait a minute.

"Ah." Thomas sat back in his chair. "I know this look well. Take your time." He sipped his tea.

I grabbed the journal we'd taken from the safe and started flipping through, scanning for a single word.

"Something you read earlier?"

"Here it is. *Another day, another disappointment. Had such high hopes for this spot, but it didn't prove out. That's three now, but I ain't gonna let it get to me. Disappointment's part of the game, and I got a good feeling about number four.*" I glanced up. "Can we take a look at Upton's things again?"

"Certainly." Thomas fetched the bundle, and the two of us stood over the bed as he emptied it out with a *clink* of glass.

"Three soil samples," I said, picking up one of the jars we'd taken from the cabin near Painted Canyon. "Three disappointments."

"He must have been attempting to pinpoint the precise location of the gold he was sensing."

"That ranch house Kit moved into . . . According to Texas Sam, Upton had already given the place the once-over and decided it was worthless. *A disappointment.* What would you like to bet that one of these samples comes from that property?"

"I shouldn't like to bet at all. I think you're probably right."

In which case . . . I turned the jar in my hand, watching the earth fall against the glass. "We hoped this might help us trace Upton's movements, but maybe Mr. Burrows can do something even more useful with it."

A slow smile spread across Thomas's face. "It's certainly worth trying. And he has been practicing."

"Practicing?" I raised my eyebrows. As far as I knew, the only arts Jonathan Burrows practiced were cognac and women.

"Hard to credit, I know, but the Foster case finally convinced him that his gift could be of some use. His luck is a good deal more refined than it once was. With a little patience, he ought to be able to track down the source of these soil samples."

"Which hopefully leads us to the cabin I saw in my dream."

"And our killer. A long shot, perhaps, but we've cracked cases with less."

I felt a lot better now that we had a way forward again, and some of the giddiness from before seeped back in. "I'm not sure I'm ready for Jonathan Burrows," I said with mock weariness. "It's been so very peaceful without that particular slice of New York in our lives."

Thomas's smile faded, and something passed through his eyes that I couldn't quite place.

Rose, you nit. That's his best friend you're making fun of. "I'm sorry, I shouldn't—"

He caught my face in his hands and kissed me. It was abrupt and a little disorienting, but that burned away in an instant, lost in the sort of desperately passionate kiss that makes you forget your own name. I went to pieces as usual, blissfully surrendering to sin. Good Catholic girls did *not* kiss this way. For that matter, neither did proper English gentlemen. We ought to have been ashamed of ourselves, I suppose, but in that moment, I felt about as far from shame as it's possible to be.

We broke off after a minute or two. I didn't want it to end, but I didn't dare stay any longer. Whatever had come over Thomas a moment ago still had a powerful hold on him; I could see it in his eyes.

Until now, I'd been relying on him to draw the line between us. That was unfair, and tonight I sensed it would also be unwise.

I cleared my throat. "Well. I should . . ." I pointed at the door.

He nodded absently. His hands still framed my face, his thumbs drifting across my cheekbones.

"Thomas?"

"Forgive me." His hands fell away. "I hope I haven't . . ."

Not this again. "Whatever you're trying to apologize for, you needn't."

He sighed. "At a minimum, my behavior has been most un-gentlemanly."

"I don't always want you to behave like a gentleman." I couldn't say it without blushing, though it was no more than the truth.

A wisp of a smile touched his lips. "Nevertheless."

"Anyway, what does that even mean in a place like this? It's like you said. We're a long way from formal society out here."

"Society will find us eventually." His voice was full of quiet regret. "Sooner or later, we must return to New York, and then . . ."

And then what? Neither of us had an answer.

"You're right. New York will find us eventually, one way or another. But not today, and not tomorrow. So in the meantime . . ." I planted a quick kiss on his lips and bade him good night.

It wasn't very brave of me—cutting Thomas short like that, retreating before he could say something I might not want to hear. But the thrill of his kiss still sparkled in my veins, and all I wanted was to savor it, to savor him, for a little while longer. Besides, I needed time to think things through. Time and a sympathetic ear, and in that moment I missed Clara painfully. Of course, I knew what she'd say if she were here.

Talk to him.

She'd been giving me that advice for nigh-on three years now, and it was high time I took it. *And so I shall,* I resolved as I turned down the lamp.

Eventually.

Thomas and I were headed for breakfast the next morning when a commotion at the end of the main street drew our attention. A herd of about a dozen horses was making its way from the livery, moving at a jog while a pair of riders whistled and hawed behind them. I spotted John Ward straightaway, and a moment later, Red Calf swerved out alongside, keeping the stragglers in line. Up ahead, Little Wolf rode at the opposite flank, waving his hat every now and then when the pace started to flag.

They're not supposed to be here, I thought worriedly. *What are they doing?*

They'd already drawn a crowd, and it didn't look friendly. Cowboys lined the boardwalk, grumbling to one another while they glared at the Lakota. Little Wolf sat proudly upright, pretending not to notice the hostility building around them. Red Calf, meanwhile, met every pair of eyes along the way, practically daring the onlookers to start something. John Ward brought up the rear, grim and watchful, rifle resting pointedly behind the horn of his saddle.

Thomas fished out his Pinkerton badge and pinned it to his chest, in case there was anyone left in town who didn't know who we were. Then he strode out into the middle of the road and threw a cheery wave at the riders. "Ho, there!" he called in a voice pitched to carry. "Good morning, my friends!"

Little Wolf reined in, shaking the hand Thomas offered him. "Are you marking your territory?" he said with a wry smile.

"Something like that. I doubt many of the townsfolk would knowingly cross the Pinkerton Agency. But there are always exceptions, as you know only too well. You and Red Calf risk a great deal by showing your faces here in town, my friend."

"We had no choice. John bought all the horses he could find at the ranches, but it wasn't enough to make a decent herd. The livery was the last place for us to try."

"But you needn't have come yourselves," I said, throwing an anxious look at the hostile faces lining the boardwalk.

The wry smile again. "John Ward is good with horses, but even he could not move this many on his own."

"Thomas and I would have been happy to—"

"What do you know of herding, my friend?"

Well, he had me there.

"Besides . . ." His smile faded. "Two Horses is my responsibility. It was my hunting party that brought him here. It is only right that I lead the party that will set him free."

Thomas sighed. "We just hope you know you're not alone in this."

"Thank you. I know you are doing everything you can. And we have John to help us."

Hearing his name, John Ward trotted up, and we brought him up to date on the doings at Cougar Ranch. It was a lot to take in— dead colleague, treacherous foreman, employer on the warpath— but as usual John received the news stoically. "Never did like George Howard. I'll bet it was him got ol' Gus all riled up, too. Probably figured going after you all"—he nodded at Little Wolf—"would keep the boss off his scent."

I gave him a rueful smile. "There you go, thinking like a detective again."

"We should not linger here," Little Wolf said. "The animals are getting restless." Grinning, he added, "The horses, too."

I couldn't help laughing. What would it take, I wondered, to subdue that easy humor? I hoped I'd never have to find out. "One more thing before you go. Some of the local ranchers just put a bounty out on the creature. A big one. It's about to get crowded out there."

John sighed. "Figures."

"Have you decided where to set the trap?" Thomas asked.

"Near Painted Canyon. There's a clearing up the northern end with a crick nearby, not too far from the spot that Jonah fella was took. White Robes is there now, looking for spoor."

Red Calf called a low warning, and we turned to find Hell Roaring Bill Jones striding toward Little Wolf with a furious expression. "You people got no business here," he barked.

"I have a pass," Little Wolf said.

"Good for you." Jones put a hand on Little Wolf's bridle. Red Calf didn't like that one bit, scowling and swinging his horse around, but Little Wolf stayed him with a gesture.

"I can show you my pass," Little Wolf said patiently. "Will you let me reach into my pocket?"

"You trying to start a shootout, son, or are you just plumb stupid?"

"Sheriff—"

"Bill—"

The sheriff silenced us all with a scowl. "Not a word from you two," he said, jabbing a finger at Thomas and me. "As for you, John Ward, I'd expect better sense."

"We ain't looking to start nothing, Bill. Wouldn't be here at all if we had a choice. Livery was the only place still had horseflesh for sale, and we got an urgent need."

"Urgent enough to get shot over?"

"Yessir."

That clearly wasn't the answer the sheriff was expecting. He frowned up at John, as if he didn't quite know what to say.

"These men are on Pinkerton business," I put in. "We tried to tell you, Sheriff."

"Oh, is that right? You're a Pinkerton now, John, is that it? Does Gus know what you're up to?"

John let out a dry laugh. "I expect he don't. You can go ahead and tell him, if you like. Now if you don't mind, Sheriff, we got important business to attend to, like the lady said."

"Damn sure don't let me stop you." Jones gestured irritably down the street. "And don't be bringing these two young bucks back here, either. I got problems enough keeping this rabble in line without Indians and Pinkertons and every other pain in my arse stirring things up."

"Lovely to see you as always, Sheriff," Thomas said.

Jones shot him a look that could curdle milk, but he released Little Wolf's bridle and turned away. "Clear the street," he hollered, hand on the butt of his gun. "You hear me, you bunch of mouth breathers? Move along."

The crowd had already started to disperse—along with the horse herd. "We best move along ourselves," John said. "Gonna take a minute to get these animals back in line."

"We'll join you on the trail as soon as we can," Thomas said. "We're close to tracking down the man behind all this, and once we learn how he made the creature, we can learn how to unmake it."

"Do you really think we're close?" I asked in an undertone as they rode away.

"We had better be," he said grimly. "Because we're running out of time."

CHAPTER 22

COMING CLEAN—OF DUCKS AND
DERRINGERS—THE ROOT OF THE
PROBLEM

The Western Express pulled into the station at a little before seven the following evening. Mr. Burrows had wired us from St. Paul, warning of his impending arrival. He hadn't said anything about a traveling companion, however, so Thomas and I were awfully surprised to see Edith Islington standing in the doorway of the Pullman car, looking absolutely exhausted.

"Good heavens!" Thomas sprang forward to help her from the train. "What are you doing here?"

"I've been asking myself that very question for the past forty-eight hours." Putting her hands on Thomas's shoulders, she let herself be hoisted down. "I couldn't bear the thought of missing out on the adventure, but I confess I had no idea the journey would be so ghastly."

"How on earth did you manage it in three days?" I asked.

"We were foolish enough to take the overnight from Chicago."

Mr. Burrows appeared in the doorway, looking red-eyed and disheveled. "I don't care to see another railway station for a very long time." Glancing about for the missing platform, he added, "And perhaps I shan't. Where in God's name have you brought us, Wiltshire?"

"May I offer you some assistance?" I smiled up at him, extending my hand in a gentlemanly fashion.

He gave me a wry look. "You certainly look as though you could manage it. Whatever are you wearing, Rose?"

"Blue jeans. They're extremely practical."

"I certainly hope so."

"Don't be a beast, Jonathan." Edith gave my arms a squeeze, looking me up and down. "I think she looks grand. A proper frontierswoman. And you, Mr. Wiltshire. Why, both of you seem . . ." She trailed off, regarding us with a puzzled smile. "Completely at home, actually."

"Well, it has been nearly a week." Saying it aloud, I marveled at how quickly the time had passed. "A lot's happened."

"And I want to hear all about it," Edith said. "But first, for the love of all that is holy, please show me to a bath."

"And a drink," Mr. Burrows added. "And if we somehow manage to stay awake for that, perhaps you can tell us why you've dragged me halfway across the country."

"Pooh," said Edith. "The water's getting cold."

"Probably for the best. If you stay in that tub any longer, you'll turn into a raisin."

"I feel as if I only just got in." She glanced over at me with that arch smile of hers. "But I see you've managed to unpack my entire trunk in the meantime. I appreciate the help, but I can manage without a servant, you know."

"I don't mind. Gives me something to do while I'm talking." Of which I'd done plenty, bringing Edith up to date on our escapades over the past week while she scrubbed three days' worth of train travel away.

"Hannah insisted on packing virtually everything I own. And yet . . ." Edith scanned the piles of clothing with a sigh. "Hardly a stitch of it seems appropriate now that I'm here. I'm going to feel very left out being the only one not in trousers."

I laughed. "It must have been a little jarring to find me looking like this."

"Not half as jarring as finding Thomas Wiltshire looking like the world's most elegant gunslinger. I thought he was dashing in evening attire, but the juxtaposition of silk waistcoat and six-shooters is just too delicious. You must be swooning all over yourself."

I hesitated in the midst of unfolding a dress. I'd never discussed my feelings for Thomas with Edith. It wasn't that I didn't want to confide in her, but the fact that she'd confessed her own feelings for him shortly after we met made the prospect more than a little awkward.

"I hadn't really noticed," I said with an offhanded little shrug.

She just laughed. "Rose, darling, have you forgotten who you're talking to? One hardly needs supernatural powers of observation to see that you're absolutely mad about each other. But as it happens . . ." She folded her arms over the edge of the tub and batted her eyelashes at me. "I have them."

My skin grew warm, and I couldn't help laughing too. "I suppose it was only a matter of time." Thomas referred to Edith's luck as *photographic memory*, but it was much more than that. Edith didn't just remember everything. She *noticed* everything. It was silly of me to think I could hide my feelings from her. "How long have you known?"

"Since that day in Mr. Burrows's parlor, with Clara and Joseph and Sergeant Chapman. The two of you were practically finishing each other's sentences. It was adorable." Sighing theatrically, she added, "And utterly heartbreaking."

I bit my lip, sinking down onto the bed. "I'm so sorry. I hope you don't think—"

"Don't be silly. I have no claim on him, and besides, how could you possibly resist? You're perfectly suited."

I gave a hollow laugh. "A former housemaid and a society gentlemen? Yes, perfectly."

She *tsk*ed. "As though that's the whole story."

"Maybe not, but the rest is just as complicated. We're partners. As it is, half the special branch seems to think the only reason I was hired was because Thomas and I are . . ." I cleared my throat. "You know."

"And?" She lifted herself out of the tub and grabbed a towel. "Are you?"

A furious blush warmed my skin. "Of course not!"

"Well, and what would be wrong with it? It's not unheard of in society circles to have a dalliance or two before marriage, even for young ladies."

"Well, we're not. Dallying, that is."

"But you are *something*, obviously."

I sighed. How could I explain when I barely knew what to make of it myself? "This place . . . It's done something to us. To him, especially. He's always been so reserved, but out here . . . There's a zest to him. A little mischief, even. It's as if I'm seeing the real Thomas Wiltshire for the first time."

"How intriguing." Edith starting unpinning her hair. "And what has he done with this newfound freedom? Has he confessed his feelings?"

"In a manner of speaking."

She smiled knowingly in the mirror. "A good-night kiss, perhaps?"

"Every night for the past few days." Confessing it made me blush even harder. Last night's kiss hadn't even included the customary apology. Just a teasing *Good night, Miss Gallagher*, and that ironically formal nod that made my heart do somersaults. "It's been . . ." I trailed off, lost for words.

Edith took both my hands in hers. "I'm so happy for you. You deserve it."

"But . . ." My smile faded. "It's a bit of make-believe, isn't it? And we both know it."

"What do you mean?"

"Out here, we can do whatever we like. But what happens when we go back to New York? Nothing's changed. All the reasons that have kept us apart until now are still valid."

She gave my hands a sympathetic squeeze. "You'll figure it out. You always do. And in the meantime . . ." Her arch smile returned. "Take what you can get. I know I would."

I laughed. "That's exactly what I'm doing. Does that make us wicked, you and I?"

"It makes us honest. Now, help me pick out something to wear, would you?"

I started sifting through her wardrobe, feeling a little lighter. I'd missed having someone to talk to, but until this moment I hadn't realized just how much. "Edith?" I turned, one of her frocks pressed absently to my chest. "I'm glad you're here."

"So am I. I've always wanted to see the Wild West. It will be an adventure."

"I'm glad you feel that way." Smiling apologetically, I added, "Because you're going to need a gun."

"Thank heavens," Mr. Burrows said, waving Edith and me over to a table at the back of the saloon. "My drinking companion has been the most dreadful bore."

Thomas ignored that, rising politely while keeping one finger on the page he'd been reading. "I trust you're feeling refreshed, Miss Islington."

"Oh, I think you can call me Edith, since we'll be bearing arms together."

"I . . . beg your pardon?"

"I gave her my derringer," I explained. "With everything that's going on around here, I thought she should be able to protect herself."

My partner looked a little nonplussed, but he didn't say anything. Mr. Burrows, meanwhile, took the liberty of yanking Thomas's Peacemaker out of its holster and examining it critically. "A bit basic, isn't it? Where's the ivory handle? The gold inlay?" He cocked the hammer.

Thomas's hands flew to the Colt, lowering the barrel and easing the hammer back down. "It is a weapon, Burrows, not a bit of finery. And unless you wish to become intimately acquainted with every other firearm in the room, I suggest you leave it alone." His glance slid meaningfully to the nearby tables, where a number of scowling cowboys were just now lowering their hands from their own guns.

"My, my." Mr. Burrows arched a golden eyebrow. "Rather a nervy bunch, aren't they?"

"With good reason," I said. "Which is why he probably needs *something*, Thomas."

"He has a derringer," Thomas said, returning his attention to the book he was reading.

"Since when?"

"Since always," Mr. Burrows said idly. "Though perhaps I ought to have something a little more powerful, given what you've told me about your exploits thus far. What about that shotgun?" He nodded at Thomas's 12-gauge, which stood propped against the wall.

Thomas didn't even glance up. "My dear Burrows, I've seen how you handle a shotgun. The derringer will be safest for all concerned."

"Come now, I'm a competent shot."

"A number of unaccountably healthy ducks would beg to differ."

Mr. Burrows smirked. "You are a perfect bastard, you know that?"

"As long as it's perfect, I am content."

Edith cut me a look. "I'm beginning to see what you mean."

Thomas glanced up, but before he could ask, I said, "Is that the book Mr. Jackson sent you?"

"Indeed, and it doesn't disappoint. In fact, I think it's given us the answer we need." He spun it around to show me, his eyes simmering with barely restrained excitement.

"*Magistellus Flora*," I read.

"A plant-based familiar. Specifically, an alraun."

You can imagine my surprise. The attack at Custer Creek had been a terrifying blur, but I definitely didn't recall being set upon by a vicious bit of shrubbery. "Are you sure that's the right entry? That thing was about every fauna known to man, but I didn't see any flora."

He gave an impatient wave. "What the creature becomes is less important than how it begins. In the case of this particular type of familiar, it begins with the root of an ash tree."

"Ash." I sighed. "That figures."

"How so?" Edith glanced between us, curious. "I thought ash was used to banish the dead."

"That is one use, certainly." Thomas flipped back to an early chapter of the book and pushed it toward her, still wearing that eager expression. "Ash has a number of spiritual properties, the most notable of which is that it acts as a conduit between the otherworld and the physical realm. Just as it can be used to banish spirits of the dead back to the otherworld, so it can be used in reverse, to summon spirits from the otherworld to ours."

"Why would anyone wish to summon the dead?"

"Any number of reasons," Thomas said. "But in this case, the spirits in question are not human at all. They are a sort of lesser fae, if you will, ubiquitous in the otherworld, as they once were in ours. Some, particularly of the lower-ranking ilk, occasionally consent to serve humans."

"Consent?" I echoed.

"They can be compelled, but it's a vicious enchantment, and difficult to maintain. The spirit is constantly trying to break free, and if it succeeds . . ." Thomas shook his head. "Let us say it does not end well for the spellcaster."

"Fascinating." Edith's voice was filled with awe. That made me feel a little better, since apparently I wasn't the only one at the table who'd never heard of such a thing.

"It is, isn't it? But here's the important part. The spell originates with a wooden figurine, carved from a root. In this case, an ash root."

"Hold on a minute." Even Mr. Burrows was interested now. "Didn't Elliot Van Dyk have one of those? That creepy little doll he used to send out at midnight to collect herbs in Central Park?"

"Just so, and that is precisely the sort of mundane task one normally expects from a familiar. Sending one on a murderous rampage is thankfully rare."

I paused, briefly overcome by the image of a tiny wooden man scurrying around Central Park picking purslane. "Is that sort of magic common among your set?"

Mr. Burrows shrugged. "It's not *un*common, especially among lucky families. Children who don't inherit the gift sometimes turn to magic instead, as a way of compensating."

The words triggered a memory. *I might not have your touch, but I have ways of my own. I read, Ben . . .* As always, remembering the dream brought a chill to my breast, and I couldn't help shivering.

"Are you all right?" Edith asked.

"Fine, thank you." I managed a weak smile. "Just remembering something, that's all. You were saying, Thomas, about a figurine?"

"Yes, the figurine." He tapped the book excitedly. "According to this, after carving the root into the desired form, the spellcaster anoints it with a drop of his blood. He then bathes it, and eventually feeds it, with the blood of the creature it is intended to mimic. Judging from what we saw of the creature, it would appear that our killer fed his alraun the blood of several different animals, all of them predators."

Well, that explained a whole lot. "So it was a cougar-bear after all."

"Not to mention wolf, otter . . . Who knows what else? One wonders if our killer found inspiration in legends of the underwater panther Little Wolf spoke of. Perhaps those stories are even rooted in truth, if you'll forgive the pun. Some other spellcaster, centuries ago, might have cast a similar spell, and the result was witnessed by the peoples native to the area."

"But if it's the same ritual Elliot used," Mr. Burrows put in, "shouldn't that have resulted in something similar to his creepy little doll? A wooden cat, perhaps?"

"In theory, yes. Unless the spellcaster found a way to amplify the magic considerably."

I groaned, dropping my face into my hands. "You were right all along, Thomas. The portal . . . It wasn't a coincidence."

He smiled grimly. "A brilliantly quick study as always, Miss Gallagher."

Mr. Burrows glanced between us, swirling his whiskey. "For the slow studies in the room, perhaps you'd care to elaborate?"

I poured out a dram of my own, since Mr. Burrows had ordered a whole bottle. I had to admit, the stuff was growing on me, even if it did bring tears to the eyes. "Remember that piece of Flood Rock we were chasing all over town? The Agency was afraid it could be used to enhance someone's luck. Apparently, portals do that. The closer you are to one, the stronger your luck, or your magic. The portal Mr. Wang showed us on the map is about twenty-five miles south of here."

"And highly visible from the road," Thomas added. "Anyone from the paranormal community would recognize it straightaway."

Bloody portals. I muttered a curse that would have made Mam blush and tossed back a mouthful of whiskey.

"But this is good news, surely," said Edith. "Now that you know what the creature is, you can work out how to destroy it! I suppose you would . . . what? Burn the figurine?"

"It's not quite that simple, I'm afraid," Thomas said. "I can only theorize that since a version of alchemy was used to create it, it would take powerful alchemy to unmake it."

In which case, I knew just the alchemist for the job. "We should send a telegram to Allentown straightaway."

"Agreed, but in the meantime, there may be a way to gain control over the creature, even if we can't destroy it outright. According to the book, the spellcaster directs the alraun by means of a talisman, usually an amulet or ring, fashioned from the same root as was used to carve the figurine. Find the talisman, and the creature is ours to command."

"Which means we need to find Kit," I said.

"Precisely. That's where you come in, Burrows."

"Oh, hurrah." Mr. Burrows was still swirling his whiskey, as though that might improve the taste. "You know I'm always happy to help, but why on earth haven't you brought a medium out here? Upton's ghost must know something of use."

Thomas and I exchanged a sour look. "That's a bit of a sore point," I said. "We wired for one days ago, but we're still waiting."

"Very well, then, how am I meant to track this person?"

We explained about the soil samples. Predictably, Mr. Burrows wasn't thrilled to learn he'd be combing through dirt, but he'd done worse for us. Like sifting through the gastrointestinal tract of a dead man, for example. That had been my idea, and I was terribly sorry for it. Mostly.

Mr. Burrows frowned at his drink. "Even if you're right about these soil samples, it's going to be a deuce of a task. Do you have any idea how long it could take?" He tossed back a mouthful, winced, and set his glass down decisively.

"We're well aware," Thomas said. "Regrettably, we lack better options."

"I'll do what I can." Mr. Burrows sighed and rubbed his eyes. "But first, I need to rest."

"Me too," said Edith. "Assuming I can fall asleep with all the heads."

"Heads?" Thomas arched an eyebrow.

She nodded at the elk trophy hanging crookedly on the wall. "There's one in my room, too. And in the lobby. And on the landing. Everywhere, heads. It's enough to give one nightmares."

"Er, speaking of nightmares . . ." Thomas and I exchanged a look, and I gave Edith another apologetic smile. "You're going to need some salt."

CHAPTER 23

A PROMISE FULFILLED—ANOTHER
PROSPECT ENTIRELY—EXPOSED

don't know what's more bracing," Mr. Burrows said as we stepped out into the morning sunshine. "The fresh country air or the fact that we can't leave the hotel without the two of you resting your hands on your guns."

I scanned the rooftops, shading my eyes under the brim of my hat. "If you'd been shot at as many times as we have, you'd do the same." Things had been quiet for the past couple of days, but Thomas and I weren't taking any chances. George Howard was still out there, and Bowie Bill too.

"Call it an excess of caution," Thomas said. "It would be foolish of our would-be assassin to make a second attempt here in town, but one never knows."

"Can't the sheriff do anything to help?" Edith asked.

"He has declined to summarily execute Two Horses, despite

the urging of a local rancher. I imagine he considers that contribution enough to our cause."

Urging was putting it mildly. We'd heard Gus Reid's bullyragging from clear down the street. He'd had a few choice words about Thomas and me as well, all but accusing us of murdering Skinny. The sheriff wasn't biting on either line, but that wasn't much of a comfort. It had been four days since Two Horses was arrested, which meant he was on borrowed time. At any moment, the order could come in from a judge, and that would be that.

"Well?" said Mr. Burrows. "Is the coast clear?" Without waiting for an answer, he hooked his arm through mine, and we started for the saloon. Lee Granger's breakfast wasn't exactly inspiring, but it was better than what was on offer at the hotel.

"Oh, look," Edith said as a rider trotted past with a pair of wolf carcasses slung over his horse. "More heads."

Thomas sighed. "Yet another hunter out for the reward. As though anyone could mistake those poor creatures for the Monster of Medora. At this rate, there won't be a wild animal left within fifty miles."

"And what about the real creature?" Mr. Burrows asked. "Any word from your friends?"

I shook my head, trying to ignore the fear wriggling in my belly. It had been two full days since we'd last seen John and the others. "I choose to believe that means they haven't found anything. A small town like this, I'm sure we would have heard if . . ." I trailed off, distracted by the sight of a dozen or so riders heading toward us at a jog. "Thomas," I murmured, resting my hand on my gun once again.

At first they were just a bunch of anonymous hats, but as they drew nearer, their features came into view. No Bowie Bill or George Howard, thank heavens, but they were heavily armed, and as they rode past, I saw that their ponies all sported the same familiar brand.

"Buckshot Outfit," I said in an undertone.

Thomas nodded. "Jonathan . . ."

"Of course. We'll see you inside." Mr. Burrows touched Edith's arm, and the two of them hurried across the street.

The riders reined in outside the jailhouse, and a moment later Bill Jones stepped out, along with Gus Reid. The sheriff looked sour as ever, and I had no doubt Reid had been working on him again, trying to convince him to hang Two Horses, or arrest us, or both.

Reid squinted up at the riders. "'Bout time you showed up. You Terrence?"

A flat-brimmed hat tipped in acknowledgment. The man called Terrence sat his horse like he'd been born in the saddle, and he wore his weapons that way, too. They all did, with their bandoliers and bowie knives and nickel-plated six-shooters. They looked like they'd ridden straight out of a yellowback novel, and only the hero could run them out of town.

"They say you're the best. That true?"

Terrence shifted a wad of tobacco in his mouth. "You got the money, we'll do the job."

"Didn't figure there'd be so many of you." Reid scanned the riders. I could practically see him tallying up the cost.

"You want it done right, this is what it takes."

"There's only a handful of 'em."

"Maybe, maybe not. Sioux's clever. He'll run decoys, make you think it's just a brave or two. So you chase 'em, and next thing you know, you been bushwhacked. I don't aim to be bushwhacked, Mr. Reid."

I glanced at Thomas, and saw my own grim thoughts reflected in his expression. Gus Reid had made good on his threat to muster a band of vigilantes—and he'd chosen the Buckshot Outfit. Under other circumstances, I could have laughed at the irony. *Damn fool. Doesn't he realize he's hiring wolves to guard his sheep?*

"You the sheriff?" Terrence asked, inclining his head at Bill Jones.

Jones hooked a thumb under his shirt. "You can see the tin, can't you?" It was no more than the growling of a chained-up dog. I could tell by the way the sheriff was standing—hands on hips, wearing that same worried scowl I'd seen the other day—he had no idea what to do about these men. "Are you gonna ask for my blessing? You won't get it, but I expect that ain't gonna stop you."

"All right, then." Terrence leaned over with an unhurried air and spat.

"Should we do something?" I whispered to Thomas.

"Such as?"

"Tell them what's going on. That Little Wolf and the others have nothing to do with—"

"They're mercenaries, Rose. They'll do whatever they're paid to do. And the sheriff has made it clear he's in no position to stop them."

I was practically shaking with fury by this point, but I knew Thomas was right. Men like these didn't care about the rights and wrongs of things. They were there to get paid, and if that meant taking lives—especially Lakota lives—that was just fine by them. "Shouldn't we at least warn John and the others?"

"They already know Reid is looking for them. If we ride out now, we'll only lead the Buckshot Outfit straight to them."

He was right about that, too.

"The best thing we can do for our friends is get our hands on that talisman, and quickly."

Thomas steered me away, but not before I caught Bill Jones's eye, and I sent him a clear message. *If there's blood, it'll be on your hands.*

He held my gaze for a moment, unflinching. Then he looked away.

"Well, I have an answer for you." Mr. Burrows set the last vial down and picked up his handkerchief, wiping the soil from his fingers. "But I don't know that you're going to like it."

I sighed. "This day just keeps getting better."

We were back at the hotel, crammed into the most discreet table we could find—which, given the size of the dining room, wasn't all that discreet. But there simply wasn't room for us upstairs, so we had to make do. Fortunately, we had the place to ourselves, at least for now, so we could speak freely.

"I'm no expert, but I think it very unlikely your Mr. Upton discovered gold anywhere near here. There isn't a trace of it in any of these vials."

"Upton did say those samples were disappointments," I pointed out.

"But then why collect them?" Thomas shook his head. "He must have sensed *something*."

"He did," said Mr. Burrows. "Something much more valuable, at least potentially." He tapped the lantern in the middle of the table.

I didn't follow. "Kerosene?"

"In a manner of speaking."

"Oil." Thomas sighed and closed his eyes. "Of course. No wonder Kit is willing to gamble the hundred thousand. He's betting on a million-dollar return."

A million dollars? My Five Pointer's brain could hardly conceive of such a sum. "Would it really be worth so much?"

"Very possibly," Mr. Burrows said. "If not more. And of course that's just the beginning. A million is easily converted into two, if one knows the right broker."

"Oh, really? Please do introduce us." I gave him a wry look.

"Yes, well." He at least had the grace to look embarrassed, dusting an imaginary speck from his ruby-red waistcoat. "All I meant was that a million dollars gives one a substantial foothold on Wall Street, which is more than enough incentive for murder."

"I suppose that explains these sketches," Edith said, holding up one of Upton's journals. She'd been reading through both of them carefully, absorbing every detail with her photographic memory. "It seems your Mr. Upton was trying to work out how to drill for oil. From what I can see, he was on the right track, too. This drawing here reminds me of an illustration I once saw of salt wells in China. The article referred to it as *percussion drilling*."

"Indeed?" Thomas looked impressed.

Personally, I didn't give a fig what Upton was looking for or how close he'd been to finding it. What mattered was whether the soil samples he collected would lead us to our killer and his pet monster. "Do you think you'll be able to retrace his steps?" I asked Mr. Burrows.

"I'll do my best, but it's going to be a dreadfully slow process. Please tell me you have at least a rough idea where to begin."

I nodded, spreading a map out on the table. "Upton's cabin is here, near Painted Canyon. He was using it as his base of operations, so it stands to reason the samples were taken somewhere in the vicinity."

"We'll look for changes in the landscape," Thomas said. "Plant life, geological features, that sort of thing, and sample them as we go. Once you get a taste for the terroir, as it were, we'll have a good idea what combination of features we're looking for, and we can adjust our course accordingly. But first . . ." He pushed his chair back. "We'll need to sort out transportation."

Mr. Burrows looked bored already. "Can't you just commandeer a couple of horses?"

"We are not the cavalry, Burrows. Come along, and bring your pocketbook. I have a feeling anything we purchase will come high."

He was right about that. As the only place in town with horses left to sell, the livery demanded an outrageous sum for two unremarkable ponies. Mr. Burrows wouldn't have minded—he was rich as a Rockefeller, and the Agency would reimburse him anyway—but then he laid eyes on Thomas's horse and began to feel he'd been very hard done by. Peacock that he was, it bruised his dignity terribly to have to "get about on some old nag" while his best friend looked positively regal astride his silver-and-black Missouri Fox Trotter. He fumed with envy the entire way to Painted Canyon, right up to the moment we reined in for our first soil sample.

"For the last time, he is not for sale at any price." Thomas looked properly annoyed as he jumped down from his saddle—but secretly I think he was a little pleased, too.

"He has a brother," I pointed out. "They're practically identical. I'm sure Reid would be more than happy to sell him."

Both men stared at me, and it was hard to say which of them looked more appalled.

Edith laughed. "As diverting as it is to imagine these two prancing through Central Park on matching ponies, perhaps we ought to focus on the job at hand."

"Easy for you to say," Mr. Burrows muttered as he tugged off his glove. "You're not the one who has to go rooting through the filth like a wild boar."

Thomas grabbed the hand drill while Mr. Burrows sank to his haunches and ran his fingertips over the ground, deciding on a spot for the sample. For my part, I slipped my Winchester out of its sleeve and scanned our surroundings. Hills crowded around us on all sides, barren flanks of clay fringed with the fresh greens of spring. They ought to have been beautiful, but all I saw was a hundred places to hide—and apparently I wasn't alone.

"It's very close here," Edith said, her glance drifting anxiously over the corrugated slopes. "I feel a little like a rat in a maze."

"I know what you mean." Thomas and I had avoided being out on the trail since the day we fled Cougar Ranch. We were exposed out here, much more so than in town. On top of which, we were uncomfortably close to the spot where we'd been ambushed by Bowie Bill—and the alraun.

"You needn't bother with the drill, Wiltshire," Mr. Burrows announced. "It's all wrong here."

Thomas sighed. "Perhaps you ought to familiarize yourself with these trees. That way, we'll know if they occur in the area we're looking for."

So Mr. Burrows handled leaves and bark and needles and berries, not to mention grass, sand, wildflowers, and anything else they could find scattered about. Then we moved on, only to repeat the ritual about half a mile away. *Dreadfully slow,* Mr. Burrows had predicted, and so it was. After the second hour, he started to flag, and by the third, he moved like one of Mr. Tesla's automatons. Edith was bored to tears, and even I was starting to feel a little sleepy under the hot afternoon sun. Thomas, though, seemed to think we were getting somewhere.

"Don't you see? You're telling me the presence of juniper and cottonwood is slight. That suggests we're looking for elevation, since wind and water would carry such material down into these ravines."

Edith perked up immediately. "One of the later entries in the field journal complains about windburn. We're sheltered down here in these ravines, but on a plateau, or out on the plains . . ."

"Which means we continue east. There, you see?" Thomas clapped his friend on the shoulder. "Courage, man. We're getting—"

A gunshot rang out somewhere nearby, the report ricocheting off the hills. In a flash, Thomas and I had our longarms in hand.

"It came from over there," I said, pointing. "But it's a ways off."

Another shot, followed by a quick answer, and a moment later, a full volley. Thomas cursed quietly. "I'll go."

Edith bit her lip. "Are you sure that's wise? What if it's the alraun?"

"It may well be. In which case, someone might be in need of aid."

"You're not the sheriff, Thomas." Mr. Burrows looked uncharacteristically grave. "It's not your responsibility."

"I appreciate the concern, both of you, but I'll keep my distance until I've a better idea what we're dealing with. There's a good vantage point up there." He gestured at a nearby hill. "I'll ride to the top and see if I can make something out. Rose?"

"We'll be fine."

"Just in case, you'd better take this." He handed Mr. Burrows the shotgun. "It's not going to do me any good at that range anyway." So saying, he spurred Gideon and disappeared around a bluff.

We waited, listening anxiously to the occasional *pop* of gunfire to the east. *It won't be John and the others,* I told myself. *They're well north of here.* At least, they were supposed to be. But if plans had changed, or the Buckshot Outfit had found them, or . . .

Stop it. Edith and Mr. Burrows were staring at me, so I tried for a reassuring smile. "I'm sure it's nothing. Just some hunters, or—"

Another gunshot, this one much closer. I took a few tentative steps down the path, listening.

That's when the screaming started.

"*Help!*" The voice carried horribly on the wind. "*Somebody help!*"

CHAPTER 24

A GRIM REMINDER—ANSWERED IN
BLOOD—THE UNEXPECTED VIRTUES OF
EXPENSIVE COGNAC

Edith gasped, her hand flying to her mouth. "Is that?"

Mr. Burrows gave a curt shake of his head. "Not Wiltshire. I'd stake my life on it."

"No." She drew a breath, visibly steadying herself. "No, you're right."

The screaming went on, and for a few terrible seconds, I stood frozen with indecision. *What if it's a trap? Or what if it isn't, and you leave your friends alone and vulnerable?*

"Go," Edith said. "We'll be all right."

"I do actually know how to use this," Mr. Burrows added, hefting the shotgun.

Still, I hesitated. Then the voice called out again, and I knew I couldn't ignore it. "Whatever happens, stay together."

Now I had another decision to make. Going on horseback would make me easy to spot, but I'd be no good to an injured man on foot. I decided to split the difference, riding a little way up the trail before dismounting and leaving Luna to wander in the brush. The voice kept calling for help, though it was growing weaker. Even so, I chose my path carefully, keeping to cover as best I could as I made my way toward the sound.

A cluster of trees lay just ahead; behind it, I heard the babble of water. *Custer Creek.* Not two miles from where we'd been attacked last time. Swallowing hard, palms sweating against the rifle, I picked my way through the brush.

The ground sloped away toward the creek bed, and that's where I found him: a lone figure lying crumpled in the sand. "Sir?"

"Oh, thank God," he sobbed. "Oh, thank you, Jesus."

The fear in that voice plucked at my heart, but still I moved cautiously, watching for any sudden movements. I couldn't see his face; he lay half on his side, his forehead pressed to the earth. I couldn't bring myself to roll him over with my boot, so I lowered my rifle and reached for his shoulder . . .

He flopped onto his back and looked up at me, and in that same instant I felt both relief and guilt. Relief, because I didn't recognize him. Guilt, because I'd taken my time getting to his side, and I knew the moment I set eyes on him that he wasn't going to survive.

"It come outta the water. It was so fast . . ."

I'll spare you the description of the poor man's condition, except to say that I briefly considered putting him out of his misery then and there. Instead, I pressed my hands feebly to the wound, but he pushed me away with what strength he had left.

"Ain't no help for it," he said, his breath rattling in his lungs. "Just don't leave me. I don't wanna die alone."

So I held his hand and prayed with him, even though every nerve in my body vibrated with fear. And when he passed, he wasn't alone.

I'd just made it back to Luna when Gideon came thundering

up the path. Thomas blanched when he saw me, but I put his fears to rest with a shake of my head. "It's not mine," I said, glancing down at the dried blood on my hands. "It's . . . I didn't get his name, actually."

Thomas swung down from his horse and grasped my shoulders. "Are you all right?"

"I told you, it's not—"

"Rose." He took my face gently in his hands. "Are you all right?"

Tears pricked behind my eyes. "I couldn't help him."

"I know. I couldn't help the man I found, either."

"The alraun?"

He nodded. "A group of hunters opened fire on it about a quarter mile to the east. The fellow you found must have got in its way as it fled. It headed back toward the river, just like last time."

I drew a deep breath, blinking the tears back and forcing myself to think like a detective. "Which means John is probably right about it retreating to deep water when it feels threatened."

"Either way, it's a grim reminder of how suddenly the creature can appear. Nowhere is truly safe." He glanced back up the trail. "On that note, we'd better get back to Burrows and Miss Islington. I think we've had enough for one day."

"But the cabin . . ."

"We're close." Reaching into his saddlebag, he produced the map. "Look here. We're less than a mile from the place the Lakota were camped last year when their horses were first stolen. Do you remember how Little Wolf described it? *Where the hills meet the prairie.* That fits what Burrows is sensing, and what Miss Islington mentioned from the journal. All of which suggests that Kit's cabin is east of here, somewhere along that ridgeline. It won't be long now."

"Isn't that all the more reason to keep going?"

"Burrows is exhausted. We all are. Pushing ourselves too hard would be counterproductive."

He's right. Exhaustion led to mistakes, and that would only cost us more time. Besides, the sun would set within the hour, and the last thing we needed was to be out here after dark. So we collected our friends and rode back to Medora, filthy and tired and more than a little glum.

"I'll report the deaths to the sheriff," Thomas said. "And then I suppose we ought to get supper."

I glanced down at the dried blood caking my hands. "I need a bath. You go on ahead."

"I don't think—"

"I can't go to supper like this." It came out more sharply than I'd intended, and I drew a steadying breath. "Don't worry, I'll be along shortly."

The hotel felt unusually cold as I walked in. Had I caught a chill on the trail, or was the ghost of Ben Upton grasping at me, angry at our lack of progress in catching his killer? I tried to put it out of my mind, heading over to the front desk to order a bath. But the clerk was nowhere to be found, and when I rang the ball, no one appeared. Shaking off a grim sense of déjà vu, I headed upstairs.

The corridor was dark. The wall lamps had yet to be lit, and no light seeped under the doors. Even so, when I heard the footsteps behind me, I didn't think anything of it. The only warning I had was a whiff of whiskey, and by then it was too late: The leather at my waist jerked as someone yanked my Colt free, and I felt cold iron pressed against the base of my skull.

"I been waiting on this moment for days." Even through the slurring, I recognized the smug tones of Bowie Bill Wallace. He stank to the rafters of whiskey, but the gun to my head felt steady enough. "Pretty stupid to go wandering about by yourself. You musta known I'd be laying for you."

"I hoped you'd done the sensible thing and got out of town." It sounded a lot braver than it felt, and it didn't earn me any points with Bowie Bill. He gripped my arm, hard.

"After what you done? That boy was my nephew."

"I'm sorry for your loss."

His fingers dug into my flesh, and he gave me a shake. "You mocking me, girl?"

"No. He was young, and nobody deserves to go like that. But it wasn't my doing."

"Might as well've been."

How did you reason with that? Even sober, I had a feeling Bowie Bill wouldn't be moved to reconsider. If I was going to live, I'd have to do something rash.

The Colt was pressed to my head, but I hadn't heard the telltale *click* of the hammer being cocked. That gave me a split second, and I took it, driving my elbow hard into Bill's ribs and twisting to grab the gun. Liquor dulled his reflexes enough that I managed to bat the revolver away, sending it skittering down the hall. But he recovered quickly, backing into a crouch and whipping out the blade that was his namesake. Just like that, for the second time in a week, I found myself facing an attacker with a knife. Only this knife was practically a saber, ten inches long and curved at the tip, with the sort of patina that testified to plenty of use.

The outlaw's lip curled into a sneer. "Better this way anyhow."

He lunged at me, quick and determined, like the striking of a snake. I met his forearm with my own, driving his attack out wide, just as I'd been taught. Again he came at me and again I turned him aside, this time deflecting the blow toward his body. Now came the hard part, and I did everything Thomas had shown me. I got hold of his wrist and twisted, but Bill didn't drop the knife. I went for his eyes, but he expected that, batting me aside with his free hand. I tried to lock out his elbow, but he was just too strong. His arm wrapped around my waist, bringing the tip of his blade against my hip; only my leather gun belt prevented the point from plunging into my flesh. Panic arced through me, and for an instant I froze.

Bowie Bill saw it in my expression, and sensing his victory at hand, he leaned in until his face was inches from mine, glaring into my eyes so he'd be the last thing I ever saw. He was so close now that I could smell the oil on the tips of his mustache.

That was a mistake, and you can probably guess what happened next.

I drove my knee between his legs, and though he didn't drop to the floor, he did crumple enough for me to snatch his revolver out of its holster and crack him over the head with it. Now he *did* fall, and he didn't move again.

The Five Points variation, I decided, really ought to be added to the curriculum.

I was winded and wobbly and just a little smug, which is probably why I didn't hear the floorboards creak behind me. I did hear the *click* of a hammer being cocked, and had a terrible instant to anticipate my death before the gunshot sounded. But it wasn't me that hit the floor, and when I spun, I found Mr. Burrows standing over the prone figure of one of Bowie Bill's boys, a delicate wisp of smoke curling from the barrel of his derringer.

"There, you see?" Mr. Burrows lowered the weapon. "A perfectly competent shot."

I couldn't disagree. The outlaw howled and writhed, clutching at his wounded shoulder, but he'd live. So would his boss—long enough to meet the hangman, anyway.

We used a curtain sash to tie Bowie Bill's wrists. That wouldn't hold him for long, but it didn't have to; already, I could hear someone downstairs shouting for the sheriff. The second outlaw had dragged himself up to a sitting position, but he was smart enough not to try anything, since Mr. Burrows and I each had one of his boss's engraved six-shooters pointed at his head.

"Thank heavens you came along," I said. "I thought you'd gone to supper."

"I found myself in need of a drink, and I couldn't bear another drop of that kerosene the saloonkeeper passes off as whiskey. Fortunately, I never leave home without a bottle of my own, so I came to fetch it."

In other words, I owed my life to Mr. Burrows's unreasonable affection for expensive cognac. Was there a lesson in there, or did the good Lord just have an odd sense of humor? Either way, I wasn't going to look a gift horse in the mouth. "You saved my hide. Thank you."

"Not at all. You'd do the same for me."

I glanced at him out of the corner of my eye. "Why do I get the impression this isn't the first time you've shot someone?"

I knew better than to expect an answer, and I didn't get one. "I'm sure I don't know."

"Jonathan." I turned to him, half exasperated, half pitying. "I hope you know you can trust me."

He flashed a thin smile. "A man without secrets is terribly dull, don't you think?"

In which case, Jonathan Burrows must have been one of the most interesting men in America. But that was a conversation for another day.

Sheriff Jones arrived on the scene a few minutes later. It being well past five o'clock, he was nearly as soused as Bowie Bill. And if I thought he'd be pleased to find the notorious outlaw gift wrapped for him on the hotel floor, I was sorely mistaken. "I'll be having to vacate my half of the jailhouse thanks to you," he growled.

"Terribly sorry for the inconvenience."

"You can be sarcastic all you like, girl, but you won't be the one under siege when Wallace's boys show up to bust him loose."

He may have had a point, but I certainly wasn't going to admit it.

Mr. Burrows collected his cognac while I washed up, and together we headed back to the saloon to join Thomas and Edith. We waited until after supper to mention my nearly being murdered. It was only good table manners.

"Good heavens!" Edith shuddered and took a healthy swallow of Mr. Burrows's cognac. "What a day!"

"It's been like this since we got here," I said, avoiding Thomas's eye. Bowie Bill had been right about one thing: it was foolish of me to go wandering off on my own. Thomas had advised against it, and I hadn't listened. He'd be unhappy with me, I knew.

"I confess that I feel a little silly," Edith said. "For coming here, I mean. Your stories always sound so exciting and glamorous, but the reality is rather different, isn't it?"

"On the bright side," said Mr. Burrows, "that's one less would-be assassin to watch out for."

"Maybe," I said, "but the sheriff's not wrong. If Bowie Bill has as many foot soldiers as they say, we probably haven't heard the last of this."

Thomas swirled his cognac with a sigh. "Human predators aside, it's clear the alraun is still on the prowl. I'd hoped that with his agent locked away, Kit might conclude there was no further value in terrorizing the local population. But it seems he has no interest in restraining the creature."

"It's perfectly horrible," Edith said. "To have so little regard for human life is bad enough, but if he's been living in the area, one has to suppose he knows most of his victims personally."

I hadn't thought about that, but she was right. "We've only been here a week, and already I can name just about every fellow in town, even the drifters. Imagine how cold-blooded you'd have to be to murder dozens of your own acquaintances."

"The worst part is, I think perhaps he's done it all for nothing." Mr. Burrows rummaged in Thomas's satchel and drew out some of the samples. "Of everything I've handled, this bit of shale tastes the strongest of oil, but even so, it's only trace amounts. This jar"—he unscrewed one of them and tapped a small amount of sand into his hand—"appears to be the same shale, ground into dust."

"The mortar and pestle," I murmured.

Mr. Burrows rubbed the sand between his fingers, closing his eyes and furrowing his brow. "It's out there, but . . ." Opening his eyes, he shook his head. "I don't know that Rockefeller himself could get it out of the ground."

"In which case, our murderer has just spent tens of thousands of dollars on worthless land." I couldn't even feel smug about it. Too many people had died for that oil, beginning with Ben Upton.

"On the bright side . . ." Mr. Burrows paused to toss back the rest of his cognac. "I do believe I'm getting a feel for it. Things will go faster tomorrow, I think. And on that note, I'd better turn in."

Back at the hotel, the four of us said our good nights. Thomas and I held each other's glance for a moment longer than was strictly appropriate, but that was as close as we could come to our customary farewell. Already, New York was creeping back into our lives, and with it all the obstacles in our path.

Even so, I was grateful to have our friends there. Edith was a comfort, and Mr. Burrows seemed confident that tomorrow would bring a breakthrough.

Which it may well have done, if only everything hadn't gone terribly wrong.

CHAPTER 25

A FORK IN THE TRAIL—SACRIFICE—
SWEET TIME

Jonathan Burrows was no one's idea of an early bird, so his failure to turn up in the lobby at the appointed hour didn't raise any eyebrows, let alone alarms. Thomas consulted his watch, Edith made a joke about too much cognac, and I watched the staircase, foot tapping restlessly as I imagined how far down the trail we ought to be by now. When, twenty minutes later, he still hadn't appeared, Thomas merely pronounced him *incorrigible* and headed upstairs to roust him.

My first clue that something was amiss was a thumping of hurried footfalls above, and a moment later, Thomas came flying down the stairs, hurtling past Edith and me on his way out the door. We found him in the middle of the street, raking both hands through his hair and looking quite lost. "He's gone."

"What do you mean?"

I already knew the answer. I just needed to hear him say it.

"They've taken him." Thomas turned on his heel and stalked back to the hotel, where he took the stairs two at a time. By the time Edith and I caught up with him, he'd already thrown open the curtains in Mr. Burrows's room and was scanning the scene with a look of fierce concentration.

"When you say *taken* . . ." Edith was doing her best to stay calm, but her hands betrayed her, twisting the fabric of her skirt anxiously. "Are you sure he isn't just at the saloon, or . . . ?"

Wordlessly, Thomas pointed at the door.

Edith shook her head. She didn't understand.

"The lock's been tampered with," I said, showing her where the paint had been stripped off.

"I saw, but . . . couldn't that have been earlier? Perhaps the hotel just didn't get around to repairing it properly."

She was just trying to convince herself, I knew. But I could see Thomas losing patience, so I tried to talk her through it. "His hat's still here," I said. "And I don't see his pocketbook anywhere."

Edith swallowed and nodded.

The bedclothes were all awry, as though there'd been a struggle, and Thomas found a few spots of blood on the pillow. "A cudgel, most likely. To keep him quiet."

That certainly settled it. Mr. Burrows had been kidnapped.

A shiver of fear ran through me, but I tried to keep a level head. "Is it possible it's just some rough holding him for ransom? His father is worth millions, after all."

"A hundred million and change," Thomas said flatly. "They may try to ransom him when they're through, but no—this is more than that. Most of the local ruffians would have no idea who he is, and besides, the timing is too much of a coincidence to credit."

Kit. He must have seen us with the soil samples and realized what Mr. Burrows was capable of. He'd know the signs, thanks to his cousin, who had a similar form of luck. "He wants Mr. Burrows to lead him to the oil."

"But there is no oil," Edith said. "None that can be extracted, anyway."

"Kit doesn't know that, and when he finds out . . ." Thomas's pale eyes were filled with so many different emotions, it was impossible to read them all. There was fear, certainly, and more than a little guilt. Mostly, though, what I saw was determination, and that stiffened my own spine.

"We'd better get moving," I said. "There's a chance we can still track him."

Thomas was already heading for the door.

"I'll speak to the sheriff," Edith said. "If he can't provide us with manpower, perhaps he can at least help us find a tracker." She gave me a quick hug. "Bring him home. And for God's sake, be careful, both of you."

Thomas and I lit out of the livery as if the Devil himself were in pursuit. It was still early, and it had rained a little overnight, giving us a clear trail to follow—at least for the first couple of miles. But our good fortune didn't last. The tracks diverged at a fork in the trail, one set veering south while another continued due east. Worse, the earth had already started to dry out, making it harder to see which tracks were fresh. "Should we split up?" I asked.

Before we could decide, a gunshot rang out, sending us scrambling behind the nearest butte. Another *crack*; a split second later, a spray of dirt leapt into the air not two inches from Gideon's hooves, spooking the high-strung stallion and nearly unseating Thomas. He swerved deeper into the embracing curve of the clay and jumped down, grabbing the rifle he'd bought off Lee Granger two days before. I did the same, and we crept back toward the trail, keeping low until we'd reached a pile of rock that offered a decent view of our surroundings. All the while, the gunfire continued.

I slid to my rump, my back resting against the cool stone. "That fire is coming from a long way off."

"Howard and his scope, no doubt." Thomas gave a bitter shake of his head. "Which means we won't be getting any farther up this road."

"We could double back. Take a different path."

"In this maze? We'd lose the trail completely, with no guarantee the sniper wouldn't have a bead on us anyway." He dropped his head between his knees. "*Damn!*"

"Thomas—"

"This is my doing. I should never have let him handle those samples in public."

His voice was level, but that didn't fool me for a second. He was fairly vibrating with anger, most of it directed at himself. I started to tell him that it wasn't his fault, but he wouldn't hear me, not right now. So I let him vent his fury, most of it in silence, a conversation between Thomas and his God and whatever passions he kept chained up inside that vault of a head.

"I should never have brought him here," he said finally.

I put a hand on his back. "You didn't *bring* anyone. We both asked him to come, and he chose to accept. It's my doing, and his too. And none of that matters."

Thomas drew a deep breath. My hand was still on his back, and I could feel his shoulder blades drawing together, as if he were literally buttoning himself up. "You're right, of course. Please forgive my outburst. Unprofessional and entirely unhelpful."

I sighed. "That's not what I—"

"The sniper has us pinned down. We don't know his position, and even if we work it out, we have no idea how to outflank him in these hills. Any one of these ravines could funnel us straight into his sights, and we'd be fish in a barrel. Our best chance is to avoid him altogether and try to find the cabin. We'll ride south and try to come in from the prairie side, where he won't be expecting us."

"But, Thomas . . ." I hesitated. "That cabin could be anywhere."

"Not quite anywhere. Within a large search radius, to be sure, but we'll find it eventually."

Eventually? Two Horses was already on borrowed time. The Buckshot Outfit was out here somewhere, hunting our friends. Mr. Burrows was being held by a madman who'd quite happily murdered his own cousin and dozens of others, and who would no doubt do the same to his captive the moment Mr. Burrows ceased to be useful. Jonathan was clever enough to string his kidnapper along for a while, but how long?

No, *eventually* wasn't good enough. Especially when we had another option.

"There's a faster way," I said quietly. "And you know it."

"No." He didn't even look at me.

"The ghost can show me exactly where—"

"*No.*"

"Thomas." I sighed. "It's not your decision."

An airy silence hung over the ravine. The breeze smelled like sagebrush and rain. Somewhere above us, a sniper crouched, peering through a scope while he waited for one of us to move.

"I can't protect you." His voice was steady, though I sensed the effort it cost him. "I don't know how. If the ghost takes you, he may never let you go. And even if he does, your mind may never be the same."

"Thomas, you don't need to tell me this. My mother—"

"Your mother speaks to her own mother. A relative, and a close one at that. It exacts a fraction of the spiritual toll. What you're proposing to do . . . If the ghost is angry . . ."

"If you're trying to scare me, it's working," I said, a little angry myself now. "But I'm not going to change my mind."

Thomas closed his eyes. "Please, Rose, don't do this. Burrows is my dearest friend, but you . . . You are my partner. Don't ask me to sacrifice one of you for the other."

"Nobody's asking *you* to sacrifice anything."

"You are so very wrong about that," he whispered. "I've been here before. Or at least someplace very like it. It nearly destroyed me."

I knew what he was talking about, or near enough. He'd lost someone—a lover, I'd come to suspect. It was a long time ago, and I knew nothing of the circumstances, but it was his deepest and most private regret.

One day, you're going to tell me about that. And maybe, just maybe, I'll finally understand you. But in the meantime . . .

"He'd do it for either of us. You know he would."

Another beat of silence. "It's your decision," he said finally. "I will do what I can to help you. But, Rose . . ."

"I know. Let's just get it done." Without waiting for an answer, I ducked back to the horses.

Edith didn't like my plan any better than Thomas had.

"What do you mean, ask the ghost? Are you quite mad?"

Not yet, but the day is young. Somehow, I didn't think either of them would appreciate the bleak Irish humor.

"You're going to allow this?" she demanded of Thomas.

"It is not my decision to make, as Rose has quite firmly reminded me."

The three of us were crowded into the Presidential Suite, formerly Ben Upton's room. I could feel him here, almost as strongly as I had the night he appeared to me. It was as though the ghost knew what was to come, anticipated it as eagerly as a wolf eying a stray calf. Tendrils of cold wrapped around my heart, though how much of that was just plain old fear, I couldn't say.

Edith glared down at Thomas, who sat on the bed. "What exactly is your plan?"

"Hypnosis. I will put her under and monitor her for signs of distress. If I see them, I will do my best to bring her out."

"Do your best?"

Thomas glanced up. I didn't see the look that passed between them, but Edith pursed her lips and subsided.

"Any advice about what I should do in the dream?" My voice sounded strangely thin, as though it were someone else's.

"Try not to anger him, but don't let him pull you just anywhere. It will be a fine line to walk."

That's it? That's all you have? But really, what had I expected? There was no magic charm here, no handy tip that would protect me. "All right." I cleared my throat. "In that case, I guess I'm ready."

That was a lie, of course, but one I needed to tell myself if I was going to get through this.

Thomas stood. "Miss Islington, could you kindly give us the room? This is not my area of expertise, and I think we'll have an easier time achieving a hypnotic state if there are no distractions. I'll bring you back in when Rose is . . . when she's under."

Edith threw her arms around me. "God protect you," she whispered. And then Thomas and I were alone.

I tried for a smile. "Is this where you swing your watch and tell me I'm feeling sleepy?"

"Not quite." He took my hand and drew me close, until his forehead grazed mine. For a moment he just stood there, staring down at my hands as if he didn't quite know what to say.

"Please don't ask me to reconsider. And don't you dare say goodbye."

He shook his head.

"This will all be over soon—you'll see. We'll find Mr. Burrows and put an end to all this, and we can go back to the way things were." I wasn't sure which of us I was trying harder to convince.

Thomas didn't say anything. He just took my face in his hands and planted a soft kiss on my forehead. Then he looked at me, and the fear in his eyes struck my nerves like a mallet hits a piano string, sending a tremor of doubt through me. Could I really do this? Risk madness and a lifetime spent trapped in a nightmare?

"Are you ready?"

I lowered myself onto the edge of the bed, knees pressed together to keep them from shaking. Thomas dragged a chair over and sat across from me. He did take out his watch, but instead of waving it in front of my eyes, he pressed it into my hand. The gold was warm from being tucked up against his chest, and I felt a gentle pulse as it ticked through the seconds. *Like holding a little heart in my hands,* I thought numbly.

"Close your eyes," Thomas said. "Listen to the watch."

I squeezed my eyes shut.

Tick. Tick. Tick.

"Take my hand." Gently, he guided my free hand to his. "Now, trace the lines of my palm."

My eyes fluttered open. "What—?"

"Focus, Rose. Listen to the watch. Feel my skin. Nothing else."

I did as I was told, trailing my thumb along the palm of his hand. It felt strange at first, as if I were searching for something without quite knowing what. But the longer my skin caressed his, the more I began to relax. My breathing slowed, and my pulse, too. The fear was there, but in stillness now, a smooth pond instead of bubbling rapids.

The hand in mine was his left, his dominant hand, and its contours spoke quiet volumes. Unmistakably the hand of a rich man, soft except where it needed to be hard, where he held a pen, or a cane, or a book. Gentle furrows in the palm. A tiny scar along the side of the thumb. Soft skin on the inside of the wrist, gently pulsing. I'd never touched anyone like this. It was incredibly intimate. Warm. Safe. The world in that moment consisted entirely of Thomas's skin, his scent, his watch.

Tick. Tick. Tick.

"You're sinking."

I'm sinking.

"You're asleep."

I'm asleep.

"Rose."

I opened my eyes. Thomas sat before me, staring straight ahead, his hand still in mine. But when I pulled away, he didn't move; his hand just hovered there, palm open. I waved my fingers before his eyes, but still he sat frozen, and for a moment I wondered if he'd gotten it terribly wrong. Did he hypnotize himself instead of me?

Then I looked over his shoulder, and there was Benjamin Upton, tall and dark and furious. His eyes met mine, sending a stab of ice through my heart. Without warning, he lunged, his huge hand seizing me by the throat.

"You took your sweet time, girl," he snarled. "And now I'm gonna take mine."

CHAPTER 26

MAGIC LANTERN SHOW—THE RIDDLE OF
THE SPHINX—CHECKING IN

What followed was so disorienting that my brain could hardly process what was happening. Upton hauled me up out of my chair—*that* part I understood clearly enough—and shoved me backward. I fell, but instead of hitting the floor, I kept falling. And falling. And *falling*. Above me was blue sky; all around me was rushing wind. I'd been thrown from a cliff and was hurtling toward the rooftops of Medora. I cried out and shielded my face with my arms—and then I wasn't me anymore.

I was a boy of nine, listening while my uncle spoke harshly of his own son right in front of him. "Lila, God rest her soul, she tried and tried to teach him, but he won't learn. And if I have another crop like I did last year, I'm done. Ben can help, can't he? He can show me where it's gonna work best, just like Lila used to. *This one* can help out with chores around here meantime. Ain't hardly a fair trade, but I'm asking."

I was a youth of fifteen, perched on a fence beside my cousin, throwing pebbles into a rusted tin can while he told me of his plans to move to Chicago. "Ain't no place for me here. I'm gonna study. Get me a real job, make some real money."

I was a man of twenty-eight, greeting my long-lost cousin with a hearty handshake, pleased as pie to see him dressed like a dandy and grinning from ear to ear. "I'm not here for Pa. That bastard can go on and meet his Maker as far as I'm concerned. It's you I came to see. I have an idea. A theory, I guess you could call it. Have you heard what's going on in the Black Hills?"

I was a man of thirty-two, drunk on success and rye whiskey, listening with rising temper as my cousin called this a *joint venture,* as though he did one lick of work. "I'm the one finding the glitter, ain't I? Look, I'm a reasonable man. I ain't gonna let you starve, Kit. But this here ain't no *joint venture.*"

Scene after scene flew past, like a magic lantern show. It was almost too fast to follow, and yet I felt as if I'd lived every one of those years. Clouded memories, not my own, crowded the corners of my mind. I even felt the passage of time in my body, the ravages of drink and hard labor taking their toll. That was a bad sign. It meant I was deeply immersed in the dream, maybe too deeply. How long had I been asleep? Minutes? Days? Years, even? The possibilities were too terrifying to contemplate.

And then, as suddenly as it all began, it was over. I was standing in the hotel room once more—except it was empty. That couldn't be right. Thomas and Edith wouldn't have left me. *Unless it really has been days or weeks or* . . . What if this was real? How would I even know? I had a fleeting image of those poor, addled souls I'd seen at the Lunatic Pavilion at Bellevue Hospital. *Is this what it's like for them? Trapped forever in some horrible in-between place, never knowing what's real?* Panic reared up inside me, but I tried to tamp it down. Giving into my fear would only make things worse.

"You see now?"

The voice came from behind me. Still angry, but a little sad, too.

"You see how it was between us? We was close, Kit and me. Like brothers."

Until you betrayed him. It was only a thought, a reflex, but this place was Upton's domain, and he heard me as clearly as if I'd spoken aloud.

"*I* betrayed *him?*"

In an instant, the room was as cold as a refrigerator. I should have been able to see my own breath, except I wasn't really there. I was a ghost now too, for all intents and purposes. And unless I was very, very careful, I'd stay that way.

Upton appeared before me now, though I hadn't seen him move. "What was I supposed to do? Just hand over everything I'd worked for? Kit had an idea. Use your gift in the Black Hills. It was a good idea. I was grateful. But how's he gonna tell me I owe him *half* of everything I got?" He towered over me, as real as any man I'd ever seen, bloodshot eyes and all. I could even smell a whiff of stale whiskey on his breath. "Do I need to show you again? Do I need to remind you what he done to me?"

Before I could answer, I was falling again, this time from the top of a butte. My stomach dropped as if through a trapdoor; my eyes teared as I gathered speed. Below me was a graying shack of hewn logs; in half a heartbeat, I'd crash through the roof and shatter my body. *Not real!* I curled my arms over my head. *Not real not real not real . . .*

And then I wasn't me anymore. I was a bruised and battered Ben Upton, tied to a chair, a madman looming over me. Everything happened just as it had before, ending with a gun to my head, and screaming.

"There, you see?"

Back in the hotel room now. Empty. Cold.

"You see what he done to me?"

"I see." The words came out in a whimper. I sank onto the edge of the bed, drawing deep breaths and willing my racing pulse to slow. I hadn't just been shot. That metallic taste on my tongue wasn't really my blood. *Don't you dare lose your grip, Rose Gallagher. Don't you dare.*

"So now, you tell me. Am I the one did the betraying? Am I to blame for what he became?"

I hesitated before answering, choosing my thoughts as carefully as my words this time. "Nothing justifies what he did to you."

The room grew a little warmer.

"He needs to face justice for what he's done."

Upton sighed. "Justice. What's that even mean? You think that's what I want—for him to hang, or spend the rest of his days rotting in jail?"

"Isn't it?"

The ghost shook his head. "Seeing my cousin swing ain't gonna bring me peace. I just wanted . . ." He sighed again, and it was like watching the air go out of a bellows. His shoulders rounded, and his head bowed. He looked sapped, as if it had cost him every ounce of energy to send me ricocheting through his life. "I just wanted someone to tell me if I done wrong by him. And I guess you think I did."

I stiffened, bracing myself for another tirade. "I never said—"

"It's all right." His gaze grew distant, as though he were lost in memory. "There's so much I woulda done different. Little things, mostly, but . . . How could I know they would add up to this?"

"You couldn't have." *But I guess that's life, isn't it?*

I'd let my thoughts get away from me again, but this time, he just nodded. "Reckon so." He glanced around the room, the way you do when you're about to leave it. "'Spose that's it, then. I got what I come here for."

Maybe *he* had, but I certainly hadn't. The ghost had shown me plenty, but not a lick of it would help me find Mr. Burrows. "The cabin where you died. Can you tell me where it is?"

He was barely listening anymore. "Time for me to go."

"Wait!" I leapt to my feet, panic gripping me once again. "Please, you can't go! Kit is holding a friend of mine captive, and . . ."

But it was too late. Already, Upton was fading, like a photograph developing in reverse. "You best wake up now," he said. "You don't wanna be here when I'm gone. You won't never get out."

"Please, wait! You have to tell me—"

He put a hand on my forehead, said, "Get gone," and shoved.

I was falling.

I woke with a gasp. Edith practically hit the rafters, clutching at her chest and giving a little shriek. Thomas did the opposite, sinking to his haunches as the air went out of him. He'd been stooped over my chair, fingers wrapped around my wrist as he took my pulse; now his head bowed, and he whispered something I couldn't hear.

"Are you all right?" Edith asked tentatively.

Thomas met my gaze, and I could see the lingering fear in his eyes. I wanted to banish that fear, to reassure him that my mind was intact, but I couldn't speak for the lump in my throat, as painful as if Upton's hand still gripped it. How could I tell him I'd failed? When I finally found my voice, it was barely a whisper. "I tried, Thomas. I really tried . . ."

Wordlessly, he gathered me in his arms.

"What happened?" Edith asked. "What did you see?"

"Upton's life. His relationship with Kit growing up." I sat back and drew a shaky breath. "It was so disjointed. And in between, I was falling."

Thomas gave me a blank look.

"He threw me off a cliff," I said, as though that explained anything. "Twice."

"How rude," Edith said with a hysterical little laugh.

Thomas handed me a glass of water. It stank of rotten eggs, but I drank it anyway, grimacing at the taste. "How long was I out?"

My companions exchanged a look. That's when I noticed the lamp burning on the nightstand. "Wait, is it . . . ?" I turned to the window, and sure enough, it was dark. "Please tell me it's still Friday, at least!"

"It's still Friday," Thomas said. "Just past seven in the evening. You've been out for nearly ten hours."

I made a little sound of despair. "And nothing to show for it."

"Are you certain of that?" Thomas took my hands and tugged me to my feet. "Walk with me. You need to get your circulation going, and pacing always helps me to think. Now, aside from childhood memories, what did the ghost show you? Anything recent?"

I tried to concentrate through the pins and needles in my legs. "I saw a saloon. In Deadwood, I think. Kit and Upton were arguing. It was Kit's idea for Ben to take up prospecting, and he thought that entitled him to a share of the profits. Ben saw it differently."

"So you saw the killer's face. Did you recognize him?"

In the dream, I'd been Upton, so of course I recognized him. But now that I was awake and thinking as Rose again, it seemed to me that I'd seen him in real life, too. I closed my eyes, trying to put his face in context. In my mind's eye, he was on horseback, spattered in blood . . .

I groaned. "Thomas, we met him. You *spoke* to him. Do you remember the treasure hunter who showed up at Upton's cabin covered in blood? The one who said he'd found Jonah?"

"I remember." Thomas sighed. "Eli, I believe it was? I thought he seemed a touch theatrical. Anxious to drive all those treasure seekers away from the site, no doubt."

"If you have a name," Edith said, "we can ask the locals about him. Maybe someone knows where he lives."

Thomas looked skeptical. "I'd be surprised if he were that careless, but it's worth trying. What about the cabin? Did you get a look at it from the outside?"

I started pacing again. "Not really. I caught a glimpse when I fell from the hilltop above, but I didn't exactly have a chance to take in my surroundings." I did my best to describe the sensation of being thrown from the top of a butte, but it's really the sort of thing you have to experience for yourself.

"How about the hill itself?" Edith asked. "Anything distinctive about it?"

"Actually . . ." My step slowed. I'd seen it before, I realized. In a dream, more than a week ago. "Mountain lion," I murmured.

Thomas cocked his head. "Come again?"

"Our first night in Medora, I dreamed of a lion the size of a mountain. At least, that's how I remembered it when I woke up, but I recall it more clearly now. What I saw wasn't a lion, it was a butte that *looked* like a lion. A bit like the one in Egypt, with the man's head."

"The Sphinx." Thomas's gaze was razor-sharp now. "And you saw this same butte near Kit's cabin?"

"Just above it. I felt as if I was going to fall right through the roof."

"Do you think you would recognize it if you saw it on the trail?"

"No need." Edith looked a little dazed, but I could already see the excitement building in her eyes. "I know exactly which butte you mean. I saw it from the train." Which meant she also knew where it was, thanks to her luck. "It's just as we thought. Where the hills meet the prairie, near the place where the tracks swing south. It's perched right on the rim of the breaks."

Thomas was already stuffing things into his satchel. "We should go now. Move into position under cover of darkness. When Kit resumes his search for the oil tomorrow morning, we'll be waiting for him."

I wasn't quite so ready to strap on my gun belt. "And then what? By my count, he has at least five men with him, including Howard. Three against six is hardly a fair fight."

Thomas paused, his satchel in one hand and a box of ammunition in the other. "Three?"

"Yes, *three*." Edith frowned. "Or do I not count?"

"With all due respect—"

"Don't you *all due respect* me, Thomas Wiltshire. Have you forgotten that I took first prize at the Newport Archery Club last August? Shooting is shooting, surely."

"Not *quite*, Miss Islington. Besides, we cannot in good conscience involve a civilian in—"

"Why not?" I said impatiently. "We involved Mr. Burrows in rescuing you last year. What's the difference?" I knew what the difference was, of course, and so did Edith. And we weren't having it.

Edith folded her arms and stuck out her chin. "I've known Jonathan Burrows for longer than the two of you put together, and I certainly have no intention of sitting idly by while his life is in danger. And with *all due respect* to your doubtless very impressive Pinkerton skills, you need me."

Thomas still wasn't convinced, but I was through arguing. "Glad that's settled. Now, what's the plan?"

Before he could answer, a knock sounded at the door, and the three of us exchanged a wary look. Thomas pulled the Peacemaker from his belt. "Yes?"

A disapproving grunt. "The Badlands have had an unfortunate effect on your manners, Wiltshire. That is hardly the greeting a gentleman expects, especially when he's the one paying the bills."

Thomas blinked, holstered his weapon, and opened the door.

Theodore Roosevelt filled out most of the doorway, his sturdy frame clad in what I can only describe as a most extraordinary costume. He wore fringed buckskin trousers and a matching fringed buckskin shirt, a neckerchief tied in a tidy little knot at his throat. Cavalry gloves (fringed) and half chaps (fringed) completed the ensemble. Lest anyone think this was all for show, an ivory-handled Peacemaker rested on his left hip (cross-draw style, naturally). Buffalo Bill Cody himself could not have looked more positively Wild West—or, at least, a New Yorker's version of it.

After a moment of stunned silence, Thomas thrust out his hand. "Sir."

"Wiltshire. Miss Gallagher. And I see you have a guest. Why, Miss Islington, is that you? Good heavens, what on earth are you doing here?"

"Oh, you two know each other?" I felt silly as soon as I asked the question. Of course they did. Families like theirs were the cream of New York society, after all.

"We've met a number of times, yes." Mr. Roosevelt flashed a toothy politician's smile. "Miss Islington is great friends with my sister, Corinne."

"We were not expecting you, sir," Thomas said.

"I imagine not, but I found your last two telegrams intolerably vague. That's not a criticism—I quite understand the dilemma of communicating by such public means—but I came to feel that the only way I could be truly seized of the matter was to come out here myself." He glanced between us, lamplight flaring off the circles of his glasses. "Your last wire mentioned Burrows, but I don't see him."

"Ah . . ." Thomas threw me an awkward look. "I think perhaps we ought to head down to the dining room. We're a touch cramped here."

"A long tale, I take it?"

"It is," said Thomas. "And I daresay you'll want to sit down."

CHAPTER 27

THE PLAN—A BIT OF
INSURANCE—STAMPEDE

Mr. Roosevelt listened with a grim expression while Thomas recounted all that had happened. "Dear me," he said at one point, and later, "Good heavens." When Thomas came to the part about consulting the ghost, Mr. Roosevelt's eyebrows flew up, and he reached across the table and patted my hand, sending that familiar buzz up my arm. "You certainly don't hesitate to throw yourself into danger, do you, my dear?"

I smiled awkwardly. "Mr. Burrows would do the same for me."

"Quite so." He gave a crisp nod. "Very well, then, I assume you have a plan?"

"We were just on our way out when you arrived," Thomas said. "Now that we know where Burrows is being held, we can move into position under cover of darkness."

"We?" Mr. Roosevelt's glance slid to Edith.

She rolled her eyes. "Don't you start."

He and Thomas exchanged a look of manly disapproval. "*Hrm*," said Mr. Roosevelt, but that was all.

"Actually," I said, "when you knocked, Mr. Wiltshire was just about to explain what comes *after* we surround the cabin. Because I'm not quite clear on that point."

Mr. Roosevelt looked at Thomas expectantly.

"Well," said Thomas. "Er . . ."

"I don't suppose Kit is just going to surrender," I said. "After everything he's done, he must know he'll get the noose anyway. He's got at least five hired guns with him. And then there's the alraun. Heaven only knows where it might be."

"He needs Burrows alive," Thomas pointed out. "That gives us an advantage."

"True," said Mr. Roosevelt, "but if you'll permit me to suggest, I believe we need some element of surprise if we're to succeed."

"We?" Edith raised her eyebrows. "I feel I should warn you, Mr. Roosevelt, that Mr. Wiltshire has strong views on the subject of civilian participation in Pinkerton operations." I wasn't sure whether to laugh or kick her under the table, and Thomas gave her the sort of look he usually reserved for Mr. Burrows when he was behaving badly. Just as that gentleman would have done, she pretended not to notice.

"What if Charlie Morrison and I were to create a diversion?" Mr. Roosevelt suggested. "Draw off some of his men, and perhaps the beast as well, if it's nearby?"

Thomas cleared his throat. "Miss Islington's witticisms notwithstanding, I do have reservations. I rather suspect the Agency takes a dim view of involving the client in a rescue operation."

"That can be smoothed over, and it's not as though you couldn't use the help. This area is the landscape of all others for hiding places and ambuscades. You need someone who knows the terrain."

I could hardly disagree with him there, but I wasn't much more comfortable with the idea than Thomas. "What about the sheriff?"

Mr. Roosevelt shook his head. "Bill Jones was my first stop. He and Snyder are holed up in the jailhouse with a raft of longarms and enough ammunition to withstand a siege. I gather they're expecting some excitement from the confederates of an outlaw called Bowie Bill Wallace."

I sighed. "They're probably right about that."

"I left Morrison with them, but he can be reclaimed easily enough. I'd round up the rest of my men as well, but there isn't time. One has to make do with what one has, my friends, and at the moment, that is me."

Thomas and I exchanged a look, but we both knew from experience that Theodore Roosevelt wasn't one to back down once his mind had been made up. "As you like, sir," Thomas said. "It's certainly true that we could use the assistance."

"Excellent. Now, do you have a map?"

"Here." Thomas spread it out on the table. "Miss Islington?"

"The butte Rose saw ought to be about here." Edith tapped her finger on a spot roughly two miles east of Painted Canyon. "I can be more precise when I see the landscape with my own eyes."

Mr. Roosevelt gave a skeptical grunt. "Are you quite certain? There are a hundred and one such formations in that canyon alone."

"*Luckily,* I'm quite certain." Edith arched an eyebrow meaningfully.

"Ah." Being lucky himself, Mr. Roosevelt understood the message clearly enough. And, as was the custom among their set, he asked no questions, it being considered unforgivably gauche to pry. "In that case, Morrison and I will create a diversion here, in these woods at the mouth of the ravine. We'll lead Kit's men on a merry chase through the maze. Then, once we've lost them, we'll station ourselves at the rim overlooking the canyon and provide covering fire. As for the three of you, I'd suggest Miss Islington remain up on the bluffs with a rifle, while the two of you cover the front and back of the cabin."

Somehow, we'd gone from discouraging Mr. Roosevelt's participation to letting him plan the entire thing. If it helped us bring Mr. Burrows home safe and sound, I wasn't going to object. But even with his help, we were still too few for my liking. "John Ward and the others are searching for the alraun not two miles west of this spot. If we could get word to them . . ."

Thomas shook his head. "We don't dare. Howard might still be watching the roads."

"In any case," Mr. Roosevelt said, "what we lack in numbers we make up for in conviction. It's a rare mercenary who is willing to lay down his life for his employer. Such a man does his duty up to a point, but a flesh wound or two will encourage him to reevaluate his priorities. If we fight fiercely enough, we will prevail."

Did he really believe that, or were those the words of a general encouraging his troops? I supposed it didn't matter. We had no choice but to try.

We collected Charlie Morrison and as much ammunition as we could carry and hit the trail. The sky was aglitter with stars, and a waxing moon shone bright over the broken landscape. Helpful for riding, but a whole lot less helpful for avoiding enemies, and I couldn't help feeling terribly exposed. It was a long ride, and difficult; what should have taken two hours took closer to four as we zigzagged our way from ravine to ravine. But long rides were nothing new to us by this point, and the closer we got to the cabin, the more my nerves started to buzz, fear and anticipation seeping into the spaces where fatigue ought to be.

Eventually we caught sight of our oddly shaped butte, and ten minutes later the five of us reined in at the lip of a heavily wooded canyon.

"We're standing on the back of the sphinx right now," Edith said. "Which means your cabin is just down that slope."

I stood up a little in my stirrups and peered over the edge. *That's it, all right.* My stomach did flip-flops at the memory. "That's not a slope, it's a cliff. How will we get down?"

"There's a trough between the peaks just there." Charlie Morrison pointed north. "You can't miss it."

"Charlie and I will hold here with Miss Islington," Mr. Roosevelt said. "When you hear the shooting, you'll know we've begun."

Thomas climbed down from Gideon's back, slinging a rifle over one shoulder and a shotgun over the other. I had my Winchester and my Colt, and Edith had a rifle Mr. Morrison had filched from the sheriff's office. "Are you going to be all right with that?" I asked her as we said our farewells.

"I'd better be, hadn't I?"

"The boss and I can go over the basics with you, ma'am," Morrison said. "We got all night, after all."

She flashed a tense smile. "Thank you. I'm a good shot with a bow, but I've never had occasion to fire a rifle. And I've certainly never shot at a human being before."

"Let us hope it won't come to that," Thomas said. "If Kit has any sense, he'll see the wisdom in surrendering without bloodshed."

I wasn't so sure about that, especially if the alraun was nearby. "If anybody sees the creature, *run.* Shooting at it only makes it angry."

Morrison frowned. "Come again?"

Mr. Roosevelt patted his foreman's shoulder. "We'll talk after we've made camp for the night. You'll want to be sitting down for this one, Charlie."

I was glad Mr. Roosevelt was finally bringing his man into the picture. Morrison needed to be able to protect himself.

As though any of us can protect ourselves if that thing decides to show up. I pushed the thought away.

Thomas and I struck out on foot, and it didn't take long to find the trough Charlie Morrison had mentioned, a steep-sided path about twenty feet wide that looked like it had been carved out by a river long ago. We followed it to the bottom of the ravine, where we found ourselves swallowed up in fragrant brush. We picked our way through the juniper, moving as quietly as we could until we came to a man-made clearing, at the edge of which stood a cabin. *That's definitely it,* I thought. The cabin I'd seen in my dream. I could tell by the stab of cold in my breast, a ghostly echo of the life that had been taken here. It wasn't a ranch house so much as a repurposed barn, with glass windows, wide doors, and the sort of tight-fitted logs that stand the test of time. It looked cozy enough, but it was steeped in death, and you'd have to be numb from the neck down not to sense it.

The orange glow of a campfire seeped through the trees. Howard's men, presumably, sleeping rough outside the cabin. Creeping closer, we counted four bedrolls. According to Parnell's ledger, there had been seven hired guns. Skinny was dead. One was mostly likely inside, guarding Mr. Burrows. That left one more unaccounted for. Was the seventh man still out there somewhere? Or was he the corpse in Deputy Snyder's pine box? I supposed we'd find out soon enough.

Thomas squeezed my hand in silent farewell, and we split up, covering either side of the cabin. I found a good spot about thirty yards away, where I could dig in behind a rock. Shielded on all sides by a thick copse of juniper, I'd be all but impossible to spot.

Now there was nothing left but to wait for the dawn. And pray.

The shooting started at a little before six o'clock in the morning, about a half mile to the southeast. At first, Kit's henchmen didn't seem much bothered, turning over in their beds and grumbling about hunters. The noise grew steadily closer, but still the men didn't stir. Then I guess Mr. Roosevelt got a little impatient, because a bullet struck the butte right above us, sending a shower of pebbles tumbling down the bluff. *That* got them out of bed quickly enough.

"What in the hell?"

"Seamus, you and Dick go take a look."

More swearing. The one called Seamus sat up, snapped his suspenders up over his long underwear, and headed for the horses; a moment later, he and his partner rode out.

Time passed. Seamus and Dick didn't come back, but the other two didn't show any sign of leaving, either. They just sat there, listening to the occasional pop of gunfire to the east.

Damn. The moment Thomas and I started shooting, the game was up. But what choice did we have?

A branch snapped somewhere close by. The roughs at the campsite reared up like cobras. "Did you hear that?" one of them whispered.

It had come from Thomas's position. Biting my lip, I watched as one of Howard's henchmen pulled out a six-shooter and headed in the direction of the sound. He vanished into the trees after only a few steps. Then came a gurgle and a crackle of brush, and nothing.

"Shit." The last man had his gun out now. He took a few tentative steps toward the place where his partner had disappeared, but he was too smart or too cowardly to go any farther. Then I saw movement in the bushes, and I made a split-second decision, whistling softly to draw the rough's attention. He whirled toward me—and Thomas flew out of the trees behind him, dropping him with a single blow from his revolver. Thomas checked the man's pulse and relieved him of his weapon. Then he crept up to the cabin, crouching behind a rain barrel and cocking his gun.

"Kit," he called.

Silence.

"We have you surrounded." Thomas's voice was smooth and businesslike, as though he did this sort of thing every day. "Toss your weapons out the door and come out with your hands up."

"I'll kill him." The voice inside the cabin sounded anything but smooth. "I'll blow his head off right now."

"No, you won't. You need him, and besides, if you kill him, there's nothing to stop us from opening fire. It would be as good as shooting yourself."

Muffled voices from inside the cabin. As expected, there was someone else in there besides Kit and Mr. Burrows.

"Surrender," Thomas said, "and we'll see to it you receive a fair trial. You have my word."

A new voice spoke. "We don't need your word, Pinkerton."

Howard. I recognized that cold growl well enough.

"How many of you is there, anyway? You and your little lady? Maybe one or two others?"

I glanced at the bluff where Edith was lying in wait. She'd have her rifle trained on the cabin by now, but I hoped she knew better than to try anything fancy.

"That ain't gonna be enough. See, I smelled you two for Pinkertons from the moment I seen you that first day on the ranch, when we was watching John Ward break that stallion. I knew you'd be trouble, so I took some measures. A bit of insurance, you might say. Ol' Gus, he don't take much convincing when it comes to Indians."

Howard hadn't struck me as the chatty type when we interviewed him on the porch. Which meant he was stalling. Hoping Seamus and Dick might come back? Or did he have another play?

Just then, a peculiar whistle sounded from the trees, and I had my answer.

"Right on time." The smugness in Howard's voice chilled my blood. "I figured you two'd show up sooner or later, so I told Terrence and his boys to be on the listen for action out this way."

Even as he spoke, I could hear the horses approaching, and my heart sank. *The Buckshot Outfit.* How many of them had we seen in town the other day? A dozen? More?

My gaze strayed to my partner, still crouched behind the rain barrel. *Well, Thomas? Any more tricks up those sleeves?* But I could tell by the way his posture slumped that he felt it too.

It's over.

We had only a split second for despair. Then someone took a shot at Thomas, sending him diving around the corner of the cabin. That wouldn't shield him for long; already, I could hear riders moving to outflank him. I started firing blindly into the trees, covering him as best I could. Thomas bolted, and he'd almost reached the tree line when George Howard came barreling out of the cabin at a full sprint, six-shooters blazing. I took aim at Howard, tracking just ahead of him to account for his speed, but then he drew up suddenly, and my shot whizzed harmlessly past. Howard barely seemed to notice, swearing and breaking off in a different direction altogether.

What the . . . ?

A rumble was building in the northwest, like an approaching earthquake. Over this steady drumbeat came a shrill staccato of war cries, and as I turned toward the sound, I met a sight that will be branded into my memory for the rest of my days. A herd of bare-backed horses thundered down the wide path into the ravine, a trio of Lakota in howling pursuit. The trees shuddered and bowed, and a moment later the herd erupted into the clearing, where it met the riders coming the other way, the two rivers converging in a frothing torrent of horseflesh and leather and shattered juniper.

I let out a *whoop* of my own as I watched Little Wolf, White Robes, and Red Calf drive their herd straight through the heart of the Buckshot Outfit. Animals and men tumbled to the ground, most of them scrambling back to their feet before scattering in all directions. Meanwhile, far above the chaos, a pair of snipers started peppering the clearing with rifle fire. I knew Edith was one, and I figured the other had to be John Ward. I prayed one of them could see Thomas, because I'd lost him in the chaos. I'd lost sight of the Lakota, too, but I could still hear them, and a steady barrage of gunfire meant they were harassing the Buckshot Outfit as the mercenaries tried to find cover.

I scurried back to the cabin, pressing my ear against the wall to listen. I couldn't hear much of anything what with all the ruckus, but the door had been shut again, so I knew Kit and Mr. Burrows were still in there. Nobody stops to close a door when they're running for their lives. I tried to peek through the window—only to jerk back with a shriek as the glass exploded, shattered by a bullet from within.

"*Christ*," I heard Mr. Burrows say, which would have been a relief if my heart hadn't been fixing to burst out of my chest.

All around me, the shootout went on, like something out of Buffalo Bill's show. I couldn't see Thomas or Howard, but I could hear them trading fire somewhere in the trees, where I'd lost sight of them. The stampede had mostly moved on by now, but a few stray animals still lingered in the trees, their panicked movements drawing fire and causing confusion. The Lakota wisely stayed hidden while patient sniper fire from above did most of the work. There were four shooters up there now, which meant Messrs. Roosevelt and Morrison had rejoined the party. They weren't aiming to kill, at least not yet; for now, shoulder and leg wounds were encouraging the mercenaries to "re-evaluate their priorities."

We're winning, I thought numbly. *We're actually winning.*

I should have known better than to tempt fate with a thought like that.

At first it was a whisper of trees. A ripple through the juniper, hurtling like a wave toward the clearing. Then the horses started going crazy.

Laughter filtered out from the cabin, high-pitched and manic, only to be drowned out by a blood-curdling roar from the trees.

"Goddamn you, Kit!" The voice was George Howard's, bright with panic.

That's when the screaming started.

CHAPTER 28

A RING OF TRUTH—THE IMPORTANCE OF INSTINCT—BONE WHITE, BLOODRED

n spite of everything, I pitied the Buckshot boys. They must have
had no idea what was coming, and when the alraun exploded into
the clearing, a sleek projectile of teeth and claws and muscle, they
panicked, opening fire from all directions and taking out several of
their own in the process. The alraun didn't even break stride, flying
straight at the nearest mercenary and tackling him to the ground. I
had to turn away from the gruesome sight, and that's how I happened
to catch Kit bundling Mr. Burrows out of the cabin and into the trees.

I had a decision to make. I didn't know where Thomas was, or
Little Wolf and his party. Could I leave them behind with that *thing*
tearing a bloody swathe through the clearing?

You have to. There's nothing you can do for them anyway.

My only chance was to get that talisman away from Kit, the
one that controlled his little pet. So I followed him, sprinting for
the tree line under a hail of bullets. Nobody was aiming at me, of

course. Nobody was paying me any attention at all, too busy trying to avoid being torn apart. That was Kit's plan, obviously: sacrifice his own allies to cover his escape. And now, I might have to sacrifice my own to stop him.

I'd lost sight of him in the dense brush, but he wasn't hard to follow. I could hear branches crashing ahead of me, not to mention a steady stream of cursing. "Move, damn you! Do you *want* to be eaten?"

Mr. Burrows did his part too, answering in a loud voice. "We both know that won't happen. You control the thing, don't you? Or are you playing with toys you don't actually know how to use?"

"Shut your mouth or I'll gag you."

The madness behind us receded as Kit moved his prisoner deeper into the trees. The distance tugged at my heart, as if each step were a betrayal. I couldn't stop thinking about what was going on in that clearing, and a moment later, I paid the price for my distraction, stumbling in the bushes and making such a racket that I might as well have fired my gun.

The footfalls ahead of me froze. Then: "Don't come any closer. I'll kill him."

I swallowed against a dry throat. "You won't. We've been over this."

"Rose, he has—"

A sickening *crack,* and then a grunt. Rushing toward the sound, I found Kit waiting for me, using his prisoner's body like a shield. Mr. Burrows looked woozy, his eyelids drooping as he sagged into his captor.

"Not another step." Kit tucked his gun under Mr. Burrows's jaw. I recognized the silver six-shooter from my dream. Ben Upton's six-shooter. It had been used to murder one man already, and I knew he wouldn't hesitate to do it again.

I had my own gun pointed right between Kit's eyes, and I pulled the hammer back.

"You shoot, he dies."

"So do you."

"Maybe. This ain't target practice, lady. Think you can make a shot like that when it counts?

Good question. I hoped for all our sakes we wouldn't have to find out. "Jonathan, are you all right?"

He blinked at me groggily. "I've been better."

Kit looked me over, sizing me up. Now that he was in front of me, I realized I'd seen him more than once. At the bar, with the other treasure hunters, and even once or twice at the hotel. *It's just like John said. You can't help running into people in this town.* He'd been right under our noses the whole time. And we'd been right under his. Small wonder he knew what we were up to.

More screaming filtered through the trees.

"Are you listening to that?" I said, jerking my head toward the sound. "Isn't there enough blood on your hands? Call that thing off!"

"You think I care about a bunch of outlaws and Indians and Pinkertons?" The mania I'd heard in the cabin was gone. An icy calm had come over him, just as it had in the dream, in the moments before he pulled the trigger.

Mr. Burrows's eyelids fluttered, and he wilted in his captor's arms. Kit jerked him upright, the barrel of his gun pointing briefly at the sky as he did so.

"What did you do to him?" I demanded.

"Just a little tap on the head. I've always wanted to do that to a plute like him."

I'll bet you have. If his cousin had driven him mad with envy, how must he feel about the likes of Jonathan Burrows? Not just rich and lucky, but young and handsome and well connected? He was everything Kit had worked for, simply because he'd been born that way. The only thing keeping him alive now was Kit's greed.

That gave me an idea. "Do you know who his father is?"

He snorted softly. "I'm not some turnip-eating farm hand. Not anymore. I've been places. I know who he is. I know you too, special branch."

I blinked in surprise.

"Yeah, that's right. I know all about you. And about this one, and his robber baron daddy. Let me guess: you're gonna tell me that if I let him go, you'll see to it I get paid."

"Well, why not?"

His lip curled. "Christ, you're all so predictable. You think you're special, just because you were born lucky. Instead of thanking the Almighty for your good fortune, you act like you deserve it. Like you're *entitled* to it. And the rest of us, we oughta be content with whatever scraps you leave behind. Wave a few dollars in front of me, and I'll be dumb enough to put my own head in the noose."

"You think *I'm* lucky?" The irony was too much; I actually laughed. "Why, because I work for the special branch? So much for knowing all about me."

He didn't even hear me. He was too busy ranting. "Just like Ben. All that God-given talent, and too dumb to know what to do with it. I was the one with the brains. The ambition. I had ideas, and the gumption to make them happen. You wanna talk about special? I made something from nothing. Little farm boy went to the big city and learned all its secrets. Then I came back to share the fruits of all my hard work with my *dear cousin*. I'm eating off *his* table? He ate off mine! But when it comes time to give me my due, suddenly I'm nothing but a burden."

The gunfire behind us was tapering off. They were running out of ammunition. Either that, or everyone was already . . . *No. Don't even think it.* Meanwhile, Mr. Burrows was fading right in front of me. "Jonathan. Wake up."

"I'm awake." He stood up a little straighter. "Just terribly bored. This conversation is dull as dishwater."

My nerves were so frayed that I actually laughed. "At least your faculties are intact."

"They are." A sudden clarity came into his eyes, and he fixed them on me. "You know what you have to do, Rose."

Kit shoved the gun right under his nose. "Shut up."

"The creature is all that matters now."

Surely he can't be suggesting . . . ? I gave him a panicked look. *Don't. You. Dare.*

Kit grew icier still. "You're not fooling anybody, Burrows. Men like you don't do noble sacrifice."

"That has a ring of truth to it, I suppose." As he spoke, Mr. Burrows's gaze slid deliberately to the gun under his nose, and the hand that held it.

The ring. There it was, on the index finger of Kit's right hand: The talisman he used to control the alraun. There was no mistaking the bone-white of ash wood.

"I think . . ." Mr. Burrows started to sag again. "I beg your pardon, but I believe I'm going to vomit."

My hands were sweating on the grip of my gun. *Damn you, Jonathan, don't you do it. Don't—*

His knees buckled.

I fired.

Kit's head snapped back, and he crumpled to the ground. Mr. Burrows dropped to his knees, but he wasn't hurt. He did, in fact, vomit.

I gave myself a moment to breathe, doubling over in relief. "Are you all right?" I panted. "I thought that was just for show."

"All the best lies are built on truth." I offered him a hand, but he pushed me away. "Don't fuss over me, just get the damned ring."

I knelt over the body, trying to ignore the shaking in my hands. Kit's lifeless eyes seemed to stare right at me. I'd never killed a man before, and I was pretty sure that was another thing you never got used to, whatever they say in the dime novels.

I twisted the ring off his finger and slipped it onto my own, but I didn't feel anything. "How do I make it work?"

"No idea."

I closed my eyes and tried to concentrate, but if there was any connection to the alraun, I couldn't feel it. "It's too big for me. Maybe if you . . ."

Mr. Burrows tried it on, but after a moment he shook his head. "Hopefully, Thomas will know what to do."

If he's still alive.

Now that Mr. Burrows was safe, the fear came rushing out like the bursting of a dam. I was sick with it, praying under my breath as we ran back to the clearing, rubbing the ring furiously as if I might miraculously stumble across the answer to making the thing work.

We found a gory scene. There was blood everywhere, human and animal, and more than a few bodies. Nothing stirred, not even the wind.

Mr. Burrows touched my shoulder and pointed, and my heart leapt for joy. Little Wolf and Red Calf perched on the roof of the cabin, bows in hand, spent rifles slung over their shoulders. And between them, disheveled but very much alive, was Thomas.

Little Wolf was the first to spot us, and he threw up a hand, warning us not to come any closer. He pressed a finger to his lips, then pointed into the trees to the south.

I rubbed the ring again. Still nothing. *What if the original spell-caster is the only one who can use it?* If that was the case, we were all as good as dead.

"What are they doing?" Mr. Burrows whispered, squinting at our friends on the roof. All three of them looked as if they were braced to jump down and were only waiting on some kind of signal.

Then a familiar voice cried, *"Now!"*

A stuttering of hooves sounded from the trees, and White Robes burst into the clearing on horseback, hollering and making herself known. It was unmistakably bait, and the alraun took it, shooting out of the brush after her. It gained on her at alarming speed, but just as it was preparing to leap, John Ward came galloping out of nowhere, swinging a rope over his head and carrying a knife between his teeth.

I don't like my chances of lassoing that thing, he'd said last week, but that's just what he did, tossing the rope perfectly around the alraun's neck. Catfish did his part, stopping cold and digging in his hooves, yanking the creature clear off its feet. As soon as the alraun's flank hit the dirt, John spurred his horse again, turning him hard about; the big bay lunged, using every muscle in his powerful frame to drag the scrambling alraun toward the cabin, where Thomas and Little Wolf were waiting. John rode straight through those wide barn doors, first the front and then the back; somewhere in between, he cut the rope. Thomas and Little Wolf slammed the doors shut, and Red Calf crouched down from the eaves, ready to give them a hand back up at the first sign of trouble.

Everyone froze, watching, but the cabin was silent. For the moment, at least, the creature was trapped.

John let out a whoosh of breath and drooped over Catfish's neck.

"Bloody brilliant!" Thomas smacked the side of the cabin in triumph. "Well done, everyone!"

"Bloody lucky, is what it is," John said, straightening. "Of all the ideas we been kicking around the past couple of days, I figured this for the longest shot." Glancing back at the cabin, he added, "Guess we're about to find out how smart that thing is. It's too big to fit through the window, but if it throws its weight against them doors . . ."

As if on cue, a fanged muzzle appeared in the broken window, snuffling. Then a massive paw reached out and gripped the window frame, its claws carving deep furrows in the wood.

"It will not fit through *that* window," Little Wolf said with a worried look, "but it might make a bigger one."

"We should go," White Robes said, sensibly.

By this point, I'd helped a slow-moving Mr. Burrows into the clearing, and I could finally throw my arms around Thomas in relief.

"Thank God you're both safe," he breathed. "Kit?"

"Dead."

"Four dead here as well, though it could have been much worse. The horses bore the brunt of it." Thomas gestured at the clearing, where half a dozen of the animals lay still. "These poor beasts saved many lives."

"What about Howard?"

"I don't know. We rather lost interest in each other when the alraun got loose. I imagine he fled along with the rest of his Buckshot friends."

"We got the talisman," I said, showing him the ring. "But we couldn't figure out how to use it."

Thomas frowned. "Strange. There was nothing in the book to suggest there's any trick to it. One simply puts it on and wills the creature to behave."

"I tried turning it, rubbing it . . ." As I spoke, my fingers explored a tiny crack in the wood. I hadn't noticed it before, and looking more closely, there seemed to be something inside it. Probably just dirt, but . . . "John, could I borrow that knife for a moment?"

"I suppose we'll have to figure it out back at the hotel," Thomas said. "Hopefully, if the alraun does escape, it will find enough fresh meat here"—he gestured at the fallen horses—"to occupy it for a while."

"My friends!" Mr. Roosevelt's shrill voice floated down from the bluffs. "I suggest we move along! Your trap is ingenious, but hardly secure."

The others set about rounding up whatever horses they could find, while Thomas went to fetch his shotgun from beside the cabin. John loomed over me on Catfish, watching as I fiddled with the knife. "What're you up to there?"

"I'm not sure." Using the tip of the knife, I worried at the crack, dislodging a few dry brown flakes. "Odd. This looks like—"

A shout of alarm went up from the far side of the clearing. White Robes pointed, and we all turned in time to see George Howard, pale and bloodied, collapse against the cabin, one hand clamped over a wound in his side. He reached for the front door, and before anyone could stop him, he opened it. Then he slumped against the wall, wearing a hateful little smile as he slid to the ground. He knew exactly what he'd done.

With his dying breath, he'd decided to kill us all.

Nobody was prepared. Most of us were on foot. And the alraun, attracted by the noise and the smell of Howard's blood, was already nudging its way out.

Now that its master was dead and there was no one directing it, the creature moved with more curiosity than haste, sniffing its way around the doorframe and blinking in the bright morning light. But that didn't make it any less deadly. Instinct was instinct, and this creature was an amalgamation of every predator in the land. Howard closed his eyes as the alraun scented him, obviously anticipating a quick end. But the creature must have figured its prey was finished already, because instead of a killing blow, it bent its head to Howard's injured flank and started lapping at the wound.

A look of pure horror came into Howard's face as he realized what was about to happen. But before he could even scream, a shotgun fired. Howard jerked once and was still. Thomas lowered his 12-gauge, his expression grim. He'd ended Howard before the man could be eaten alive, but I'm not sure Howard deserved the mercy. Especially since Thomas must have known what would come next.

The alraun turned, yellow-green eyes fixed on the man who'd just peppered it with buckshot.

Everyone did what they could. Rifles cracked from the bluffs. John yanked out his revolver and started shooting. None of it mattered. The alraun dug its front claws into the earth, preparing to spring. It might have been invulnerable, but it still had the instinct to defend itself when attacked.

I had an instinct too, and I prayed it was right. Jerking the knife blade across my palm, I clenched my hand into a fist. *Please, God. Please.*

The alraun charged. Thomas didn't even try to run; there was nowhere to go. It pounced, tackling him to the ground. I heard a scream from up on the bluff, and down here in the clearing, too. One of them was my own, a single syllable of terror.

No!

The alraun had Thomas pinned beneath its bulk. It leaned in, so close that a drop of blood dripped from its muzzle onto Thomas's silk scarf. Thomas squeezed his eyes shut and turned his face away as the creature sniffed at him. It *whuffed,* blowing the hair from Thomas's forehead. And then it climbed off him and walked away.

I fell to my knees, shaking so hard that I could barely hold myself upright. I felt sick to my stomach, dizzy with fear and relief as I gazed down at my bloodied hand. The talisman, bone-white beneath the crimson of my blood, blazed with heat. *The spellcaster anoints it with a drop of his blood.* I'd used a lot more than a drop, but when the man you love is about to be torn to bits, you don't take chances.

And speaking of taking chances . . .

"Rose . . ." Thomas's voice, full of fear.

The alraun was making for me in swift, liquid strides. A stalking gait, head low, gaze focused. I looked it right in the eye.

I waited.

CHAPTER 29

THE BURDENS OF COMMAND—BEAUTY IS
IN THE EYE OF THE BEHOLDER—NO MORE
MISCHIEF—A TREATISE ON TROUSERS

The alraun stood over me, so close that I could feel the heat of its breath. It scented me the way a cat does, openmouthed, narrow-eyed, *tasting*. I could sense its focus—and a whole lot else besides. The enchanted link between us obviously ran both ways, and a wave of sensations crashed over me. Confusion. Anger. Most of all, despair. It filled my chest like ballast, cold and heavy and aching. I could feel the spirit tugging against me, trying to break free of the enchantment, but it was like Ben Upton struggling against his bonds after two days of captivity: weak, resigned, without any real hope of success. Its anguish swelled inside me until it felt as if I would burst.

Go.

Yellow-green eyes met mine.

Just go. I won't try to stop you.

I don't know if the spirit understood me, but if so, it didn't seem able to obey. It just crouched miserably onto its belly like a chained dog.

"What's happening?" It was White Robes who spoke, but they all stood over me in various shades of awe and fear.

I shook my head, unable to speak around the lump of grief in my throat.

"She commands it." Thomas knelt beside me and put a comforting hand on my arm. "They are connected through the ring. She feels what it feels, and apparently what it feels is—"

"Pain." I swallowed hard. "It's trapped and dying, but it's such a slow, agonizing death. And it's hungry. So hungry, but it knows it will never fill its belly." I shook my head again. "How did Kit endure this for more than a year without going mad?"

"I'm not sure he did." Thomas squeezed my arm. "Are you going to be all right?"

I looked down at my hand, still bleeding freely. "I'll have to be, won't I? If I take the ring off, who knows what it'll do?"

"I think we all know what it will do," Mr. Burrows said grimly.

White Robes sank to her knees before the creature. That was a whole lot of trust to put in an enchantment I barely knew how to use, but she seemed perfectly calm. Tentatively, she placed her hand in front of the alraun's nose. It sniffed at her, though without much interest. I could feel the hunger twisting inside it—permanent, insatiable—but I'd already informed it, silently but firmly, that White Robes wasn't prey. "This is witchcraft?" she asked.

"An ancient form of it," Thomas said. "From across the sea. The spell draws upon the land, its trees and wildlife. This creature is born of ash and the blood of many animals."

"Ash?" Little Wolf hummed thoughtfully. "We make our bows from this wood."

"So you've said, and I doubt that's a coincidence. Your ancestors were most likely aware of the spiritual properties of ash, just as our

European ancestors were. That knowledge is largely lost among our people, but there are still some who know the truth, especially where the reach of the Church has been limited. I'd hazard a guess there are more than a few among your people as well."

"Then I will find them," Little Wolf said, "and ask them to teach me."

White Robes was only half listening, entranced by the impossible creature before her. "It's beautiful," she murmured.

Some would certainly say so. Its lustrous coat was the sandy gold of the hills, with subtle swirls of color like layers in the stone. Its long, sleek frame had echoes of the familiar, the face vaguely canine and the body feline, except for the powerful tail and slightly webbed toes. Those yellow-green eyes matched the keen gaze of a cougar with the soulful eyes of a bear. But no matter how long I stared at it, or how much its predicament tugged my heart strings, there was no getting past those claws, massive and bloodied, curving out from paws the size of supper plates. I'd seen what those claws could do to human flesh, and all I can say is that beauty is in the eye of the beholder.

White Robes must have guessed my thoughts, because she said, "What happened was not its fault. If what you say is true, and it is bound by the ring, then the man who commanded it to kill is responsible."

"I know. I don't blame it." *I just can't look at it.*

"Its eyes are full of pain," she said. "We must find a way to end its suffering."

"We believe we know someone who can. In fact . . ." Thomas took out his watch. "She should be arriving this evening. We'll need to make a few preparations, but hopefully we can have this taken care of tomorrow."

The sound of approaching riders put everyone briefly on edge, but it was only the rest of our party coming down from the bluff, leading Luna and Gideon behind them. Edith and Charlie Morrison reined in well back of the creature, but Mr. Roosevelt rode right up to it. "Good heavens. Isn't that extraordinary?" Dismounting, he looked it over with a naturalist's eye. "Why, just look at it! The power in those shoulders. And those jaws! I'll wager it cracks bones as handily as any hyena." He shook his head wonderingly. "A pity this creature doesn't exist in the wild. What a hunt it would give you!"

"Just think," said Edith, "you could put its head on a wall."

The Lakota exchanged a *look*.

If Mr. Roosevelt noticed, he chose to ignore it. "You fellows certainly know how to make an entrance. Good to see you again . . . Little Wolf, wasn't it? We met on the hunt last year, I believe. And John Ward. How are you, sir?"

"Alive, just about."

"Indeed, indeed." Mr. Roosevelt nodded gravely. "I imagine it was all the shooting that brought you this way? Miss Gallagher did mention you were camped nearby."

"We was on the move, actually," John said.

Little Wolf gestured at the dead mercenaries. "These Buckshot men were tracking us. They were getting close, so we decided to move camp under cover of night. When we heard the guns, John and I rode to the top of the plateau to scout, and we saw them riding this way. That's how we knew there was trouble."

"Wasn't hard to figure Howard was mixed up in it somehow," John said. "Him and his Buckshot buddies have been mixed up in everything. And we figured trouble with Howard probably meant trouble for these two." He hooked a thumb at Thomas and me.

"We owe you a great debt," Thomas said. "Things would have turned out very differently if not for your timely arrival."

"Well, and now what?" Mr. Roosevelt's glance shifted back to the alraun. "It's quite under control, obviously. Who has the talisman?"

I raised my bloodied hand as if I were in school.

"Dear me. That looks like it wants stitches. And . . . I say, are you sure you're all right, Miss Gallagher? You look awfully low for a woman who just saved the day."

"It's the alraun, sir." I explained again about the connection between us, how I was experiencing the creature's emotions as if they were my own.

"*Hrm*. I'm afraid there's not much I can do about that, but as to the stitches, at least, there's a doctor in town. Are you able to leave the creature behind safely?"

"Yes. It won't do anything unless I tell it to." I wasn't sure how I knew that, but I did.

"In that case," Thomas said, "perhaps the best thing would be for it to stay just where it is. There's plenty to eat and drink, and it's a remote enough location that no one is likely to stumble across it."

"I will stay with it," White Robes said.

Her husband didn't think much of that idea, and there was a brief exchange in Lakota. But there was little doubt who would come out on top, and eventually Red Calf just sighed. "Then I will stay also. As long as it is safe."

"It's safe," I said. "He knows you aren't prey."

"He?" White Robes echoed.

I nodded. I wasn't sure how I knew that, either, but I was glad I didn't have to check the old-fashioned way.

"If we leave him here," said Little Wolf, "how will we prove to the townsfolk that he exists? We should bring him with us, for all to see."

Mr. Roosevelt's eyebrows flew up. "We will do nothing of the kind, sir. The mere rumor of this creature has been damaging enough. Ordinary folk must be told that it was a giant cougar, or perhaps a bear."

Little Wolf's gaze grew cold. "That is not for you to decide. You do not speak for us."

Mr. Roosevelt's own expression hardened, and for a moment it looked like things would get unpleasant, so I figured I'd better step in. "If I may, the immediate concern is getting Two Horses out of jail. He's been wrongfully accused, but the sheriff made it clear that he wouldn't release him without proof of his innocence."

"Leave Bill Jones to me," Mr. Roosevelt said. "I'll have your friend out by this afternoon, you have my word."

"I will accept your help with thanks," Little Wolf returned, "but I will not *leave* it to you. This is my hunting party. Two Horses is my responsibility."

Mr. Roosevelt grunted. "Spoken like a true leader. Very well, we'll go together. Does that satisfy you? In exchange, I ask only that you refrain from speaking of this creature with my people. What you choose to tell your own is of course your affair."

Little Wolf hesitated. "It's not just the sheriff. The ranchers, the people in town . . . many of them blame us for killing their cows. These Buckshot men were hired to bring us in for cattle rustling."

"Any cattle rustling in these parts was done at the behest of George Howard, and I will make sure everyone knows it. Charlie here will say the same, as will Mr. Ward. The three of us are well respected in this community, so our combined word will carry considerable weight."

"What about Gus Reid?" I asked. "From what I saw, he won't be persuaded by any amount of evidence."

"Maybe not," said John, "but he'd be a fool to go on making trouble. Howard was his man. If he ain't careful, there's gonna be a whole lotta folks looking to him to make good for what his foreman done. I reckon Gus is smart enough to know that, but if he ain't, there's a few of us ready to spell it out for him."

Thomas smiled. "I'd very much like to see that, but I suspect it won't be necessary. Most likely, this will all blow over once cattle are no longer being slaughtered."

"It will," Mr. Roosevelt said confidently. "As I said before, this is hard country. People are accustomed to lurching from one catastrophe to the next. There will be a brush fire in the summer, or a drought, or a range war, and all this will be forgotten. Sad to count upon such things, but it is the reality."

Little Wolf glanced at Red Calf and White Robes, and they both nodded. "Very well. If the sheriff releases our hunter, we will not speak of this creature among your kind."

With that settled, we gathered up our things. Mr. Burrows was still feeling wobbly, so John Ward offered to take two on his big draft horse. Charlie Morrison poured some whiskey over my cut and tied it up with a handkerchief, and we were on our way, promising to return at first light tomorrow. The alraun watched me go, and I could feel its yellow-green eyes tracking me all the way to the tree line. It felt strange to leave it behind, but I knew with iron-clad certainty that it wasn't going anywhere unless I told it to. It wouldn't even feed without my permission, so I gave it.

A little while later, I had the odd sensation of feeling as if I'd just eaten, even though I hadn't. Which was just as well, because it was going to be a long while before I had an appetite of my own.

We arrived in town to a welcome sight: Bowie Bill Wallace, hand-cuffed, being led from the jailhouse by a tall, gaunt fellow with coal-black hair and the most extraordinarily bushy mustache I'd ever seen. (Which is saying a lot, considering where we were.) It was the sort of face that looked like laughter had never touched it—at least until he spied us coming up the road, at which point the mustache quirked, and a spark of wry humor came into his eyes. "Late, as usual," he called, loading his sullen charge into the back of a wagon.

"What do you mean? It appears I'm right on time." Mr. Roosevelt leaned down from his horse to shake the man's hand. "How are you, Bullock?"

"Was it you poached this one, too?" Bullock inclined his head at the wagon.

"Poached indeed. When are you going to let that lie? He was my horse thief as much as he was yours."

"Maybe, but he was mine first."

"So you say. As for this fellow, I had nothing whatever to do with his arrest. You'll have to address yourself to my companions here. Mr. Wiltshire, Miss Gallagher, may I present Seth Bullock, sheriff of Deadwood."

Bullock eyed us with that same wry look. "These the Pinkertons Bill Jones speaks so fondly of?"

As if on cue, the gentleman in question appeared on the porch of the jailhouse. He glanced over our ensemble with his usual enthusiasm, but he didn't say anything, which I figured was down to the presence of Seth Bullock. His stance had the wary deference of a lower-ranking wolf in the presence of an alpha.

Not quite so hell-roaring now, are we?

Aloud, I said, "The feeling is mutual, I'm sure. But actually, proper credit goes to Mr. Burrows here."

"Well, whoever got him, I'm much obliged. He's been a very bad boy."

Thomas glanced at the wagon. "Are you not concerned his confederates will waylay you on the road?"

"Oh, we met his *confederates* already, just outside of town. One of 'em ended up in the back of that wagon. The rest . . . didn't." Bullock didn't expand on that, but we could fill in the blanks well enough.

"In a similar vein," Thomas said, turning to Bill Jones, "I don't think you'll have further mischief from the Buckshot Outfit, at least not for a good long while."

Jones narrowed his eyes. "That so?"

"I'll fill you in on the details by and by," Mr. Roosevelt said. "Quite a tale, I assure you."

Bullock scanned our odd little party with another quirk of his mustache. "I'll just bet it is. I'd like to hear it myself, but we'd best be getting on. Wouldn't want these fellas"—he nodded at the wagon again—"getting up to any *mischief*." He shook hands with Mr. Roosevelt and Bill Jones and touched his hat at the rest of us. Then he climbed onto the seat of the wagon, twitched the reins, and trundled off, flanked by a pair of deputies.

"Now, then." Mr. Roosevelt climbed down from his pony, gesturing for Little Wolf to do the same. "This young fellow and I have some business to discuss with you, Bill." Throwing a friendly arm over the sheriff's shoulders, he steered Jones back inside.

The rest of us carried on to the doctor, and from there to the hotel, where a round of very hot baths was ordered. This was followed by a good deal of napping, and finally a visit to the saloon, where everyone, with the exception of Mr. Roosevelt, took a generous sampling of Mr. Burrows's cognac or Lee Granger's forty-rod, depending on his or her preference.

I took the whiskey.

"Look, no one is denying trousers are practical," Mr. Burrows was saying by the time Granger brought out the third bottle. "In fact, they're quite indispensable. Society as we know it could not exist without trousers. But they are not beautiful. They *cannot* be beautiful. Bad enough that one half of the population should be confined to them. If women start wearing trousers, the sartorial art as we know it will be utterly lost."

Edith *tsk*ed. "This from a man who spends hours each week contemplating the delicate interplay between waistcoat and scarf."

"Precisely why I am an expert. I assure you, there is nothing to be done about trousers. Tell them, Wiltshire."

"I quite agree. Trousers cannot be decorative, no matter how finely tailored."

"There, you see?"

"I dunno," said Charlie Morrison. "The boss has some interesting buckskin pants."

"Oh dear." Mr. Burrows laughed. "How do you answer this charge, Roosevelt?"

"Leave me out of it. Mr. Ward and I have far too much sense to wade into such treacherous waters. Isn't that right, John?"

"Reckon so."

Alas, Little Wolf was not present to offer his views on trousers, having taken Two Horses back to rejoin the others.

I would have chipped in my own two cents, but I was afraid of ruining the celebratory mood. Even with several miles between us, I could still feel the alraun's despair. On top of which, I was fighting a growing melancholy of my own. I'd killed a man today, and I couldn't stop replaying it in my mind. The Rose Gallagher who returned to New York would not be the one who'd left. It would be a different version of Thomas, too, and that was still another unhappy thought. All in all, I wasn't feeling very sociable.

Pushing my chair back, I offered an apologetic smile. "I'm suddenly feeling terribly tired. I hope you all won't think me rude if I turn in for the night."

"Turn in?" Edith glanced at the clock on the wall. "It's five thirty!"

"The Western Express will be arriving soon," Thomas said. "Are you sure you wouldn't like to greet our guest?"

"I would, very much, but I'm exhausted. Please give her my apologies."

"Very well, I'll walk you." He pushed his own chair back.

I started to tell him that I didn't need an escort—we'd taken care of just about everybody who wanted us dead, after all—but I could see he was worried about me, so I gave in gracefully and bade everyone else an early good night.

"Do you fancy a cup of tea?" Thomas asked as we crossed the road.

Which was Thomas Wiltshire for *Can we talk?*

My mother was fond of saying that there was nothing a good cup of tea couldn't fix. I had a feeling we were about to put that theory to the test.

CHAPTER 30

DREAMING—AN OLD FRIEND—GOODBYES

A re you all right?" Thomas asked while the tea steeped. "It's been a difficult day, especially for you."

"Why, because half the people I care about in this world almost died?" The darkness of the thought surprised even me.

"Among other things." His pale eyes scanned me with concern. "The enchantment is affecting you. Is it painful?"

"Not physically. And I'm already getting used to it, at least a little. It's more . . . in the background, I guess you could say. But I still don't see how Kit put up with it for so long without going completely barmy." I'd heard of people developing terrible nervous disorders because they had a constant ringing in their ears. What would it do to you to have someone else's rage and despair dragging at you, day in and day out, for over a year? "Why he would go to such lengths is beyond me. Surely there was another way to get what he wanted? Something a little less . . . flashy?"

"I rather suspect that was the point," Thomas said, pouring out two steaming cups. "From what you've told us, it sounds as though he went through his whole life feeling as if he had something to prove."

"Too bad the people he was trying to prove it to were already dead. First his father, then his cousin."

Thomas added a lump of sugar to my tea and gave it a stir. "I think the person he was most trying to prove it to was himself."

"Right up to the end. Why couldn't he have just surrendered? He didn't have to make me kill him."

Thomas sighed. "It's a terrible thing, taking a life. I'm sorry you had to do it, but as you say, he left you no choice."

"You'd think that would help, but . . ." I accepted the cup Thomas offered me and sank into a chair. "I just keep seeing his face. It's as if I've traded one sort of ghost for another." *And speaking of ghosts . . .* I glanced around the room. "At least Ben Upton has found peace."

"Does that mean you no longer sense him?" Thomas sat across from me, cup and saucer balanced in his lap.

"Not a trace. It's as if he was never here."

"I'm glad. He may have had his faults, but he surely didn't deserve what happened to him."

My glance fell to my tea, to the drawn reflection I saw in its dark surface. I looked every bit as beaten down as those cowboys in the saloon, the ones whose sorrows didn't have the decency to be drowned. "I still can't believe all this happened because of one man's greed. It seems so . . . petty."

"In my experience, that is often the case with murder."

"It's true, isn't it?" I shook my head wonderingly. "The cases we deal with . . . luck, witchcraft, ghosts . . . all these supernatural things, and yet when it comes right down to it, the motives are so very *ordinary*. Greed. Politics. Revenge. The same as any old case that might land on Sergeant Chapman's desk."

"Is that so surprising? Luck and magic are just tools, after all. The men and women who wield them are the same flawed human beings as the rest of us."

"I suppose so." I'd often thought about how much my world had changed when Thomas first told me about the existence of the supernatural. For a long time, it felt as if everything around me were new and foreign, but that wasn't really true. At the end of the day, people were people, just as Thomas said. The rest of it was just a bag of tricks.

"At any rate, at least it's over."

"Amen to that," I said, taking a grateful sip of my tea. "Things can finally go back to normal in this town, and we can go home."

Home. The word landed between us like a stone. Both of us stared at it for a moment, our gazes fixed on the same invisible spot on the floor. *Home* meant going back to all the things that kept us apart. It meant the end of the pretty little daydream we'd been living in, and we both knew it.

The silence stretched until the air was taut with it.

"Thomas—"

"Rose—"

We smiled awkwardly at one another. "Please," he said, gesturing for me to start.

I'd agonized over what to say when this moment finally came, but now that it was here, none of the things I'd planned seemed right. I needed Thomas to understand that I hadn't been trying to trap him. That I'd known from the start that what was happening between us was fleeting and there would be a reckoning eventually. That despite it all, I'd decided it was worth it for even a brief taste of how it could be between us if things were different.

It sounds simple enough, doesn't it? But in that moment, with the witch's brew of emotions bubbling inside me, it felt anything but simple.

"It's hard to put into words," I said. "This past week has felt almost like a dream. As if it weren't quite real."

Thomas didn't interrupt. He just watched me intently, those pale blue eyes unreadable in the lamplight.

"I hope that doesn't sound silly. It's just . . . This place is unlike anywhere I've ever been. It's so . . . unshaped, I guess, like raw clay. Full of possibilities. And I felt unshaped too, or at least like I could be reshaped. These clothes . . ." I glanced down at my trousers, at the gun belt around my hips. "And nobody here but you and me . . . even the ghost, in a way, pulling me out of myself, and . . ." I trailed off with a sigh. "I'm not making any sense, am I?"

"You're making perfect sense," he said quietly. "Please, go on."

"I guess what I'm trying to say is that I've felt free. Maybe for the first time. And it's been wonderful, and I don't regret a moment of it."

Thomas shifted a little in his seat. There was clear tension in his posture now, apprehension in his eyes. *He's bracing himself,* I thought. *He's afraid you're going to put him on the spot.* I started talking faster.

"But of course I knew from the start that it couldn't last. That it was a life for *out here,* and here is where it would have to stay. Nothing has changed for us back home. We're still partners. I'm still . . ." *Beneath your station. A scandal waiting to happen.* I couldn't be that blunt. It would only make him uncomfortable. "I'm still making a name for myself as an agent. All the things you said that night in the parlor six months ago . . . they're still true. It's still complicated."

He sighed and glanced away. "More than you know."

What does that *mean?* I started to ask, but what would be the point? We just had to get through this and be done with it. Like pulling a tooth, or tearing off a sticky bandage. "It's just as you said, isn't it?" I tried for a brave smile. "Civilization was bound to catch up with us eventually."

"And now it has." He stood abruptly and crossed the room, fetching the teapot. "Would you like another?"

He said it cool as you please, as if we were merely discussing the journey home. *Shall we overnight in St. Paul, or press on to Chicago?* I suppose I shouldn't have been surprised. Nobody buttoned himself up faster than Thomas Wiltshire. "No, thank you. I just wanted you to know that it's all right. When we get home, everything will be as it was."

He poured himself some tea.

I waited, but he didn't say anything. "Your turn."

He shook his head. Abandoning his tea, he walked over to the window and gazed out into the street. "I find I have little to add."

"That's hardly fair."

I could see his reflection in the glass, and a spasm of pain crossed his features. "What would you have me say, Rose?"

"Whatever you feel. What's so hard about that?"

He sighed and closed his eyes. Then he turned back and took my hand, pulling me up out of my chair. "Everything is hard about it. But I will say this. If it was a dream, it was one we shared. And in spite of everything, it's been the happiest time of my life. Thank you for that."

Hard as that was to hear, it was a balm, too. It meant I hadn't imagined the feelings between us. Later, when I let myself, I'd be furious at the world for standing in the way of that happiness, but right now it was enough to know that we'd both felt it, however briefly. It gave me hope that maybe someday, somehow, we'd find a way.

Thomas reached for me, his gaze wistful as he brushed the hair back from my face. "Just as it was, then?"

"Just as it was."

He nodded and let his hand fall away. "Good night, Rose."

"We're not in New York yet."

A sad smile. "Aren't we? The decision is made. What would be the point of pretending for one more night?"

"The same as it's always been. Because we want to."

"Yes, but it will only—"

"Thomas Wiltshire, you think too much." I pulled his head down into a kiss, and we stayed in the dream just a little longer.

"Oof," said Henny Weber. "That is a big kitty."

She regarded the alraun with a twinkle in her eye, as if the moment we turned our backs she would slip him some sweets. Henny Weber looked at everyone that way, which was why she was not only my favorite witch, but one of my favorite people in the world, period. I hadn't seen her since the Hell Gate incident, when she'd sealed the leaking portal in the East River, but she looked just the same as I remembered: round and rosy, her cherubic face framed by golden hair streaked with gray. She smelled the same, too: like cookie dough, with sprinkles of mischief.

Maybe the alraun thought so too, because he sniffed at her with obvious interest, and when she started whispering sweet nothings in German, he actually relaxed a little. "I think he understands you," I said, sensing it all through the enchantment.

"Of course he does. The magic is German." She laughed.

I was pretty sure she was joking, but either way I was glad her presence brought the creature some comfort. We had a long ride ahead of us to reach the portal, which meant his suffering— *our* suffering—would continue for a while longer. His sadness still weighed me down, and though I grew a little more accustomed to it with each passing hour, I couldn't wait for it to be over.

"Will you be able to help him?" White Robes asked.

"Oh, yes. I can send him home. And don't worry, it will be painless. Like going to sleep, no?" Henny murmured to the alraun some more.

White Robes looked relieved. "My brother and I would like to accompany you. Is that possible?"

"Of course," I said. "We'd be happy to have you."

And so we set off: Thomas and me, Henny and Mr. Roosevelt, and White Robes and Little Wolf, with the alraun padding along behind us. We stuck to the back trails to avoid being seen, and by the time we reached the looming white spire that marked the portal, it was already well into afternoon.

"Where would you like this, Mrs. Weber?" Thomas gestured at the bundle of wood tied to the back of his horse.

"Just there, please, at the foot of the monolith. We will need the fire to burn down to coals first, so we had better get started."

It was a little odd, the six of us gathered around Henny's fire as though we were a group of friends out camping. *Just a couple of Pinkertons, a politician, two Lakota hunters, and a witch. Oh, and a very big kitty.* The alraun crouched a good distance from the rest of us, which was just as well, because he made the horses terribly nervous.

"Tell me, Wiltshire," said Mr. Roosevelt over the crackling fire, "are you quite confident the portal played no role in these affairs? Other than magnifying the magic, that is?"

Thomas sighed. "Can one ever be truly confident when it comes to portals? I scanned it quite thoroughly with Mr. Tesla's luck detector, and there was no sign of radiation. The portal isn't leaking, which means my initial theory about an elemental was incorrect."

"Not necessarily," Henny said conversationally.

Thomas blinked. "Come again?"

"Oh, I'm sorry." She laughed. "I didn't mean to speak out of turn. I don't know anything about your mysterious winter. I only know that a portal doesn't have to be leaking for an elemental to come out."

"Excuse me," said White Robes, "what is an elemental?"

"A winter spirit," Little Wolf explained. "Rose and I talked about this on the way here. There are some among the white men who believe the bad winter was the work of such a spirit."

White Robes furrowed her brow. "White men don't believe in such things."

"Some do, obviously." Little Wolf shrugged. "Just as some of us do not. I will not remind you that you didn't believe in this creature."

"Thank you for not reminding me," she said wryly.

Thomas, meanwhile, looked a little pale. "Mrs. Weber, would you mind expanding on that? Why wouldn't the portal have to be leaking for something to come out?"

"A leak is an accident, yes? Something broken. An elemental does not need something to be broken. It can just . . ." She mimed drawing a curtain aside. "Just like the fae."

"Wait." I felt the blood draining from my face, too. "Are you saying the fae can come and go as they please?"

"Of course! They don't, but they can."

"Good heavens," said Mr. Roosevelt. "What a disconcerting thought."

Disconcerting wasn't the word I'd have chosen. "I thought the whole point of the monoliths was to seal off the passages between their world and ours."

"The point is to keep us out," Henny said. "Not to keep them in. But we shouldn't worry. They left because they didn't like what we do to the world. They will not come back."

Even Thomas looked disturbed at the notion. "I'd like to speak more about this at some point, if you don't mind. It sounds as though you bring a perspective not widely represented in our circles."

"We Germans have long memories," she said with a wink.

"But what does it mean?" I asked. "If an elemental did come out, it would leave the same radiation, wouldn't it? And we didn't find a trace of it."

"True enough," Thomas said, "but it's been months. Perhaps it just dissipated in the meantime." Sighing, he turned to Mr. Roosevelt. "I'm afraid we may never have an answer for you, sir. It's simply too long after the fact to establish anything with certainty. Unless it were to happen again . . ."

Mr. Roosevelt patted his shoulder. "If those are my choices, I'll take the mystery, and gladly. I hope we never see a winter like that again, at least in my lifetime. I far prefer this nice warm weather, don't you?"

"Talking of warm . . ." Henny poked the fire with a stick, breaking down some of the wood. "These coals are ready. It's time to begin. Come, kitty."

At my wordless direction, the alraun walked over.

"He must lie down in the coals there. Don't worry, he won't feel any pain. He is not vulnerable to fire, any more than to bullets."

Even with that assurance, it was hard to watch the creature step into the glowing coals. I bit my lip, expecting a howl of protest, but he didn't seem to mind, flopping down onto his belly. Perhaps the spirit trapped inside understood what was happening. That this was the only way it could be free.

Henny knelt over the coals and poured out several vials of liquid, sending little puffs of odd-smelling vapor into the air. Then she held out her hand to me, and I slipped off the ring and gave it to her. She dropped it onto the fire, poking around with her stick until it was buried in the coals, and then she stepped back. "There," she said. "It won't be long now."

"Really?" Mr. Roosevelt looked a little disappointed. "I expected something more elaborate."

She smiled. "Alchemy is like chemistry, no? Maybe sometimes you get smoke, or something fizzes or goes *boom*, but that is not the usual. Most of the time, what happens is quiet. But that does not mean it's not powerful. Just wait."

So we waited. In the meantime, White Robes and Little Wolf

knelt by the fire, each of them placing a bundle of herbs in the coals. "Sage," White Robes explained at my questioning glance. "To honor the spirit, and the animals that gave their lives to bind it here."

The sage took light, sending fragrant smoke into the air. The alraun, meanwhile, didn't have so much as a singed hair . . . and yet something was clearly happening. The ground beneath our feet grew warm, like a stone under a strong afternoon sun. Then, slowly, the smoke around the creature began to coalesce into a distinct form, a bit like a cloud assuming a familiar shape.

"My word," Mr. Roosevelt murmured.

First, it was a long-legged cat with a short tail. Just an outline, a shadow made of smoke, but there was no mistaking its form. The bobcat sprang away from the alraun's back and vanished like . . . well, like *smoke* . . . only for another animal to rise up in its place: a long, slim rodent that might have been a weasel, or a mink. It too scurried off and scattered in the wind.

One after another they lifted like steam from the alraun's fur: coyote and bear, fox and otter, cougar and marten and wolf. The breeze blew each of them away in turn, making room for the next. And as each shadowy form materialized, the alraun itself grew a little paler, more faded, until at last it was white as bone.

No, not bone. Ash.

I realized it in the same moment the wood finally caught flame, and the figurine carved by Kit, made life-size by magic, began to burn. I lifted my gaze to the sky, watching as the smoke curled into the endless blue. A tremendous feeling of relief came over me. Of *release*. Some of that feeling was my own, but much of it, I knew, came from the spirit. Reaching out with my thoughts one last time, I bade it farewell. *Wherever you are, I hope you find peace.*

By the time I looked back it was over, and all that was left of the monster of Medora was a glowing pile of coals and the lingering perfume of burnt sage.

The goodbyes came hard upon one another after that. First, to Little Wolf and White Robes, at a crossroads heading back to town. "Do you think you will ever come this way again?" White Robes asked me.

"I don't know. I hope so, someday. What about you? Will your people hunt here again next year?"

Little Wolf shook his head. "We will wait a year or two. Let the animals recover." Grinning, he added, "And the game, too."

I never did find out what it would take to repress that humor, and I was glad of it.

After that it was John Ward, who'd gathered up his things from Cougar Ranch and was planning to head west. "Helena," he told us when we asked. "After that, who knows? I'm looking for a new line of work."

"Perhaps we can help with that." Thomas took out a silver business card and wrote something on it. "If you're interested, get in touch with this gentleman in Chicago."

John Ward lifted an eyebrow. "Pinkertons?"

I smiled at him. "Why not? You already think like a detective."

"The special branch is looking for resources out west," Thomas said. "An experienced frontiersman such as yourself would be a tremendous asset."

Finally, it was our client, who would be staying on for a day or two to get things straightened out with the sheriff and anyone else who came around asking after recent events. There was the matter of Kit's lands to decide, too, along with any leftover gold they turned up at his cabin. "We'll sort it out, don't you worry," Mr. Roosevelt said, shaking our hands. "In the meantime, I'll see to it your hierarchy hears of your good work."

"Thank you, sir," Thomas said. "Until next time."

"And there will be a next time, I imagine." Mr. Roosevelt flashed a toothy grin. "If I should continue to serve in public life, that is."

I would take that bet. Both of them.

One goodbye we would not be making was to Luna and Gideon, much to my relief. Thomas had arranged for them to travel in the livestock car, and though I didn't think they would much enjoy the journey, I promised Luna I'd make it up to her with a luxurious paddock in Mr. Burrows's stables.

The last goodbye, and maybe the hardest, was to Medora itself, and I couldn't suppress a pang of melancholy as the train pulled away, feeling like I'd left a little piece of my heart behind. I had no doubt the ride home would feel twice as long as the one we'd taken to get out here, but at least I had good friends to help pass the time. Edith, Mr. Burrows, Thomas, Henny, and I played a lot of cards over the next four days. Euchre and hearts, but mostly poker.

I really did get to like that game.

CHAPTER 31

ONE-WAY TICKET—RINGING IN THE NEW
YEAR—TIME

Porca Madonna!" Pietro sat back in his chair, wide-eyed. "Was everybody in the whole of Dakota trying to kill you?"

We were in the parlor, enjoying the sunshine streaming in through the big bay window. I'd been home for two days already, but this was the first opportunity I'd had to tell Pietro the *real* story—or at least, the parts of it that didn't involve the supernatural. Maybe someday, we'd agree on a policy of full disclosure, but until then the Containment Protocol was firmly in place in this household. That meant Mam got fluffy tales of elegant parties in Oyster Bay, while Pietro got the gritty truth—minus the bulletproof cougar-bear.

"Some days it felt that way," I said, sipping my tea. "It really is the Wild West out there."

"How did you manage with all the cowboys? They probably hadn't seen a dress in months."

I laughed. "They didn't see one on me, either. I ended up looking just like them in the end."

"And now you've got a horse. What are you going to do with it?"

"Why, ride her, of course. Mr. Burrows's groom will take good care of her while Thomas gets his own stables in order, and I can take her around Central Park on Sundays with Thomas and Edith."

Pietro's expression curdled, as it always did when a certain name was mentioned. "It's *Thomas* now, is it?"

I *tsk*ed. "It's been Thomas for a year, and you know it. Really, Pietro, you're going to have to give up this silly dislike you have. Just because he's wealthy doesn't mean he's a bad person."

"That's not why I don't like him."

I made a wry face.

"All right, but not only. He's dangerous for you."

"My *job* is dangerous. And I wouldn't have it any other way."

"Oh, I know." He shook his head and put his empty teacup aside. "For now, anyway. One day, maybe, you will have your fill of it. Believe me, danger stops being exciting after a while. You get tired of running for your life, and you learn to appreciate something like this." He gestured at the sunny parlor.

"It sounds like you're speaking from experience."

Now it was his turn to make a wry face. "I'm an orphan from Five Points, Fiora. Of course I am speaking from experience. So . . ." He pressed his hands together and pointed them at me. "For now, you go and earn your money, and then when you have enough, you can quit and you and me and Mama will grow tomatoes and drink tea and not have to worry about nobody getting shot."

I laughed. "It all sounds lovely. But for now, I have work to do. Which reminds me . . ." I glanced at the clock. "I'd better get going. I promised Thomas I'd look over the report he's sending to Chicago. Tell Mam I'll be home by five. And Pietro . . ." Jumping up from my chair, I gave him a quick hug. "Thanks for looking after her. I'd be lost without you."

He shrugged. "I care about your mama, and besides, I get to live here. Everybody is happy, no?"

I thought about that on the train on my way uptown. I *was* happy, in spite of the little cracks in my heart. What happened between Thomas and me would hurt for a while yet, but we'd get past it. Things would settle into the familiar rhythm soon enough. And maybe someday, with a little ingenuity and a dollop of good fortune, we'd find a way to turn our partnership into something more. Until then, there were cases to solve and adventures to be had, and that was enough.

Such was my thinking, at any rate, as I climbed the steps at 726 Fifth Avenue. But I knew the moment I walked in that something was wrong. Clara was standing at the foot of the stairs, hands on hips, gazing up at Thomas's study with a worried frown. We hadn't seen each other for more than two weeks, and yet she greeted me with only a brief hug, visibly distracted.

"What's going on?"

"Hang it if I know. Mr. Wiltshire about bit Louise's head clean off a minute ago, and for no good reason."

"Thomas? That's not like him at all."

"You don't have to tell me." She shook her head, still staring up at Thomas's study. "I reckon it's got something to do with that letter he got yesterday, but it's no excuse. I'm gonna let him cool down a spell, and then he'll have a piece of my mind."

"What letter?"

She made a dismissive gesture. "You know him. He'd never say, and I'd never ask. But it has to be bad news, 'cause he's been moping about ever since. Haven't seen him but for a moment here or there, on his way out and so forth. He didn't even come down for breakfast this morning."

"A death in the family, maybe." I followed her gaze with a pang of anticipated grief. "I'd better see if he wants to talk."

I went upstairs and knocked softly on the door, but there was no answer. "Thomas?"

A pause. "Come in."

I found him seated at his desk with a faraway look. A letter was spread out before him, as though he'd been going over it again. I had to fight the urge to try to read what was on the page, but that would have been unforgivably nosy. So I just sank onto the sofa, not quite sure what to say. "Are you all right? Can I bring you some tea?"

"No, thank you."

"Clara says . . . Well, she mentioned you weren't feeling yourself."

He sighed and rubbed his eyes. "Shameful behavior. I'll apologize to them both when everyone's had a moment to settle."

"Do you want to talk about it?"

Another pause. "There is something we need to discuss, yes."

He didn't turn to face me. Instead, he pivoted toward the desk, almost as if he were taking cover behind it. Not a good sign.

"I've been thinking a great deal about our talk the other night, in Medora."

I swallowed. *Definitely* not a good sign. "All right."

"We agreed to go back to the way things were." He spoke softly, as though the words themselves were fragile. "But the truth is, I'm not sure we can. Too much has happened between us. To pretend otherwise will be all but impossible. And even if we could . . ." Propping his elbows on the desk, he knit his fingers and bent his head toward them, almost as if in prayer. He stayed like that for a moment, until finally he closed his eyes and shook his head. "I can't bear it, Rose."

I didn't know what to say. I could see he was hurting. I could feel the shadow of that grief spilling over me, warning me of the blow about to fall, but I didn't know how to stop it. So I just stood there, waiting for the inevitable.

"Seeing you every day . . . Not being able to . . ." He shook his head again. "Even if I had the strength, it's terribly unfair to you. You deserve someone who can give you everything. But so long as I am here, haunting your every step, I fear you may never find that person. May never become who you were meant to be. How can I, in good conscience, allow that to happen?"

"You're leaving." Even as I said the words, my gaze fell on the train ticket on his desk. A ticket like that was only good for twenty-four hours. Which meant he'd be gone by tomorrow.

"I've requested a transfer to San Francisco. Sharpe approved it this morning."

"I see." The words spoke themselves. I was too numb to frame a thought more complicated than that.

"I know this is terribly abrupt, and I'm sorry for that. There are other factors at play, but regardless, I believe this is the right thing for both of us. I want you to know that it has been the greatest privilege of my life to serve as your partner. You have flourished, Rose. And I have no doubt you will flourish even more without me casting a shadow over you. Personally, and professionally."

Scattered questions swirled in my brain. Who would be my partner now? Would I even have one? What would Clara do? They rustled through my mind like dead leaves on the breeze, without any real feeling attached to them. As if they weren't even really my thoughts at all.

I must have been quiet for a while, because Thomas closed his eyes and pressed his chin back to his knit fingers. "Please say something."

"What should I say? You've made your decision. You've even bought your ticket, I see."

"I am not one to linger over something painful."

"Evidently." I stood up. "So I won't keep you."

"Rose . . ."

"It's all right," I said, and I was surprised to find that I meant it. Not that it didn't feel as if someone were twisting a knife in my heart, because it very definitely *did*. But even in that moment, I knew there was more than a little truth to what he was saying. And as much as this hurt, it would hurt even more if we parted on bad terms. So I did my best to put on a brave face—for him, but mostly for me. "I'm grateful for everything you've done for me. You've been an incredible mentor and a good friend."

I couldn't read how those words landed with him, but in that moment, *at that precise second*, I stopped trying. I'd never been able to decipher Thomas Wiltshire, and that wasn't going to change. It was time to accept that.

"I am sorry," he said. "For so much, but mostly, that things couldn't be different." I could see he wanted to say more. But as usual, he didn't know how, so I decided to spare us both the struggle.

"Me too, but you're right, there's no point lingering over it. The world is the way it is. I wish you the very best in San Francisco. I'll say goodbye before I leave, but just now, I'd like to spend some time with Clara. I haven't seen her in ages."

I left the study and closed the door behind me. I heard him lock it as I walked away, and that was all right with me.

I was through knocking.

"He's a coward." Clara fairly vibrated with outrage, her finger tapping a furious rhythm against her teacup. "A no-good coward."

I'd told her the story in reverse, beginning with the transfer to San Francisco and working back through everything that had happened between us in Dakota. There was a lot of ground to cover, since I hadn't managed to answer her letter. But she listened to it all, and the more I talked, the angrier she became. At one point, she actually got up and left the room, presumably to spare me the sight of her losing her temper. Either that, or she'd gone upstairs to thump him one. As for me, I was still numb. I could feel the grief lurking around the corner, but it hadn't pounced yet. It didn't quite feel real.

"I'm sure it has something to do with whatever was in that letter." He'd all but said as much. *Other factors,* he called them. I couldn't imagine what those might be, but just now, I didn't much care.

Neither did Clara. "Hang the letter. After what you all have been through together, he's gonna just leave? *Tomorrow?*" She shook her head. "A coward and a sneak."

"That's unfair. I might not like how he's handled this, but I know he wants what's best for both of us."

"He don't even know what's best for himself, let alone you. He don't wanna hurt. Well, who does? Anyway, if it hurts so bad, why don't he find a way to fix it?"

If only it were that simple. "Being with me would ruin him, Clara. He'd probably be fired from the Agency. At the very least, his reputation would be left in tatters, and not just at work. He'd never be able to show himself in society again. Why should he have to sacrifice everything? For that matter, why should I? I'd be fired too, and unlike Thomas, I don't have a reputation to rebuild from. I'd be a laughingstock from here to Chicago, the girl who only got her job because she was sleeping with the boss. It would be worse on Fifth Avenue. I wouldn't be able to walk out that door without people whispering behind their hands." I shook my head. "No, thank you."

Clara listened to this speech with a stony expression. "You really believe all that, or are you just trying to convince yourself?"

Sometimes, your friends can know you a little *too* well.

"It's all true," I said, which was part of an answer, at least.

The doorbell rang, and a moment later, a familiar voice sounded from the entryway. "Where is he? I'm going to kill him."

The poor maid stammered out something inaudible.

"We're in here," Clara called.

Edith burst through the kitchen door. "Oh, Rose," she said, flinging her arms around me. "Oh, my dear."

"How did you—?"

"I called her," Clara said. "Figured you needed reinforcements."

So that's where she'd disappeared to.

Edith took me by the shoulders. "He's a beast, and I'm going to tell him so right now."

"Please don't."

"A coward, and that's all there is of it."

Clara hoisted an eyebrow at me. *See?*

I couldn't help laughing, in spite of the ache in my chest. "Stop it, both of you. His reasons are perfectly valid."

"Valid. *Hmpf.*" Edith plonked herself onto a chair and started tugging off her gloves. "A man should be prepared to fight for his beloved."

"This isn't a storybook. And anyway, who says I'm his beloved?"

"Don't be absurd. Of course you are."

"He never told me so. He never made any promises. On the contrary, he was clear from the start that we shouldn't become involved, that it would only bring us grief. He has feelings for me, sure. But feelings aren't necessarily love."

Clara narrowed her eyes at me. "Did you tell him?"

"That I loved him?" I hitched a shoulder self-consciously. "Not in so many words, maybe, but it's not as if he doesn't know it."

"Says who? You just finished saying feelings aren't necessarily love. He knows you got feelings, but how's he supposed to know how deep if you don't tell him?"

Maybe she was right, but just then, I was rather glad I hadn't. Mam would call that pride, and maybe it was. But if you ask me, a little pride is no bad thing when your heart's just been broken.

"What I don't understand," Edith said, "is where this all came from. Why the sudden volte-face? Did the two of you talk about it at all in Dakota?"

"Some. We agreed to go back to the way things were before."

"You agreed? Both of you?"

"Pardon?"

Edith bit her lip. "I'm sorry, I shouldn't pry. It's just that in my experience, people often talk past one another. They make all sorts of assumptions, fill in all sorts of gaps. Especially when they're emotional."

That was certainly true. And I hadn't been in the best frame of mind when we'd spoken. "It doesn't really matter, though, does it? The bottom line is that we can't be together. Thomas doesn't want to be reminded of that every day, and I can't blame him."

Clara sighed, reaching across the table to squeeze my hand. "Rose, honey, you're strong as an oak, and everybody knows it. But it's just us chickens here right now. Ain't no shame in admitting he hurt you. We love you just the same."

And that, right there, was the moment the grief finally pounced. Tears pricked my eyes, and my chest grew so tight I could hardly breathe. And then Clara's arms were around me, and Edith's, and we took a moment, just the three of us. There would be more moments, I knew, in the days and weeks to come. Hurt like this didn't just vanish overnight. But I'd get through it, just as Clara said. And in the meantime, even though my heart was cracked, it was full up too, because I had no shortage of love in my life.

After a minute or two, Edith drew back with a sniffle. "Well, then." She flicked a tear from her cheek. "I think we had better drink, don't you?"

"Oh." I dragged my sleeve across my eyes. "I almost forgot. I brought this back for you, Clara. A little taste of the Dakota Territory." Reaching into my handbag, I produced a bottle of Lee Granger's forty-rod.

Clara took it with a bemused expression. "I appreciate the thought, but I don't drink whiskey."

"In that case, you needn't worry," said Edith. "Whatever that is, it isn't whiskey."

Clara laughed. "I'll get some glasses."

So there we sat, sipping kerosene and denouncing the perfidy of men, and all I can say is if tea is the world's greatest problem solver, Dakota moonshine ain't too shabby. It sanded down the edges of my hurt, and after a couple of drams, I was starting to feel downright reflective. "Maybe this all happened for a reason. Something Thomas said keeps coming back to me, about needing to grow outside his shadow. I think he's right about that. This case . . . it was the first time I truly felt like a full-fledged agent in my own right. Like I didn't need to look to him for advice at every turn. I think it'll be good for me to be on my own for a while. Gain a little independence."

"Funny," Clara said, "I was thinking along the same lines a minute ago. How maybe this is the push I need to get on with nursing school."

"Ladies, you are paragons of modern womanhood, and I salute you." Edith raised her glass. "To independence."

Glasses clinked, and it felt a little like toasting the New Year. Which, in a way, I suppose we were.

I helped Clara pack up the house after Thomas had gone. It was strange, seeing Number 726 empty like that, all the furniture covered up and the curtains drawn. Walking through it made me feel a little like a ghost. I was seeing ghosts, too. In the parlor, two partners sharing a passionate kiss. In the bedroom, a fledgling agent getting ready for her first ball, as if she were Cinderella. In the study, a wide-eyed housemaid listening as her employer showed her "the gears inside the watch," introducing her to a world she never knew existed.

Clara found me in Thomas's room. I hadn't set foot in there since I left his service, but as a housemaid, I'd lingered here often. Lifting one of his ties to my face, or perusing his bookshelves, or straightening his cuff links *just so*. It was the closest I could come to knowing the man. Maybe it was the closest I ever really got. As hard as I'd tried, I never truly knew him. For a long time, that had felt like my tragedy, but I saw now that it was his.

"Here you are. Been looking all over for you."

"Sorry." I smiled at her. "Just lost in memories. It's going to be strange, not seeing this place."

"For me too. 'Course, I'll be here now and then. He wants me to check in every so often, make sure it hasn't burned down, I guess. As though that earns the pay."

"Pay?" I cocked my head. "I thought he let you and Louise go."

"He did. *Due severance,* he calls it. I don't know what's due about it, but if he feels guilty, that's his business. I plan to put that money to good use in school."

How things change. Not so long ago, Clara would have been too proud to accept anything she didn't feel she'd earned. She was still angry, obviously. I hoped it wasn't entirely on my account, but either way, it was between them. "When do you start?" I asked.

"In the fall. Not sure what I'm gonna do with myself in the meantime."

"How about learning to ride? It's going to be a lovely summer in Central Park."

She snorted softly. "Sure."

"Why not? Mr. Burrows has plenty of horses you might borrow."

Clara shook her head, but she was smiling, too. "We'll see. Meantime, we oughta be on our way, but before I forget, I found this for you in the study." She handed me a sealed envelope, heavy, with my name written in Thomas's tidy handwriting. "I'll give you some privacy. See you downstairs."

Opening the envelope, I found a familiar brass badge.

PINKERTON NATIONAL DETECTIVE AGENT, NEW YORK.

There was something else, too, wrapped in velvet to protect it from the badge. A glint of rose gold peeked out between the folds, and I caught my breath. There, ticking softly in its velvet bed, was Thomas's Patek Philippe.

My first thought was that it must have been a mistake. He would never leave that watch behind. But no . . . one didn't just drop a gold watch into an envelope accidentally. For whatever reason, he'd decided I should have it. There was no note, of course. Heaven forbid Thomas Wiltshire should explain himself.

Clara was waiting for me outside. I paused in the darkened entryway, taking a last look at the place that had changed me forever. The Patek Philippe tugged at the breast pocket of my dress, ticking softly.

It's time.

Turning, I stepped out into the world.

AUTHOR'S NOTE

Growing up in a city that proudly brands itself "Cowtown," I've always been fascinated by the Old West—or at least the stereotypical version of it peddled by Hollywood. I was determined, from the earliest days of planning this series, that Rose and Thomas should eventually pay a visit to the great American frontier, but I wasn't quite sure how the opportunity would arise. Happily, the question all but answered itself once I'd decided on Theodore Roosevelt as an important side character in book two (*A Golden Grave*). TR famously had a foot in each world. On the one hand, he was the quintessential Knickerbocker of Gilded Age New York. But he also came to be intimately associated with the West—the "Cowboy President," whose inaugural parade included fifty Dakota cowpunchers under the leadership of the legendary Seth Bullock, U.S. marshal and onetime sheriff of Deadwood, the most iconic U.S. lawman ever to come out of . . . well, Canada, actually. But I digress.

Roosevelt's adventures in the Badlands began in the fall of 1883, when he embarked on a buffalo hunt. Thus began, in his words, "the greatest romance of my life," a sentiment that imbues the language he used to describe it:

> It was still the Wild West in those days . . . the West of the Indian and the buffalo-hunter, the soldier and the cow-puncher. . . . It was a land of scattered ranches, of herds of long-horned cattle, and of reckless riders who unmoved looked in the eyes of life or of death. In that land we led a free and hardy life, with horse and with rifle. . . . We knew toil and hardship and hunger and thirst; and we saw men die violent deaths as they worked among the horses and cattle, or fought in evil feuds with one another; but we felt the beat of hardy life in our veins, and ours was the glory of work and the joy of living.[1]

Given the outsize profile it would assume in his legacy, one could be forgiven for assuming TR's career as a cowboy was a long and storied one. But while the latter was certainly true—due in no small part to Roosevelt's own shrewd cultivation of the legend—his stint in the Badlands was actually relatively brief, beginning in the fall of 1883 and already on the wane by the time this novel takes place in the spring of 1887. Even so, he threw himself into it with typical TR zeal, and if he went a little overboard with the trappings—fringed buckskin, monogrammed ivory-handled Peace-maker, and even a sombrero at one point—he was no mere pretender. Unlike most of his fellow eastern capitalists, who were content to leave the rough business of driving, roping, and branding to their ranch hands, Roosevelt insisted on being in the thick of it. What

---

1. Theodore Roosevelt, *An Autobiography*.

he lacked in skill he made up for in determination, and those who initially dismissed him as just another eastern dude quickly learned that he had "sand in his craw aplenty."

One particularly famous incident involved a scene straight out of a dime novel:

> I heard one or two shots in the bar-room as I came up, and I disliked going in. But there was nowhere else to go, and it was a cold night. Inside the room were several men, who, including the bartender, were wearing the kind of smile worn by men who are making believe to like what they don't like. A shabby individual in a broad hat with a cocked gun in each hand was walking up and down the floor talking with strident profanity. He had evidently been shooting at the clock, which had two or three holes in its face. . . . As soon as he saw me he hailed me as "Four eyes," in reference to my spectacles, and said, "Four eyes is going to treat." I joined in the laugh and got behind the stove and sat down, thinking to escape notice. He followed me, however, and though I tried to pass it off as a jest this merely made him more offensive, and he stood leaning over me, a gun in each hand, using very foul language. He was foolish to stand so near.[2]

Roosevelt, who'd had a brief boxing career in his Harvard days, made short work of the ruffian, rising as if to comply with the demand to buy drinks, only to knock the man out cold.

I love this story for three reasons. First, because it shows that as exaggerated as tales of the "West Wild" have become, some of the legends are true. Second, because of the sublimely eastern manner in which this western story is related. (Roosevelt's patrician disdain

2. Ibid.

for shabby individuals using strident profanity is worthy of Thomas Wiltshire.) Most, of all, though, I love this story because it shows TR at his most TR, walking softly while carrying a big stick. As a New York aristocrat, Roosevelt was first and foremost a man of diplomacy. But where diplomacy failed, he was always ready—perhaps a little *too* ready—for war.

Another fellow who was reportedly "good with his fists" was Hell Roaring Bill Jones, Sheriff of Billings County. I say *reportedly* because I couldn't find much on Jones, and what I did turn up could almost always be traced back to a single source—i.e., his sometime deputy Theodore Roosevelt. As he appears in TR's autobiography, Jones is something of an erratic figure, whose "unconventional" approach to law enforcement seems largely to have consisted of beatings and the threat of beatings. (Though, to be fair, that was hardly unusual for the time.) Jones came to Medora via Bismarck, where he'd served as a police officer until he pistol-whipped the mayor, at which point he was politely asked to resign. According to one source, his real name was Patrick McCue, an Irish immigrant who began his career in the United States as a New York firefighter. (Those familiar with the history of firefighting in New York City will appreciate how very appropriate this choice would have been for a man of pugilistic inclinations.) A "gun-fighter" and "thorough frontiersman," Jones was nevertheless "a little wild" when drunk, at least according to TR. Sadly, that condition became the exception rather than the rule, which may have contributed to his eventual demise in a blizzard in 1905.

The Buckshot Outfit is loosely based on the Aztec Land and Cattle Company, better known as the Hashknife Outfit. Formed in Arizona in 1884, the Hashknife Outfit was once the third largest cattle company in America, boasting a range of over a million acres and some thirty-three thousand head of cattle. Its chief claim to fame, however, was the reputation its ranch hands garnered as the "thievinist, fightinest bunch of cowboys" in the West. While some were doubtless ordinary, law-abiding ranch hands, others could be found rustling, brawling, train robbing and gunfighting, and their brand—which resembled the hash knife used by camp cooks on the roundup—was allegedly spotted in some of the region's most notorious range feuds, including the Pleasant Valley War of the late 1880s.

The winter of 1887 was unusually harsh in many parts of the United States, but nowhere was its impact more devastating than in Wyoming, Montana, and the Dakotas. The Winter of the Blue Snow decimated cattle herds, bankrupted ranches, and marked the beginning of the end of open-range ranching in the West. A hot, dry summer in 1886 left the grasses dry and withered, and the grazers that depended on them were weak and undernourished going into the winter. Then, a disastrous blizzard in January 1887 sent the mercury below fifty degrees Fahrenheit, and the Great Die-Up began. Cattle perished on their feet, their hooves imprisoned in ice. Others were buried in snowdrifts. Those that didn't freeze to death went mad with hunger, drifting listlessly into town to chew tar paper off the buildings. When spring arrived, the range was littered with carcasses—many of them still on their feet, edible statues torn open by scavengers. Some sources claim as many as 90 percent of open-range cattle perished. The human toll is less well recorded, though there were reports of children freezing to death and settlers turning their guns on themselves and each other when it seemed as if the howling winds might never relent. For Roosevelt, who had sunk much of his fortune into Elkhorn and Maltese Cross, the losses were devastating, financially and emotionally, claiming 50–65 percent of his "backwoods babies." It was around this time that Roosevelt's visits out West began to taper off, and it's tempting to speculate how history might have been different were it not for that disastrous winter.

Last but certainly not least, John Ward is inspired by John Ware, one of my hometown's most legendary figures. Born into slavery on a cotton plantation in South Carolina, Ware headed west after emancipation, arriving in Texas at the age of eighteen and finding work on a ranch. Like many cowpunchers of the day, he lived a nomadic life, driving herds north from Texas along the Western Cattle Trail. One such drive, in 1882, brought him to the Bar U Ranch in the foothills southwest of Calgary, after which he stuck around, finding his skills in great demand. Almost immediately, the legend of John Ware began to take shape. He could stop a steer head-on and wrestle it to the ground. He could walk across the backs of cattle, and even lift small cows. He had never, ever, been thrown from a wild horse. Take this glowing testimonial from the *Macleod Gazette* in 1885:

> John is not only one of the best natured and most obliging fellows in the country, but he is one of the shrewdest cow men, and the man is considered pretty lucky who has him to look after his interest. The horse is not running on the prairie which John cannot ride.

Ironically, it was a fall from a horse that eventually killed him, at the age of sixty, when his mount stepped in a badger hole and crushed him beneath its bulk. Ware's funeral was said to be one of the largest ever held in Calgary.

Researching this piece was a delight for many reasons, but mostly because it gave me an excuse to get back to my Cowtown roots, spending a little time in the saddle and reacquainting myself with the legends I loved growing up. If the first two books of this series are love letters to New York, this one is, at least in part, a love letter to Calgary. My hometown has more than a little in common with Medora: the ranching history, the Great Plains . . . and just now, the negative-40-degree temperature.

That last part I could do without.

Calgary, Canada
January 2020

New York Tribune,
Feb. 26, 1905

ROOSEVELT'S INAUGURATION [FROM THE *TRIBUNE* BUREAU]

COW PUNCHERS IN LINE

Seth Bullock, Sheriff of Deadwood, idol of South Dakota, picturesque plainsman, and withal a gentleman, who enjoys the personal friendship of President Roosevelt, is busy out in the hills of the Northwest gathering together a band of genuine Western cowboys, whom he will bring to Washington arranged in all their fantastic regalia to participate in the inaugural parade. Seth is a conservative man, but even he admits that when these sun browned boys of the West prance up and down Pennsylvania-ave on their ponies the multitude will be delighted, and the inaugural visitors will enjoy a real cowboy treat.

President Roosevelt has expressed a wish that the men who "round up" the herd, "hog tie" and "cut out" big wild eyed steers, "bust" broncos, ride "cayuses" and conquer "outlaws" shall be represented in the inaugural parade, and it is in obedience to this wish that Captain Bullock has undertaken the project, which bids fair to add that final touch of picturesqueness to the inaugural ceremonies. Cow punchers have never before taken part in an inaugural parade, and with their "chaps" and lariats and "big horn" saddles should prove a feature of the pageant.

Captain Bullock has addressed himself to the task of "rounding up" the cow punchers for their journey to Washington with characteristic energy and enthusiasm, and promises to bring with him to the national capital the rarest bunch of "wild and woolly" Westerners that ever passed along a civilized boulevard. Captain Bullock is to command them, and the famous old frontiersman, while giving them sufficient license and liberty to insure their riding naturally, will yet subject them to discipline and hold them strictly accountable for their deportment. He declares that he will tolerate no "foolishness" on their part, and they all understand that he will see to it that what he says "goes."

Captain Bullock expects to bring with him not less than fifty men and ponies. He says he could easily take a hundred and fifty or two hundred if it were practicable to accommodate so many, for well nigh every cow puncher in the Deadwood region has signified his desire to be present.

Among the well known Western characters that will come along with the cow punchers is "Deadwood Dick" Clark, the once famous scout, bandit hunter and leader of the "shotgun men," who guarded the Wells-Fargo Express treasure coach from Deadwood to civilization a quarter of a century or more ago. The small boys whose hair has stood on end as they read of the escapades of "Deadwood Dick" in dime novels will peek out from under the protecting arm of their fathers or big brothers, just to get a glimpse of the wonderful man, who to them is far greater than the President of the United States.

"Tex" Burgess, the king of the cowboys on the big Hyannis range, in Nebraska, is another. Captain Seth Bullock, "Deadwood Dick" and "Tex" Burgess constitute a trio that alone would be worth travelling two thousand miles to see in an inaugural parade. The fame of Captain Bullock and "Deadwood Dick" extends, or once extended, from ocean to ocean, and the deeds of valor and daring they performed in the early days in the Western hills would make a tale stranger and more thrilling than any romance ever written.

[Said "Tex" Burgess,] "You just bet I'm goin'. I wouldn't miss it for $1,000. We all want to go, but Captain Bullock says he can't accommodate all of us, so some of us will have to stay at home. We are mighty pleased at the invitation to take part in this show. It shows that the President thinks a cow puncher is as good as anybody else as long as he behaves himself, and you can bet we'll behave ourselves."

New York Tribune,
February 20, 1887

LEFT TO DIE IN THE SNOW

THOUSANDS OF HEAD OF CATTLE LOST IN DAKOTA AND WYOMING

Rapid City, Dak., Feb 12—A journey down the western slope of the Black Hills to the plains of Wyoming in winter adds more to a man's information than pleasure. The severity of the weather has been felt throughout the country; but on these western plains, sheltered by the mountains, where rough wintry storms are little expected and no provision is made to resist them, the winter has assumed a grim and terrible aspect. The writer, in company with the manager of a Dakota cattle company which keeps 10,000 head of cattle wintering on the ranges of western Dakota and eastern Wyoming, recently made the journey down the western slope of the Hills to the Wyoming plains to observe how the herds survive the storms of winter without food or shelter.

Long before reaching the principal ranch or headquarters of the company, evidences of the fatal severity of the winter storms were found in the carcasses of cattle half buried in the snow that lay scattered over the plain. Looking in any direction, a horn, a nose or an upturned leg could be seen projecting above the snow. In a drive of fifty miles along the western skirt of the Hills, there was scarcely a moment when the carcass of an animal was not visible within a few rods of the track. Sometimes ten or a dozen lay in a group on the south side of a knoll or in a narrow ravine, where water might once have run. Many of them have frozen stiff while standing on their feet. Here and there an animal or a group of animals could be seen standing motionless and dead with noses resting in the snow. Troops of hungry coyotes come prowling down from the Hills to gorge themselves on the frozen carcasses. Many an animal can be seen near the foot of the Hills standing stiffly on its feet among the drifting snow with great holes torn in its sides by these tarnishing creatures.

Four days were spent at the ranch of the Dakota Company, and I had an opportunity of more carefully inspecting the winter's havoc among the herds. Three months ago more than ten thousand cattle owned by this company were grazing upon this range, all of them fat and healthy. It would take the appliances of a Spanish Inquisition to extort from the owners a confession of their present number.

The living cattle go about among their frozen mates and are, if possible, a more pitiful sight than the heaps of carcasses. Thousands of cattle are staggering in the snow so feeble that they would never regain strength if spring should open tomorrow. The strongest are little more than skeletons.

It is as yet impossible more than vaguely to guess the amount of loss suffered by the grazers of these Dakota and Wyoming ranges. The owners of these herds are extremely cautious in their statements.

The New York Times,
June 27, 1886

THE CUSTER MASSACRE

A DESCRIPTION OF THE BATTLE BY
THE SIOUX CHIEF GALL

Custer Battlefield, Montana, June 26—The celebration of the tenth anniversary of the Custer massacre by a few of its survivors took place yesterday. The great Sioux Chief Gall went over the field and described the manner in which Custer's command was destroyed. Gall is a fine-looking Indian, 46 years old, weighing over 200 pounds. He was reticent at first, but finally told his story with dignity and emotion. He said:

"We saw soldiers early in the morning crossing the divide. When Reno and Custer separated we watched them until they came down into the valley. The cry was raised that the white soldiers were coming, and orders were given for the village to move. Reno swept down so rapidly upon the upper end that the Indians were forced to fight. Sitting Bull and I were at the point where Reno attacked. Sitting Bull was the big medicine man. The women and children were hastily moved down the stream where the Cheyennes were encamped. The Sioux attacked Reno and the Cheyennes Custer, and then all became mixed up. The women and children caught horses for the bucks to mount, and the bucks mounted and charged back on Reno, checked him and drove him into the timber. The soldiers tied their horses to trees, came out and fought on foot. As soon as Reno was beaten and driven back across the river, the whole force turned on Custer and fought him until they destroyed him. Custer did not reach the river, but was met half a mile up the ravine now called Reno Creek. They fought the soldiers, and beat them back step by step until all were killed."

One of Reno's officers confirms this, saying: "It was probably during the interval of quiet on Reno's part that the Indians massed on Custer and annihilated him." Gall continued: "The Indians ran out of ammunition and then used arrows. They fired from behind their horses. The soldiers got their shells stuck in the guns and had to throw them away. Then they fought with their little guns [pistols]. The Indians were in couples behind and in front of Custer as he moved up the ridge, and were as many the grass on the plains. . . . The warriors directed a special fire against the troopers who held the horses, and as soon as a holder was killed, by waving blankets and great shouting the horses were stampeded,

which made it impossible for the soldiers to escape. The soldiers fought desperately and hard and never surrendered. They fought standing along in line on the right. As fast as the men fell the horses were herded and driven toward the squaws and old men, who gathered them up.

"When Reno attempted to find Custer by throwing out a skirmish line, Custer and all who were with him were dead. When the skirmishers reached a high point overlooking Custer's field the Indians were galloping around and over the wounded, dying, and dead, popping bullets and arrows into them. When Reno made his attack at the upper end he killed my two squaws and three children, which made my heart bad. I then fought with the hatchet. . . . When the big dust came in the air down the river [meaning Terry and Gibbon] we struck our lodges and went up a creek toward the White Mountains. The Big Horn ranges were covered with snow. We waited there four days and then went over to the Wolf Mountains."

ACKNOWLEDGMENTS

My research library for this series continues to grow, and while I find myself reaching for many of the same volumes over and over, a few new additions merit particular mention. They include *Mrs. Astor's New York: Money and Social Power in a Gilded Age* by Eric Homberger; *The Journey of Crazy Horse: A Lakota History* by Joseph M. Marshall III; *Black Elk Speaks* by John G. Neihardt; and *The Taming of the West: Age of the Gunfighter: Men and Weapons on the Frontier, 1840–1900,* by Joseph G. Rosa (with special thanks to Uncle Harry for the loaner).

As always, the behind-the-scenes support for this series is incredible. Special thanks to my amazing editor, Nettie Finn, and the entire Minotaur team; to Lisa Rodgers, Joshua Bilmes, and everyone at JABberwocky; to Evan Pritchard for providing such a thoughtful sensitivity/authenticity read; and a special shout-out to Rowen Davis, David Baldeosingh Rotstein, and Gary Redford, who keep outdoing themselves with gorgeous cover designs and cover art for this series. I'm also grateful to the wonderful Barrie Kreinik, whose narration of the audio series continues to delight. Thanks also to my family and friends for their continued support, in particular Tammy Smith for her help with Serbo-Croatian, and Suzanne Ambrogetti for her help with Italian. And finally to my husband, Don, who always knows when to be there for me, and when to be somewhere else. Because as any writer's spouse will confirm, you got to know when to hold 'em, when to fold 'em, when to walk away . . . and when to run.

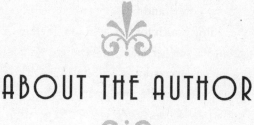

ABOUT THE AUTHOR

ERIN LINDSEY has lived and worked in dozens of countries around the world, but has only ever called two places home: her native city of Calgary and her adopted hometown of New York. In addition to the Rose Gallagher mysteries, she is the author of the Bloodbound series of fantasy novels. She divides her time between Calgary and Brooklyn with her husband and a pair of half-domesticated cats. Visit her online at erin-lindsey.com, facebook.com/ELTettensor, and twitter .com/ETettensor.